4.25

Responses and Evaluations

Responses and Evaluations
Essays On Canada

by
E.K. Brown

Edited and with an introduction
by David Staines

General Editor: Malcolm Ross

New Canadian Library No. 137

McClelland and Stewart

Introduction Copyright © 1977 by
McClelland and Stewart Limited

0-7710-9252-0

The Canadian Publishers
McClelland and Stewart Limited
25 Hollinger Road
Toronto, Ontario

Printed and bound in Canada

Contents

Introduction

".. . no one, I think, in his generation made a more lasting imprint upon Canadian literary taste than this brilliant native of Toronto, who was barely forty-six when he died. The explanation of his influence is easily found; he was a man of delicate literary perception, catholic critical taste, and extremely well-informed judgment in all matters relating to expression in both the English and French languages, and he found in the current poetic output of Canada a sufficient quantity of worthy work to justify his spending a great deal of his time and abilities in his study and evaluation of it." In these words the essayist B. K. Sandwell paid tribute in *Saturday Night* (May 8, 1951) to E. K. Brown, the first Canadian critic to look at the literary world of his country with intelligence and discernment. With his knowledge of many literatures, his interest in the close textual analysis of the New Criticism, and his personal commitment to his Canadian heritage, Brown brought high and informed standards to bear on a literary world which was only beginning to assert itself. To the pleas of such writers as Duncan Campbell Scott and A. J. M. Smith that Canada lacked intelligent literary criticism, he responded with sensitive and perceptive critical essays which set a new standard for his contemporaries and his successors.

Edward Killoran Brown was born in Toronto on August 12, 1905. After attending the University of Toronto Schools, he entered University College in the University of Toronto where he graduated in 1926 with his bachelor's degree and the Governor-General's Medal in Modern Languages. On a Massey Fellowship he travelled to the University of Paris where he received the *Diplôme d'études supérieures* in 1927, the *Elève titulaire de l'Ecole de Hautes Etudes* in 1928, and the *Docteur-ès-Lettres* in 1935; he wrote his major thesis in French, "Edith Wharton, étude critique," and his minor thesis in English, "Studies in the Text of Matthew Arnold's Prose." The three years in Paris (1926-1929) were a shaping influence in his literary career as he studied the literatures of England and the United States under the leading scholars of the Sorbonne, including Louis Cazamian, Professor of English Literature and Civilization, and Charles Cestre, who held the chair of American Literature and Civilization. They introduced Brown to the methods of the New Criticism, broadened his literary perspective, and taught him to avoid the narrowness of a merely provincial outlook in approaching a country's literature.

Brown returned to University College in 1929 to become an Instructor in the Department of English; in 1931 he became an Assistant Professor. With the exception of two years, 1935-1937, which he spent at the University of Manitoba as the youngest chairman of an English department in Canada, he taught at University College until 1941. In his teaching career as in his four undergraduate years, the tall, dark, and bespectacled Brown was a figure of distinction in the halls of the College. A reader who relished the opportunities to broaden his knowledge and understanding, he was always a sensitive and enthusiastic student of literature. Popular in a dignified way with both faculty and students, he had a ready wit and a delightful sense of humour which often included self-deprecation but never permitted laughter at the expense of another person. In the classroom he was a patient and demanding teacher who conveyed his enthusiasm and instilled interest and understanding in his students; his high and rigid standards of criticism were imposed with kindly tolerance.

In his first six years as a member of the faculty of University College, Brown championed the teaching of American literature in Canadian universities, and his article, "The Neglect of American Literature," is his documented assessment of one facet of Canadian ignorance of the literature of the United States. Such neglect did not bode well for the future of Canadian literature; he knew too well that ignorance of neighbouring literatures would lead only to cultural provincialism in a country which was struggling to develop its own literature. Later years would find Brown arguing with equal force and effect against the prevailing ignorance in the United States of Canadian Letters. His interest in North American literature complemented his major interests in the novel and in Victorian literature, and this period saw the publication of his articles on Arnold, Forster, Wharton, Hawthorne, Melville, and Wilder; in addition, he brought out an English translation of Louis Cazamian's *Carlyle* (1932). In 1935, the year of his departure for the University of Manitoba, his two theses were published.

During the thirties Brown became actively involved in the realm of Canadian periodicals. His first article in the *Canadian Forum,* "The Abbé Groulx: Particularist," appeared in October, 1929, and in the next ten years he published more than fifty articles and reviews in the *Forum.* The range of his inquiries is wide, from Chaucer to T. S. Eliot, and his reviews take him into the literatures of Canada, the United States, England, France, Spain, and Russia. Yet here too his major areas of investigation were threefold: Victorian England, the world of the novel, and Canada. From December, 1930 until December, 1933, he served as Associate Editor of the *Canadian Forum.*

Complementing his commitment to the *Canadian Forum* was an even stronger dedication to another new periodical, the *University of Toronto Quarterly,* which first appeared in 1931. Brown contributed to the first volume, and nearly every volume in the next ten years contained one of his long articles; the list of subjects included Arnold and Swinburne, Wharton and Cather, Wilder and T. S. Eliot, Thomas Wolfe and Edmund Wilson. From 1932 until 1941 he served as joint editor of the *Quarterly,* and he was largely responsible for the creation of the annual survey of Canadian Letters which first appeared in the *Quarterly* in 1936; Brown himself conducted the annual survey of Canadian poetry and his fifteen yearly assessments did much to establish new standards for Canadian criticism.

In 1941 Brown left Canada to assume the chairmanship of the Department of English at Cornell University. In the following year he took a six-months' leave of absence to serve on the wartime staff of Prime Minister Mackenzie King. He went to Ottawa as a distinguished scholar-gipsy who believed in an active participation in life as well as learning. His reflection on this period became the substance of his candid article, "Mackenzie King of Canada," a study which still remains of much importance for its personal insights into this enigmatic character. In 1944 Brown left Cornell to become Professor of English at the University of Chicago, a position he held until his untimely death in 1951.

It was during the forties that Brown began to focus his attention increasingly on Canada. This decade saw the publication of his second book on Arnold, *Matthew Arnold – A Study in Conflict* (1948), two enlarged revisions of his 1936 edition of *Representative Essays of Matthew Arnold* (1940 and 1945), an anthology of *Victorian Poetry* (1942), an edition of *Four Essays on Life and Letters by Matthew Arnold* (1947), and his own translation of Balzac's *Père Goriot* (1946). At the same time, however, Canada began to occupy a central position in his critical investigations. Though his departure from the University of Toronto forced him to relinquish his role as joint editor of the *University of Toronto Quarterly,* he continued to write the annual surveys of Canadian poetry. In 1941 he edited a special number of *Poetry: A Magazine of Verse* (Chicago) devoted to new Canadian poetry and criticism of Canadian poetry. Before he left Toronto, he had finished two major studies, "The Contemporary Situation in Canadian Literature" (*Canadian Literature Today,* 1938) and "The Development of Poetry in Canada, 1880-1940" (*Poetry: A Magazine of Verse,* 1941), which were later incorporated in his important study *On Canadian Poetry,* published in 1943. "Less an historical enquiry than a critical essay," as Brown noted in his preface, *On Canadian Poetry* remains a landmark in Canadian criticism. Perceptive and incisive, thorough and accurate, the volume eschews patriotic fervour in favour of a reasoned and sensitive evaluation. *On*

Canadian Poetry received the Governor-General's Annual Literary Award for 1943. With the editorial assistance of Duncan Campbell Scott, Brown also spent much time editing *At the Long Sault and Other New Poems by Archibald Lampman* (1943) and "Two Canadian Poets: A Lecture by Archibald Lampman" (*University of Toronto Quarterly*, 1944). In 1944 he published a revised and expanded version of *On Canadian Poetry*.

In the last year of his life when he knew he was dying of cancer, Brown set aside his major project, a critical biography of Willa Cather, which was already near completion, in order to write a memoir of Duncan Campbell Scott as an introduction to a new edition of Scott's poetry. So deep were his respect and affection for Scott that he feared a proper edition of the poetry might not appear; only a few months after Brown's death the Ryerson Press brought out *Selected Poems of Duncan Campbell Scott with a Memoir by E.K. Brown*. It remained for Leon Edel, a friend of Brown's since their graduate days at the University of Paris, to complete the Cather volume; *Willa Cather – A Critical Biography* was published in 1953.

Canada was always a major centre of Brown's interest, and Toronto had a special place in his heart. When he criticizes Morley Callaghan in "The Problem of a Canadian Literature" for the novelist's failure to depict adequately his home town of Toronto, he is the loyal Torontonian who cannot hide his civic pride: "Most of Mr. Callaghan's novels and shorter tales are about the city in which he lives, Toronto; but it seems to me, and I speak as one who was born and brought up in that city, that Mr. Callaghan's Toronto is not an individualized city but simply a representative one. I mean that in reading Mr. Callaghan one has the sense that Toronto is being used not to bring out what will have the most original flavour, but what will remind people who live in Cleveland, or Detroit, or Buffalo, or any other city on the Great Lakes, of the general quality of their own milieu . . . When I walk through the parts of Toronto that Mr. Callaghan has primarily dealt with, the poor areas towards the centre and a little to the north-west of the centre, or the dingy respectability of the near east end, it is only with an effort that I remember that he has written of them at all. It is a notable fact that never once in all his novels does he use the city's name."

A special honour came to Brown in 1949 when he returned to University College as the twentieth Alexander Lecturer. Established in 1929, the Lectureship honoured W. J. Alexander, the first Professor of English at University College, who occupied the chair of English from 1889 until 1926. Alexander had been the professor, as Brown later wrote, "from whom I first learned the meaning of literature and of literary study." And Brown was Alexander's first student to be invited to this Lectureship. He delivered his four lectures, *Rhythm in the Novel* (published in 1950), to four overflowing audiences in Hart House Theatre. Occupying a Lectureship established to honour his first teacher of literature and following in a tradition of Lecturers which began with Louis Cazamian, Brown's principal teacher at the Sorbonne, Brown returned home for his last official visit.

Shortly before his death Brown was informed that the Royal Society of Canada would confer upon him at the June, 1951 meeting the Lorne Pierce Medal in Canadian Letters, the highest literary award in Canada. On April 23 Brown died in Chicago at the age of forty-five. In the April 25 issue of the *Toronto Globe and Mail,* a long editorial concluded: "Dr. Brown had always been a teacher and a student of English. Literature and life, for him, were synonymous; and he deeply felt that the decline of interest in good literature meant a decline in civilization itself. He sought to remedy this by his own knowledge and enthusiasm, and thousands of students and fellow-professors – not least at the University of Toronto, where he taught for nine years – will attest that his efforts were not in vain. The seeds he sowed in two nations will be harvested for many years to come." On April 26, a funeral service for Edward Killoran Brown took place in Saint Simon's Church and Mount Pleasant Cemetery in Toronto.

E. K. Brown attended university at a time when the search for Canadian criticism was a topic of continual discussion and debate. In his 1922 presidential address to the

Royal Society of Canada, Duncan Campbell Scott defined the ideal Canadian critic, the critic Brown himself would become: "We talk too often and too lengthily about Canadian poetry and Canadian literature as if it was, or ought to be, a special and peculiar brand, but it is simply poetry, or not poetry; literature or not literature; it must be judged by established standards, and cannot escape criticism by special pleading. A critic may accompany his blame or praise by describing the difficulties of the Canadian literary life, but that cannot be allowed to prejudice our claim to be members of the general guild. We must insist upon it. If there be criticism by our countrymen, all that we ask is that it should be informed and able criticism, and that it too should be judged by universal standards." And in his famous 1928 article, "Wanted: Canadian Criticism," A. J. M. Smith decried the absence of a Canadian literary critic: "One looks in vain through Canadian books and journals for that critical enquiry into first principles which directs a new literature as tradition guides an old one. Hasty adulation mingles with unintelligent condemnation to make our book reviewing an amusing art; but of criticism as it might be useful there is nothing." In the following year Brown returned to Canada and began his career as a literary critic.

The importance of E. K. Brown in the historical context of Canadian criticism has been clearly outlined by Northrup Frye, the distinguished critic who succeeded Brown in writing the annual surveys of Canadian poetry in the *University of Toronto Quarterly:* "E. K. Brown was the first critic to bring Canadian literature into its proper context. Before him, the main question asked was 'Is there a Canadian literature?' After him, the question was rather 'What is Canadian literature like?' He started out with an interest in contemporary literature which in his generation marked a quite unusual originality, and he worked at first mainly on American authors, including Edith Wharton and Willa Cather. Thus, when he came to Canadian literature, he was able to see it, not simply as a local product growing in the surrounding woods like a hepatica, but as a literary development within, first, its North American context, and, secondly, in its international context. He was aware of the British and colonial affinities of earlier Canadian literature, but did not exaggerate their importance as earlier critics had tended to do."

Throughout his life Brown assailed the poverty of good Canadian criticism as one of the main obstacles in the way of the development of Canadian literature. The scarcity of unbiased and objective criticism brought out his disappointment with his country. "There are two types of criticism going on in Canada," he said in 1949, "newspaper and academic. The newspapermen seem to have chips on their shoulders – if a book is written by an academician, that seems to be enough to condemn it before the paper is off the outside. Take the case of Barker Fairley's first book on Goethe which came out in 1932. A Toronto critic – who ought to know better – gave it quite a raking although he showed a rather embarrassing unfamiliarity with the subject of Professor Fairley's book." The academicians also provoked Brown's disfavour. "There's a supercilious or patronizing air often detectable in academic appraisals of Canadian work because it *is* Canadian," he complained. "Surely there is some common objective ground on which the two camps can approach Canadian work without sacrificing principles." The common objective ground is the realm of Brown's literary criticism. Though he was not a theoretical critic, he did pause in his survey of the Canadian poetry of 1948 to define his critical method as he studied his country's literature: "The criticism of poetry as of any art must first interpret. If in the exercise of his interpretative function a critic writes chiefly of what is genuine in a poem, what is notable, what is *there*, rather than of what is spurious, what is negligible, what is not there, his doing so need not mean that he is abandoning another of his functions, the making of judgments. Careful interpretation, conducted with insight and a measure of sympathy, must precede judgment, and in writing of recent or contemporary poets it is much wiser to make sure that one's interpretation is adequate than to press on to judgment. The history of criticism is strewn with examples of how the slighting of the critic's interpretative function has led to false and absurd judgments."

Essays on Canada is the first collection of E. K. Brown's writings on Canada. With the exception of the studies which were incorporated in *On Canadian Poetry,* this volume brings together all of Brown's pronouncements on his country; I have included, however, the opening chapter of *On Canada Poetry,* "The Problem of a Canadian Literature," since this study is Brown's important and authoritative account of the conditions of authorship in Canada. As he studies the varied aspects of Canada's literature and culture, Brown presents penetrating and judicious interpretations which always reflect his high critical standards, his extensive knowledge of French, English, and American literatures, and his deep attachment to Canada. His fondness for his country does not blind him to the inadequacies of its literature, and his criticism, though always uttered with a sympathetic understanding of the cultural milieu, is candid, incisive, and impressive. His wide knowledge and learning bring a new perspective to his studies of the Canadian literary world.

The many articles which comprise this collection are complemented by two extended series of related studies. "Canadian Poetry (1935-1949)" is the series of fifteen annual surveys of Canadian poetry which originally appeared in the *University of Toronto Quarterly.* In this crucial period of poetic growth in Canada, Brown presents the most accurate, comprehensive, and enlightened perspective on the field. These fifteen years saw the publication of major volumes of poetry by Earle Birney, Ralph Gustafson, A. M. Klein, Irving Layton, Dorothy Livesay, P. K. Page, E. J. Pratt, and James Reaney, to name only a few. Here, indeed, is a wealth of Canadian poetry, and the surveys offer an important critical and historical assessment of these writings. The fifteen surveys almost form a unified group as Brown, aware of his imminent death, pauses in his final survey to reflect on the entire fifteen-year period. The second series of studies is "Causeries," a more informal and colloquial form of criticism which reflects Brown's genuine interest in journalism. In 1946 the *Winnipeg Free Press* began a series of Saturday causeries, informal, chatty articles on literary subjects; it was not one author that spoke, but several writers who chatted, each in their turn, about some literary topic of interest. One of these contributors was E. K. Brown, whose affection for his sometime home of Winnipeg prompted him to write a monthly causerie. Between September 27, 1947 and March 24, 1951 he wrote thirty-eight. For this volume I have chosen the eight causeries which talk about the Canadian scene.

Essays on Canada is a testimony and a tribute, a testimony to the ideals of criticism E. K. Brown espoused and a tribute to his fundamental contribution to the world of Canadian criticism. To his contemporaries and to his successors, he sets an example, and that example is an ideal.

David Staines
Harvard University

Acknowledgement Notes

The Problem of a Canadian Literature

From *On Canadian Poetry* (Toronto: The Ryerson Press, 1943), 1-27. By permission of McGraw-Hill Ryerson Press and the estate of E. K. Brown.

The Abbé Groulx: Particularist

From the *Canadian Forum,* October, 1929, 19-20. By permission of the *Canadian Forum.*

Henri Bourassa

From the *Canadian Forum,* August, 1932, 423-424. By permission of the *Canadian Forum.*

The Neglect of American Literature

From *Saturday Night,* November 21, 1931, 2-3. By permission of *Saturday Night.*

The Immediate Present in Canadian Literature

From *Sewanee Review,* 41 (1933), 430-442. By permission of *Sewanee Review.*

Mackenzie King of Canada

From *Harper's Magazine,* 186 (1943), 192-200. By permission of *Harper's Magazine.*

Our Neglect of Our Literature

From *Civil Service Review,* 17 (1944), 307-309. By permission.

To the North: A Wall Against Canadian Poetry

From *Saturday Review of Literature,* April 29, 1944, 9-11. By permission of *Saturday Review.*

A. J. M. Smith and the Poetry of Pride

From *Manitoba Arts Review,* 3 (1944), 30-32. By permission of *Manitoba Arts Review.*

The Poetry of Our Golden Age

This study, hitherto unpublished in English, is E. K. Brown's original English version of his French article, "L'age d'or de notre poésie," which appeared in *Gants du Ciel,* 11 (1946), 7-17. By permission of the estate of E. K. Brown.

Now, Take Ontario

From *Maclean's Magazine,* June 15, 1947, 12; 30-32. By permission of *Maclean's Magazine.*

Canadian Literature Today

From the *Winnipeg Free Press,* October 30, 1948 and October 29, 1949. By permission of the *Winnipeg Free Press.*

Duncan Campbell Scott: A Memoir

From *Selected Poems of Duncan Campbell Scott With a Memoir by E. K. Brown* (Toronto: The Ryerson Press, 1951), xi-xlii. By permission of the estate of E. K. Brown.

Canadian Poetry (1935-1949)

From "Letters in Canada," *University of Toronto Quarterly,* V-XIX (1946-1950). By permission of *University of Toronto Quarterly.*

Causeries

From the *Winnipeg Free Press.* By permission of the *Winnipeg Free Press.*

The Problem of a Canadian Literature

Towards the end of his life Matthew Arnold expressed his disapproval of a tendency in the United States to speak of an American literature. American authors should be conceived, he suggested, as making their individual contributions to the huge treasury of literature in the English language. It was wrong to deal with the Americans who made such contributions as if they formed a group apart, with a peculiar unity of its own. The reality of the unity among American writers is now so obvious as to be accepted by everyone who is not a crank. It has been demonstrated in histories, anthologies and critical studies, and not once but a hundred times, that to consider an American writer or a group of American writers as American is one of the most illuminating approaches one could make. There are, it need scarcely be said, other illuminating approaches: just as it would not be sufficient for the student of Carlyle to consider him solely in relation to his British predecessors, and contemporaries, so it would not be sufficient for the student of Emerson to consider him solely in relation to other Americans. But the study of Emerson against his American background is just as rewarding as the study of Carlyle against his British background. This is what is meant by saying that American literature is a useful concept, and the study of American literature an illuminating study. In expressing his disapproval of such a study Arnold was satisfied that he had reduced the idea to absurdity by pointing to an unbelievable future which would see histories of Canadian and

1

Australian literature. "Imagine the face of Philip or Alexander at hearing of a Primer of Macedonian Literature! Are we to have a Primer of Canadian Literature, too, and a Primer of Australian?" I think the time has come when to doubt the value of the concept of a Canadian literature, or an Australian, is to be a crank: a beginning has been made towards demonstrating that among Canadian, and Australian, writers, as among Americans, there is a peculiar unity, a unity sufficiently important as to make the approach to Canadian or Australian writers as Canadians or Australians a sharply illuminating approach. As I said above, in speaking of American writers, the national approach is not adequate, it is not the only illuminating approach, but it is valuable, and it throws into relief significant aspects which would otherwise fail to attract the attention that is their due.

At the beginning of his *History of English Canadian Literature to Confederation* Professor R. P. Baker defines his scope when he says that "it is wiser to consider only those authors of Canadian descent who maintained their connection with their native country and those of European birth and education who became identified with its development." In accepting this definition I should like to develop it to a point where it will have greater precision. By Canadian literature I shall understand writing by those who having been born in Canada passed a considerable number of their best creative years in this country, and also writing by those who, wherever they may have been born, once arrived in Canada did important creative work and led much of their literary life among us. Although this definition continues to have an element of indefiniteness, it will, I believe, serve to cover every author who will come before us in the development of Canadian poetry. I should add that, like Professor Baker, I shall include among Canadian writers those who wrote in any of the British colonies which now form part of the Canadian confederation even if at the time when they wrote their place of residence was outside what was then described as Canada: the significance of this addition will be to include all the Maritime authors whose lives, or literary lives, had ended by the time that the Canadian Confederation came into existence.

There is a Canadian literature, often rising to effects of great beauty, but it has stirred little interest outside Canada. A few of our authors, a very few, have made for themselves a large and even enthusiastic audience in Britain or in the United States or in both. Among these the first in time was Thomas Chandler Haliburton, a Nova Scotian judge, who would not have relished the claim that he was a Canadian. A curious blend of the provincial and the imperialist, he ended his days in England, where long before he himself arrived his humorous sketches were widely read, so widely that Justin McCarthy has reported that for a time the sayings of his most ingenious creation, Sam Slick, were as well known as those of the more durably amusing Sam Weller. Haliburton's papers were also popular in the United States, and their dialectal humour and local colour have left a perceptible stamp upon New England writing. At the mid century, when Sam Slick was already a figure in English humour, *Saul,* a huge poetic drama by a Montreal poet, Charles Heavysege, had a passing vogue in Britain and in the United States, impressing Emerson and Hawthorne and inducing Coventry Patmore to describe it as "indubitably one of the most remarkable English poems ever written out of Great Britain." Its vogue was lasting enough for W. D. Lighthall, a Montreal poet of a later generation, to recall that "it became the fashion among tourists to Montreal to buy a copy of *Saul.*" Today, along with Heavysege's other works, his *Count Filippo* and his *Jephthah's Daughter,* it is unknown within Canada and without. Even the songs and sonnets of Heavysege are absent from recent Canadian anthologies. At the turn of the century the animal stories of C. G. D. Roberts extended the range of North American writing in a direction it might naturally have been expected to take with equal success somewhat sooner – the imaginative presentation of the forms of wild life characteristic of this continent in their relationship to the frontiers of settlement. These tales, simple and at times powerful, continue to hold a high place in the rather isolated and minor kind of literature to which they belong; but there is no doubt that in our time they are more talked of than opened except by youthful readers. There is little need for comment upon the writings of a handful of Canadians who at about this same time began to make their huge and ephemeral reputations as best-selling writers. Gilbert Parker soon left Canada to establish himself in Britain, and it is to English literature, to that group of British novelists who followed in the wake of Stevenson's romantic fiction, that his work belongs. Preëminent among the others, Ralph Connor, L. M. Montgomery and Robert Service, continued to live in Canada, the first two until they died, Service till middle age. They were all more or less aggressively unliterary; and their only significance for our inquiry is the proof they offered that for the author who was satisfied to truckle to mediocre taste, living in Canada and writing about Canadian subjects, was perfectly compatible with making an abundant living by one's pen. The lesson they taught has not been forgotten: fortunately it has not been widely effective.

More recently Canadian work of value comparable with that of Haliburton's sketches and Roberts's animal tales has become known outside the country. There were the humorous papers of Stephen Leacock, the best of which have delighted not only Americans and Englishmen, and the peoples of other parts of the British Commonwealth, but also some Europeans. I can remember hearing M. André Maurois read to a group of students at the Sorbonne the charming study called "Boarding House Geometry"; and I never heard merrier laughter in Paris. The endless Jalna chronicles of Miss Mazo de la Roche maintain a large audience in Britain, and a sizable one in the United States; and in a more restricted group in the latter country the short stories and, to a less degree, the novels of Morley Callaghan are valued. I think that I have mentioned all the Canadians who have acquired considerable popularity or reputation as imaginative authors, either in the United States or in Great Britain. To the reader outside Canada such works as have been mentioned have not been important as reflections of phases in a national culture; the interest in the work has not spread to become an interest in the movements and the traditions in the national life from which the work emerged. Canadian books may occasionally have had a mild impact outside Canada; Canadian literature has had none.

III

Even within the national borders the impact of Canadian books and of Canadian literature has been relatively superficial. The almost feverish concern with its growth on the part of a small minority is no substitute for eager general sympathy or excitement. To one who takes careful account of the difficulties which have steadily beset its growth its survival as something interesting and important seems a miracle.

Some of these difficulties, those of an economic kind, may be easily and briefly stated. Economically the situation of our literature is, and always has been, unsound. No writer can live by the Canadian sales of his books. The president of one of our most active publishing companies, the late Hugh Eayrs, estimated that over a period of many years his profit on the sales of Canadian books was one per cent; and I should be surprised to learn that any other Canadian publisher could tell a much more cheerful tale, unless, of course, the production of text-books was the staple of his firm's business. Text-books make money in any country. In general the Canadian market for books is a thin one, for a variety of important reasons. The Canadian population is in the main a fringe along the American border: nine out of ten Canadians live within two hundred miles of it, more than half within a hundred miles. The one important publishing centre is Toronto; and a bookseller in Vancouver, Winnipeg or Halifax must feel reasonably sure that a book will be bought before he orders a number of copies which must be transported across thousands of miles. Books like *Gone with the Wind* and *The White Cliffs* – to keep to recent successes – he will order in quantity with confidence; but the distinguished work, the experimental novel, the collection of austere verse, the volume of strenuous criticism, is for him a luxury. The population of Canada is less than that of the State of New York; if our population were confined within an area of the same size the problem of distributing books would be soluble. Even if

5

our fewer than twelve million people were confined within the huge triangle whose points are Montreal, North Bay and Windsor – enclosing an area comparable with that of the region of New England – the problem might be soluble. But it is hard to see how the cultivated minority is to be served when its centres are separated by hundreds if not thousands of miles in which not a single creditable book-store exists.

Of the fewer than twelve million Canadians who are strung along the American border in a long thin fringe, almost a third are French-speaking. These read little if at all in any language except French, apart from a small, highly conservative minority which studies the classics and scholastic philosophy, and a rather larger minority which keeps abreast of books in English that treat of political and economic subjects. In French Canada the sense of cultural nationality is much stronger than in English Canada, but the nationality is French Canadian, not Canadian *tout court*. French Canada is almost without curiosity about the literature and culture of English Canada; most cultivated French Canadians do not know even the names of the significant English Canadian creative writers, whether of the past or of the present. Occasionally an important Canadian book is translated from the original into the other official language; but it is much more likely that the work of a French Canadian will be translated into English than that the work of an English Canadian will be translated into French. Louis Hémon was a *Français de France,* but it was because *Maria Chapdelaine* dealt with French Canada that a distinguished Ontario lawyer translated the novel into English, making one of the most beautiful versions of our time. W. H. Blake's translation of Hémon's book is a masterpiece in its own right; no French Canadian has as yet laboured with such loving skill to translate any book that deals with English Canada. A symbol of the fissure in our cultural life is to be found in the definition of sections in The Royal Society of Canada. Three sections are assigned to the sciences, one to mathematics, physics and chemistry, another to the biological sciences, and the third to geology and allied subjects; in these sections French and English fellows sit side by side. But in the two sections assigned to

6

the humanities the French and English fellows are severely separate: in each the subjects run the impossible gamut from the classics to anthropology. It is not too much to say that the maximum Canadian audience that an English Canadian imaginative author can hope for is fewer than eight million people.

To write in the English language is to incur the competition of the best authors of Britain and of the United States. Every Canadian publisher acts as agent for American and British houses; and it is as an agent that he does the larger and by far the more lucrative part of his business. Every Canadian reviewer devotes a large part of his sadly limited space to comment on British or American books. Every Canadian reader devotes a large part of the time and money that he can allow for books to those which come from Britain and the United States. Some angry critics have contrasted the plight of Canadian literature with the eager interest that Norwegians take in the work of their own authors. It is obvious that the accident by which Canadians speak and read one of the main literary languages of the world is a reason why they are less likely to read native books than a Norwegian is, speaking and reading a language peculiar to his own country.

Our great distances, the presence among us of a large minority which is prevailingly indifferent to the currents of culture that run among the majority, the accident of our common speech with Britain and the United States – here are three facts with enormous economic importance for literature. The sum of their effect is the exceedingly thin market for the author who depends on Canadian sales. Unless an author gives all or most of his time to writing for popular magazines he can make very little indeed; and even the resort of the popular magazines is a precarious solution. There are few of these – they, too, are affected by the factors that have been mentioned. They are in almost ruinous competition with American magazines, they cannot pay very much, they print a good deal written outside Canada, and they live so dangerous an existence they commonly defer slavishly to the standards of their average readers.

The serious Canadian writer has a choice among three

modes of combining the pursuit of literature with success in keeping alive and fed. He may emigrate: that was the solution of Bliss Carman, and many have followed in his train. He may earn his living by some non-literary pursuit: that was the solution of Archibald Lampman, and it has been widely followed. He may while continuing to reside in Canada become, economically at least, a member of another nation and civilization: that is the solution of Mr. Morley Callaghan. Each of these solutions is open to danger and objection.

The author who emigrates becomes an almost complete loss to our literature. It is probable that in the end, like Henry James or Joseph Conrad or Mr. T. S. Eliot, he will take out papers of citizenship in the country where he has found his economic security and to which he has transferred his spiritual allegiance. If he goes to Britain, the choice will not arise in this form, but he will be at best simply a citizen of the Empire ceasing to be an authentic Canadian. No one thinks of Grant Allen as a Canadian author nor did he so consider himself though he was born in Ontario. How the creative powers of a writer are affected by expatriation is much too vast a problem to receive adequate consideration here. Only this I should like to say: the expatriate will find it more and more difficult to deal vigorously and vividly with the life of the country he has left. Joseph Conrad did not write about Poland. When towards the end of his career Henry James read some of the early tales of Edith Wharton, before he had come to know her, he urged that she should be tethered in her own New York backyard. His own experience persuaded him that exile disqualified one from treating the life of one's own country without admitting one to the centre of the life in the country to which one had fled. If one compares the later novels of Edith Wharton, written after she had lost contact with New York, with the earlier ones which rose out of strong impacts that New York made upon her sensibilities, it is immediately evident that the colours and shapes are less vivid and definite, and that the works of her elder years are less significant. I should argue that Bliss Carman, our most notable exile, suffered a grave loss by passing his middle years in the United States, that he did not become an

8

American writer, but merely a *déraciné,* a nomad in his imaginary and not very rich kingdom of vagabondia.

People often ask why an author cannot satisfy himself with the solution of Archibald Lampman. Lampman, after graduating from Trinity College, Toronto, entered the employ of the federal government as a clerk in the Dominion Post Office at Ottawa. Why, people inquire, cannot a writer earn his living as a clerk, or a teacher, or a lighthouse keeper and devote his leisure to literature? The answer to this question must be an appeal to experience. One of our most gifted novelists, Mr. Philip Child, once remarked to me that a writer must be the obsequious servant of his demon, must rush to write when the demon stirs, and let other things fall where they may. If you fob off the demon with an excuse, telling him to wait till you can leave the office, he will sulk, his visits will become rarer and finally he will not return at all. Temperaments differ; and some writers may, like Anthony Trollope, give fixed hours to authorship and the rest of the day to business and pleasure. Even the Trollopes of this world would prefer to be free from their unliterary employments, since it is not to manage a post-office that a Trollope came into this world. Temperaments less phlegmatic than Trollope's find even the mild yoke of the post-office too heavy for them. Lampman did. He had easy hours, from ten to four-thirty, work which did not exhaust, and long holidays; but he was irked by his employment and made desperate and always unsuccessful efforts to escape from it. One has only to read his letters to realize that he believed that his task-work was fatal to his full development, and one has only to read his poems to believe that there was something in Lampman that never did come to full fruition, something that would have led to deeper and wiser poetry than he did write except in snatches. It appears to me so obvious as to require no argument that whatever success a particular writer may have had in combining the practice of his art with the business of earning a living by work which is remote from letters, the notion that a whole literature can develop out of the happy employment of the odd moments of rather busy men is an unrealistic notion, and one that shows an alarming ignorance of the process by which great works are normally

9

written. I suggest that the richness of Canadian poetry in the lyric and its poverty in longer and more complicated pieces, in epic, or dramatic composition, is related to the need of Canadians to be something else than writers in most of their time through their best creative years. Some of them have, like Matthew Arnold – also as a poet the victim of his unliterary employment – left unfinished their main poetic attempt.

There remains a third solution, Mr. Callaghan's solution. It is possible to write primarily for an American or a British audience. Most of Mr. Callaghan's novels and shorter tales are about the city in which he lives, Toronto; but it seems to me, and I speak as one who was born and brought up in that city, that Mr. Callaghan's Toronto is not an individualized city but simply a representative one. I mean that in reading Mr. Callaghan one has the sense that Toronto is being used not to bring out what will have the most original flavour, but what will remind people who live in Cleveland, or Detroit, or Buffalo, or any other city on the Great Lakes, of the general quality of their own milieu. If one compares Mr. Callaghan's Toronto with Mr. Farrell's Chicago, the point becomes very plain. When I pass through Mr. Farrell's Chicago, that part of the South Side which has been deserted by the Irish to be seized by the Negroes, the memory of what he has written of a life which has ceased to exist becomes very moving. When I walk through the parts of Toronto that Mr. Callaghan has primarily dealt with, the poor areas towards the centre and a little to the north-west of the centre, or the dingy respectability of the near east end, it is only with an effort that I remember that he has written of them at all. It is a notable fact that never once in all his novels does he use the city's name. Just as Mr. Callaghan uses his Canadian setting for its interest for a larger North American audience, so Miss Mazo de la Roche sets her emphasis on those exceedingly rare aspects of rural Ontario life which would remind an English reader of his own countryside and the kind of life that goes on in it. In the work of both writers an alien audience has shaped the treatment of Canadian life. Whether this peculiarity has injured the novelist's art as art, whether the characters and the setting are less alive and moving than the characters and setting in, let us say, Mr. Farrell's novels or Arnold Bennett's is not the immediate question; but there is not a scrap of doubt that the methods of Mr. Callaghan and Miss de la Roche have interfered with their presentation of Canadian life in the terms most stimulating and informing to Canadian readers. One of the forces that can help a civilization to come of age is the presentation of its surfaces and depths in works of imagination in such a fashion that the reader says: "I now understand myself and my milieu with a fullness and a clearness greater than before." Many a Russian must have said so after reading *Fathers and Sons* or *War and Peace.* It is difficult to believe that a Canadian will say this or anything of the sort after reading the work of Miss de la Roche or Mr. Callaghan.

I should like to turn for a moment to the question momentarily put aside, the question whether the solution adopted by such writers as Mr. Callaghan and Miss de la Roche is injurious to their art, whether it reduces the worth of their fiction for readers who are not Canadians, and not interested in the problems peculiar to Canada as the ideal Canadian reader must be. A great opportunity has been refused by Mr. Callaghan – the opportunity of drawing the peculiarities of Toronto in full vividness and force. This is a subject that no writer has yet treated. Most Canadians who are not born and bred in Toronto emphasize that there is a quality in the life of that city which is to them mysterious, and obnoxious. To make plain what that quality is, perhaps to satirize it as Mr. Marquand satirized something peculiar to Boston in *The Late George Apley,* perhaps to give it a sympathetic interpretation as Arnold Bennett interpreted the Five Towns in *The Old Wives' Tale* – here was a great theme calling aloud for imaginative treatment. Had Mr. Callaghan not been essentially a part of American civilization, it would have forced itself upon his perceptive and completely realistic mind. There is also something unique in the life of rural Ontario, something that no novelist has succeeded in catching, and Miss de la Roche has refused an opportunity perhaps no less golden than Toronto offers.

IV

The difficulties that have so far appeared, unlike as they are, all have economic roots. It is time to turn to the psychological factors, implied in much that has been said, against which the growth of a Canadian literature must struggle.

Among these the most obvious, the most discussed, although *not* the most potent, is the colonial spirit. Long ago Harvard's President Felton doubted that Canada would come to much since a colony was doomed to be second-rate. In a later generation an American who knew us much better than Felton and who wished us well, William Dean Howells, used almost the same language. In *Their Wedding Journey* he conducts his couple from Niagara Falls by way of Kingston and Montreal to the east coast, giving sharp little pictures of the Canadian towns; he concludes that in comparison with the free nation to which they belong this colony is second-rate in the very quality of its life. Just a year or so ago the Halifax novelist, Mr. Hugh MacLennan, gave to one of the colonially minded characters in *Barometer Rising* the same thought: "I've wasted a whole lifetime in this hole of a town. Everything in this country is second-rate. It always is in a colony." These are probably independent judgments. What do they mean? That a colony lacks the spiritual energy to rise above routine, and that it lacks this energy because it does not adequately believe in itself. It applies to what it has standards which are imported, and therefore artificial and distorting. It sets the great good place not in its present, nor in its past nor in its future, but somewhere outside its own borders, somewhere beyond its own possibilities.

The charge that English Canada is colonial in spirit is the most serious of all the many charges that French Canada brings against us. Speaking in the 1942 session of the Canadian House of Commons, Mr. Louis Saint Laurent, the leading French member of the government, illustrated what he meant by our colonialism when he cited an interchange that is supposed to have occurred within the last few years between the two living ex-prime ministers of Canada. One said to the other, on the eve of his departure to live in England: "I am glad to be going *home*," and the other replied: "How I envy you!" For these two men – if the interchange did occur – Canada was not the great good place; and every French Canadian would regard their sentiments as justifying his practice of referring to us not as *Canadiens Anglais,* but merely as *Anglais,* or when his blood is up, as *maudits Anglais!* Colonialism of this kind is natural to emigrants. One can easily forgive Sir Daniel Wilson, although he spent almost his entire active career in Canada, for wishing to lie in Scottish earth; and yet for a Canadian who knows what Scotland is like in November it is an awe-inspiring thought that Sir Daniel on one of our autumn days, full of the crashing scarlet glories of the Canadian forests or the mellow radiance of our Indian summers, wished to be amid the "sleety east winds" his native land. What is odd, and unsatisfactory, is the perpetuation of this kind of colonialism in the descendants of emigrants even to the third and fourth generation. It is clear that those who are content with this attitude will seek the best in literature, where they seek the best in jam and toffee, from beyond the ocean. That anything Canadian could be supremely good would never enter their heads.

It is important to distinguish this attitude of pure colonialism from another, which is steadily confused with it by all French Canadians, and combined with it by a good number of English Canadians. As the nineteenth century drew on and the concept of empire in Britain herself assumed a new colour, the Kipling colour, some Canadians spoke and wrote of a Canada which would be a partner in the destinies of a great undertaking in which Britain would not be the master, but simply the senior partner. Charles Mair, our first important political poet, expressed the view I have in mind when he wrote, in 1888:

> First feel throughout the throbbing land
> A nation's pulse, a nation's pride –
> The independent life – then stand
> Erect, unbound, at Britain's side.

Another poet, Wilfred Campbell, coined an impressive phrase for Canada's destiny: Canada was to be a part of "Vaster Britain." "Stronger even than the so-called Canadian spirit," he wrote, "is the voice of Vaster Britain." It is unjust to speak of this version of the imperialist ideal as showing the "butler's mind": it contemplated not serving Britain, but sharing Britain's glories. The psychological source of this intoxicating imperialism was not perhaps so much loyalty to Britain, but rather discontent with the dimensions of the Canadian scene. Canada was at the close of the last century a poor country, mainly concerned with material problems, and steadily losing many of her people to the large, rich, exultant land to the south. Imperialism was a kind of beneficent magic which would cover our nakedness and feed our starving spirits. The imperialist dream still lingers, but it is only a dream, for the mode in which the empire has evolved has been centrifugal – away from the concept of imperial federation – and there is nothing sufficiently rich and various to which the loyalty the dream evokes can attach itself. In practice the imperialist has drifted unconsciously into a colonial attitude of mind.

As the idea of imperial federation receded – and it was an idea that we may well judge impractical since French Canada could never have shared it, nor the Dutch in South Africa, nor the Southern Irish – Canada entered upon a period in which thinking was extremely confused. I cannot attempt to provide here any account of the extraordinary political evolution of the Dominions within the past generation. But the confusion is obvious if one notes merely a few significant political facts. Canada has no distinct flag, and no single distinct anthem although Mr. Mackenzie King paused on the very brink of asserting the latter; the relations between Canadian Provinces and the federal government are subject to review in London; and the Judicial Committee of the Privy Council, also in London, is our highest court. But Canada has her own ministers in foreign countries, makes treaties without reference to Britain, and declares, or refuses to declare, war by the instrument of her own Parliament. Is it any wonder that Canadian thinking about Canada is confused, that one set of clear-thinking men demand that we cease sending ministers and signing treaties and declaring war for ourselves, and that another set of clear-thinking men demand that we provide ourselves with a distinct flag and anthem and end the ingestion of the British Parliament and the British Privy Council in our affairs? The average English Canadian would still like to have it both ways and is irritated, or nonplussed, by the demand that he make a resolute choice; at heart he does not know whether Canada or the Empire is his supreme political value.

In the contemporary world autonomy is the most luxurious of privileges, one which this anxious country cannot now afford and will not be able to afford in any measurable future. It is not an unmixed good. Autonomy almost always breeds chauvinism, and usually brings as an immediate consequence an unwholesome delight in the local second-rate. Its advent opposes strong obstacles to international currents of art and thought. This is to be set firmly against the notion that out of autonomy all good things soon issue. Still it must be appreciated just as clearly that dependence breeds a state of mind no less unwholesome, a state of mind in which great art is most unlikely to emerge or to be widely recognized if it did. A great art is fostered by artists and audience possessing in common a passionate and peculiar interest in the kind of life that exists in the country where they live. If this interest exists in the artist he will try to give it adequate expression; if it exists in the audience they will be alert for any imaginative work which expresses it from a new angle and with a new clearness. From what was said a moment ago it will be obvious that in a colonial or semi-colonial community neither artist nor audience will have the passionate and peculiar interest in their immediate surroundings that is required. Canada is a state in which such an interest exists only among a few. I have pointed out how Mr. Callaghan and Miss de la Roche have written as they could not have written if they had possessed such interest. It is the same with Canadian readers. A novel which presents the farms of the prairie, or the industrial towns of southwestern Ontario, or the fishing villages in the Maritime Provinces will arouse no more interest in the general reader than a novel which is set in Surrey or in the suburbs of Chicago. Canadian undergraduates are much less likely than Americans to write stories about their immediate environment; their fancies take them to nightclubs in Vienna (rather than

Montreal), islands in the South Seas (rather than the St. Lawrence), foggy nights in London (rather than Halifax). It is almost impossible to persuade Canadians that an imaginative representation of the group in which they live could clarify for the reader his own nature and those of his associates. To the typical Canadian reader such a notion is arty folly. I give this as a fact; and I offer as a partial interpretation, at least, that most Canadians continue to be culturally colonial, that they set their great good place somewhere beyond their own borders.

Somewhere beyond their borders – not necessarily beyond the seas. Canada is colonial not only in its attitude towards Britain, but often in its attitude toward the United States. It is true that the imprint of a London publisher, or of a British university press is a more impressive guarantee of a book or an author than any Canadian sponsorship, even a Governor-General's. When the late Lord Tweedsmuir remarked that a Canadian's first loyalty should be towards Canada (rather than towards Britain or towards the empire) it was believed in some circles, and these not the least cultivated, that he had been guilty, as one journalist phrased it in cynical fun, of "disloyalty towards himself." It was inevitable that a Scottish man of letters should think in such terms, Scotland being almost wholly free from the spirit of colonialism. Pleas that we should seek to free ourselves from our colonial feelings towards Britain are met with cries of "ingrate!" or "traitor!" There can, of course, be no question of such open and violent objection against efforts to free us from a colonial attitude towards the United States. Our colonialism in relation to the United States is unavowed, but it is deep. The praise of a couple of New York reviewers will outweigh the unanimous enthusiasm of Canadian journals from coast to coast. There is every reason to suppose that as Canadian feeling becomes more and more friendly towards the United States, as it has done during the past quarter century, our cultural dependence on the Americans will grow. If it does, our literature may be expected to become emphatically regionalist; of the dangers of regionalism something will be said a little later.

One consequence of our colonial or dominion status, and

of our growing dependence on the United States and growing sense of security in American power, claims special note. Taking stock of our literature in 1891, and thinking in particular of the lack of national feeling or thought in it, Archibald Lampman wrote: "The time has not come for the production of any genuine national song. It is when the passion and enthusiasm of an entire people, carried away by the excitement of some great crisis, enters into the soul of one man specially gifted, that a great national poem or hymn is produced. We have yet to reach such an hour, and we may pray that it will not come too soon or too late." In the earlier years of the Confederation, when there was still some suspicion of the friendliness of the United States, Canadians felt that they had a strong defence in the force and prestige of England; and in later times the force and prestige of the United States as well has been conceived as an assurance that Canada need not fear aggression. There has been no moment in our history comparable with what England knew on the eve of the Elizabethan efflorescence, when the Armada approached her shores, or at the height of the Romantic achievement, when Napoleon gathered his forces at Boulogne, or in the early summer of 1940, when the salvation of the country depended upon itself alone. Nor has Canada known an internal crisis at all comparable to the War between the States. It is probable that, as Lampman supposed, a national crisis of supreme intensity would call forth emotions of such a strength and purity as to issue in a significant expression in the arts. We are probably as far, or almost as far from such a crisis in 1944 as in 1891. The only tension to become impressively more dangerous is that between the French and the other strains in the Canadian population; and this tension, alarming as it is, stopped far short of crisis on the two occasions when it has become acute, 1917 and 1942. The essential orderliness and forbearance of the Canadian character allows one to believe that the inter-racial tension will not escape from control. On some other issue at some time not yet to be foreseen the passion and enthusiasm to which Lampman looked will surge up and there will ensue a fierce coming of emotional age. Our Whitman is in the future.

V

A more powerful obstacle at present to the growth of a great literature is the spirit of the frontier, or its afterglow. Most Canadians live at some distance from anything that could even in the loosest terms be known as a material frontier; but the standards which the frontier-life applied are still current, if disguised. Books are a luxury on the frontier; and writers are an anomaly. On the frontier a man is mainly judged by what he can do to bring his immediate environment quickly and visibly under the control of society. No nation is more practical than ours; admiration is readily stirred, even more readily than south of the border, by the man who can run a factory, or invent a gadget or save a life by surgical genius. This kind of admiration is a disguised form of the frontier's set of values. No such admiration goes out to any form of the aesthetic or contemplative life. The uneasiness in the presence of the contemplative or aesthetic is to be ascribed to the frontier feeling that these are luxuries which should not be sought at a time when there is a tacit contract that everyone should be doing his share in the common effort to build the material structure of a nation. That a poem or a statue or a metaphysic could contribute to the fabric of a nation is not believed. In a gathering of ruminative historians and economists, speaking their mind one evening in Winnipeg years before the war was imminent, the unanimous opinion was that a destroyer or two would do more than a whole corpus of literature to establish a Canadian nationality. The dissent of two students of literature was heard in awkward silence. If there were any belief in the national value of art or pure thought, the strong desire of the frontiersman that what is being built should eclipse all that was ever built before would make a milieu for art and thought that would at the root be propitious.

In a disguised form of frontier life what function can the arts hold? They are at best recreative. They may be alternatives to the hockey match, or the whiskey bottle, or the frivolous sexual adventure as means of clearing the mind from the worries of business and enabling it to go back to business refreshed. The arts' value as interpretation is lost in the exclusive emphasis on their value as diversion, and even their value as diversion is simplified to the lowest possible form – a work of art must divert strongly and completely. It must divert as a thriller or a smashing jest diverts, not as an elaborate and subtle romance or a complicated argument diverts. In a word, Canada is a nation where the best-seller is king, as it is on the frontier.

A third factor telling against the appreciation of art is our strong Puritanism. Every foreign observer notes with amazement, both in our French and in our English books, the avoidance of the themes that irk the Puritan, or the language that now irks him more. Canada has never produced a major man of letters whose work gave a violent shock to the sensibilities of Puritans. There was some worry about Carman, who had certain qualities of the *fin de siècle* poet, but how mildly he expressed his queer longings! Mr. Callaghan has fallen foul of the censors of morals in some of our more conservative cities, and even among those of his own Roman Catholic faith a novel as *Such Is My Beloved* has had an uneasy path; but how cautious in the description of sordor and how chastened in language he has always been! Imagination boggles at the vista of a Canadian Whitman, or Canadian Dos Passos. The prevailing literary standards demand a high degree of moral and social orthodoxy; and popular writers accept these standards without even such a rueful complaint as Thackeray made in warning that he could not draw his Pendennis as a full man, since no hero of an English novel intended for the general public had been drawn in full since Fielding went to his grave.

Even our Canadian Puritanism, however, has not been proof against the international currents of moral relaxation which have coursed so strongly during the past quarter century. In the poetry of those who are now approaching their fortieth year, there is a broad range of emotion, which does not stop short of carnality, and an equally broad range of speed for which nothing in the Canadian literary past gave a precedent. This poetry does not yet circulate at all widely, most of it is still locked away in periodicals read by few, and it is not possible to be sure whether it could even yet pass the moral test of the general reading public.

If Puritanism operated simply to restrain the arts within the bonds of moral orthodoxy, its effects, though regrettable, would be much less grave than they are now. Puritanism goes beyond the demand for severe morality: it disbelieves in the importance of art. It allows to the artist no function except watering down moral ideas of an orthodox kind into a solution attractive to minds not keen enough to study the ideas in more abstract presentations. At its most liberal Puritanism will tolerate, a little uneasily, the provision through the arts of an innocent passing amusement which is expected to leave no deep trace on character. To popularize orthodox morality and to provide light, clean fun – that is the very limit of what the arts can be allowed to do without alarming the Puritan mind. For the Puritan a life devoted to one of the arts is a life misused: the aesthetic life is not a form of the good life. That profane art, both for artist and for audience, may provide the contemplation of being, may offer an insight into the life of things, is for the Puritan mist and moonshine.

Puritanism is a dwindling force, and the time is not far off when it will no longer exercise its ruinous restraint upon the themes or language of a Canadian writer who is addressing the general public. Regionalism, another force which tells against the immediate growth of a national literature, cannot be expected to dwindle so fast. Canada is not an integrated whole. The Maritime Provinces recall the days – only seventy-five years in the past – when they were separate colonies; Nova Scotia, for instance, has re-established its colonial flag, dating from the eighteenth century and flying now from the Province House at Halifax; French Canada is a civilization apart; Ontario unconsciously accepts itself as the norm of Canadian life; the Prairie Provinces are steeped in their special vivid western past; and British Columbia has a strong sense of its preconfederation life and of its continuing separate identity. Geography confirms the influence of history. Ontario is separated from the Maritime Provinces by the solid enclave of Quebec; between the populous southern part of Ontario and the prairies the Laurentian shield interposes another huge barrier; and this barrier is no stronger, if broader, than the Rocky Mountains create between the prairies and he coastal province of British Columbia. There is little doubt that the Fathers of Confederation, or the majority of the leaders among them, expected and planned for a much more unified whole than has so far come into being. In time of war the tendency to self-aggrandizement on the part of the Provinces is arrested, and even reversed; but here is ground for fearing that the return to peace will start into vigorous being once more. Among most Canadians here is little eagerness to explore the varieties of Canadian fe, little awareness how much variety exists, or what a peril that variety is, in time of crisis, to national unity. It may be that the next important stage of Canadian literature will be strongly particularist and regionalist: one remembers what a force regionalism was in American literature in the years after the Civil War.

Regionalist art may be expected to possess certain admirable virtues. One of these is accuracy, not merely accuracy of fact, but accuracy of tone; and throughout our literature there has been a disposition to force the note, to make life appear nobler or gayer or more intense than Canadian life really is in its typical expressions. It would help us towards cultural maturity if we had a set of novels, or sketches, or memoirs that described the life of Canadian towns and cities as it really is, works in which nothing would be presented that the author had not encountered in his own experience. It should also be acknowledged that a warm emotion for one's *petit pays* can lead to very charming art, as in Stephen Leacock's humorous transposition of Ontario town in his *Sunshine Sketches*. In the end, however, regionalist art will fail because it stresses the superficial and the peculiar at the expense, at least, if not to the exclusion, of the fundamental and universal. The advent of regionalism may be welcomed with reservations a stage through which it may be well for us to pass, as a discipline and a purgation. But if we are to pass through it, the coming of great books will be delayed beyond the life-time of anyone now living.

VI

What I have been attempting to suggest with as little heat or bitterness as possible is that in this country the plight of literature is a painful one. People who dislike to face this truth – and most Canadians do – have many easy answers. One is that Canadians have been so busy making a new world that it is harsh and unrealistic to expect that they might have written a large number of important books, read them with strong and general interest, and set a distinctive literary tone for their civilization. To this answer one may retort by pointing to what had been achieved in the United States a century ago, calling the roll of the names of those Americans who had written works of the first order, of national and international importance, by 1844 – Edwards, Franklin, Jefferson, Irving, Cooper, Poe, Hawthorne and Emerson. In certain other ways the American environment up to 1844 was more hospitable to literature than ours has been up to the present time; but there can, I think, be no doubt that Americans were in the century and a half preceding 1844 just as busy building the material structure of a nation as we have ever been. Another easy answer is often put in such terms as these: "If a Dickens begins to write in Canada we shall greet him with a cheer, we shall buy his books by the scores of thousands, get him appointed to the Senate of Canada, and request the Crown to give him an O.M. Meanwhile, don't bother us with your complaints. You can't point to a single man of anything approaching the calibre of Dickens who has written in this country. We have neglected no one of great importance. Wait till our Dickens comes along, and then we'll prove to you that we know how to honour a great writer." The line taken here depends on the belief that literature is an autonomous thing, a succession of single great men, each arising accidentally, each sufficient to himself. On this view you will get your great literature when you get your great men of letters, and meanwhile there is no problem worth discussing.

Thinking of this sort ignores a fundamental fact: that literature develops in close association with society. I should not deny that a single man of genius might emerge and express himself more or less fully in a society which was inhospitable to literature; but I find it significant that the most original of our poets, E. J. Pratt, has maintained:

> The lonely brooding spirit, generating his own steam in silence and abstraction, is a rare spirit, if indeed he ever existed, and as far as one may gather from scientific discussions on the point, there is no biological analogy for this kind of incubation. Rather, the mountains come to birth out of the foothills, and the climbing lesser ranges. The occasional instance cited in literary history, of personal isolation ignores the context of spiritual companionship with books and causes and movements.

The ways of genius cannot be fully predicted; but the "occasional instance," the single man of genius, is not a literature and does not bring a literature into being. No doubt if a Browning or a Yeats were to write in Canada and to make himself felt in Canada, the effect on Canadian literature would be considerable. But the stimulus such a writer could give, great though it would be, and much as it may be wished for by all who hope for the growth of a great literature in this country, would be a passing stimulus, unless it were assisted by social conditions friendly to creative composition. A great literature is the flowering of a great society, a vital and adequate society. Here I must reluctantly take leave of the subject, for it is not in the province of a student of letters to say how a society becomes vital and adequate.

In the observations I have offered it will be thought by many Canadians that the note of pessimism, or at least of rigour, is too strong. On the side of hope and faith it should be said that the future of Canada is almost singularly incalculable: none of the factors that now tell so strongly against the growth of our literature is necessarily eternal, and many of them are likely to diminish in force. Every reflective Canadian must feel a mixture of disturbance and delight in our inability to foresee even the main stresses of the Canada that will exist a hundred years from now.

The Abbé Groulx:
Particularist

French Canada has had three significant native historians, Garneau, Chapais, Groulx. These, the greatest names in French Canadian historiography, are probably the greatest in the broader field of French Canadian prose as well. Time has dealt harshly with Garneau. His massive history is almost altogether superseded as a work of reference: it is likewise antiquated in method and recalls the cumbersome histories of Garneau's contemporaries and masters, the historians of the Second Empire and early decades of the Third Republic. It is important to keep in mind that Garneau was never a really sound pillar of the French Canadian structure; his vivid particularism led him to doubt the value to French Canada of that international organization, the Catholic Church. Garneau would never have manned the walls of Rome; he would perhaps have been among the first to clamber through the Porta Pia. In his marked preference of the French Canadian for the Catholic faith, Garneau was a mirror of a large body of his compatriots; but this is a mirror into which they do not care to look too closely.

After Garneau, Chapais. For many years the occupant of a chair of history at Laval, a chair in the Legislative Council of the Province of Quebec, and a third, more lucrative chair in the Federal Senate, Thomas Chapais is one of the most attractive figures in the history of French Canadian culture. The several courses on the history of Canada which he has presented from the Laval chair of history, and reprinted substantially as delivered, form probably the most noteworthy and durable contribution to the political history of Canada, extant in either language. Senator Chapais is conscience and precision incarnate. He offers to his

24

readers no deceptive vistas of speculation, such as Garneau and the Abbé Groulx contrive; his business is with the determination of fact and the destruction of fiction and prejudice. Senator Chapais is no longer an oracle to the *élite* of Quebec; he lingers from a time when it was still admirable to think nationally rather than provincially, to sustain the policy of racial collaboration which was Laurier's in his prime, to acclaim Laurier as the greatest of his people, to regard with mild and measured contentment the imperial connection.

The young men of Senator Chapais's province have turned to a turbulent prophet for their catch words; turned to the Abbé Lionel Groulx, Professor of Canadian History at the rival and junior University of Montreal, and, for many years now, Editor-in-Chief of the slashing and smashing particularist review, the title of which was in 1927 changed from *L'Action Française to L'Action Canadienne-Français.* The cult of the Abbé Groulx and of the review which he ably directs, now evident in the students of Laval as well as of Montreal, and, indeed, in the Quebec intelligentsia generally, is an ominous sign of the times. The genesis of the cult is to be found in the dramatic events of a decisive decade in Canadian history; the second decade of this century.

The decade opened with the arrival at Ottawa of a number of fire-eating Quebec enthusiasts who sheltered their heretical doctrine beneath the empty euphemism – 'nationalists'. It saw the sequels to the Bourne *Gaffe,* – the Fallon letter, and an open rift in the Ontario Catholic hierarchy and laity. It saw the pathetic reversion of Laurier to the status of a racial leader. It saw the reluctance of French Canada, responsive to its popular tribune M. Bourassa, to transfer efforts in the battle for the welfare of French culture to a continent three thousand miles away. It was a decade of civil tragedy. Of this torrid decade the Abbé Lionel Groulx is a type; its history is his, and his works are the elaborate projection of his personal history.

This is not to deny that his patriotism is of long standing. Indeed he is a patriot to the manner born; Jean Grou, first and last of the name to cross from France died in defence of his farm and family and died a victor; – the Indian marauders, disheartened by the fighting power of the hand-ful of colonists gathered and led by Jean Grou, withdrew. For the Abbé Groulx, his ancestor is another Dollard des Ormeaux and the fight he fought another Long Sault. Born and bred in the county of Vaudreuil, of which he has writ-ten passionately in the early chapters of the pseudonymous novel *L'Appel de la Race,* the thought of Long Sault visited him often and was his guarantee of the invincible purity of French Canadian patriotism. The record of the ordinary events of his rural childhood is to be found scattered in the sheaf of sketches to which he gave the savoury title *Les Rapaillages.*

Later, as a student at Laval he made it his distinction that when for a Latin essay prize the theme presented was a Massachusetts orator urging upon a local meeting the demolition of French power in Canada, Lionel Groulx declined to compete. This was in the eighteen nineties; and for the Abbé Groulx then was the zero-hour of Canadian history. As a priest and teacher at Valleyfield, where he went soon after graduation from the University of Laval, he developed his interest in provincial history and pub-lished a brief but substantial history of the local com-munity on which it is now difficult to lay hands.

His important works come much later and are products of his activities in Montreal, courses delivered from his chair, papers contributed to his review. His great work remains unwritten; he aspires to be a philosophic historian of French Canada, to give a luminous and penetrating account of what Barrès called 'the Canadian miracle'. But the mass of his important writing has long been considera-ble; let us consider the provisional reputation which it justi-fies.

Where is the distinction of the Abbé Groulx? It is first of all in his striking powers of expression and emotion. No matter how worn his subject, or how ponderous and arid his facts, he has the secret of suffusing all he writes with an unforgettable and divinizing radiance. He writes with equal ability of the Canadian Vaudreuil thwarted by Montcalm (whose continental birth is for the Abbé Groulx a presumption of inferiority, if not an indelible sin); or of *patriotes* of 1837 mown down by the veterans of Waterloo or of the sullen eloquence of Antoine Dorion, exposing the spider's web of federation; or of the school-children of Green Valley striking for the right of instruction in the language of Champlain and Dollard and Jean Grou. Whenever a French Canadian does a deed of moment, he becomes by the recreative power of the Abbé Groulx's imagination something more than an individual, at once a factor and a type of the race's unending struggle for the immaculate preservation of its identity. It is in the recreative process that the historian's eloquence is fired, the eloquence of an academic Chateaubriand, the most luxuriant in Canadian prose. One may carp and cavil, set him down for a pulpit historian, smile at the disproportion between the minute event which prompts the outburst, and the outburst's magnitude; but sooner or later, if one is at all sensitive to the rhythm of excited French prose, the Abbé Groulx has won another admirer.

But what of the Abbé Groulx as an historian? As a polemist in the field of Canadian history he has but one French Canadian equal, M. Bourassa. He relies on emotion where Bourassa would appeal to *le bon sens';* he is vehement and verbose where Bourassa would be pointed and incisive. But as an historian? No one will deny that his study of Canadian history has been comprehensive and exhaustive. From the time of Cartier to the time of Laurier, no important source or secondary authority has escaped his search. But he appeals to these, not to correct or nuance his theses but to verify them. His principal thesis, his hobby horse, is that the credit and prosperity and prospective autonomy of French Canada belongs exclusively to the French Canadians. He finds in the French regime a large measure of ignorance and incompetence, in the British regime a much larger measure of intolerance and oppression. The protagonist in the drama of Canadian liberation is the shrewd obdurate *Canadien,* whose strict labour and populous families made Canadian life independent of the blunders committed by French worldlings, whose Norman slyness married to Breton stubbornness extorted from a nonplussed British parliament what Canadian life required. The Americanization of Canada is the Abbé's present bugbear, a menace of degradation and dissolution.

English Canada, ruled by lodges and congregations of fanatics, he regards with malevolence as a nursery of heresy and intrigue. The vials of his wrath are, it will be seen, copious; but in their flow, the British lion has the lion's share. The Abbé Groulx's references to Britain are mostly in the strain of a popular song which long ago ran like wild-fire through Quebec: –

> *Les Français aiment l'equité,*
> *Les Anglais la duplicité,*
> *Voilà la différence.*

This, if a little distressing, is explicable. The Abbé Groulx exhorts, he does not expound; history is to him a mine not for science, but for art, and in particular for the art of preaching. The emphatic justification for the study of Canadian history is its contribution to national pride. So opines the Abbé Groulx and this opinion debars him from the writing of scientific history.

Particularism is the doctrine correlative with the emotion of national pride. The Abbé Groulx is as ravenous a particularist as any Alsatian. He is a particularist in economics: he adjures the Quebec employer to protect the provincial resources from the tentacles of foreign capital, and the employee to protect his unions from foreign organizers. The economic world of French Canada is to be a unit, autonomous and complete. He is a particularist in religion: he adjures the clergy and laity of Quebec to maintain an intact identity in resistance to 'the Irish peril'. He is a particularist in politics: he anticipates, although he will not precipitate, the disruption of Confederation, and, in consequence, wishes Quebec provided with all the organizations proper to a nation's life. In law, in education, in literature, domains to which he has given less attention, his particularism is radical and unvarying.

As I write these words, within hearing of the din, and almost within sight of the frippery of the annual Orange parade of the principal city in the Dominion, it occurs to me that in the drastic but plausible doctrines of the Abbé Lionel Groulx, there is a menace to Canadian unity far more disquieting than all the activities of all the lodges in the land.

Henri Bourassa

The respect which M. Henri Bourassa commands almost everywhere in the province of Quebec as well as among all English-Canadians who do not take a worm's eye view of national affairs is based on a recognition that he has a clear, complete, and tenable political philosophy. One of the chief tendencies in French-Canadian thought during the past fifteen years has been the progressive depreciation of the eloquent parliamentarians who have seen no need for such a philosophy and are content to be the phonographs of their constituents and their party. Sir Wilfrid Laurier – 'that opera-star' as M. Bourassa calls him – has perhaps suffered more from the new exigencies of Quebec than anyone else; but Laurierites like M. Rodolphe Lemieux and M. Jacques Bureau have shared in a large measure their leader's fate. And M. Bourassa, who for forty years has professed a philosophy unchanging in its essentials and preached it in the House of Commons, on platforms and in the columns of *Le Devoir,* has become a figure vastly more influential than they. You know where to have him. The war of 1914-1918 proved the rigorous consistency of his attitude: no man of our time has endured more petty gibes, more slanders, more threats of physical violence, and M. Bourassa endured them month after month, year after year, without bating a jot of his doctrine.

He has written no great book. Perhaps his life has been too packed with action and contention to allow for the long quiet incubation such a book would require. Perhaps, and it is more likely, he has not the sort of mind which expresses itself in a few matured and finished works. He has put in circulation what is more precious than a great book: an idea of capital importance traced along all its ramifications. He has defined Colonialism and he has instructed us how to purge ourselves of it. He was not the first to see the havoc wrought by Colonialism: Papineau and D'arcy McGee, to name but two, saw its dangers and worked to forestall them. M. Bourassa has pressed his analysis further than they; he has revealed Colonialism at the bottom of many wells where its contamination was not suspected; above all he has pointed out the way of escape more effectively than anyone else.

Political Colonialism he has attacked since the outbreak of the South African War. That war, he said, concerned England and the Boer states. Not only was it possible to justify Canadian abstention from it: it was impossible to justify Canadian participation. For Canada to participate was to prove herself for the first time a militant and causelessly aggressive power. A decade later when the proposal came up that Canada should contribute to the maintenance of the British navy he spoke out again. Was Canada herself in a state of adequate defence? Could Halifax and Vancouver withstand attack? Was the Saint Lawrence fortified? Was there a satisfactory pact for mutual defence between Canada and the formidable nation to the south? To put a few watchdogs on our own doorsteps would be the best initial act for Canada as an armed power.

M. Bourassa's gift for asking unpopular questions was shown again during the European War. He wished to know whether there was ground to think that Germany was proposing to annex or invade Canada and whether there was any specific quarrel between the two states. If the right answer to these questions was No, then as a peaceable people it was our duty to remain neutral. French Canadians were urged by their English compatriots to rush to the defence of France if they had no patriotic feeling for England. A blatant piece of special pleading, said M. Bourassa in *Le Devoir*. If England were at war with France, the English-Canadians would sing another tune. Anyhow French-Canada owed no debt to France. A Colonialist attitude toward the impious Third Republic was worse than a Colonialist attitude toward England; even the French monarchy

30

had proved a cruel and then a neglectful step-mother to the French-Canadians. Naturally a newspaper-editor who in war-time spoke his mind with such frankness did not do so with impunity. We have our own example in J. A. Macdonald. The offices of *Le Devoir* were ravaged by a drunken mob. Once when M. Bourassa was addressing a gathering in Ottawa, soldiers in uniform broke up the meeting and, as he says, added to the crime of disorderly conduct that of insult to an allied nation when they ignorantly hissed the Marseillaise. Fifteen years later M. Bourassa's insistence that the only reasonable attitude for Canada in the domain of foreign affairs is one which asks not what the Empire wants but what is the peculiar interest and the peculiar duty of Canada seems almost commonplace. We have travelled a long way on M. Bourassa's path from colony to nation and are now in small danger of overestimating the scope of our imperial obligations or talking idly of the lioness and her whelps. A French-Canadian leader with the imperial outlook of Laurier is now inconceivable.

The subtler menace of social and moral Colonialism is what besets us today. Sixty years ago William Dean Howells, who knew Canada extraordinarily well, remarked: –

The constant reference of local hopes to that remote centre beyond the seas, the test of success by the criterions of a necessarily different civilization, the social and intellectual dependence implied by traits that meet the most hurried glance in the Dominion, give an effect of meanness to the whole fabric.

Howells had English-Canada in mind when he drafted that comment: and even today, English-Canada is without a distinctive culture or civilization and almost entirely ignorant of the nascent culture and civilization of Quebec. Some of our traits we describe, when we encounter them in the man across the way, as English, others as American. We should be hard pressed if a visitant from Sirius were to ask us to name some trait which was neither English nor American. If we succeeded it too would be derivative – our Scottish attitude towards the Sabbath, for example. Professor Norman Rogers in his review of Professor Brady's *Canada* stated that our culture could be authentic even if imitative; and in such a statement he represents almost the whole of English-Canada. Surely this is to rob the idea of authenticity of all meaning. What in Professor Rogers' view is a spurious culture?

Now the French Canadians have gone far beyond us in the development of an indigenous culture. There is a discernible cohesion between the sermons of the patriotic clergy, the articles of the political philosophers grouped about the Abbé Lionel Groulx and the *Librairie d'Action Française,* the linguistic purists of Laval and the authors of sketches and novels of the *terroir*. M. Bourassa, along with the Abbé Groulx, M. Edouard Montpetit, and Canon Emile Chartier, has striven to harmonize and unify the particular activities and aims of such varying groups as those mentioned. Besides he is an effective policeman: he has his eye on the renegades who from snobbery or sycophancy or the desire for great wealth betray the French-Canadian cause and go over to the English society of Montreal and Ottawa.

Most English-Canadians fail to distinguish between the political philosophy of the Abbé Groulx and that of M. Bourassa. The distinction is fundamental. As I pointed out in a paper published in THE CANADIAN FORUM for October 1929, the political ideal of the Abbé Groulx is a French-speaking republic on the banks of the Saint Lawrence. That ideal M. Bourassa has always opposed. Such a republic, he says, would stand to Anglo-Saxon North America in about the position in which Monaco stands to France. Moreover, to achieve it Quebec would be obliged to break faith with the French-Canadian settlements in Ontario and the western provinces. M. Bourassa prefers to accept the Canadian Confederation as the permanent frame for French-Canadian destinies. The Abbé Groulx once complained that certain French-Canadians had adopted 'a too broadly Canadian patriotism' merging the loyalty due to the race in loyalty to a shadowy nationality. M. Bourassa is disposed to be as broadly Canadian as English-Canadians will allow him; and when one reads the reports of his speeches in the House of Commons with the frequent and fatuous interruptions of Ontario Orangemen one is grateful for his longanimity.

At one point even the most tolerant English-Canadian will properly reject M. Bourassa's political philosophy; and it is a point on which M. Bourassa would never compromise. He is not merely a devout Catholic, but a clerical as violent as Louis Veuillot; and it is difficult to conceive of a clericalist philosophy shaping a nation in which Catholicism is not the religion of an overwhelming majority. Clericalism has been one of the stumbling-blocks in the way toward national unity in France and Germany; and M. Bourassa gives us no reason to think that it would be less of a peril in Canada. While I am in the chapter of reproaches, let me implore M. Bourassa not to charge English-Canada with *'matérialisme'*: the first desideratum in an indictment is that the person indicted should understand it; and there is probably not one English-Canadian who has the least glimmer of what the French-Canadians mean when they use that conveniently comprehensive word. They use it so often they should pay it extra.

It was one of Lowell's soundest generalizations that before there could be an American literature there must be an American criticism. If he had had the shameless honesty of Bernard Shaw, he would have said that what America needed was as many Lowells as she could stand. That is exactly what we in Canada need today. Goldwin Smith is the nearest to this type of critic that English-Canada has come; Henri Bourassa comes nearer to it than any other French-Canadian. It is a pity that French-Canada has profited so little from the first of these masters and English-Canada so little from the second.

The Neglect of
American Literature

The study of American literature has a very small place in the Canadian universities. In several of them it has indeed no place at all, and students may go out to teach English without having read an essay of Emerson or Lowell, a poem of Whitman or Lanier, or a novel of Hawthorne or Henry James. In only one of our universities is American literature given a place more generous than Anglo-Saxon is given. Arranging the Canadian universities in three groups, – the Maritimes, the Central and the Western, – let us see just how odd our treatment of American literature has been.

In the Maritime provinces only one university provides for the study of American literature. Neither Mount Allison, nor New Brunswick, nor Saint Francis Xavier, nor Dalhousie is officially aware of its existence. Yet Dalhousie for more than eight years has had a full course of two hours a week throughout the session on *Literary Movements in Canada.* I say "yet" because the mind which responds to the claims of Canadian literature is seldom averse to the academic study of American literature. Acadia does make generous provision for American literature; here there is a course on *Contemporary English and American Drama;* some consideration of the American poets in a survey of *Modern English Literature;* and a course of three hours a week throughout the session on *American and Canadian Literature.* The calendar describes the American half of this course in these words: "A general study of American literary activity from the beginning to the present time, with special attention to the New England and the New York schools of writers." It is a disappointment to find that the content of the course reveals a strange scale of values: *Uncle Tom's Cabin* and a novel of the New England Winston Churchill (horresco referens) are here, and Herman Melville and Lafcadio Hearn are not.

Of the central universities, Queen's is the only one which provides at all generously for the study of American literature. At McGill a quarter of a course is allowed; although in justice I must add that in the two courses on the English novel American authors are given their due. At McMaster no provision is made; and at Western Ontario – where there is a full course on Canadian literature as extensive as that at Dalhousie – there is the same scorn of American work. If one were to trust the University of Toronto calendar, Toronto would be in the case of McMaster; but the truth is that for four or five years an optional course on American literature has been furnished in one of the four colleges. At Queen's there is a full course on *American and Canadian Literature.* The American course "rapidly surveys the field indicated, emphasizing the work of Irving, Cooper, Bryant, Poe, Emerson, Hawthorne, Lanier, Whitman, Mark Twain, Henry James and other writers."

In the western universities an attitude as niggardly as in the others is found. The programmes are more elastic in these universities, the authority of British tradition is less solid, and there is a greater number of American professors. At Manitoba there is a course similar to that given at Queen's, but including certain contemporary poets. And here as at Saskatchewan Emerson is allowed a place in general courses on nineteenth century prose. There is no systematic study of American literature at Saskatchewan, nor, – if the calendar is to be trusted – at Alberta. At British Columbia there is "a survey of the principal writers of this continent during the nineteenth century", a survey similar in scope to the course at Queen's.

What is done in other countries? Is the study of American literature a domestic occupation? What is done at Oxford? Neither at Oxford nor at any other university in the British Isles or in the Dominions other than Canada is American literature a subject of study. But in France and

Germany it is. Let us examine what is done in France.

At the University of Paris and at the University of Lyons there are instructors who devote all their time to the teaching and investigation of American literature; and at Paris there has been since 1926 an endowed chair in the subject, the professor being a former professor of English literature at Bordeaux. In these two universities there is a certificate in American literature equivalent to the certificate in English literature except for those who purpose to teach. In the final comprehensive examination in English, the *aggregation,* it is not unusual that one-third of the programme should be American. More important still is the fact that a remarkable number of theses for the State doctorate in English are studies of American matters. I say "more important" because it is the holders of the State doctorate who mold the programmes and policies of the French universities. There are two pairs of these on Whitman and on Poe; there is a thesis on Hawthorne which Barrett Wendell thought to be the best study of Hawthorne that he had read; there is a thesis on Cooper; there is a thesis on French influence on American poets, good enough to please the exacting taste of Mr. Edmund Wilson. Besides these there are many theses for the University doctorate, some of them of high value. To the mild and ineffectual displeasure of some of the elder *anglicistes* more and more of the younger French scholars in Anglo-American matters are turning their eyes to American literature. The more spirited critics are moving with them.

The French enthusiasm for American literature is of special interest since the French are proverbially indifferent to foreign literatures. It should lead us to inquire whether American literature has not a universal significance, an absolute value. Dr. Havelock Ellis writing in *The New Spirit in Literature* asserted that apart from the novelists there were five American writers whose importance was "universal": Emerson, Thoreau, Poe, Whitman, William James. Each of these has had foreign recognition; Emerson almost everywhere; Thoreau in England; Poe in France and England; Whitman in France, England and Germany; William James in France, England and Italy. Of the American novelists, universal significance can be predicated of Melville and of Henry James, if one remembers to assert that their future is likely to be greater than their past abroad as at home. Stuart Sherman, who was until his last years essentially a student of English rather than American literature, claimed in 1923 that in the following list of parallel writers the American was in all cases the more significant. "It is not too soon," he contends, "to declare that, if a choice must be made, the American student should choose to be familiar with 'The Federalist', rather than with the Letters of Junius, with Irving rather than Leigh Hunt, with Emerson rather than Carlyle, with Thoreau rather than Richard Jefferies; with Whitman rather than William Morris, with Mark Twain rather than Oscar Wilde, with Henry James rather than George Moore, and with Theodore Roosevelt rather than Queen Victoria. In every case I have mentioned the preference of a native writer would also, I believe, be the preference of a greater personality." The only comment this catalogue of comparisons prompts is that Stuart Sherman, doubtless with full consciousness of what he was about, understated the case for the Americans, by choosing English writers very markedly their inferiors. There has never been a time when a reputable English critic would set more store by Richard Jefferies than by Thoreau, by Leigh Hunt than by Irving, by William Morris than by Whitman.

The absolute value of American literature lies in the work of the five writers named by Dr. Ellis, in the work of most of those named by Stuart Sherman, and in the work of three or four who did not enter into the context of these catalogues. Their works are irreplaceable; their value is absolute in the sense that if we did not pass the portals of their works we should be evidentially the poorer. We should be the poorer if we did not know the Emersonian doctrine of self-reliance with its supreme formulation of the *non serviam,* "if I am the Devil's child I will live then from the Devil"; we should be the poorer if we did not know the ethical shudder of Hawthorne and his twilight world of symbols; we should be the poorer if we did not know Melville's grandiose orchestration of the Byronic themes of guilt, loneliness and fatality; we should be the poorer if we did not know the scrupulous civilization of Henry James and the homely culture of Thoreau; we should be ineffably the poorer if we did not know Poe's ravenous love of the exotic and the monstrous and his prolific from which emerged all the exquisite poetry of the symbolists; and we should be ineffably the poorer if we did not know the plasticity of Whitman's verse and the overpowering completeness of Whitman's honesty. These are the voices of the American experience; and since the American experience has been both unique and significant, the voices which have made it articulate are precious in an absolute sense.

Apart from the absolute value of the major works of its greatest writers, American literature has a special value for Canadians, as the literature of the higher rank which is morally and socially nearest their own experience. No matter how devoted we may be to our national literature, we cannot for a moment appraise it a literature of the first rank, a literature which will provide students with the aesthetic experiences and the drama of literary development into which they must be initiated. All the English departments in Canada act upon the conviction that these experiences and the sense of this development are to be sought wholly or nearly wholly in the literature of England. They do not perhaps adequately recognize that "even the best modern authors of England — accessible though they are and closely related — are imperfect equivalents for the native authors that we need to express for us the individual adventures and the social sense of men and women who live under our own national conditions". The professors of English at Saskatchewan did recognize this when the prescribed *Maria Chapdelaine* and *The House of the Seven Gables* in their freshman course.

It will be said that an American writer is not a native author. But our "individual adventures" are far more like an American's than an Englishman's; and in most parts of the country this is true of our "social sense" as well. Perhaps I can best illustrate this if I contrast for a moment *The Old Wives' Tale* with *The American Tragedy*. *The Old Wives' Tale* is essentially a study of the middle class in the North of England; and *The American Tragedy* is essentially a study of the middle class in the Northern states. How much in Bennett's novel is remote from normal Canadian experience. In our industrial cities do people often die in the houses in which they were born? Do affluent merchants and their wives acknowledge social superiors? Do their sons drift into being artists? Do such cities recoil from consolidation as a threat to local identities? To a young Canadian of the middle class this novel of the English middle class leads into another world and bewilders as it leads. With *The American Tragedy* there is no bewilderment. The upstate New York city in which most of it occurs might be Hamilton or Windsor; the factory, the operatives, the owners, the society dominated by the young unmarried set; the social success of a young man, handsome, well dressed and nice mannered; the gravity of his being poor and his resentment of this barrier to happiness; the luxurious "camps" on the northern lakes which might be Rosseau or Muskoka; everything in *The American Tragedy* from the sordid to the gorgeous is Canadian, everything but the electric chair.

Of all the great poets Whitman is the one most suited to the Canadian experience. The huge lakes, plains and mountains of Canada; its fierce extremities of heat and cold; its diversity of races and creeds; its loyalty to mere power and mere money; the thinness of its culture and its national consciousness, a culture and a consciousness in the earliest stages of formation; all the aspects of the Canadian scene prepare us to find our "individual adventures" and our "social sense" in *Leaves of Grass*. Is there any experience lying in wait for the Canadian who reads English poetry that can arouse his emotions as readily as a passage like this from *By Blue Ontario's Shore:*

> The separate States, the simple elastic scheme, the immigrants,
> The Union always swarming with blatherers, and always sure and impregnable,
> The unsurvey'd interior, log-houses, clearings, wild animals, hunters, trappers,
> Surrounding the multiform agriculture, mines, temperature, the gestation of new States,

Congress convening every twelfth-month, the members duly coming up from the uttermost parts,

Surrounding the noble character of mechanics and farmers, especially the young men,

Responding their manners, speech, dress, friendships, the gait they have of persons who never knew how it felt to stand in the presence of superiors,

The freshness and candour of their physiognomy, the copiousness and decision of their phrenology,

The picturesque looseness of their carriage, their fierceness when wrong'd

The fluency of their speech, their delight in music, their curiosity, good temper, and open-handedness, the whole composite make,

The prevailing ardour and enterprise, the large amativeness,

The perfect equality of the female with the male, the fluid movement of the population,

The superior marine, free commerce, fisheries, whaling, gold-digging,

Wharf-hemm'd cities, railroad and steamboat lines intersecting all points,

Factories, mercantile life, labour-saving machinery, the North-east, North-west, South-west,

Manhattan firemen, the Yankee swap . . .

There is nothing in Browning or Tennyson, in Housman or the Sitwells as "available" as this; and *By Blue Ontario's Shore* is not of Whitman's best. Yet even in the University of Western Ontario, situated in the city of Dr. Bucke, one of Whitman's most important associates, a city in which there are priceless Whitman manuscripts, students graduate with honors in English and know no more of Whitman than if they came from Trinity College, Dublin. Without thanks the librarian of Trinity College returned to Edward Dowden his gift of a copy of *Leaves of Grass*; and one hesitates to predict what havoc the more austere citizens of Western Ontario might work on the treasure in their midst.

There are two dovetailing explanations for the Canadian neglect of American literature. One of these is the practice of the universities in the British Isles. Up to 1800 there were few American works of more than national significance; and the universities in the British Isles are still inhospitable to the English writers of the past hundred and thirty years. A professor of English at the Sorbonne once confided to me his astonishment at the English belief that there was more dignity and merit in occupying oneself with Spenser than with Browning, with Sidney than with Pater. And the second Merton Professor of English Literature at Oxford announced in his inaugural lecture in 1923 that he had no pity for the undergraduate who had been so busy with Beowulf that he had been obliged to skimp his study of Keats. The anomaly has its cause in the fact that at Oxford and Cambridge there were chairs in Anglo-Saxon long before there were chairs in English literature. Since the war, it is true, more ample provision is being made for the study of modern English literature in the country in which it has been written.

If American literature has not shared in this belated justice, it is because the English attitude toward American culture is still somewhat *maratre*. "The common blood", as Lowell perceived, "and still more the common language, are fatal instruments of misapprehension." They lead the Englishman to set the American down as "a counterfeit Briton whose crime appeared in every shade of difference". It is not long since a writer in one of the great quarterlies alleged that the only art in which America could pretend to excellence was the art of the negro spirituals. It is not much longer since the author of a handbook of criticism denied that there was an American poet. Two or three years ago the American author most popular among English undergraduates was Sinclair Lewis; and their delight in him was a simple case of his procuring them the holier-than-thou mood. These are detached instances, it will be said, but no one would say they were misrepresentative after reading the reviews of American books which appear in the Literary Supplement of *The Times*. There is nothing obsolescent about Lowell's essay *On a Certain Condescension in Foreigners*. In the things of the mind and the spirit, Americans are still "treated as a kind of inferior and deported Englishman whose nature they (the English) perfectly understand, and whose back they accordingly stroke the wrong way of the fur with amazing perseverance". The universities are seldom in advance of the critics and reviewers – although it must be held to Oxford's honor that Lowell himself was invited to take her chair of English literature; and not until the generality of cultivated minds accepts American culture as a culture of the first order, are the universities likely to admit American literature to their programs. There is one hope, however; Oxford accepted Lord Northcliffe's gift of a chair in American history; there is no reason to fear that Oxford would reject a gift from, shall we say, Lady Astor of a chair in American literature.

Infallibly such a gift would have its repercussion in the Canadian universities. Many a Canadian professor would begin to evince an interest in American culture. There would still remain, however, our particular Canadian form of snobbery which is, as Professor Underhill has said, a conviction of our superiority to the Americans. There is no cause for humiliation or concern in the superiority of the general body of English literature to the general body of ours, or of the contemporary English productions to ours. The superiority is so overwhelming and it is so clearly explicable that there is no sting in it for us. It is something of a humiliation and it may well give us anxious concern to remember the glory of American literature in a period as remote as that from 1830 to 1860. To those thirty years belong the later works of Irving and Cooper; the whole of Edgar Allen Poe; all that matters of Emerson, Hawthorne, and Melville; *Leaves of Grass, Walden, The Oregon Trail, The Autocrat* and *The Professor at the Breakfast Table.* And there are minor works of notable importance in a very large number. Well may Mr. Lewis Mumford describe such a period as The Golden Day. Seventy years later, what have we to place beside such a garner? It is difficult to be snobbish, it is difficult to remain erect when one has taken stock of what we have. With what an English classicist calls our "blank, bland blonde optimism" we avert our eyes from the American performance and keep them resolutely fixed not on our own but on the English.

The Immediate Present in Canadian Literature

The present state of Canadian literature is economically unsound. No poet or critic or even novelist could live decently on the Canadian sales of his works. No dramatist could exist at all on the proceeds of the Canadian performances of his plays. Three alternatives are before the literary artist who has had the doubtful luck to be born in Canada. He may, like Grant Allen or Bliss Carman, emigrate and become a part of another culture. Or he may, like Mazo de la Roche or Morley Callaghan, become, economically at least, a part of another culture without emigrating. This is a precarious thing to do and it is doubtful whether it can be successful, artistically, or economically, in the long run. The third alternative is to earn one's living in an unliterary, or semi-literary, occupation and to create only in one's leisure. Such a solution was permanently satisfactory for Charles Lamb in the office of the East India Company or for Joris Karl Huysmans in the French Ministry of Foreign Affairs. In North America the tempo of commercial and financial life is too swift and too exhausting to permit of such achievements as Lamb's unless the artist be a man of prodigious vitality. The writing of Canadian literature, then, goes on under economic difficulties almost overpowering.

Canadian attitudes to Canadian literature are also unsound and disabling. There is, first of all, the attitude of the small but precious group of Canadians of cosmopolitan culture. These people are to be found in small numbers in almost every city or large town in Canada and in somewhat larger numbers in our musical, dramatic, political, and educational centres. Nowhere are they powerful enough to exert an open influence. Nowhere do they determine the form or the flow of local life. These citizens of the world care for good books; they read them as closely as they are read in London or New York; they are, many of them, excellent judges of literary values. They do not care particularly where a book is published. Many of them have never read *Jalna,* some of them know Morley Callaghan only by vulgar report, very few of them knew even the name of the man whom I esteem our greatest living poet, Abraham Klein. There is, perhaps, a drop or two of hostility in their attitude to Canadian literature. So often at the suggestion of enthusiastic friends have they wasted an evening with a mediocre Canadian novel or volume of verse!

In direct contrast to the attitude of this group is that of another, scarcely, if at all, larger, the group of the truculent advocates of Canadian literature. This is a more coherent group. "Nothing is more pleasant to man than incorporation", said Lord Shaftesbury the essayist. The members of this group are incorporated in many local and national societies; and they have an open if not very extensive influence upon the Canadian public. A colleague of mine, addressing one such group a year or two ago, ventured to suggest that our lyric poets, of the last generation, Carman, Lampman, and Roberts, were not quite the equals of the masters of English romantic poetry in whose school they learned most of their best lessons. He was taken to task as a traitor. Now anyone who believes that our lyric poets are the equals of Shelley, Keats, and Wordsworth will believe anything. In Lewis Carroll's phrase, he will believe as many as seven impossible things before breakfast. It would, however, be a grievous injustice to dismiss the advocates of Canadian literature as merely or mainly unreasonable. Their tone is the result of a natural and justified resentment of the somewhat scornful indifference of our cosmopolitans and, even more, of the attitudes of the third group now to be considered.

This third group is the general reading public in Canada. If the present state of Canadian literature is economically unsound, as I asserted at the beginning of this paper and as I could easily prove if proof were necessary, the chief responsibility lies here, with what Virginia Woolf calls, with no hint of disparagement, the common readers, the immense number of men and women whose main concern in life is not with literature. The Canadian public is not hostile to Canadian literature but it is indifferent. It does not know good prose from spineless sprawling prose, and therefore it endures the Canadian press. It does not know great drama from infantile melodrama and hoodlum comedy, and therefore it endures the English and American movies. It does not know competent and stirring painting from sentimental wash of color and therefore it endures the pictures sold in our emporia. The public of the American Middle West and Far West is much the same. American critics, attempting to explain the aesthetic insensitiveness of this public, invoke the concept of the frontier, evolved a generation ago by Professor Turner. Most Canadians live at some distance, physical and mental, from the frontier; but their attitude to life has still many elements natural to the frontiersman. Attitudes to life change much more deliberately than the material conditions of life. There is always what the sociologists call a cultural lag. Now, the material conditions at the frontier place a premium on action, physical strength, will, patience. Not only was there no function for the artist on the frontier; the desires in people which appeal to the artist for satisfaction, the desire for beauty, the desire for knowledge of life in general, the desire for the representation of complex and subtle relationships between individuals, were out of place on the frontier and tended to atrophy. The material conditions of the frontier have passed away from most Canadian towns and cities, but we have not attained the balance of mind which exists at the centres of civilization. We are, most of us, in the frontiersman's attitude to literature. Literature is a luxury. The reading of books is primarily a means of killing time, a substitution for a cigar, or a rugby game, or a movie. The cultivated and observant mind of Mr. Louis Bromfield states the North American cultural dilemma in these words:

Life is hard for our children. It isn't as simple as it was for us. Their grandfathers were pioneers and the same blood runs in their veins, only they haven't a frontier any longer, they stand . . . these children of ours . . . with their backs toward this rough-hewn middle west and their faces set toward Europe and the East and they belong to neither. They are lost somewhere between.

Most Canadians have not yet squarely turned their backs on the frontier, but they are turning them. When they have done so they will begin, as so many Americans have already done, to perceive the great and indispensable function of the artist, the priest of truth and beauty, and I venture to prophesy great artists will then be born.

In our present phase, in which the artist is not an integral part of the national life, the attitude of sincere and profound writers will and must be one of protest and revolt. The few living masters of Canadian literature dare not accept the present mould of Canadian life. One of the greatest of them, and one of the most reflective, Frederick Philip Grove, remarked a year ago in the *University of Toronto Quarterly* that "as far as the general public goes, Canada is a non-conductor with regard to any kind of spiritual current." That is the gravest indictment that any artist can make against a community, for, as a great American expatriate wrote to James Russell Lowell, the artist's first need is "an audience which can understand what is good and what is bad." Without such "a sounding board", he continues, "the heart grows into stone". The hearts of our Canadian masters have every excuse for stoniness: but the fact is that the best of them are turbulent and indignant rather than petrified.

I should serve no useful end by passing in rapid review the names and works of the worthy Canadian writers of today. I prefer to select three writers who appear to me to justify hopes for Canadian literature and who exemplify the attitude of protest and revolt in the three literary types which seem to me the richest and most significant in Canada today, – the novel, the lyric, and the critical essay.

II

Any serious reader of Canadian fiction of the past decade will admit that its three masters are Mazo do la Roche, Frederick Philip Grove, and Morley Callaghan. I shall pass over Mr. Grove despite my high regard for his fiction. His best work seems to me to lie outside the novel in such books as *Over Prairie Trails* and *The Turn of the Year,* books in which his bleak, grim power is extremely impressive. I shall also pass over Miss de la Roche. I believe that *Jalna* is the most neatly constructed novel ever written by a Canadian, and I also believe that in that novel and the sequel *Whiteoaks of Jalna* the grandmother Whiteoaks is the most memorable character created by a Canadian artist. For two reasons, however, I prefer to deal with Mr. Callaghan. The Jalna novels, the best of Miss de la Roche's work, are in their manner somewhat antiquated, written in the way consecrated by Thomas Hardy, and in their matter somewhat foreign, dealing as they do with an English family curiously self-contained, and living in southern Ontario much as they might live in the English Midlands. In an absolute sense neither of these peculiarities is a defect; but in an examination of tendencies in the present literature of Canada it is natural to choose something more characteristic of the present and more characteristic of Canada.

That something is the work of Morley Callaghan. He is no less bleak than Mr. Grove, but his bleakness is less frankly revealed. His characters swear and drink and misconduct themselves in an extremely brutal, in an oddly inarticulate way, like people deadened by a misery too great to be borne. That misery is the mere fact of being alive. If they had the analytical mind of George Eliot they would say, as she did, that in their birth an irreparable injury was done them. They are ordinary folk, however, and they merely feel what George Eliot defined. Such characters do not make good material for a full-length novel, unless that novel is to be sensational melodrama. Mr. Callaghan is too modern, that is to say, too serious, too austere, to tolerate melodrama. He has wisely confined his novels to a remarkable brevity. Still it is in his novelettes and his short stories that he has done his best work. The novelette

In His Own Country seems to me to be the very best of Mr. Callaghan; and on it I wish to pause.

It is an episode in the life of Bill, a young journalist in a town on the shore of Georgian Bay. Bill is very ignorant and very ambitious. One day he reads in a Sunday Supplement of the achievement of Saint Thomas Aquinas in reconciling the philosophy of Aristotle with the dogmas of the Christian Church. "Bill understood readily that Saint Thomas was the superman of the Middle Ages." It occurred to Bill that "a man like himself, willing to work hard, might become the Saint Thomas of to-day" if he could "make a plan of different fields of science and show definitely that it could become one fine system in accordance with a religious scheme". Bill loses interest in the card games and movies which had occupied him and his wife Flora in the evenings. Flora, completely unable to comprehend what Bill is doing, is slowly alienated. Bill loses his job, neglects his wife, and, unforgivable sin, becomes in the view of his townsmen an eccentric, a "nut". His wife leaves him, his health gives way, and still his progress with Christian theology and the principles of science is negligible. The story ends with Bill an invalid, his wife returning to nurse him and assuring the priest's housekeeper "You may be sure he'll not bother again with studyin' and too many books."

Even if one does not inquire into the ultimate meaning of *In His Own Country,* the novelette is a striking achievement, a life-like record of a Canadian town. It is for its deeper meaning, however, that I have chosen it as a sample of Morley Callaghan. Bill, with his pathetically grandiose ambition, is an emblem of the creative spirit, and Bill's relation with his wife, and his community, is an emblem of the artist's relation with Canada. Even if Bill's wife and the townsmen of that little railway junction on Georgian Bay had known what it was Bill wanted to do, what was the nature of the vast and intricate system evolved by Saint Thomas, what were the issues between religion and science, his task would still have been an arduous one. The task of the great creative and critical minds is always arduous, whether it is carried on in a Canadian town or in the British Museum or the halls of the Sorbonne. But after all, as

Emerson cheeringly says, "Cicero, Locke, and Bacon were only young men in libraries when they wrote these books" of theirs. The history of thought and of art is full of the stories of men who grew up and lived in remote villages, and yet added to the world's store of knowledge and beauty irreplaceable treasures. They have not, any of them, lived in Canadian villages. There, admirably hidden behind Mr. Callaghan's scrupulously dispassionate presentation of an episode in the life of Bill, whom his wife and his townsmen deemed a "nut", is the proper gesture of protest and revolt against the present form of Canadian life.

III

Among critics and in the reading public at large there is no unanimous, or even current, opinion of the relative importance of the dozen worthy Canadian poets of the day. Our important poets, it seems to me, are of two kinds: those who work in the manner and with the matter of Lampman and Carman, and those who, feeling in themselves moods unknown to the gentle minds of Lampman and Carman, seek a matter and manner more modern, new to Canada, or in one or two instances, almost absolutely new. It is in poets of this latter sort that one finds most clearly revealed the tendencies of the immediate present. Among these poets I single out as the most original, Wilson Macdonald, E. J. Pratt, Dorothy Livesay, and Abraham Klein. Wilson Macdonald the most versatile of the four, seems to me imperfectly modern: side by side with strident scornful poems, comparable with the work of Sandburg and Masters, are suave and graceful lyrics which might have been the work of Carman, for whom Mr. Macdonald has a tender admiration. E. J. Pratt, born on the rock-bound Newfoundland coast, shows his disdain of contemporary Canadian life by escaping in his greatest poems to the sea and to the primitive immensities of the emotions it nourishes and satisfies in those who live on and by it. Like Mazo de la Roche, he is not fully a part of Canadian culture; and in the rare poems in which he deals with modern life on the land he lacks, so it appears to me, both the emotional force and the fierce blasting rhythms, which make him, in such a poem as *The*

Cachalot, one of the great poets of the sea. The work of Dorothy Livesay is no less original than his. She has found in the lyrics of Emily Dickinson and Elinor Wylie, or perhaps simply in a mind akin to theirs, something which has no precedent in Canadian poetry, an oddity of imagery, an artfully simple ease of expression, and a startling alternation of ecstasy and cynicism.

More significant than any of these three is, in my opinion, Abraham Klein, whose poetry is so original, that no publisher has as yet brought out a volume of his verse. His work must be sought in collections such as *The American Caravan,* and in such magazines of the *avant-garde* as *The Canadian Forum.* There is but one contemporary poet whose work Mr. Klein's resembles – T. S. Eliot; and, I imagine, nine out of ten of the younger poets and careful students of poetry in Great Britain, in the United States, and in Canada, would rate Mr. Eliot's poetry higher than that of any other written in our time. Mr. Klein is in no significant sense an echo of Mr. Eliot. In the first place Mr. Klein is a Jew. His culture seems to me to be broader and more intense than that of any other Canadian poet; but in that culture the central element is Jewish. In his great poem on Spinoza he finds words and images and cadences for the philosopher's prayer which recall not the Authorized Version but the literal truth of the Old Testament's art:

The wind through the almond trees spreads the fragrance of thy robes; the turtle dove twittering offers diminutives of thy love; at the rising of the sun I behold thy countenance.

Yea, and in the crescent moon, thy little finger's finger-nail...

On the swift wings of a star, even on the numb legs of a snail, Thou dost move, O Lord...

A babe in swaddling clothes laughs at the sunbeams on the door's lintel: the sucklings play with thee; with thee Kopernik holds communion through a lense.

One of the chief sources of Mr. Eliot's power to move us is his recognition of the city as the best material for the poetry of a civilization which more and more centers in vast confused urban conglomerations. The city is more real to most of us than

> The silence that is in the starry skies
> The sleep that is among the lonely hills.

Mr. Klein, too, is a poet of the city. After Judaism, Montreal is the most powerful factor in his work. *The Diary of Abraham Segel, Poet* open with these lines:

> No cock rings matins of the dawn for me;
> Morn in russet mantle clad,
> Reddens my window-pane; no melodye
>
> Maken the smalle fowles nigh my bed...
>
> No triple braggadocio of the cock,
> But the alarm of a dollar clock,
> Ten sonorous rivetters at heaven's gate;
> Steel udders rattled by milkmen; horns
> Cheerily rouse me on my Monday morns.

In the same poem he presents the street car in which he rides to work; the newspaper "he reads over his neighbor's shoulder"; the fellow workers at the factory; the boss and his fatuous wife; the Northeastern Café and the food he eats there; dinner at the family table; the amusements of the city; and finally the escape in the company of his sweetheart to the top of Mount Royal when:

> They see again, the eyes which once were blear,
> His heart gets speech and is no longer dumb...
> Upon the mountain top Abe Segal walks,
> Hums old-time songs, of old-time poets talks,
> Brilliant his shoes with dew, his eyes with starts.

All this is far removed from Mr. Eliot's view of the city, the view of a jaded, fastidious cosmopolitan, for whom London or Vienna or Alexandria is repulsive merely by its miscellaneous vulgarities, its filthy sights, its raucous sounds, its total consecration to materialism. Mr. Klein's poetry of Montreal is not cosmopolitan but, to take his own

51

epithet, "industrial". The poet is a part of the vulgarity, he cannot escape the filth, he is a victim, in body and intelligence, if not in spirit, of the materialism. His protests are more vehement, his pictures more intimate, since he is infinitely more exposed to what he scorns and hates.

Mr. Klein is in full revolt from Canadian life. In Abe Segal he gives us a symbol of the creative spirit at war with its circumstances, a symbol more powerful than Mr. Callaghan's Bill, for Abe Segal is a conscious accuser as well as a victim. His revolt finds fierce and highly poetical expression in the poem, – a companion piece to the *Diary, – Soirée of Velvel Kleinburger*. Here the bemused Velvel, a symbol of the weakness of the worker, reflects on the Canadian form of society, as he fools aimlessly with a pack of cards. The misery of the poor; the hypocrisy of the rich; the chasm between them so difficult to bridge; the desire of the poor for what the rich flaunt: such are the reflections of Velvel Kleinburger, poor in brains as well as in dollars, envious of the luxurious motors and the Paris-gowned and diamond-jewelled women of the rich. And the bitter voice of the poet breaks in upon his reflections:

> Hum a hymn of sixpence
> A table-ful of cards
> Fingers slowly shuffling
> Ambiguous rewards,
> When the pack is opened
> The pauper once more gave
> His foes the kings and aces
> And dealt himself the knave.

There is Mr. Klein's comment on the wild hopes of the utopists who go about persuading the millions of Velvels that they have a technique for reshaping Canadian society and settling permanent happiness upon every corner of the land. Mr. Klein knows too much of the mainsprings of life to lose his head: *his* heart is in the house of mourning.

The outlook is brighter for our poetry and fiction than for our criticism; and since to write great criticism supposes culture, as well as large information and excellent taste, the plight of our Canadian criticism need not surprise us. Culture is not a national god in Canada. (By culture I mean nothing exotic, but only the knowledge and love of the best that has been thought and said, a recognition of the excellent and a resolution to rest satisfied with nothing less, a liberation from the vulgar, the superficial, the provincial. Culture leads one to care more for Lear and the Fool upon the blasted heath than for any tear-sodden film that Hollywood or Elstree, to care more for the last cantos of the *Paradiso* than for the hymns in any of our hymnals, to care more for the sharp, chastening laughter of Molière and Shaw than for the aimless guffawings that make the radio a nuisance. By caring I mean not simply saying that Shakespeare is better than Joan Crawford or the Bennett girls, or Shaw better than Ed. Wynne and Amos and Andy, but feeling that Shakespeare and Shaw are a day-to-day necessity and the others are not. Catch a man hurrying to a cinema or reaching to turn on his radio and he will certainly say that Shakespeare, (if not Shaw), is about the greatest artist in the world's history; but it is not with Shakespeare that he intends to spend the evening. To prefer Shakespeare to the radio and the movies for the evening's leisure is to invite the label "highbrow." An educated man need not, I admit, be a highbrow. There is an alternative, – he may be a traitor. We have a reasonable number of scholar-critics, who address a limited international audience, and whose importance is international rather than national. During the past few years our scholar-critics have published important books on subjects as diverse as Plato and Heine, the English lyric and the plays of Henry James. A scholar-critic may have a powerful impact upon the national culture in one of two ways: he may evolve a new critical method which others can then apply to national problems, as Taine did in his history of English literature, or he may devote his scholarship, as most of our historians do, to the study of Canadian culture. No Canadian has, to my knowledge, made an important change in the methods of criticism, nor has any of our scholar-critics, except Professor James Cappon in his elaborate study of Bliss Carman, written a book on a literary Canadian subject which could be compared favorably with the books on Plato or Heine or the others instanced in their company. The primary reponsibility of our scholar-critics is international; and it is no reproach to them, if it is a matter for our regret, that they habitually address an international audience.

Another reason for the proverty of our criticism claims mention here. As Mr. Norris Hodgins remarks in the excellent introduction to his recent collection *Some Canadian Essays:* "Essays are rarely written in bookfuls." Essays flourish where literary periodicals flourish; and literary periodicals do not flourish in Canada. How many of Mr. Paul Elmer More's essays would have remained unwritten had he not edited the New York *Nation?* or of Mr. Middleton Murry's, had he not edited *The Adelphi,* or even of Mr. T. S. Eliot's, without his *Criterion* as a platform? We have no periodicals of importance in which literature is the sole concern, or even the admittedly chief concern. The periodical which seems to me to have done most for the erection and diffusion of critical standards in Canada is *The Canadian Forum;* I dare not enlarge upon that complimentary judgment since for the past three of its thirteen years of life I have been a member of its editorial board. It is in the number of its writers that I should expect to find the best of our critics: and the critic I shall single out for comment was in fact a member of the *Forum* committee from its inception until the present year – Mr. Barker Fairley. In speaking of him I shall not suffer the embarrassment incident to praising a colleague academic or editorial, since, after twenty years in Canada, Mr. Fairley recently resigned his professorship in German at University College, Toronto, (and concurrently his editorship of the *Forum*) to accept the chair of German at Manchester. Mr. Fairley is a scholar-critic as well as a commentator on Canadian culture. His recent book on Goethe's Poetry takes rank with the best contributions to international culture written in Canada. It falls, however, far outside the scope of this

54

paper in which Mr. Fairley's Canadian importance is what matters.

"Whatever the American men of genius are", says an English critic, "they are not young gods making a new world." Similarly, Mr. Fairley's attitude to Canadian literature may be expressed thus: "The creative spirits of Canada are not the fierce enthusiasts one would expect, revealing the violent beauties of the Canadian landscape and of the Canadian struggle to make a nation." He complains of the lack of intensity in the Canadian:

> Sitting daily in the street-car I scan the faces of my compatriots but never a sign do I see of rapture or despair . . . of course if I stay with these countenances I take them for granted, but a trip across the water and a few weeks sojourn among those volatile European faces disaccustoms me again and I return, hungry for the signs of emotional experience in the human features around me. This illogical desire lasts for days and days till at last it dies of starvation and I settle down again, defeated rather than reconciled, and resign myself to the conviction that we have all agreed to play a perpetual game of poker.

Americans of cosmopolitan experience, Henry James and W. C. Brownwell and Edith Wharton, confess to just such disappointments with their countrymen. It would seem that all we North Americans pipe our energy into our work and leave our personal life a shell over a great emptiness. And in a more bitter protest against the complacency of the official eulogists of Canadian literature, Mr. Fairley exclaims against "the notion that if only there is enough soft soap and back scratching all will be well with Canadian literature", a notion the exact opposite of the truth which is that the kind of author we need is an Aldous Huxley, one of "the Mephistophelean type, who will dispel our mists and mirages and let us see this great country of ours – excuse me, it slipped out! – in its true and therefore its best light." Here Mr. Fairley voices the attitude of all who care and hope for Canadian culture; so different a mind as Dr. Lorne Pierce's expresses itself with at least equal vehemence: "The last enemy to be conquered is the rhapsodist, the undiscriminating braggart who deals wholesale in fleece-lined caressive garments of praise". I have done Mr. Fairley an injustice if I have implied that in his rebellion against the attitudes of the Canadian public and the panegyrical enthusiasts of Canadian literature he is merely a specimen of the cosmopolitan Canadian. His hot advocacy of the Group of Seven in the early dangerous days when these painters were commonly regarded as a menace or a laughing-stock, and his immense sympathy with the work of such writers as Mr. Grove, Mr. Klein and the late Raymond Knister, are absolute proof of his difference from the cosmopolitans. Like Mr. Klein and Mr. Callaghan he looks at Canadian life through his own eyes: like them also he is a rebel against it.

So rapid a survey as this requires no conclusion. Instead of a conclusion I wish to add a foot-note. I do not claim that the great artist is always and everywhere essentially a rebel against his community. The greatest artists, a Dante, a Leonardo, a Goethe, a Shakespeare, express not merely a personal attitude to life, but the attitude of the best of their community and generation. What I claim is, merely, that here and now the Canadian artist is properly in rebellion against the Canadian community: that his rebellion is in some sort indispensable to his intellectual and artistic integrity; and that the guilt for his rebellion lies not with him but with the community of which he is, by its own tacit wish, no organic part.

Mackenzie King
of Canada

William Lyon Mackenzie King is one of the hardest men in North America to meet but he is one of the easiest to see. Any superficially respectable person who visits Ottawa when the House of Commons is in session – as it is for about half the year in wartime – may have a ticket for one of the galleries. If he uses it at 3 P.M., when the official day begins, he is almost sure to see just after the opening a bald, short very heavily built man with a brief case under his right arm, making his way with an odd sliding walk toward his place on the front benches to the Speaker's right. The heavily built little man will make a low and impressive bow to the Speaker and sink loosely into his seat. Mackenzie King is a House of Commons man, devoted to its decorums and its dignities. Despite the burden of his endless desk work, he dislikes to be absent from his place. From three to four each afternoon, when questions are asked, he expects that all his ministers will be present if they are in Ottawa and can walk; he is careful to set the example himself.

In the course of the question period he is almost certain to rise either as Prime Minister or in one of his other capacities as President of the Privy Council or Secretary of State for External Affairs. In answering a question he is uniformly grave and quiet and he is almost always courteous. He departs from courtesy – the sign that his temper is about to flare is the twiddling of his pen – only when he is quite sure that the question is a trap; and he especially resents the repetition at intervals of a few days of some question which is intended to stab him into quick action. The habit of his mind is deliberate and he believes that any full-witted member knows that he is not to be driven out of his habit. Whatever question he may be answering Mackenzie King always has the ear of the House, which knows its master.

If the visitor is in luck he may hear Mackenzie King make a speech; he does so at least once a month during the session. His speeches are of two kinds. Usually, at least during his present administration, he has a complete manuscript from which he reads in an agreeable and clearly audible voice, but with scarcely any change in pace or deepening to tone and almost without gesture. Speeches of this kind are addressed to the nation and to posterity, not to the House, and seem better in the columns of the morning paper. Now and then he will deliver quite another sort of speech, what is known in Ottawa as "one of the old man's fighting speeches"; he will have only a few notes, he will warm to his theme, and draw on the great resources of voice and expression which he commonly spares. The listener will know that he is hearing one of the last of the great parliamentarians in the Victorian manner, the manner of Gladstone and Laurier. And the listener will be exasperated if on a later visit to the House he sees Mackenzie King drawing from his brief case a thick manuscript.

If the House is not in session the Prime Minister can be seen by the casual visitor to the capital in a rather different sort of gathering a few hundred yards to the west along the same street. Mackenzie King is a faithful attendant at St. Andrew's Presbyterian Church. Sunday evening usually finds him in his seat. His feeling for his Church and for the Christian doctrine and way of life is exceedingly strong. The depth and reality of Mackenzie King's religion is evident to anyone who assists at a Presbyterian service when he is of the company; and no criticism affects him more deeply than one uttered by a responsible divine of his denomination. The recent death of the minister at St. Andrew's was as grievous a blow to him as if he had lost one of the members of the War Committee of his Cabinet.

This man, devoted to Church and Commons, is one of the loneliest beings alive. Most of those for whom he has cared most deeply have died. A year or two ago, speaking at a Liberal dinner given in his honor at Toronto, he said that the strongest influences upon his development had been those of his mother, her father, and the Lauriers. All have long been dead.

Mrs. John King, his mother, was a woman of intense feeling, considerable general culture, strong interest in public affairs, and strong ambition for her two sons. It is almost forty years since, in his oddly elaborate way, Mackenzie King remarked: "It is rarely, if ever, that men, especially young men, stop to estimate the influences which are the most potent in their lives, and it is rarer still, in seeking this estimate, that they become conscious, with any true degree of proportion, of the extent to which home, as compared with other influences, has contributed to the result." Such a reproach could never have been directed against the author of the sentence: in public and in private Mackenzie King's appreciation of the home in which he grew up is constantly given the warmest expression. His mother died in 1917, a year after her husband; the happiest household Mackenzie King had known since his childhood was the one he established for his parents in their last years, when one was blind and the other almost an invalid. It is doubtful if he has ever been completely happy since the day of his mother's death.

Her father, William Lyon Mackenzie, from whom he takes his protracted name, he never saw. But from infancy he was taught to revere the furious little Scottish-Canadian printer who is one of the chief heroes in the development of Canada toward responsible government and autonomous status. Mackenzie's editorials lashed and stung; when his efforts at orderly reform were frustrated by a cynical little group of colonial fat cats he rose in armed revolt. The rebellion of 1837 is one of the white milestones in Canadian history, and in the savage events of '37 no one was bolder or more ingenious than Mackenzie. With the threat of execution for high treason hanging over his head, Mackenzie fled to the United States. There during his exile, in a home of poverty and fear, the mother of the Prime Minister was born. Neither she nor her son would forget. When he was a young boy Mackenzie King read his grandfather's fine Scottish-sounding profession of faith: "Well may I love the poor, greatly may I esteem the humble and the lowly, for poverty and adversity were my nurses, and in youth were want and misery my familiar friends; even now it yields a sweet satisfaction to my soul that I can claim kindred with the obscure cotter and the humble laborer of my native ever-honored, ever-loved Scotland." It is often on the Prime Minister's lips; it has helped to keep him critical of those whose care is wealth or power or glamour; it has helped to keep his democracy real and simple and honest.

II

The Lauriers were the admiration of Mackenzie King's young manhood. A graduate of the University of Toronto in political science (class of '95), Mackenzie King studied at Chicago and Harvard. He specially concerned himself with depressed classes and areas, living at Hull House, and later at the Passmore Edwards Settlement in the East End of London. During one vacation spent in Toronto with his parents he investigated and exposed shocking sweatshops, some of them engaged in government subcontracts. His revelations bore on practices in the Post Office and drew him to the notice of Sir William Mulock, now approaching his hundredth year and still a cherished adviser, then Postmaster-General of Canada. Mulock's interest in the young zealot led to an invitation whose acceptance was the turning point in Mackenzie King's life. He was asked in 1900, when he was but twenty-five, to become the Dominion's first Deputy-Minister of Labor. Sir Wilfrid Laurier was then at the beginning of the second of his four consecutive administrations; and from the outset of their relations he manifested the deepest confidence in the new deputy's abilities and made abundant use of them. Young King, he used to say, had the best brains in Canada.

In 1908, after resigning his post, Mackenzie King was elected to the House of Commons for Waterloo North, in central Ontario, the home of his childhood and youth; and in the following year when a full-fledged ministry of Labor was set up, Sir Wilfrid took the step, highly unusual in Canadian practice, of inviting the former deputy to become the minister. The most vigorous of Sir Wilfrid's younger colleagues, astute in committee, impressive in debate, with the prestige rare in a Canadian minister of expert knowledge of the highest order, Mackenzie King was almost at once thought of as chief claimant to the succession, should the old leader retire or die. The defeat of the Laurier administration in 1911 – in which Mackenzie King lost his seat – brought the young man and the old man into even closer association and confidence. Mackenzie King became a sort of *chef de cabinet* for his leader; they were much in each other's company; and since Lady Laurier shared her husband's pleasure in Mackenzie King's society, he was very often at their home, the home she was later to bequeath to him.

From Sir Wilfrid, a great teacher, Mackenzie King learned a precious lesson which has proved ineffaceable. In Laurier's view the crucial Canadian problem was the preservation of national unity. At a time when other statesmen and students of statesmanship devoted themselves to the problems of transcontinental transport or the grain economy or the encouragement of immigration, Sir Wilfrid rose above finance and industry (the only figures that he understood, as one editor bitterly remarked, were figures of speech) and fixed his mind on methods of averting friction between French and English. Sir Wilfrid was probably too much the realist to believe that the two races would ever really love each other, though he often spoke as if he had nothing short of reciprocal love in mind; he was implacably determined that they should not hate each other. Although he had come out of the depths of Quebec province, where he had been for years a small-town lawyer, Laurier was well-read in the classics of English letters and politics; his conception of Liberalism was almost purely English; and he was that exceedingly rare creature, a French-Canadian at home in English-Canada, even in Toronto. Upon his young assistant he urged that the greatest of all Canadian tasks, the task incumbent on the leader of a political party, was that of preventing the fissures between French- and English-Canada from widening.

In Laurier's last years, when he was leading the opposition after fifteen continuous years of office, national unity was threatened as never before. In 1917 the Conservative government was reorganized to include representatives of the English-speaking Liberals who favored the enactment of conscription for service overseas; and the new Union government, with such conscription as its main plank, went to the country on December 17th. That was a black day. In the eight predominantly English provinces Sir Wilfrid had the merest handful of elected supporters – in some he had none; but Quebec, apart from three seats in the English part of Montreal, had given him every last constituency. The two races glared at each other across the House with a nearer approach to absolute hostility than at any other time in the national history. Anglo-Saxon ascendancy was complete. The French nursed their wrath and meditated an adequate revenge when the war should have ended. Many French-Canadians included Laurier in their anger, feeling that national unity, the gospel he had preached for so long, was a sinister catchword enabling the English majority always to get its own way under cover of fine mouth-filling language.

With the death of Laurier in 1919 the last of the major influences upon Mackenzie King had passed from the scene. When most of Laurier's ex-ministers and chief lieutenants among the English-Canadians had deserted the old chief to join or advocate the Union government, Mackenzie King, the youngest of them, the one with most to lose had stood firm. In the grim elections of 1917 he had gone into one of the most bigoted parts of English-Canada, where Laurier's supporters were reviled as near-traitors, and had fought a hard battle in which, as was to be expected, he was thoroughly beaten. But he had demonstrated to French-Canada, that one at least of the most eminent English-Canadian statesmen was no fair-weather friend. French-Canada took note and did not forget. In the *Memoirs* of Sir Robert Borden, the Union leader, it is reported that Mackenzie King meditated deserting his leader if he were offered a seat in the coalition; but the report is false. To have joined in a government of Anglo-Saxon ascendancy would have been to desert the principal cause of Mackenzie King's political life, to depart fatally from his historic role. The desertion did not take place and it was not meditated. When Laurier died Mackenzie King was of all English-Canadian statesmen the closest to the chieftain, the most in his company, the most in his confidence.

A few months later the party met to name a new leader. What was required above all was a great conciliator who could drive the oddly assorted team of French liberals who had come to doubt the whole of English-Canada and English liberals most of whom had just returned to the party reservation. Mackenzie King, trusted by the Quebec delegation, was chosen on the fourth ballot. He immediately showed that he had learned Sir Wilfrid's lesson that in public life there is no place for the cherishing of resentment. He took into his confidence a number of those who had deserted in 1917, and when in 1921 he assumed the prime ministership some of the principal departments were given to former Unionists.

During the 'twenties he formed two new and significant friendships. One was with Ernest Lapointe, who succeeded Laurier in one of the Quebec City seats and after a time as spokesman for French-Canada. Lapointe, who died in 1941, was one of Mackenzie King's chief finds – a huge bear of a man, looking as if he had just come off a farm in Normandy, he combined with immense political astuteness a lovable simplicity and warmth of nature and a profound broadly national idealism. In the province of Quebec the Liberal government was known as *"le gouvernement King-Lapointe"* and it was felt by habitant, priest, and bigwig that nothing contrary to the interest of French-Canada would be designed as long as Lapointe was at the council table. Lapointe loyally and enthusiastically saw to it that the trust his people had in him was spread to include "Rex," as he called his Prime Minister and admired friend. Confidence between the two was unlimited; and when they were seen chatting together as they sat side by side in the House one's mind was carried to the most impressive of the monuments on the bank of the Ottawa, which celebrates the friendly union a hundred years ago between Robert Baldwin, the Liberal leader of Upper Canada, and Sir Louis Lafontaine, the Liberal leader of Lower Canada. The partnership of King and Lapointe is one of the great alliances of Canadian political history.

The other friendship was with a much younger man,

Norman McLeod Rogers, who left his chair of history in small maritime college to become Mackenzie King's principal secretary, and in 1935, after teaching for some years at Queen's University, entered active politics to become Minister of Labor. History seemed to be about to repeat itself. Rogers was young, he was a master of political and social questions, and an intellectual with great practical gifts; he was assuming the very role his Prime Minister had played a quarter-century before. Mackenzie King, who is seldom at home with the young and even less disposed either to accord them his confidence or to take account of their judgment, leaned heavily upon Rogers. At the outbreak of the war he transferred him to what was expected to be the most onerous and the most glorious of cabinet posts – the ministry of National Defense. Rogers's death in an airplane crash was a devastating blow not only to the conduct of the war and to the general councils of the Cabinet, but to a weary and lonely old man. The places of Lapointe and Rogers in Mackenzie King's Cabinet have been honorably filled; no one will ever replace either of them in his inner forum.

He lives much in the past. For him in the deepest of all senses the dead vote; he is always asking himself what William Lyon Mackenzie would have done, what Laurier would have said, what his mother and Ernest Lapointe and Norman Rogers would have advised. As you meet him on his way to his office in the East Block – an office which is almost as Sir Wilfrid left it – you think that you are face to face with a chunk of the nineteenth century at its best. The heavy comfortable clothes cut in a spacious old-fashioned way, the high stiff collar, the pearl tie-pin, the thick black cord that hangs from his massive spectacles, the elaborate cane – all these, and the air of immovable dignity, suggest some contemporary of Sir Wilfrid. Looking at Mackenzie King, one is taken back to leisurely days in small Ontario cities, before there were motors, when the leading citizens passed the summer evenings bowling on the green and thought twice before they removed their vests in the company of ladies. He makes one nostalgic for the city of Kitchener (then called Berlin) in which he grew up, the Toronto in which he was an undergraduate, the Ottawa of the opening years of the century.

But Mackenzie King's mind is also on the future. Everyone in Ottawa knows that he is compiling voluminous memoirs, and that all his utterances and actions are calculated partly for the position they will have in the written record. What he says and does must satisfy the ghost of Sir Wilfrid; it must also satisfy the future historians of our time to whom he is demonstrating, no doubt, that everything he has said and done is of a piece, forming a pattern of flawless consistency and symmetry.

III

Preoccupied with the past and the future, Mackenzie King is in peril of failing to understand the fullness of the present. So far as memoranda and monographs and press clippings can give an understanding of immediate facts, Mackenzie King is faithfully served. But his has always been an intuitive mind and the intuitive mind must see and feel what it is dealing with. In the old days when he was in the Labor department it was seeing and feeling, not poring over bluebooks, that lay at the root of his successes. Take, for example, a passage in his report as royal commissioner on a strike of telephone girls at Toronto in 1907:

> There is physical strain through the reaching necessary to make connections at switchboards and through inability to relax the long sitting in one position . . . There is a drain on the nervous force. The liability to occasional injury from shocks, the irritation caused by the intermittent glowing of lights reflecting the impatience of users, the occasional buzzing and snapping of instruments in the ear, the sense of crowding where work accumulates, the consciousness of supervision, the sense of responsibility in response to calls, and the inevitable anxiety occasioned by seeking to make necessary connections whenever a rush takes place, all combine to accentuate the strain upon the nervous energies of an operator.

That final sentence could have been written only by one who had gone to the spot where the thing was happening. Today Mackenzie King rarely goes to the crucial spot, and so he deprives himself of the proper materials for an intuitive judgment. His mind requires personal associations and contacts with assemblies which would put before him the expressions on people's faces and the inflections in their voices. The Cabinet, the House of Commons, the congregation of St. Andrew's Church, and a few, a very few trusted members of the civil service are not enough. The almost broken contact between the Prime Minister and the people is a grave loss to them as they undergo their greatest crisis; it is a grave loss to him too.

The loss is the sadder to contemplate because Mackenzie King is instinctively on the side of the common man. He has never been the victim of a foolish admiration for the maker of millions, the loudmouthed railway-builder, the Rabelaisian stockbroker, the mining pirate. The big in any shape, even the big Empire, is without any magic for him. Saving money impresses him more than making it, and he has never been in the least interested in accumulating wealth. Pomp and flunkeyism are distasteful to him: his favorite home is a small cottage on the shore of a little lake a few miles from the capital. Here he retires for week-ends even during the winter and here he makes his headquarters after the House rises at midsummer. At Kingsmere he lives in the utmost simplicity, usually answering the telephone himself, strolling across the fields with his dog, stopping to chat with the neighboring farmer. In a less exacting time he might often be found in the heavy humid afternoon asleep in his hammock, a volume of Browning's poems or Arnold's beside him on the grass.

There is nothing grandiose in his way of life at Laurier House, his winter headquarters, an ugly gray-brick building with bilious green trimmings. On the top floor Mackenzie King had a number of windows set into the south wall, and in the room they light he has established his real office, with thousands of books lining the other sides, deep comfortable chairs and davenports, thick rugs and a roaring fire. Here he thinks, drafts his speeches and statements, and talks to most of the few whom he admits to see him. His study is a charming informal place and the man who sits facing the fire is entirely unpuffed up by fifteen years in the highest post in the nation. No farmer or factory hand or private soldier would be long oppressed by his presence.

Conversation with him is a constant surprise for one who has known him only from public appearances and general reputation. The Mackenzie King legend is not a pleasant legend, and it is a perversion of a reality which is pleasant. Mackenzie King has never been widely popular in English-Canada; to-day he is less popular than before. The citizens of Toronto and Winnipeg and Vancouver are always devising stories which turn him into ridicule and cover him with scorn. They are tiresomely alike, and the most innocuous of them is that of the drunk on the Toronto streetcar who threatened to speak the two foulest words in the language, and after everybody had exhausted the utmost resources of persuasion to prevent him, turned just as he was getting off and said: "I *will* say them! Here they are! *Mackenzie King!*" When War Loan campaigns are held, the posters represent Churchill and Roosevelt, not the Canadian Prime Minister. When Canadians are urged to "support their leader" the face beside the script will be that of General McNaughton, the commander of the Canadian army overseas. It is true that General McNaughton is magnificently photogenic and the Prime Minister is not: photographs always fail to catch the quality of Mackenzie King's eyes, which are of a singularly full and impressive blue, sometimes commanding, sometimes simply amiable and winning. Nor do they suggest the strength of his thin mouth, the lines of firmness in his chin, or the general air he has of integrity and distinction. But it is not just because the Prime Minister falls so far short of being photogenic that his face does not appear on posters; what his countrymen believe his character to be does not at all satisfy their notion of a national leader.

Canada is a pioneer country still and the Canadian notion of leadership requires vigor and color. Mackenzie King has preferred to be conciliatory and unobtrusive. His conciliatory powers probably surpass Laurier's – the greatest conciliator and charmer the nation had previously had – and they are set down by multitudes of his countrymen as timid shilly-shallying. His careful unobtrusiveness is sneered at as weakness of fiber. The needs of the Canadian imagination and the needs of the Canadian situation have been at variance ever since Confederation. With its two nations within a single state, its strong sectional feelings, its precarious economy, Canada can be effectively governed only by a conciliator. Those Canadian statesmen who have not been conciliatory have not risen to the prime ministership or their stay in the office has been brief and uneasy. It is worth noting that most of the gibes at Mackenzie King as a wartime leader would apply also to the Canadian leader in the First World War. Sir Robert Borden was a learned, prudent, rather stolid Halifax lawyer who never succeeded in exciting his countrymen but who impressed them as an ideal national trustee – efficient and upright and adequate. It is possible of course to be conciliatory and colorful too – Macdonald and Laurier are there to prove it. The private personality of Mackenzie King has rich veins of color. Those who have known him well at any time during the past twenty years know that he is capable of impulsive and violent speech, that he is full of compassion and easily stirred to resentment of injustice. There is a disquieting nimbleness in the movement of his mind and his judgments are often the flashes of a brilliant moment. He has deep pieties and loyalties deeper still. But none of these traits is generally known to the people of Canada, who set him down as an astute old fellow who will never take a straight course when he can find a crooked one, or say a simple word when he can think up an ambiguity or circumlocution.

IV

I can recall clearly the first time I heard Mackenzie King speak. Twenty years ago he addressed a student audience in the University of Toronto, speaking of the liberal way and illustrating from one of his heroes, Louis Pasteur. I can recall the restrained emotion with which he spoke, and how deathlike a silence fell upon the room. Everyone felt that for the moment he was in the presence of human greatness. The man who gave that address still lives, but he is buried under layers of fatigue and an increasing weight of awareness how appalling are the problems with which Canada must cope in war or in peace.

There are many Canadians – no doubt Mackenzie King is of the number – who believe that the Prime Minister is an indispensable, that no one now in public life or close to it could take his place. But one may believe this and also believe – and thousands do – that the public personality of Mackenzie King is very far from what a national leader should mean to his countrymen. A single visit to the study at Laurier House is enough to make one sure that Canada would be a far stronger nation in the crisis of today if Mackenzie King could and would leave upon his people the imprint of his real character.

Mackenzie King is in the most eminent degree a man of peace. I do not merely mean that he shares the aversion to war which is the surest mark of the authentic democratic statesman of the present century. To him war is not only hateful; it is monstrous; it is as alien to his idea of human life and destiny at its present phase as blood-sacrifice or suttee. His deep humanitarianism suffers daily at the thought of human flesh exposed to the cruel tearing force of the instruments of modern war. His imagination – the imagination that put him in the place of the tired telephone girl – paints pictures of merciless clarity. That highly developed modern societies such as that of Germany should resort to war with exhilaration, regarding it as the normal condition of man, gives the lie to his whole reading of earth, his whole conception of the promise of human life. It is a personal tragedy that this supremely peaceful man should have had the final responsibility for taking his country into a world conflict. Mackenzie King spoke from the depths of his being when he said that he was sure he would never again, no matter how long he lived, be required to assume a burden so heavy as the one he bore when he rose to ask the House of Commons to declare that a state of war was to exist between Canada and the German Reich.

If we are to see into those depths from which he spoke, a little book will help us. I have said that Mackenzie King's thoughts are much with those of his friends who are dead, but I have not mentioned the most intimate of his friendships as a young man. In 1900 when he was appointed Deputy Minister of Labor he brought with him to Ottawa as his principal aide Henry A. Harper, a classmate of his in political science at Toronto and his closest friend. In December of the following year Harper was skating on the Ottawa late one afternoon when a couple he knew fell into a space of open water; he hurried to the rescue and, told by the girl that all effort would be futile, cried out "What else can I do?" and plunged in and died with the girl he had despairingly tried to save. The manner of Harper's death became one of the formative experiences in Mackenzie King's life. The subtle mind circled round and round about the theme and finally built about the diaries and letters of Harper a memoir called *The Secret of Heroism*.

The style of this memoir is extraordinarily old-fashioned. The mastodon sentences with their Latinized phrases, their formidable regularity of rhythm, and their starched stiffness tell a good deal about Mackenzie King. This is the prose of one who sees a bewildering variety of aspects to a fact, seeks to elicit their bearing one upon another, is sure that they can be set in a genuine order, and hesitates to admit others to the inner sanctum in which his complicated mental processes are going on. It is entirely wrong to call this early style of Mackenzie King's commonplace; it is one of the most revealing styles ever used by a Canadian.

A single sentence will suggest what it is like at its best: "Harper and his friend (Mackenzie King) had lodgings in common and his diary is full of mention of the evenings they spent together in company with books from which each in turn read aloud to the other, and which were laid aside only that a deeper searching of the heart might follow, accompanied by pledges of mutual loyalty and resolve, long after the embers had burned out upon the hearth, and all things were in the sacred keeping of the night". The harsh concrete word never comes; the world is wrapt in a musical dream. The style suits a man for whom spirit is real and matter unreal, for whom emotions are dangerous things to be touched lightly and with infinite caution. It would be foolish to say that to understand *The Secret of Heroism* is to understand the Prime Minister. Thirty-five years of active political life, fifteen years in the siege perilous will deeply affect a character; but *The Secret of Heroism* will tell what is deepest in Mackenzie King, now as always.

The idealist chose a practical career in 1908; he did not fumble it, he grew into the most astute politician of his day and country. The astuteness does not arise from the idealism; it is however an expression of something that often goes along with idealism – sharp intuitive insight into men, the kind of insight a poet has or a painter. Mackenzie King's aphorisms in conversation remind one of Emerson's. The processes of his mind are not intelligible to the lawyers who surround him – when did lawyers understand a poet? In England a prime minister with a poet's mind has given the most notable leadership his country has known in this generation; in Canada a prime minister with a poet's mind leaves his people with the sense that they are leaderless. Winston Churchill is magnificently articulate; Mackenzie King cannot find or will not utter the right words for what is in his spirit. Nowadays, to use a phrase from one of his favorite poets, "a common grayness silvers everything". If one were to ask Mackenzie King why his prime-ministerial utterances are so colorless and cautious I do not know what he would reply. I think he would say that one cannot be too careful, that one must be certain he is understood, and that by this he would mean that Canadians are practical folk and will have confidence in the soundness of a man who talks in his fashion and only distrust for the leader who comes out with such notions as "the sacred keeping of the night". He has been Prime Minister even longer than Sir Wilfrid Laurier – he should know. And yet one remembers Sir Wilfrid's incomparable *panache,* his spectacular phrases, his operatic bearing, his warmth and gaiety and inescapable charm, and the tears that come into the eyes of hard old men when they speak of him a quarter century after his death.

Our Neglect of
Our Literature

I have been asked to speak to you this evening about the state of our national literature, and particularly about some of the difficulties our authors have to meet, and what we might do to lessen those difficulties. To lessen them, I say, not to remove them, for it is not in our power to remove them at present. I have been asked to talk about these topics because I have recently brought out a book called *On Canadian Poetry* in the course of which I tried to show why our literature was not in a healthy condition, and suggested that the great things some of our writers have done (and some of them have done great things) have not been as widely read and appreciated as one would wish.

On the cover of every issue of the Chicago magazine *Poetry* appears the saying of Walt Whitman: "To have great poets there must be great audiences too." It is true of most literature that to get it written requires the assurance that it is going to be wisely and appreciatively read. I have recently had the privilege of going through the notebooks of our greatest poet Archibald Lampman. In one of them I found the text of a lecture that he gave to the Literary and Scientific Institute in Ottawa, in 1891. Lampman speaks there of the problem of a Canadian literature, and speaks sadly. He says that the world around him was not ready to read. The people of Canada, fifty years ago, were making money, building the material fabric of a nation, and so plunged in materialism that they could read only in off moments, and even the reading they did was not, Lampman believed, wise reading, not really discriminating and appreciative. It will take two generations, Lampman says, before there will be good readers in the country, enough good readers to stimulate the writing of good books. Well, two generations have come and gone, or almost. What would the great poet say if he were alive today? Would he be satisfied with the quality of reading in Canada today?

I cannot believe that he would be satisfied. Allow me to tell you a story. Some five years ago when I was professor of English at the University of Toronto I was asked to address a meeting of a fraternal society in that city and I was advised that the subject I ought to treat was our national literature. In the course of my address I spoke with warm praise of E. J. Pratt, whose *Brébeuf and His Brethren* so many of you have heard over the air. Afterward one member of the audience came up to me and said he had been particularly interested in what I had said about Mr. Pratt. They had been classmates at Victoria College thirty years before; he had seen Mr. Pratt off and on over the years – as was natural since they both lived in Toronto; but this was the first time he had heard that Mr. Pratt had written any poems. There is something wrong in the national attitude towards literature when this is possible.

I will tell you some of the things that are wrong. In the first place literature is not taken seriously. It is regarded as one of the things that don't really matter. It is seen wholly as amusement. It is amusing to read some novels, and to see some plays. At least a good many people find it amusing and the rest will concede that it is a respectable amusement. Now I know very well that literature ought to be amusing, that it ought to entertain. But there is something else it can do. Literature is not a subject of instruction in our schools and colleges because it is amusing or entertaining. It is a subject of instruction, and a very fundamental one, because it interprets life. Shortly after the Russians entered the war, two New York publishers brought out editions of Tolstoy's great novel *War and Peace*. I do not know how many copies one of them sold, but the other within a year had sold, I believe, three hundred thousand copies. Why was *War and Peace* bought in such quantities in 1941 and 1942? Because it was amusing? Certainly not. Three hundred thousand copies were bought because *War and Peace* interprets Russia, because it shows the sort of people the Russians are, and especially what they are like in time of war.

If you wish to find out what a nation is really like, the history books will tell you something, but the great novels will tell you more. A modern British critic, Mr. St. John Ervine, has said that if he wanted to get to the heart of England as it was in the eighteenth century he would not go to the great history of W. E. H. Lecky, but to Henry Fielding's great novel, his great panorama of English life in country and town, *Tom Jones*. If I wanted to show a Russian what Canada was like, I would give him as the first two books Louis Hémon's *Maria Chapdelaine* and Stephen Leacock's *Sunshine Sketches of a Little Town.* Now I do not think that Canadians in general hunger after literature as an interpretation of their lives. That is the first great thing that is wrong. We do not take literature seriously because we do not understand how much it could do for us if we would let it. Novels, if they are really great, can interpret our lives for us, can make us understand ourselves better than we did before we read them. Once you have provided yourself with enough to eat, with a good roof over your head, and clothes to keep you warm (or cool), there is nothing so urgent as understanding the sort of person you are and the sort of persons your associates are, your friends, your fellow workers, and your enemies (if you have them).

We do not take any literature seriously, but particularly we do not take our own literature seriously. This failure to do justice to our own authors is partly because we do not do justice to our own country. My friend Mr. Ferguson, the editor of the *Winnipeg Free Press,* has recently returned from a visit to England. The articles he has been writing have shown that the English are deeply impressed with our war effort, that they see us as a great power in the world today, and destined to be a greater power yet in the world tomorrow. It is healthy for us to hear this. We are in no danger of swelled heads. Our danger is in hanging heads. We do not know our own strength. We do not think that we are likely to do things that are really first class. Now we have in this country some artists of the first class. They suffer from not being accorded the serious attention, the thoughtful criticism, the discriminating appreciation by which an artist becomes better. It is not as bad as it was in Lampman's day. A poet can get his work published now without much delay or any cost to himself. But it does not sell very widely; it is not very carefully reviewed; it is not much talked about; he is not likely to overhear the next passenger in the street car talking about it. Not very long ago a young Canadian poet now in the army, Earle Birney, brought out a book of verse called, from its title poem, *David.* The poem *David* is a narrative of a tragedy in the Rockies. Two young men go mountain climbing, one of them a man of experience, the other a novice. The novice gets into difficulties, the man of experience comes to his rescue, and in doing so falls a sheer hundred feet, and breaks his back; he asks his companion to push him from the ledge which had caught him, and let him fall straight to the valley far below. The companion is very reluctant to do so; but in the end he yields. That, along with the feelings and thoughts the companion has, makes the poem. It is a moving piece, and it is beautifully written. It made a stir in a small way when it came out; there was a second edition; but now the book is out of print. It ought not to be out of print. Hundreds have bought it, perhaps a few thousand have read it; but thousands should buy it; and scores of thousands should read it. It is something that matters to us. We should not let it go.

Another thing that we very much require is a number of magazines in which the author of short stories and sketches may reach a Canadian public. Our magazines have a hard time, I know. They face very severe competition from the Americans. American magazines circulate everywhere in Canada; and Canadian magazines are almost unknown in the United States. We cannot maintain magazines for our writers as easily as the Norwegians or the Swedes can; for our language is not peculiar to us. I will tell you what should be done. One of the best of the American magazines, the *New Republic,* exists because of the generosity of one family. It is richly endowed. We too need endowed magazines, we need them more than the Americans do. Hospitals are endowed in Canada; art galleries are endowed. Why cannot we have an endowed magazine? While I am on the theme of endowments let me mention to you another American generosity. At Saratoga Springs, in New York State, there is a large estate called Yaddo. Yaddo was endowed by the late owner as an institution where authors and other artists might come and work at their projects for months and sometimes years, with board and lodging free, and with the provision of ideal studios in which the book or painting or musical composition could go forward. The existence of Yaddo has meant the difference between success or failure for many a man and woman. We need a Yaddo. Certain American publishers, the Houghton Mifflin Company for instance, award what are called literary fellowships carrying with the award enough money for the support of a man, even of a married man, for a whole year. This kind of award enables an author to give his total time and energy to his book.

That is the opportunity so many Canadian authors need – to have all their time and energy, at least for long periods, free to give to a book. How few of them get the chance! In earlier days when the pace of business was slower an author could be a civil servant or a lawyer or a doctor or a teacher and still count on enough leisure to write a great deal of good literature. The greatest authors, it is true, were in the main ones who served only the one god-literature. Today it is very difficult to earn one's living by some other occupation and write in one's spare time. Moreover, the continuous overwork implied in carrying two kinds of work abreast is probably unhealthy for the mind as well as for the body.

Another step we could and should take is to make more of our literature in the Canadian universities. When I taught at the University of Toronto I lectured on Canadian literature, and I sought to make its great qualities plain. I do not think I spent enough time on it, and in general I think the subject is dealt with too briefly in our universities. As a result the graduates, a large potential buying public, are not sufficiently impressed with the merits of our literature, or sufficiently instructed in its great names. Of course our literature is not as yet comparable, either in quality or in extent, with American literature. American literature is today one of the great literatures of the world. Still the always increasing stress on American literature in the universities of the United States is a movement from which we can learn a good deal. It is to be noted, also, that in our Canadian universities there is an always increasing stress on Canadian history, and from this too we can learn a good deal.

The note on which I would close is this: what we as a people owe to our writers is interest, intelligent and appreciative interest. It would be a misfortune if we came to think that ours was the greatest literature in the world – but that is an error we are incapable of making. The misfortune is that almost all of us now seem to think that ours is a literature of so little worth and power that time spent in reading it is likely to be time wasted. It is for interest, above anything else, that I plead; if we could take a strong and discriminating interest in what is being written in Canada and about Canada, everything else would come right before many decades had passed. Surely this war, and the great exploits of our armed forces in it, and the great powers of endurance of the civilian population, should give to us a decent and reasonable pride in ourselves. When we acquire that pride our literature may appear to us a vital expression of our national genius. In the best works of our best writers, especially the best poets, that is what it is today.

To The North:
A Wall Against
Canadian Poetry

In the summer of 1940 Mr. George Dillon asked me to collect and introduce a Canadian number of *Poetry*. When this appeared in the following April it was accompanied by a terminal note in which the editors explained why they had conceived the project: Canadian poets were not "discovered" by American readers as poets from England and the continent were; they did not readily find American publishers; they did not make their way into textbooks and anthologies. Some special effort to make them known in this country was called for. Mr. Dillon was the first of many to make such an effort. In 1942 Mr. Ralph Gustafson, a young Canadian poet and critic living in New York, brought out an "Anthology of Canadian Poetry" in the Pelican Library, which has circulated widely in America as well as in Britain. In the following year he edited two smaller anthologies, a Canadian number of *Voices* and, for New Directions, "A Little Book of Canadian Poets." Meanwhile another young Canadian poet and critic also living in this country, Professor A. J. M. Smith of Michigan State College, used his period as a Guggenheim fellow to complete his "Book of Canadian Poetry." I am not at one with Mr. Smith in all his judgments, but I do not think anyone can doubt that in the four hundred and fifty pages of his anthology, chosen with a poet's sensitiveness and representing Canadian poetry from the beginnings to pieces that were still in the drawers of gifted novices, the range and power of this poetry was clearly shown.

And yet the wall that prevents Canadian poetry from becoming known in this country still stands high and firm. In the same issue of *The New Republic* which dismissed Mr. Smith's book with a pleasant pat on the back (in the form of a brief notice written out of good-natured ignorance) there was a careful column-long review of a recent anthology of translations from Latin American verse. I have yet to see in an American periodical an adequate review of the two important books of Canadian poetry published in 1943, Mr. Smith's "News of the Phoenix" and Mr. E. J. Pratt's "Still Life."

The wall is a new erection, at least it is much higher and firmer than it used to be. In the last twenty years of the nineteenth century the best of the Canadian poets appeared regularly in the best of the American magazines. Archibald Lampman, who lived in Ottawa as a civil servant from 1883 to his death in 1899, and had practically no literary connections with this country, had five poems in the *Atlantic,* eight in *Harper's,* and twenty-five in *Scribner's.* Bliss Carman and Charles G. D. Roberts, who lived in New York for years, did better.

I cannot say why the wall should be there now, but I should like to see it blown up, and here I should like to suggest what lies behind it today.

There is the extensive work, the twelve volumes, of E. J. Pratt. Mr. Pratt is over sixty. Born in a Newfoundland fishing village, he came inland to Toronto when he was in his middle twenties; after studying theology, philosophy, and finally psychology, he taught the last named of these subjects at the University of Toronto until 1919, when, deeply dissatisfied with abstract thought of any kind, he removed to the department of English, and began to put together his first collection of poems, "A Book of Newfoundland Verse." This came out in 1923, and by 1926, with the appearance of "Titans," he was recognized in Canada as the most original and variously gifted of the newer poets. Eighteen years later he is not even a name in this country; nothing of his had come out in *Poetry* before the Canadian number of 1941; I have never seen a poem of his in any of the larger American magazines; he is represented in none of the anthologies. And yet he is a poet in whose work it is easy to take pleasure, and the pleasure he can give is rather different from what can be found anywhere else. Mr. Pratt's revulsion against the terms of social life in our time has led him to scholarly but also ruggedly vigorous evocations of the prehistoric world, to narratives of the sea in which learning, humor, and emotional intensity mix in a wild and powerful amalgam, to epic reconstructions of the Canadian past, to meditative lyrics in which force and a certain essential aloofness and unexpected coolness work together to shape a unique mood and texture. I should like to mention the response of one of the most eminent American academic men of letters to the reading of one of the meditative lyrics, "Silences": "This is a man to whom one would go on pilgrimage."

Technically Mr. Pratt is always interesting. He has devised a bounding, resonant tetrameter which is all his own, he has found a grave, slow-moving kind of blank verse perfect for epic, and his use of the polysyllable is a miracle of deftness. The unique texture of his verse depends on a startlingly original temperament, and also, perhaps, on the order in which the main layers of his experience have come. First there was the contact with exciting and spectacular crude realities in Moreton Harbor, where as a youth he used to row around the whales that had been dragged home and moored in the bay; then there were the fifteen years of abstraction, with the amassing of heaps of theories and terms about God, the universe, and man; then came the discoveries in elder authors, particularly in the English Renaissance; and much later the sympathetic explorations in recent verse techniques. I have no hesitation in saying that this poetry of Pratt's is a bigger thing than Robinson's or Masefield's ever was, that it offers something comparable with what you can get from Jeffers. Next fall his collected poems will appear in Toronto.

I think that Mr. Pratt's work is the most startling single thing now concealed behind the northern wall. But there is a vast variety of excellence. In the period from 1900 to 1920 there were two notable achievements, Marjorie Pickthall's and Dr. Duncan Campbell Scott's. Marjorie Pickthall was in her late thirties when she died in 1922. She is a delicate poet, of the kind that writes line by scrupulous line, pausing to reconsider each detail with eye and ear. At her best she could do a moving and beautiful dramatic monologue, or a nature lyric exquisitely fine. I do not know that she ever awakened any response in this country, and yet for me, as for many in Canada, she is one of the best women poets of her time.

Dr. Scott's is a more substantial achievement. His first collection came out in 1893; from that time on he was steadily growing until in 1905, with "New World Lyrics and Ballads," he stood with Carman as the best Canadian poet alive. He has had a great career in the federal department of Indian Affairs which he directed for rather more than ten years before his retirement in the early nineteen-thirties; and the mark of his long imaginative association with his charges is upon much of his surest poetry. His Indian poems are, quite simply, the best I have ever read, vigorous, firm, and always with a suggestion either of the tragic past of the race, or of its positive pathetic present. In his reflective pieces he has more intellectual weight and precision than Carman, who was so much better known in this country. Indeed in some of his nature poems the depth and intricacy of his thought is so unusual that only now is interpretation beginning to cope adequately with it. Here and there in his collected poems, published in 1926, and in the later volume, "The Green Cloister," are meditative lyrics of admirable fineness and clarity. In all his best work – and he is still adding to it at eighty-one – there is a beautiful fusion of intensity and restraint.

And there are younger poets of high distinction. In the past three years there have been three first collections that I value very highly. Mr. Abraham Klein's "Hath Not a Jew ..." was published in New York and has been praised in the Jewish press. Mr. Lewisohn (who wrote a preface) found it the best example of authentically Jewish poetry in the English language. It abounds in Talmudic erudition, touched with humor no less genuine for being learned; it has the powerful Coleridgean charm of the strange made to seem natural and familiar; and if the form is sometimes careless there are bursts of sudden splendor in rhythm and image. Then there is Mr. Earle Birney's "David." "David" is a story of a mountain tragedy in which the note of ordinary attitude and action is sternly kept until the close, when the reader is suddenly and surely carried through an emotional experience which is among the most memorable to be had from recent poetry. Finally, just a few months ago, appeared Mr. Smith's "News of the Phoenix," long awaited in Canada, and in perfection of technique undoubtedly the finest first volume since Archibald Lampman's "Among the Millet" came out in 1888. Mr. Smith has undergone the same influences that went to shape the difficult younger poets in this country. He is their analogue – and their peer. In his work is a distinctive note, the note of a temperament which is, as I have said elsewhere, "proud, hard, noble, and intense."

I am forced to omit so many names that I am oppressed by a sense of committing simultaneously a multitude of acts of injustice. Those I have mentioned are, I think, the greatest, but so rich is the field that choice is deeply embarrassing. And what I am most concerned to do is to suggest the general richness, to urge that Canadian poetry is great and important, that beyond the northern wall there is far more for the American reader than he supposes.

A. J. M. Smith
and the Poetry
of Pride

It is eight years since the first appearance of a group of Mr. Smith's poems within the covers of a book. In the anthology *New Provinces* were twelve of his pieces, varying in their force and beauty from the sharp packed metaphysical imagery in "The Two Sides of a Drum" –

> that country under dream
> Where Eternity and Time
> Are the two sides of a drum

– to the cool conversational manner of Kenneth Fearing in "News of the Phoenix" –

> They say the Phoenix is dying, some say dead.
> Dead without issue is what one message said.
> But that was soon suppressed, officially denied.

At last Mr. Smith has brought out a collection of his own. My first feeling, at the mere sight of the book, was one of disappointment. It is a little book; it holds but thirty-nine poems, spread over about as many pages; and among the thirty-nine are the twelve from *New Provinces,* and others well known to the readers of more recent anthologies of Canadian verse. One had hoped for evidence of greater fertility. A poet who has added but twenty-seven pieces to his canon in seven years, and these the years from thirty-five to forty-two, is either the barren fellow that Johnson called Fielding, or else a most exigent critic.

It is an exigent temperament that this collection reveals, even a haughty temperament. In one of the most admirable poems, Mr. Smith espouses the "cold goddess Pride" and announces that it is to the "barren rock" he addresses his "difficult lonely music". In another, his most explicit exercise in criticism, he counsels a younger writer to aim at achieving the effect

> of a hard thing done
> Perfectly, as though without care.

The tone of that, as well as the idea, recalls the elder Yeats, to whom, in a memorial essay, Mr. Smith paid significant tribute, speaking of him as an "eye made aquiline by thought". Well, Mr. Smith, too, is aquiline, and it is temperament as much as thought, as it was with Yeats, that has made him so.

The eagle's vision is in that picture of the Canadian landscape called "The Lonely Land". This is a scene girt with sharp jagged firs and pines that a ceaseless wind has bent, spume is blown high in the air, and at the centre are wild ducks calling to each other in "ragged and passionate tones". The essence is stirringly caught in these lines:

> a beauty
> of dissonance
> this resonance
> of stony strand,
> this smoky cry
> curled over a black pine
> like a broken
> and wind-battered branch
> when the wind
> bends the tops of the pines
> and curdles the sky
> from the north.

In this harsh world Mr. Smith takes an austere and intense delight. The natural setting for his beautiful "Ode: on the Death of W. B. Yeats" is almost the same. His Ireland has nothing in common with George Moore's or Elizabeth Bowen's: it is no place of soft contours, rich greenery, and gentle rain; his Ireland is the bare hills and rough coast of

Synge, and of Yeats in his elder years. If a tree is conceded blossoms, it is a twisted tree; if a white swan flies through the poem, the air is cold, and the clouds above upheave.

Almost equal severity stamps the religious poems with which the collection closes. In 1936 religion was a minor theme in Mr. Smith's work, it was scarcely more than an armoury of imagery. Now it is almost in the dominant place. The choice of religious topics is revealing: Good Friday, Calvary, Christian death. A line or two here and there is infused with gentleness:

> And His face was a faded flower
>> Drooping and lost

but lines such as these are among the least successful in the book. The main effect is that of the Bellini portrait of Christ: haggard, stricken, at odds with life.

Mr. Smith's theory of poetry leaves an honoured place for satire and light verse. In the introduction to his important anthology, *The Book of Canadian Poetry,* he quotes with approval Mr. Auden's warning that it will "do poetry a great disservice if we confine it only to the major experiences of life". "Far West" is a lightly satirical suggestion of a London girl's feelings as "among the cigarettes and the peppermint creams" she enjoys a movie about cowboys. More acrid are "On Reading an Anthology of Popular Poetry" and "Son-and-Heir". In these Mr. Smith's disgust with bourgeois values has a searing strength. "Son-and-Heir" is an arraignment of bourgeois civilization in terms of the reveries an average bourgeois couple might have as they plot the ideal future for the baby. The quality of the reveries is cheap, but Mr. Smith would emphasize not only the cheapness, but the danger of having reveries at all. He is as much the foe of revery as Irving Babbitt. I mention Babbitt because the enmity Mr. Smith holds to romanticism is as deep as Babbitt's: the drubbing he gives to the anthology of popular poetry shows this to be so. Most of his phrases of contempt in the poem upon it might be paralleled in Babbitt, except that Mr. Smith, as a poet, properly heightens the feeling. He speaks of the "sweet sweet songs", the soft melodious screams", the "old eternal frog in the throat that comes with the words, *Mother, sweetheart, dog*". I have spoken at such length of Mr. Smith's satiric poems because I think that they, more clearly than any others in the book, make plain the pride and severity of his temperament. Read first, they will help prepare one for the emotions that lie within and behind the more difficult and more important pieces.

That Mr. Smith is a difficult poet he would not himself deny. There are phrases here and there in the book to which I cannot assign a clear meaning. Why should Buffalo Bill be described as "toxic"? I assume that it is because from the screen he entices to reverie. I can offer no suggestion why politeness should be compared to a "mezzanine floor". But whatever the difficulties it presents, this collection demonstrates again and again not merely triumphant virtuosity, but perfect keeping between substance and form. It is a book in many manners, but one can see why there must be many.

A proud, hard, noble and intense book, *News of the Phoenix* makes one regret that Mr. Smith has not been more fertile, or, if he has kept much back, that he should not have given us some peeps into the laboratory in which he works his wonders.

The Poetry of
Our Golden Age

During the past decade there has been a revival of poetry and of interest in poetry without a parallel in the present century. The hard school of a lingering depression, a troubled international scene, a war which has strained every one's energy to the last sinews, has been stimulating and purifying for poetry. It has also been stimulating and purifying, although inevitably to a less degree, for the people in general, whose ears are not so wholly closed to the words of the seer or the music of the craftsman as once they were. Every year has brought with it at least one volume excellent and original: 1935 E. J. Pratt's *The Titanic;* 1936 *New Provinces, Poems by Several Authors;* 1937 E. J. Pratt's *The Fable of the Goats;* 1938 Kenneth Leslie's *By Stubborn Stars;* 1939 Anne Marriott's *The Wind Our Enemy;* 1940 E. J. Pratt's *Brébeuf and His Brethren* and A. M. Klein's *Hath Not A Jew . . .;* 1941 E. J. Pratt's *Dunkirk;* 1942 Earle Birney's *David;* 1943 A. J. M. Smith's *News of the Phoenix;* 1944 A. M. Klein's *Poems* and Dorothy Livesay's *Day and Night;* 1945 Frank Scott's *Overture.* Anthologies large and small, comprehensive and sectarian, costly and cheap, have enabled the new poetry to circulate in many milieus. A group of critics sympathetic to the new poetry has come forward to interpret and recommend it. The beginnings, indeed rather more than the beginnings, of a renewed respect for our poetry in the United States are already perceptible. No one admires more than I the epic energy and resonant music of Pratt, the high-spirited spontaneity and curious learning of Klein, the severe emotion and careful art of Smith, the considered simplicity of Birney. On this occasion others will pay homage to their poetry.

It falls to me to examine the poetry which preceded the new movement. I confess to feeling some anxiety at discerning in the works of some of its leaders, in the verses of some of their imitators, and in the criticisms of some of their allies a tendency to dismiss the earlier poetry with indifference or to approach it with patronage. To the academic critic, familiar with the history of letters, it is a truism that the success of a new movement results in a passing injustice to the movement it has displaced. So it was when Malherbe succeeded the Pléiade, when the Romantics won the dubious victory of *Hernani,* when one of the symbolists described Leconte de Lisle as a *marchand de quinquaillerie.* Such knowledge makes one patient, but it need not reduce one to silence. There is no reason why one should not anticipate the judgment of posterity, at least in part, why one should not call for the old idols, or some of them, to be brought forth from the lumber-room and set in the niches which will later be theirs forever.

I

I do not hesitate to claim that the most admirable body of poetry which has yet been written in English-speaking Canada within a short period belongs not to 1935-1945, but to 1885-1900. It appeared at a time much less propitious to poetry than ours: when it was much harder to get one's verses published in Canada, when there was a much smaller audience, when there was a stronger tendency to be interested only in the product of the region in which one lived. The poets overcame these handicaps as best they could; their work made its way slowly, it did not tell upon the life of the community even in the limited degree in which the work of our poets tells today. But the work itself was authentic and graceful.

A recent poem abusing the poets of the past ends with the line of reproach:

And Lampman turning his back on Ottawa.

The author considers that instead of burying himself in the

woods and meadows Lampman should have done something with the material that Ottawa offered. One has only to read Lampman's poetry with some care, not very much care but just a little, to know that he did not merely turn his back on Ottawa. He has written stinging sonnets on corrupt politicians and malefactors of great wealth – I do not think that in substance they have been surpassed, and I am sure that in form they have not been surpassed, by more recent social poetry. In longer works Lampman expressed his contempt for the material preoccupation he observed on all sides: he knew it was debilitating to the national society and he said so. He went further and formulated, in the tradition of Shelley and Morris, perhaps the noblest tradition of English nineteenth century social idealism, his conception of the right standards of life, the true quality of life, in human societies. *The City of the End of Things* is a passionate suggestion of what he found to be wrong, *The Land of Pallas* is an idyllic and utopian statement of what he thought to be right, Lampman was not a great social poet, he was no Whitman, no Hugo. What is significant is that he knew exactly what Ottawa was, what the society which it had called it into being was, before he decided that his best (but not his only) subject lay in nature. "For the poet," he declared, addressing the Literary and Scientific Society of Ottawa in 1891, "the beauty of external nature and the aspects of the most primitive life are always a sufficient inspiration". What he meant was that he did not think himself crippled as a poet by the dismal condition of society as he found it about him; there was for him, as there was not for the novelist or the biographer, an escape, not a cowardly escape, not an ignominious flight – an escape into a world of permanent values, meaningful, beautiful, inexhaustible. His decision was not unlike that made in our time by Robinson Jeffers, similarly afflicted by the sense that the American society about him was an inadequate and a corrupt society. Mr. Jeffers observes in the forward to the selected edition of his verse:

Prose, of course, is free of all fields; it seemed to me reading poetry and trying to write it, that poetry is bound to concern itself chiefly with permanent things and the permanent aspects of life. . . . Prose can discuss matters of the moment; poetry must deal with things that a reader two thousand years away can understand and be moved by. This excludes much of the circumstance of modern life, especially in the cities. Fashions, forms of machinery, the more complex social, financial, political adjustments, and so forth, are all ephemeral, exceptional; they exist but will never exist again.

Lampman would have liked that. He hoped that what he saw and divined in Ottawa would never exist again. It was one of the more dreary stretches in the growth of the nation. In the past there had been great deeds and thoughts; and there would be again. But he did not see expressions of greatness in Ottawa in the last two decades of the past century. I do not think he was myopic.

The landscape of Canada awaited him. To it he brought a mind stored with the visions of Wordsworth and the pictures of Keats; he brought too his sensitive and acute eyes and ears; and he brought his passion for Canada, his imperative need to discover and to celebrate something in Canada which was beautiful and intense – and unique. It was inevitable that his subjects should often be taken from the nature that lay about him, the hills on the Quebec side, the river in its varied moods and aspects, the fields on the outskirts of the town. Considered as a part of the Canadian social and economic structure, Ottawa itself assumed beauty and a satisfying meaning. Lampman was a hardy spirit, and he drove his body beyond its strength; he took pleasure in long tramps, sometimes on snowshoes, on the most nipping winter days. The beauty of snow, especially in the delicate light of dawn and sunset, is admirably caught in his poems. But the seasons in which the spectacle of nature aroused the deepest excitement in him were the quick violent northern spring and the dreamy lingering end of summer. They were Keats's seasons too. The sense of a threat suspended over the end of summer is beautifully expressed in the final stanza of his *September:*

Thus without grief the golden days go by,
   So soft we scarcely notice how they wend,
And like a smile half-happy, or a sigh,

The summer passes to her quiet end;
And soon, too soon, around the cumbered eaves
   Sly frosts shall take the creepers by surprise,
And through the wind-touched reddening
   woods shall rise
October with the rain of ruined leaves.

The last line is grand with the announcement of a resistless change to come, and poignant with the poet's lament. It makes a strong and immediate impression; but perhaps most readers will not immediately appreciate how much of its power comes from the strategy by which it has gradually been prepared. The rest of the stanza is exceedingly quiet; the poet strews through earlier lines sounds which are approaches to lamentation – in "soon, too soon," there is more than an approach, there is a lamentation itself – and in the penultimate line develops a preluding movement which is exciting and full of suspense.

In Lampman's work the note of *September* is repeatedly struck, and it is one of the finest notes in our poetry. He was also at home as man and as poet in the wilder parts of the country. He often devoted his vacations to canoe trips in the northland. In 1896 the trip was from Lake Temiskaming to the Hudson Bay post at Temagami. In 1898 on sick leave, in his last escape from the city, he made his way by La Tuque to Lake Wayagamack, though by now he was not strong enough for a veritable expedition. In the poems on the northland he used a starker diction and a more austere movement. Intimate as his treatment of this wilder nature could be, it was not Lampman but his friend Duncan Campbell Scott who expressed the fullness of the emotion that arose in a sympathetic temperament in contact with the northland.

The death of Lampman in the winter of 1899 was, in my opinion, the greatest bereavement our poetry has ever suffered. As Duncan Scott has beautifully said, he was turning leaves in some book that Death forbade him to write. Among the new themes in the poems of his last years was his evocation of a great moment in Canadian history, the feat of Daulac at the Long Sault. It was my privilege to decipher in the delicate script of his notebooks the text of this narrative in which, more perhaps than in any other work, he shows that at the end his genius was renewing itself, as Tennyson's had done at about the same age. The image which dominates the central part of the poem is that of a moose beset by a pack of snarling wolves and in the end brought down. It is worked out with passion and vigour. But at the close the gentle spirit of Lampman reasserts itself. The Frenchmen are dead, the Indians in retreat, the scene is illuminated by a quiet May moon. The lyric begins at Montreal, the prize whose safety was assured by the sacrifice, and passes to the Long Sault, where the sacrifice was offered:

All night by the foot of the mountain
  The little town lieth at rest,
The sentries are peacefully pacing
  And neither from East nor from West

Is there rumour of death or of danger:
  None dreameth tonight in his bed
That ruin was near and the heroes
  That met it and stemmed it are dead.

But afar in the ring of the forest
  Where the air is so tender with May
And the waters are wild in the moonlight
  They lie in their silence of clay.

The numberless stars out of heaven
  Look down with a pitiful glance:
And the lilies asleep in the forest
  Are closed with the lilies of France.

This lyric, in which the anapaests work so persuasively on the emotions, in which serenity and tremulousness are so perfectly fused, was written late in 1898. In the February of the following year the poet was dead.

II

A note very like that of the lyric which closed *At the Long Sault* had been sounded some years earlier by a poet of the same generation, Bliss Carman. Carman, whose fame outside Canada has been broader than any other English Canadian poet has yet won, brought out in 1893 his first collection, *Low Tide on Grand Pré*. The titular poem is, like Lampman's lyric, at once serene and tremulous. As was Carman's way, the way of Shelley and Swinburne, he developed his theme to a greater length than it required, and lost himself in exquisite music. The opening stanza shows what music there was in Carman:

> The sun goes down and over all
> These barren reaches by the tide
> Such unelusive glories fall,
> I almost dream they yet will bide
> Until the coming of the tide.

It is an incantation: and the key words of the charm are "unelusive glories fall." The poet's coinage "unelusive", "glories" – one of the most richly musical words in the language, and the dying note in "fall" are admirable taken individually, and as a group have a rich and liquid effect. They are moreover framed with the most cunning art both as to diction and movement. Carman was a more sensuous being than Lampman, and to the serenity and the tremulousness he adds, even in so simple a piece as this, something of luxuriance. The temptations of verbal and musical luxuriance he was unfitted to resist or control; he was all too often soft or vague; his ear was more acute than his eye, and thus his images lack the appropriateness he could give to his rhythms. Poetry like his is today under a specially heavy cloud; but the time will surely come when our present indifference to Carman will amaze both the general reader of poetry and the historian of Canadian letters. If a personal note may be permitted, I should like to say that I now believe that in the past I have been too grudging in estimating this poet, so attractive in the sweep of his music and the sensuous sincerity of his language. At all times in his long career, except perhaps at the very beginning, his performance was uneven; but we must forget the inferior work, which towards the end predominated, and make our way back until we can read the young enchanter without the painful consciousness of how the enchantment was to lose its power.

The later poetry of Duncan Scott in no way obscures the excellence of his early collections. Excellent these indeed were; but his talent developed slowly, and it is after 1900, and not before, that his finest work was written, in poems such as *The Height of Land, Variations on a Seventeenth Century Theme,* and *The Forsaken.* For my present purpose I shall confine myself to *The Magic House,* which appeared in the same year with Carman's *Low Tide on Grand Pré,* and *Labour and the Angel* which followed after five years. Unlike Lampman and Charles G. D. Roberts, he has seldom used the sonnet, but there are few modern sonnets in which art and emotion are so admirably allied as in *The Onondaga Madonna.* The sestet will show its quality:

> And closer in the shawl about her breast
> The latest promise of her nation's doom,
> Paler than she her baby clings and lies,
> The primal warrior gleaming from his eyes;
> He sulks and burdened with his infant gloom,
> He draws his heavy brows and will not rest.

The solemn movement is appropriate; but the suggestive power, as is usual in Scott's poetry resides rather in the idea and the image than in the music. This is one of the many striking poems in which Scott has dealt with the Indian; and he has indeed treated the Indian theme with greater power than any other English-speaking Canadian writer. The Indian for him is not a noble savage, nor yet the sordid victim of the potlatch: the Indian is simply a human being belonging to a class which has had difficulty in adjusting to a complicated social structure for which its background has not been a preparation. The entire active career of Duncan Scott, from his appointment to the civil service in 1879 as a junior clerk to his retirement in 1932 was passed in the department of Indian Affairs, which for twenty years he directed. His Indian poetry is the fruit of long experience, deep wisdom, and serene benignity.

In reaching out towards the Indian theme Scott showed his sensitiveness not merely to a social class which was depreciated and which he sought to establish in the national society, but no less to the primitive elements in that part of Canada which civilization had barely touched. Not only the Indians, but the landscape of the Rockies and the Selkirks and the pre-Cambrian shield were congenial to his imagination. It is to him we must go for the most suggestive evocations of the terror and strangeness of the north and the northwest, as readers in French Canada have gone to *La Forêt* and *Le Pin Du Maskeg*, those remarkable works of M. Georges Bugnet.

But, always a devoted admirer of Rossetti, and the tradition that stems from him, there is in Scott no less than the primitive the subtly civilized. In his first collection the subtly civilized strain is dominant; and in the second appeared *The Piper of Arll,* a work of extraordinary delicacy, which won John Masefield for poetry. This is one of those voyages into a dream world strange and intense in color and line in which the English poets of the later nineteenth century delighted. And the movement of the verses is as admirable as the imagery. *The Piper of Arll* is not the kind of poetry to which at this particular moment we first turn, or turn with the most eager delight. So much may be admitted; but it should also be firmly said that if there is a provincialism of place – the provincialism against which the poets now most admired inveigh – there is also a provincialism of time. To let one's taste in poetry take its limits from the vogue of the moment is to succumb to the provincialism of time.

Lampman, Duncan Scott, Carman, these are the great names of the fifteen years I have been considering. But they were not alone. The mellow classical idylls, the homely regional pictures of Charles G. D. Roberts; the stormy eloquence and dreamy landscapes of William Wilfred Campbell; the picturesque and racy narratives of W. H. Drummond – of which Louis Fréchette wrote with such generous and discerning appreciation – in all these the spirit of true poetry is sometimes present, and vital.

It was a romantic spirit. And for some years poetry has been insurgent against romanticism. The insurgence will end; in France, where so often a new movement takes form before any other culture is aware of it, strong romantic currents are flowing again. In the poetry of Pratt the romantic spirit is almost always recognizable. He will help us, and the poets of yesterday will help us, if we approach them with neither scorn nor indifference, to escape from the characteristic limits of the taste of our time. Escape is necessary if we are to read poetry as whole men, and escape is the only means by which we may win the respect of the future, and in our degree aid that future to come into being undistorted and sane.

Now, Take Ontario

This is the last in the series of reports on the regions of Canada. If the report on Ontario could not come first, it should come last and crown the whole.

No Ontarian will ever concede that his province is on all fours with the others. Ontario is the apex, the present culmination of the national achievement. Because all we Ontarians believe this as a primary article of faith, we are widely disliked. This dislike is all the more acute because we either do not know it exists, or forget to remember it exists. When it is pointed out to us by some solitary exile from the indigent Maritimes or from the more desolate parts of the prairies we are not perturbed.

"It is not dislike at all," says the typical citizen of Hamilton, or London, or Smiths Falls, "it is just envy".

For my part I think that other Canadians (the French Canadians, of course, excepted) would do much better to concede that Ontario is the heartland of the nation, and then blame us in Ontario for what goes wrong. Of course, we are blamed for that anyhow.

Ontario is the apex, the heartland. More than a third of the Canadian population lives within our borders: in Toronto, Hamilton, Ottawa, Windsor, and London we have five of the 11 largest Canadian cities. From Ontario comes more than 40% of the total production of Canada. Just less than a quarter of the forest products, rather more than a quarter of the farm products, almost half the mineral products and more than half the manufactured products of Canada are the outcome of Ontario hands and Ontario skill.

Forty per cent of the national income goes into Ontario pockets and purses – more into the pockets; and a bit more than 40% of the retail sales made in Canada are exchanged for what comes out of those pockets and purses – a good deal more comes out of the purses.

In the cultural and religious life of Canada the record has long been equally impressive, and is today perhaps more impressive than ever.

The blue-ribbon distinction for a scientist who is a British subject is fellowship in the Royal Society; Ontario has and has long had the bulk of Canadian F. R. S.'s. The only Nobel prize that has ever come to Canada was awarded to professors in the University of Toronto for the discovery of insulin. The one really fully developed school of graduate studies in Canada, the focus for the greatest intellectual energies of the Canadian people, is in this university.

Toronto has long been the centre of Canadian music. In Toronto, and in the wild landscape of the pre-Cambrian shield in northern Ontario, the Group of Seven had their roots, and it was by their daring that Canadian painting took its longest forward step. The two greatest Canadian poets of our time live in Ontario, Duncan Campbell Scott in Ottawa (where he was born and where he had his entire brilliant career in the department of Indian Affairs) and Edwin John Pratt in Toronto (where he has lived and taught since he first came to Canada from his native Newfoundland 40 years ago).

Toronto is the centre of the United Church of Canada and of the Church of England in Canada. In Toronto the Roman Catholic Church has the one English-speaking Canadian Cardinal and the centre of Catholic intellectual life, the Pontifical Institute of Medieval Studies.

Yes, it is easy for the Ontarian to see that his province is the Canadian heartland. What he does not usually see at all is that Ontario, like every other part of Canada, is also a region with its own characterizing traits, some good, some bad, some comic, some pathetic, but all helping to mark it off, all leading it to diverge from the Canadian norm. The Ontarian simply believes that Ontario is the norm; the way Ontario does things and the way Ontario approves and disapproves are, he believes, exactly what the laws of Canada, of human nature and of God Himself ordain. I am not sure that the Ontarian would admit that the flickering light in a southern Ontario electric light bulb is a regional oddity. In Buffalo they have got rid of that flicker; but the flicker is already an Ontario tradition, and the Americans are generally supposed by Ontario to be a rashly innovating people.

Discovery in Manitoba

I had my first real perception that Ontario was a region one day in the autumn of 1935. Just before the Dominion elections of that year Mitchell Hepburn spoke in Winnipeg. I had taken my first job outside the boundaries of Ontario a month or so before, and with a homesickness that every exiled Ontarian will understand, whatever his politics, I made a point of finishing my dinner at Moore's restaurant on Portage Avenue (where the lights do not flicker) in time to go and listen to him.

Nothing at all of what Mr. Hepburn said has stayed with me; but I shall always remember a comment in the Free Press on his "warm Ontario accent". So Ontarians had an accent! I had supposed that every one else had, but not we. Perhaps – the destructive idea began to insinuate itself – we had not only an accent which sounded a little queer in the ears of other Canadians, but also our own ways of thinking and feeling, and could it be that these might seem queer to the mind and heart of a man from Calgary or Fredericton?

Now, I am a hardened Ontarian. I was born in Toronto and my father and mother were born in rural Ontario. I went to school and to college in Toronto. I spent my vacations in Muskoka. At 21 I had scarcely been outside Ontario. I have been away a good deal in recent years, but more than three quarters of my life has been lived in Ontario, and there is no other place in the world where I feel freely and easily at home.

The central and northern parts of Toronto are where I am most at home. The narrowness of lower Yonge St., the rows of its shabby and sometimes seedy shops between College and Bloor, the huddling curves of South Rosedale, the vista from Casa Loma, the shadeless streets of that suburb so oddly named Forest Hill, they are all beautiful in my eyes.

Not Really Drab

When I meet any really grown-up Torontonian who claims to know the city well, I have a question for him, a test for his credentials. Did he know the whistler?

The whistler was a middle-aged man with a thick pepper-and-salt beard, strikingly red protrusive lips, and a bent back, who hurried along the streets with a loping stride, making indescribable birdlike sounds. I have met him in almost every part of Toronto, once and most memorably late on a below zero night on the Main Street bridge; then, as always, he paid no attention as he hurried past whistling with an energy and volume which compensated for the lack of melody. There was a man with a life of his own, who lived it as he would. I should like to know what has become of the whistler. I hope that someone who reads these lines will tell me. It is a long time since I last saw him.

He may stand here for a fact of immense importance, which Ontarians almost always forget, or at least play down: that there is color in the life of Ontario. By the rest of the world we Ontarians are thought to be far over on the drab side; some of us even like to think that we are dull, thoroughly dull, for in thorough dullness is safety. But we really know better. The life of Ontario has far more color than we say.

Our Ontario history has color. The War of 1812, which was very much an Ontario war, had heroic episodes and grotesquely comic episodes, but it had no dull episodes at all. It may have been a small war, and our rebellion in 1837 was certainly a small rebellion. But it was a lively rebellion; there is not a really dull page in its history. Whatever may be said of our political leaders in Ontario, most of them have been, like George Drew and Mitch Hepburn, men of vivid and fiery personality. Their vividness has not prevented their re-election.

George Brown, probably our greatest newspaper editor, dipped his pen in something at least as bitter as gall, and was assassinated in the building where he conducted the old Globe. Even to one who now lives in the same city with Colonel Robert R. McCormick's Chicago Tribune, the leading Ontario papers of today are anything but dull.

They have a fine devotion to invective. When I sat a few weeks ago in the office of George McCullagh, the publisher of the Toronto Globe and Mail, and listened to his views on the state of the province, the nation and the world, I could not find a trace of timidity or dullness in the man or in what he said. To use an old American expression, Mr. McCullagh is about as intense as he can live. He sees life in intense oppositions and great urgencies. He gives the lie to many illusions we Ontario people have formed about ourselves. He has the mind of a prophet.

The murder of George Brown was not an exceptional event in the history of Ontario. Stewart Wallace's fascinating record, "Murders and Mysteries," can stand on the same shelf with William Roughead's accounts of Scottish capital crimes. Ontario has been the scene of some of the purplest murders in the annals of passion. And since Mr. Wallace wrote a decade or so ago there has been no decline in the number or quality of our murders.

The Spell of the North

Color has run through our history and runs through it today. Today the greatest single source of color in the life of Ontario is in the northland. A remark of John W. Dafoe's – like so many of the best Westerners he was Ontario born and Ontario bred – first brought home to me the unity of Ontario's existence. The towering skyline of Toronto in the 1930's, he said, depended on the mines in the northern ranges of Ontario. The height of the one was in balance with the depth of the other.

That northern country is the home of every Ontarian's imagination, if he has any; I believe far more Ontarians have an imagination than will own, even a little sheepishly, to that unpredictable and therefore perilous power. In the best book written on Canada, André Siegfried said that the crucial factor in a country's history is the particular dream that haunts the imagination of its people. The Ontario dream is of the north, the land of mines and lakes and forests, the margins of civilization, the approaches to the unknown. That is why so many Ontarians leave cool and comfortable houses, shaded by some of the most beautiful maples and elms in the world, to spend as much of the summer as they can in primitive and monstrously ugly summer hotels with a few scrubby jack pines scattered among dull rocky hillocks, or in even more primitive cottages. Nothing could entice me into one of them now or forevermore. But then I nourish my northern dream on other materials, on painting and poetry. Our Ontario folklore, the tales that are told but seldom written down, and yet linger from decade to decade and pass from town to town, are largely about the north. Before any one generalizes about Ontario, he must think about the mining towns, and the kind of people in many southern cities and farmhouses who are in touch with them either through their families or through their pocketbooks.

The north country is vividly present to the economist and to those whom the economist has taught, when they look at the Toronto or Hamilton skyline. Our painters too have seen it, and have loaned out their imaginations so that when any of us goes to the art gallery in an Ontario city, or examines the Christmas cards in almost any Ontario store, he may bring the essence of the north before his mind.

To our painters we owe a debt that only a few of us fully realize and that we are never likely to pay. When I was a boy drawing-rooms, dens and dining rooms were hung with discouraging oils and grim engravings, the oils usually in sombre browns and greens, the engravings a moribund gray. Now it is different. Tom Thomson and his associates have brought the emphatic lines and the fierce and splendid colors of the northern landscape to the walls of our rooms – the reproductions are almost everywhere, at least when a young person has had a hand in decoration. To speak for myself, a little Tom Thomson reproduction in color, bought at the Art Gallery in Ottawa, is always on my desk. I should not care to work without it.

At first Ontario would have nothing to do with the wild new paintings. They are called, to choose one of the milder terms, the "products of a deranged mind." The general opinion was that they were the outcomes of frantic duels between maniacs hurling gobs of paint at long distance. But before very long – it seemed long enough to the painters – something very deep in Ontarians began to respond. I have always thought that Mr. and Mrs. Vincent Massey made one of the most successful contributions toward the popularity of the Group of Seven by hanging many of their works on the walls of Hart House at the University of Toronto where, in the course of years, thousands upon thousands of still quite impressionable young Ontarians grew accustomed to them and slowly came to like them. The violent colors and decisive lines in which these painters presented our own landscape showed us something strong and decided in ourselves. Perhaps we did not at first like to be found out behind our drab defenses; but in the end we have admitted the truth and enjoyed having our painters tell it to us.

Snobbery and Timidity

We in Ontario are franker about ourselves and our circumstances than we used to be. There are still reticences which do us nothing but harm. The most unpleasant form of Ontario reticence is our unfriendliness. We are about as unfriendly as a people can be.

Just as an Englishman's social reserve may make him appear rude to those to whom he has not been introduced, so does the reticence of the Ontarian make him unfriendly to those he does not know.

We in Ontario have not the expressive friendliness of people in the West, or of people in the United States. I do not ask for the high courtesy of Virginia, or for the warm-eyed neighborliness of Winnipeg, but we might perhaps get some of the ice out of our eyes and our voices.

It is this same reticence which accounts for most of that insufferable toploftiness in so many of our Leading Citizens, and their sons and daughters. I know a little about the sons and daughters for I had them about me in the 10 years when I taught at the University of Toronto. Whether they come from London or Brantford or Ottawa or Toronto they hold apart. They hive together. They join the same few fraternities and sororities. They do not make very warm overtures to students from simpler backgrounds.

Snobbery is a very ugly word, one of the ugliest in the language. A snob, said Thackeray who wrote a "Book of

Snobs," is one who meanly admires mean things. That definition does not seem to fit the Ontario species of snobbery. Ontario snobbery is timidity, another form of the reticence which underlies so much of what is wrong with us. Our Leading Citizens are not really sure of themselves; they don't quite know what has made them leading citizens, or what will keep them leading citizens. They have wealth, most of them, but they are intelligent and they know that wealth by itself is not a real superiority, and cannot form a recognized class. They have power of one sort or another, but they know too well how they or their ancestors acquired the power to rest very secure in a belief that power argues a real superiority and makes a recognized class. In their insecurity they crowd together. So do sheep.

The Fear of Self-Reliance

This reticence underlies another unfortunate trait. Since teaching is my trade I shall illustrate it from the classroom, but it is just as often present in the factory or the office. When you ask an American or a western Canadian student a complicated question, his main wish is to crow over what he knows. The whole class would like to talk, and the student you single out would like to talk as long as you will let him. Your problem is to save some time for yourself to say something.

But when you ask the same sort of question in an Ontario classroom, what the student you single out wants above all is not to give himself away, not to reveal any ignorance or misinformation, or any impolite excess of information. He will say as little as he can. He does not trust himself. From his point of view it is a breach of the code to trust yourself conspicuously. He writhes when some outlander or some Ontarian who is unfaithful to the customs of the tribe (and there are such, quite a number of them, affectionately recalled at this moment) speaks out frankly, cheerfully and at serene and happy length. That man, the rest of the class appears to be reflecting, as they look at their books, or at their fingernails or ostentatiously out the window, is dangerous.

It is just the same when you ask an Ontario student to

read a report. True, he will read it; that is the bargain, and an Ontarian will normally keep the letter of a bargain grimly. But he will gabble it as fast as he can and with as little expression as possible so that all his fellows will know that he does not really wish to impose his thoughts upon them, that he only does so because he is obliged to, and that at least he is making the exhibition of himself as brief and as colorless as the vocal chords will allow. Thus he expects to be pardoned; and he is.

And yet I could tell him that he has at least as much to say as the Western student or the American, perhaps much more. For there is nothing wrong with his mind judged as a machine, and in its recesses ideas are turning over which have originality and value. A German poet has said: "It is certain my conviction gains infinitely the moment another soul will believe in it." The conviction of an Ontarian would gain infinitely the moment he would fully believe in it himself. And he would gain as a personality, he would become more generous in his judgments on others, more friendly in his responses to the lesser breeds without the law.

I should like to see every high school student in Ontario reading Emerson's great essay on "Self-Reliance." "Trust thyself," says Emerson, "every heart vibrates to that iron string." And again: "Nothing can bring you peace but yourself."

If we in Ontario could acquire a decent measure of self-reliance, it would be more valuable to us than even the discovery somewhere in the province of an inexhaustible deposit of anthracite. For, until we acquire that self-reliance, we cannot make the full and right use of the great resources we already have – the land, and the metals, and the lumber, the roads and rails and planes, and all the other bases for a flourishing civilization.

If we people of Ontario had that self-reliance, people elsewhere in Canada would be powerfully drawn towards the heartland, would trust our leadership and work with us. No lesson in algebra, or in Latin grammar, or in any of those odd newfangled subjects which have been introduced since I last sat at a desk in a Toronto school, and are credited with the magical power to make whole men and whole women, would have as much persistent influence as the enthusiastic and effective teaching of that essay of Emerson's written just a little over a hundred years ago. The Americans have absorbed its doctrine; you cannot live among them without seeing that. We have shied away from it; you cannot live among us without seeing that.

The choice that lies before us, so far as we have a choice, is between the set of values which are represented by the north country – the qualities of vividness, strength and self-reliance which are latent in us – and the set of values represented by too many Leading Citizens and their admirers – timidity, dullness and caution. The war shook us up, and gave the first and better set a temporary triumph. What we have to do now is to shake ourselves up and make that triumph lasting.

Canadian Literature Today

1948

In any fair-minded consideration of the present moment in Canadian writing in English there are a number of blessings to be counted first.

The past few years have brought a number of solid novels that are honest, deeply felt and extremely readable. This is a novelty. The greatest success has gone to Gwethalyn Graham's "Earth and High Heaven"; and that competent and passionately sincere study of race prejudice deserves all the popular approval it won. Miss Graham's skill enabled her to avoid preachiness, and to embody her assault upon the vicious anti-semitism that marks too many Canadian groups in a number of living characters who do credible things, and enlist our emotional participation. In "Two Solitudes" Hugh MacLennan took up another aspect of racial prejudice, and if he was less skillful in art, his sincerity and passion were as moving as Miss Graham's. The preachiness, the tendency to long essay-like passages, decreased in his more recent novel "The Precipice". That book is not so good a novel as Miss Graham's; but it is tending in her direction.

There has been no memorable war-novel, as yet. Probably there are better war-novels to come. But the level of maturity and straight competence in writing is higher than it was in the Canadian novels that followed the first world war.

Imaginative Insight

The novels of the past few years have been notable for imaginative insight into crucial national issues. These issues have also been illuminated by the historians. One of the best achievements in recent Canadian writing has been the re-interpretation of Canadian life in terms of its past and its economic and social setting. There was a signal for a new and richer sort of historical writing in Bruce Hutchison's fascinating "The Unknown Country". In Donald G. Creighton's "Dominion of the North", Edgar McInnis's "Canada" and A. R. M. Lower's "From Colony to Nation" history has become much more complex and also much more interesting than it used to be. To write history well in the terms imposed today requires a combination of intellectual, ethical and artistic qualities seldom combined in one man. The younger Canadian historians – and there are others of great note and worth besides those named – are among our greatest national assets.

Poetry has not thrown up a rival to E. J. Pratt who is now in his middle sixties, and at work on one of the most ambitious themes he has ever considered. But Earle Birney and Dorothy Livesay, the chief literary figures of British Columbia, have found highly individual ways of expressing a rich fusion of feeling and thought. They are mature and notable artists, and their insight into Canadian social forces is trenchant, if not profound.

We continue to lack a dramatic literature; but the lack should not surprise us when the theatre languishes across the country. Dramatic writing for radio is making extraordinary advances; and in Miss Gwen Pharis there is the promise of a playwright for the more traditional kind of stage.

Magazine Gap

The desperate gap is in magazines. The poverty of magazines, financial or intellectual, and in some cases both, is one of the chief obstacles to the advance of culture in this country. The academic quarterlies are not read, and few know of their existence. The more popular magazines, although most are noticeably better than they were a decade ago, continue to be afraid of anything that demands real thinking, and in some of the most widely circulated there is an absurd insistence on a childish simplicity of approach. What is needed is a magazine in the manner of "Harper's", a monthly expertly written and admirably edited, devoted above all to a clear incisive and mature examination of the main problems in the intellectual and social life of the times. "Harper's" makes reading about such problems as easy and as agreeable as the best writing and editing can. But the editors of "Harper's" know that when the problem is a complicated one, it cannot be presented adequately and honestly without demanding some thought from the reader. It would be a great stimulus to our national maturity if we had a magazine which would raise the level of Canadian essays and comments on questions of the day to the level sustained year in and year out in half a dozen American magazines which exercise real influence on currents of opinion in the United States. There might be some money in the venture, too.

1949

A story, a poem, an essay, is not written in a vacuum. Even when a writer takes to the woods, he responds, the moment he uses his pen, to pressures in the society in which he grew up, and to which he cannot avoid belonging. Even when he says, and sincerely believes, that he is expressing some experience he has had and valued, he is always expressing more than something that happened to his individual self. He is affected by the kinds of people that make up his nation, and the kinds of things that they are interested in.

James Joyce (whose Ulysses is now admitted to Canada, thus lightening the suitcases of hundreds of returning Canadians each year) certainly did not write for the Irish. But the kinds of Irish people he had known before he angrily left Ireland in his early twenties affected every book he wrote. His revolt against the kinds of things they were interested in affected the way he wrote.

A Close Interest

The literature we have in Canada is our reflection: it shows very clearly what we are and what we are not. A great many of us have a close interest in the history of Canada, and we have excellent historians, as good as any in England or in the United States. Scarcely any of us are closely interested in the great abstractions – the exact definition of freewill, for instance – and we have no original philosophers or theologians.

The best theological and philosophical writing done in Canada has come from Europeans, who seldom remained in the atmosphere that was not propitious to abstract thought.

The best things in Canadian novels are akin to the writing of history. Our novelists know how to describe and analyse a man in relation to the framework of the social and political institutions of our country. In "Two Solitudes" and "The Precipice" Hugh Maclennan has given important and often profound accounts of Canadians at grips with racial and social prejudices and traditions.

But our novelists do not show the same degree, or anything like the same degree, of insight into an individual's more intimate concerns, into love or religion, or the quest of one's own self through what Keats called the "vale of soul-making". We have no novels with a tithe of this insight as shown by Dostoevski, or on a smaller scale by E. M. Forster or Elizabeth Bowen.

Psychological Depths

Our recent poetry has been strong in the rendering of the same kind of relationships that appear in Hugh Maclennan's novels. Our older poetry was strong in expressing another lasting Canadian interest and enthusiasm – for the landscape, and man's relation to it. But we have very little poetry that penetrates, as so much of the greatest poetry does, into the nature of love and religion and the quest of one's self. I have mentioned Keats: we do not have any poems that even remind us of the psychological depths in his odes.

It is the same story with our essays. These are best when they attack some specific problem, and weakest when they attempt something more general, more profound. They are the work of men who do not have an ingrained habit of reflection, but think cogently about a limited issue that seems susceptible of quick solution.

Our greatest books lie ahead of us. It is fun to watch the first signs that they are looming up.

Duncan Campbell Scott:
A Memoir

Duncan Campbell Scott was born August 2, 1862, at Ottawa, in a parsonage that used to stand near the corner of Queen and Metcalfe Streets, two short blocks from Parliament Hill. His father, William Scott, born at Lincoln in England October 4, 1812, was converted to Methodism in boyhood; and when an early marriage, to Maria Slight, closed the way into the English conference of his church, came out to New York with his wife in 1834. After two years or so of work on the editorial side of a magazine in that city he was received on trial for the ministry of the Methodist Episcopal Church. The British connection meant more to him than he had thought, and in 1837 he came to Canada. In 1839 he was ordained, and from 1841 to 1847 was attached to the St. Clair mission, ministering to the Indians along the eastern shore of Lake Huron, on Manitoulin Island, and at Amherstburg on the southwestern tip of what is now Ontario. His interest in the Indians was to be lifelong, and one of the main bonds with his son Duncan. After 1847 he undertook regular parochial work, chiefly in the Ottawa and Kingston districts and, to the south of the St. Lawrence, in the so-called "eastern townships" of what is now Quebec. By his first marriage there were four children; it ended in 1857 with the death of Maria Scott. Two years later William Scott married Isabella Campbell MacCallum, who was born in 1827 at Ile aux Noix on the Richelieu River near the Vermont border. John MacCallum, her father, and her mother, Isabella Campbell, who had the Gaelic, were emigrants from Killin in Perthshire. By this marriage there were three children, of whom Duncan was the second, and the only boy.

"The birthplace of a Methodist minister's son in the days of the itinerancy is fortuitous", Duncan Scott has said in his memoir of Walter J. Phillips, "it may be here or there, it carries with it no ancestral ties or even lengthy residence." Although he was born in the city where he was to pass the whole of his mature life, throughout his childhood Duncan Scott lived in small towns and villages. He soon became curious about the ways of life among French Canadian neighbours, and looked on, or heard about, some of the wild happenings among the lumbermen. He was a restless inquisitive boy and appears to have felt the pressure on an itinerant minister's children to avoid offending by an unusual act or word the more censorious members of the parish. The family was large, and the stipend small; it fell far short of "the hundred dollars a month" mentioned in that work of his old age, "The Circle of Affection," as "affluence in the Ottawa of the seventies" – it was sometimes as little as three hundred a year. William Scott, a large bluff man, had some independence of spirit, and besides was well read beyond the round of his profession. "In his library," Duncan Scott has said, "were the standard works, translations from the classics, essays, poetry, Carlyle, Emerson, etc." Emerson's "Self-Reliance" was an early discovery, and Duncan Scott was lastingly grateful for its doctrine. Isabella Scott had a strong feeling for music, and encouraged Duncan in the study of piano, which he began when he was seven. His interest in art began with the woodcuts in *Good Words* and *Good Words for the Young*, which came regularly to the parsonage where the bound volumes were carefully preserved. In these periodicals he could study the work of Millais, Holman Hunt, and Rossetti, and to the end of his life they gave him pleasure. "These books," he recalled shortly before his death, "were the possessions of happy children brought up by indulgent parents whose influence was ever for the best in letters, music, and in art, and who encouraged every evidence of talent". The "first perception or what might be called *pang* of poetry" was in the high school at Smith's Falls, where William Scott had a charge in 1874 and 1875:

it was "when the master wrote on the blackboard these words from Tennyson's 'Dream of Fair Women':

"One sitting on a crimson scarf unroll'd;
A queen with swarthy cheeks and bold black eyes,
     Brow-bound with burning gold."

There was to be a good deal in Duncan Scott's poetry in the vein of this description of Cleopatra, and to Tennyson, as to Emerson, the attachment was lasting. In 1877 the family moved to Stanstead, where Duncan delighted in the hilly landscape, and attended the recently founded Wesleyan College. He was beginning to think of medicine as his profession, probably under the influence of his mother's brother, Dr. Duncan Campbell MacCallum, who had the chair of midwifery and diseases of women and children at McGill University from 1868 to 1883, and for some years afterward was a leading physician in Montreal. Like most children who have borne it, Duncan Scott was unhappy over the constant flitting from place to place; but in retrospect his childhood and boyhood seemed to him to have been good. He was never given to repining.

He did not repine when there was no money for a medical course. When he had come to the end of such instruction as was given at Stanstead his father was nearing retirement. William Scott arranged for Duncan to have an interview, in December, 1879, with the Prime Minister of Canada, Sir John A. Macdonald, and Sir John, who had a request before him from the department of Indian Affairs for a temporary copying clerk, endorsed it: "Approved – employ Mr. Scott at $1.50." Duncan Scott did not at once give up hope of a course at a university; but salaries in the lower ranks of the civil service were very small, and after William Scott's superannuation Duncan's responsibilities to his mother and his sisters grew. Besides, somewhat to his surprise, he found that he liked the civil service, and Ottawa he liked very much, even the long winters. How highly his abilities were valued was shown in 1889. In a recommendation that he be made a first-class clerk at $1,-400 a year, the Deputy Superintendent General wrote: "the duties and responsibilities wh. attach to the office appear to render it advisable that the officer should hold the rank of first class clerk. Mr. Duncan C. Scott, who at present fills the position, is a very competent book-keeper and a person of good business capacity". The person of good business capacity had meanwhile built the red brick house at 108 Lisgar Street, within ten minutes' walk of his birthplace, which was to be his home for the rest of his life.

Duncan Scott was making friends, chiefly in the service. Chief among them was Archibald Lampman, one year his senior, who came to the Post Office department in 1883. Lampman had published a number of poems before his arrival in Ottawa; but the landscape of the Ottawa Valley at once began to move him to much better verse than he had been able to write in central Ontario. Lampman was unhappy in the service; he chafed at the narrowness of life in Ottawa; he was disgusted by the chicanery and syco-phancy he saw all about him. With Duncan Scott he could share his interest in nature, in music, and in books. They spent many evenings in literary talk, tramped the fields and woods around the little city, and often spent the liberal vacations of the service in canoe trips to wild parts of Ontario and Quebec. It was by the stimulus he took from Lampman that Duncan Scott began to write. "It never occurred to me" he has said, "to write a line of prose or poetry until I was about twenty-five – and after I had met Archibald Lampman." The viola, which he had lately taken up, was laid aside, and most of his indoor leisure was given to writing.

When I asked him some few years before his death which was the first of his poems to be printed, he could recall no other so early as a sonnet, "Ottawa Before Dawn." (He was never a sound sleeper, and would say with humorous tartness that Lampman saw "precious few sun-rises," phenomena with which he was himself all too famil-iar.) This first sonnet does not appear in the collected *Poems;* but it may be seen in W. D. Lighthall's *Songs of the Great Dominion.* It was composed because an Ottawa bookseller and stationer was dissatisfied with a poem he had requested from "Seranus" (S. Frances Harrison) for an illustrated card, and turned to Duncan Scott. "Ottawa Before Dawn" is a significant, if not at all a brilliant, begin-ning. In it Scott combines the exact rendering of nature

> the Chaudière fills
> The calm with its hushed roar; the river takes
> An unquiet rest,

the romantic appreciation of beauty in the city

> fair as a shrine that makes
> The wonder of a dream, imperious towers
> Pierce and possess the sky,

and the faith in the future of the nation

> the star of morning dowers
> The land with a large tremulous light, that falls
> A pledge and presage of our destiny.

It is rhetorical, a little stiff, and has other qualities that are common in occasional verse. The second poem he wrote was, he said, "The Hill Path," which is among the collected *Poems,* and first appeared in *Scribner's Magazine* for May, 1888. It is a light lilting love poem that gives no indication of what was to come.

It was in 1893 that Scott's first collection was published, *The Magic House and Other Poems.* The name of the Ottawa bookstore of J. Durie and Sons appears on the title page of the copies distributed in Canada, as it had appeared five years before on that of Lampman's *Among the Millet;* but unlike Lampman, Scott refused to accept the ugliness of type and format that Canadian manufacture imposed on a book – with excellent result he had the book printed and bound in Great Britain, where Methuen distributed it. Reviewers were astonished by the extraordinary range in quality, and in the end the author accepted the criticism when he excluded many of the poems from the collected edition; but there is a sufficient number of good poems to make this first collection something more than a work of apprenticeship. Some of these are in the manner of the title piece, delicate fantastic expressions of a dream world akin to the most refined effects according to the Pre-Raphaelite formula. Scott's dreams were always to be a main source of his poetry. The prosody in the dream poems is often original to subtle result, and seems to have been affected by the poet's experience as a musician. On other poems, not so fine as the dream pieces, but nevertheless attractive, the mark of Lampman is plain: they abound in pictures and aural suggestions of nature. "The Fifteenth of April" was appropriately dedicated to "A.L." – there are many dedications in this book which like this one have been suppressed in reprintings. The debt to Lampman's admirable "Heat" is evident in such lines as these:

> Ringing from the rounded barrow
>   Rolls the robin's tune;
> Lighter than the robin; hark!
>   Quivering silver-strong
> From the field a hidden shore-lark
>   Shakes his sparkling song.

"At the Cedars," which had appeared in Lighthall's *Songs,* is a first proof of power in robust narrative in verse; if this tale of death in a log-jam lacks much of the finish and ease that mark the beautifully composed tales of Indian life that were to follow, it has their force. The most personal of the poems, and I should say the best, is an elegy, "In the Country Churchyard: To the Memory of My Father." William Scott had died in 1891 at Ottawa; during his last years he had a post in the same department with his son. Surprisingly, the poem has no trace of personal or intellectual intimacy; there is no account of the father's character or career; and there is no sense of filial bereavement. Like Gray's "Elegy," with which it has an affinity so close as at first to be disturbing, the work is a record of the poet's casting up his own account with life, on the suggestion in his father's passing that life does not last forever. The attraction of the semi-wild neglected churchyard – the most vivid element in the poem – is rendered in Lampman's manner; and the attraction of this quiet homely place, and of death, is resisted by the poet because:

>   the world is beautiful,
>   And I am more in love with the sliding years,
>   They have not brought me frantic joy or tears,
> But only moderate state and temperate rule;
>   Not to forget
> This quiet beauty, not to be Time's fool,
>   I will be man a little longer yet.

ıe beauty of nature is one of the reasons for the wish to be man a little longer yet, but it does not have the primacy, it is not felt with the passion, that would have appeared in a poem of Lampman's.

The sliding years from 1890 to 1895 were among the most important in Duncan Scott's life. In 1891 a third poet of the same generation, William Wilfred Campbell, entered the civil service; and from February, 1892, to July, 1893, Scott and Lampman joined with him to write "At the Mermaid Inn," an informal weekly column for the Toronto *Globe*. If it invited more controversy than was quite welcome to Duncan Scott's pacific disposition, it led him into clear formulations of his ideas about poetry and literature generally, and although to this he was almost indifferent, it gave him something of a name in the broad region where people experienced some difficulty in distinguishing between the pronouncements of the *Globe* and those of the Bible. The column stopped partly because of the resentments stirred by Campbell, but Scott felt that it would have petered out, that there was not enough to write about at the level of a newspaper when Canadian culture was so thin and Europe so remote. It is impossible to trace any direct debt of Duncan Scott's to Campbell's vehement and argumentative personality or to his practice of poetry, although he did admire Campbell's rendering of nature; but no one could associate with Campbell without being provoked to harder thinking and sharper statement. The three Ottawa poets were steady contributors to *Scribner's Magazine* throughout the eighteen-nineties. Duncan Scott was also writing narrative prose; as early as 1887 there had appeared in *Scribner's* the first of the sketches which were to make up *In the Village of Viger,* published at Boston in 1896. "In the Country Churchyard" is, like Matthew Arnold's "Thyrsis," "a very quiet poem"; and these are very quiet sketches, gentle, sensitive, even. They made no stir, and could not; but they wear almost as well as the sketches of such a master as Sarah Orne Jewett, although they do not have quite her perfection of phrase. The publication of *In the Village of Viger* was not the most important of Duncan Scott's ties with Boston at this time. It was indeed the result of another: the manuscript went to the small company of Copeland

and Day because, on October 3, 1894, Duncan Scott married Belle Warner Botsford of Boston.

Belle Botsford had been, in Duncan Scott's words, "a student of violin at the Paris Conservatory of Music; she was afterwards a favourite pupil of Léonard and later of Marsick (both of them famous teachers of violin in Paris at the end of the last century) and had a short but distinguished career as a professional violinist, appearing on the concert platforms of Great Britain, the United States and Canada." Duncan Scott met her when he was her accompanist at a recital in Ottawa; and from the time he knew her, music became an ever larger part of his life, with effects of increasing and finally of extraordinary beauty on his poetry. Their tastes in music were very much alike, for the delicate and austere. In later years Duncan Scott was strongly attracted by the more massive and mysterious music of the nineteenth century, and curious, and perhaps more than curious, about recent American compositions. Belle Scott was energetic, high-strung, and imperious. She had much of the characteristic New England zeal to remould persons and circumstances nearer to her heart's desire. She was a stimulating companion, and she cared about poetry; but a man of Duncan Scott's disposition, shy and slow to mature, might sooner have come to a full self-understanding if he had not lived in the shadow of so dominant a wife. It is likely that there were deeper and earlier sources of repression – the vulnerability of a minister's son in a small town, the sharp social cleavages and the strong demand for conformity in the middle class urban society of central Canada. "The trouble," he wrote in one of the few letters in which he analyses himself, "is that the moment I endeavour to write or speak about myself something intervenes and I become shy and inarticulate and anything that I write or say seems affected and banal. I suppose this makes ordinary intercourse with me difficult but I cannot change my spots now." A perceptive woman, the wife of one of his most intimate friends, used to say that Duncan Scott's habitually fixed and melancholy expression was "not his real face," but a mask that had formed upon it. One deep reason for his melancholy was the rift with his mother and his sisters that came soon after he married, for

119

what precise reasons is now unknown. His relation with his mother was permanently ruined; at a much later time he was again on a footing of intimacy with his sisters, one of whom died in 1938, and the other in 1947.

In 1898 Copeland and Day published the second volume of his poetry, *Labor and the Angel,* dedicated to his wife. The most remarkable of the new poems is a dream piece, "The Piper of Arll," a far more disturbing and thrilling work than "The Magic House." On its first appearance in the Christmas number of *Truth,* a New York weekly, it was read by a young man who was working in a carpet factory at Yonkers; it was the first poem by a living writer to touch him to the quick – no poem would ever give him more pleasure – it "set him on fire." He got by heart its forty stanzas, and could repeat them half a century later. This was John Masefield, who has explained in his autobiographical study, *In the Mill,* how "The Piper of Arll" had determined his impulse to become a poet. William Archer, in his essay on Scott in *Poets of the Younger Generation,* complained that the allegory in the poem eluded him; but in these days of difficult and implicit poems the allegory should not tax anyone's imaginative understanding. Even for those who with Masefield have declined to struggle with its intricacies the main power of the poem is accessible – a series of moods, rendered with a delicacy and intensity that are achieved with such fullness much more often in music than in words. In this second volume of verse, Duncan Scott's impressions of the Indians begin to appear. Notable among them are the twin sonnets, "Watkwenies" and "The Onondaga Madonna." Both are built on a feeling for the contrast of the savage powerful past of the race with its humbled present and hopeless future; the clear images of the two women are involved in suggestions of the theme. The sonnet was not a form in which Scott was often at ease; he was right in his belief that it was too rigid for the expression of what was flexible and elusive in his nature. But the rigidity of the sonnet is appropriate for what he felt about the Indians in the eighteen-nineties; later his feelings would become more complex, and for these, too, he would find a medium.

In the summer of 1897 Scott and Lampman took the last of their long canoe trips together. They ascended the Gatineau, made their way across country to the Joseph, a small river full of obstructions, and from it made the difficult portage to Lake Achigan. Duncan Scott has set two of his stories, "In the Year 1806" and "Clute Boulay," on the shores of "the still lake surrounded by sombre spruces." In his unpublished novel, written towards 1905, Lake Achigan had an important role. It was one of the special places for his imaginative life. Lampman revived with every mile of distance from his desk; he talked with a gaiety and a force he could no longer summon in Ottawa; and Duncan Scott was always to remember these days in the Quebec forest as evidence that in Lampman's mind and personality there was something for which his poems gave no full expression – boldness in thought and feeling that was only beginning to stir in his last works. A few months after their return Lampman became seriously ill, and although he lived more than a year, dying on February 10, 1899, his health was broken. Duncan Scott went through the score of notebooks Lampman had filled with pencilled drafts, many of them on the verge of the illegible, and compiled a memorial edition with a biographical and critical introduction that remains the most valuable of all his pronouncements on the poetry and character of his friend. It came out in 1900, the year after Duncan Scott succeeded to Lampman's seat in the Royal Society of Canada. To the end of his life no man ever filled the place that Lampman had held for almost fifteen years. To me he usually called his friend "our poet," with a special sad inflection; sometimes when he spoke of the circumstances so many and so various that had combined to prevent Lampman from giving his full measure as man or poet, he would say in a whisper "Poor Archie!" and fall silent. It is impossible to convey how much feeling he put into the simple phrase.

With the circumstances of his own life he was reasonably content. On July 22, 1895, his one child, Elizabeth Duncan, was born; and there are many poems concerning her, full of a sensitive, sometimes whimsical affection, now and then with an intensity at which the poet himself seems frightened. Elizabeth, who had her mother's red hair and small face, also had something of her disposition: she was imaginative and independent, swift in her movements, sharp in her discriminations, odd in the opinion of her friends. In 1896 his "moderate state" was heightened, when he became secretary of the department of Indian Affairs, began to shape policy, and to take more journeys of inspection into the wilder parts of the country which were to have so large a part in his best poetry. One of these, taken in the summer of 1899, led to the writing on his return to Ottawa of those extraordinary pieces, "Rapids at Night" and "Night Hymns on Lake Nipigon." He had become intimate with Pelham Edgar, a son of Sir James Edgar – once a speaker of the House of Commons – and from 1897 a member of the staff at Victoria College, Toronto. Edgar and Duncan Scott were appointed editors of the *Makers of Canada,* a series of biographies. They were devoted editors, pruning and enlivening the prose of their associates, softening expressions of prejudice, and trying to escape with honour from mistaken commitments by the publisher to authors who had lapsed into senility or laziness. Their correspondence over the years in which the series was in preparation shows how excellently they understood each other, how skilful they were in soothing sensitive biographers, notably Stephen Leacock, and how careful they were in meeting the objections raised by living relatives of the "makers," although in one famous instance a grandson did prevent the publication of a biography.

For the series Duncan Scott wrote the volume on John Graves Simcoe, the first lieutenant-governor of Upper Canada. He was unhappy about the quality of the book, which misses being a good biography mainly because of the extreme incompatibility between author and subject. Simcoe was an old world Tory Anglican professional soldier, a museum specimen of the type. Duncan Scott, for all the warmth of his belief in the British connection, was a man of the new world; during the eighteen-nineties he had been active in the Ottawa group of the Fabians; he had an inherited distaste for an established religion, and his personal religion was exclusively spiritual; he found the Toryism, formalism and militarism of Simcoe sometimes comic, sometimes repellent. The most animated passage in the biography is where Duncan Scott describes Simcoe's vision of a provincial capital for Upper Canada: "There was to be a sort of worship of the British Constitution, there at every street corner was to be a sentry, there the very stones were to sing 'God Save the King!' and over it all there was to be the primness of the flint box, and the odour of pipe-clay." The value of the book is not in the portrait of Simcoe, executed with reluctant conscientious respect, or in the perfunctory account of the political and military incidents of Simcoe's time, but in the admirably composed pictures of life among the pioneers and Indians in the last decade of the eighteenth century. Because of these pictures, in which the poet and writer of short stories take the pen from the biographer, the book remains alive, a more pleasing work than most in the series. But one wonders why Duncan Scott chose among the "makers" to write the life of such a dullard as Simcoe: can it have been simply because no one else cared to, and he thought the series would have been weakened by its absence?

The year in which the life of Simcoe appeared, 1905, is much more important in the record of Scott's life because of *New World Lyrics and Ballads,* a collection in which the Indian poems and the poems about the wilderness are for the first time dominant. "On the Way to the Mission" and "The Forsaken," which is founded on a story told the poet by the Hudson's Bay Company factor at Nipigon House, are narratives that turn on primary passions and demand the acceptance of painful truths. In "The Mission of the Trees," a slightly earlier piece, the primary passions and painful truths are enfolded in a dreamlike rhythm and landscape:

> Then the cloud was spent at midnight
>   And the world so gleamed with snow,
> That the frosty moon looked downward
>   On a moon that glowed below . . .
>
> Then the weary partridge-hunter
>   Hears amid the rustling hush,
> One, two, three, the triple tonguing,
>   Mellow as a calling thrush.

In a collection where darkness, violence and despair are frequent, the most terrifying poem is a ballad, "Catnip Jack." The central incident in it – two men dragging through the bush a stone-boat that bears a corpse and shouting *Picotte!* (smallpox) – was told by a friend but the framing of it was imaginary. The rhythms in "Catnip Jack" have the sound of Kipling's at their most ominous; at the crucial point in the narrative there is a doubleness of vision by which the reader is made to lose any moorings he may have kept, and is exposed to the full threat of the emotional effect. The melancholy reflective tone that was to rule so many of the best among the late poems runs through "Rapids at Night," a memory of a moment in one of the journeys of inspection. "The little light cast by foam under starlight" seems desperately precarious amid the massive darkness of the cedars that crowd the banks and of the mountains that rise behind. In a clump of glimmering birches suddenly a thrush breaks into song. The note of joy, an echo of the south, seems as alien in the threatening northern silence as the lighted foam in the darkness. Both are insubstantial challenges to "the sadness that dwells at the core of all things." The sadness appears also in the solemn sapphics of "Night Hymns on Lake Nipigon." The aspect of Nipigon which Duncan Scott judged to be "the most heroic of all the lakes" – "the lonely loon-haunted Nipigon reaches" – impressive in itself, becomes a part of a heroic history as the paddlers sing in "the long drawn Ojibwa, uncouth and mournful" one of the great hymns, "Adeste Fideles." There are links between the poems about the Indians and the wilderness and such a poem as "The Piper of Arll" – the links of intensity, terror, and gloom; but what link is there between them and the poems in which Duncan Scott is working out his thought, such a poem as he had written just before the *New World Lyrics and Ballads* appeared, but did not include among them, the "Meditation at Perugia"? He was not ready to make that link.

A pendant to the collection of 1905 is a brochure of seven poems, emphatically of the new world, which came out the next year. The poems in *Via Borealis* were written during an official journey, taken during the summer of

1906, one of the longest and probably the most interesting that Scott made in the north country. In 1905 he had been appointed a commissioner to negotiate treaties with tribes in northwestern Ontario and the James Bay region and has described the journey taken in that year in an article, "The Last of the Indian Treaties," which appeared in *Scribner's* for December, 1906, and has been gathered into *The Circle of Affection*. The party left the Canadian Pacific transcontinental line near the Manitoba-Ontario border; travelled by canoe through much of the Lac Seul water system; crossed the height of land dividing the waters that flow towards Superior from those that flow towards Hudson Bay; descended to James Bay, and paused at a number of settlements and gatherings along the Bay. In 1906 the Commissioners entered the northland by a more eastern approach. The first of the poems, "Night Burial in the Forest" (May 9th), was a reconstruction of an incident that had occurred long before the journey at a spot the travellers passed. When the story was told him Scott left the encampment alone, and paddled to the site of the quarrel over a woman which had ended in one man's death and another's flight into the wilderness. The second, the longest in the brochure, "Spring on Mattagami" (June 1st-3rd), is perhaps the least satisfying. It is the only one of his longer poems with which I ever heard Duncan Scott say he was dissatisfied. It was undertaken to comply with a suggestion of Pelham Edgar, who accompanied the Commissioners and was then under the spell of Meredith's poetry, with "Love in the Valley" as the model, and one can trace Meredith's pressure on the prosody, and even on the approach to the subject. Meredith was not a poet with whom Scott had a deep congeniality, and the poem is often patently artificial. To the end of his life he was gnawed by a wish to recast it; but he did not go beyond the improvement of a line here and there such as:

Here in the wilderness less her memory presses,

where, if he did not follow Tennyson's advice and throw the hissing geese out of the boat, he did remove the greatest concentration of sibilants by substituting "solitude" for "wilderness." "Dream Voyageurs" was written at Crawfish

Lake (July 18th) and "The Half-Breed Girl" at New Brunswick House (July 26th). "Ecstasy," written at Split Rock Portage (August 12th), is superior to either, and it is not difficult to see why. It is a pure lyrical outburst. The other two poems, with their weight of observation and thought, and their elaborated language, are of the kind that Duncan Scott could do well only after his imaginative insight had had time to play flexibly and variously with his material.

In the summer that Duncan Scott took this northern journey, his wife went to Europe with Elizabeth and arranged for her to spend a year in a convent near Paris. In April, 1907, Duncan Scott was granted a four-month leave, and after he and his wife had spent a short time with Elizabeth they went to Spain at the end of May. When they left Elizabeth she was in perfect health; when they reached their hotel in Madrid a few days later Duncan Scott was handed a telegram which read with brutal simplicity, *"Elizabeth morte."* This blow was the hardest he ever received. "I think," he wrote to Pelham Edgar in July, "every fibre of our souls was ingrown and tangled with hers." He copied into the notebook in which he made the drafts of his poems these lines from *Much Ado about Nothing:*

> The idea of her life shall sweetly creep
> Into his study of imagination;
> And every lovely organ of her life
> Shall come apparell'd in more precious habit,
> More moving – delicate and full of life
> Into the eye and prospect of his soul
> Than when she lived indeed.

One of Duncan Scott's intimate friends, R. H. Coats, still recalls the inconsolable grief of the parents on their return to Ottawa. It was to be four years before Duncan Scott could write to any effect. Always a very nervous man, even his handwriting, which was normally angular and decisive, became a shaky formless thing. To the end of his life he was deeply distressed by any reference to Elizabeth, and it was understood among his friends that no admiration for his elegy, "The Closed Door," should lead one to speak of her. The affection for small children that led him to write so many of the best among his final poems – one was addressed to my own son Deaver, whom he had never seen – had its pathetic source in his preoccupation with his own grief.

In 1913 Duncan Scott was promoted to the highest post in the department of Indian Affairs, the Deputy Superintendency General. Hard intelligent work during thirty-four years would not by itself have won him this post. The men who held it before and after him were politicians who received a reward for services to party. He was not a party-minded man – he preferred the Conservatives to the Liberals mainly because they were sounder in all that had to do with the British connection – but in his own round of activity he had an acute political sense. He knew how to defend the interests of his department when it came into conflict with others, and his own interest within the department. His conception of the national duty to the Indians was simple and sound. It was the result not of close ethnological study, but of immense experience and imaginative understanding. The poet in him and the civil servant agreed in believing that the future of the Indians, if it were not to be extinction or degradation, depended on their being brought more and more nearly to the status of the white population. Special safeguards were a temporary necessity; but meanwhile by education and encouragement the Indians were to cease being interesting exotic relics and practise trying to hold their own in a society which could not be bent in their direction. Sometimes Duncan Scott felt that he should stress the special safeguards, the peculiar status, but it was to the end of bringing the Indians into the national society that he strove with that mixture of guile and idealism that is the mark of the highest sort of civil servant.

It was nine years after the death of Elizabeth before the next collection appeared, *Lundy's Lane and Other Poems*. The poem that furnished the title and came first in the book, "The Battle of Lundy's Lane," was one of the few written soon after his bereavement: it is dated 1908. Something of his own grief enters into the rendering of the grief of an old man and an old woman for their son killed in battle forty years before the poem is supposed to be uttered.

But even the transfusion of grief does not make "The Battle of Lundy's Lane" a living work. It is a dramatic monologue, a form Duncan Scott seldom attempted, and for which he did not have the special imaginative power required. The chief poems in the book are, it is obvious, "Lines in Memory of Edmund Morris," written in the winter of 1913-1914, and "The Height of Land," written in November, 1915, but an outcome of the great northern journeys of 1905 and 1906. "The Height of Land" is the nearest equivalent in verse to the evocation of the northern country in the work of so many of our painters. It is strongly felt, and the strength gives depth as well as force to the expression of the country that was for Duncan Scott the imaginative centre:

> The lonely north enlaced with lakes and streams,
> And the enormous targe of Hudson Bay
> Glimmering all night
> In the cold arctic light.

Some of the pictures have an almost ferocious energy:

> Where a bush fire, smouldering, with sudden roar
> Leaped on a cedar and smothered it with light
> And terror.

Now and then in the midst of so much force and fear there is an islet of simple beauty, in which the strange combines with the familiar:

> On a wide blueberry plain
> Brushed with the shimmer of a bluebird's wing,

The observation and the feeling are merely the admirable circumstances for the process of thought. "Poetry," he had come to believe, "must have brain at the bottom of it or it is nothing." Believing this, it was to be expected that he would link with his emotions among the Indians and in the wilderness the general ideas that had received a preliminary formulation in such poems as "Meditation at Perugia." The height of land leads Duncan Scott to think not only of the wilderness and its denizens, but, with perspective and a perfectly conveyed sense of renovation, of the world he has left and will return to. These are the surroundings in which his insight is sharpened and refined, and in "The Height of Land" he rises to impressive intellectual power. The poet to whom he is nearest in thought, here, and often in form as well, is Matthew Arnold, a lifelong admiration of his; but he shows a mind which, if not more powerful than Arnold's, is less discursive and more convinced of the validity of the conclusions to which it comes. He had been nearer to Arnold's mood in the "Meditation at Perugia," where his suspicion of science and belief in intuition stream out in cadences that recall "The Scholar Gipsy." But now he has a faith firmer than Arnold could attain. In the moments of illumination that are possible in ideal circumstances, the individual, Duncan Scott is telling us, is restored to a state that is natural to him:

That seems more native than the touch of time.

It is a state that cannot be formulated in words, but it is "the zenith of our wisdom." He was to be more explicit in a poem not so moving in its rhythms or its images, "The Fragment of a Letter," originally called, when it was written in May, 1919, "A Note to Pelham Edgar." Although it was not published until in 1921 Duncan Scott brought out his next collection, *Beauty and Life,* it properly comes in here not only as a completion of the statement in "The Height of Land," but as another derivation from the great journeys of 1905 and 1906. The new description of illuminations is this:

what we gain from living
When we possess our souls or seem to own,
Is not the peak of knowledge, but the tone
Of feeling; is not the problem solved, but just
The hope of solving opened out and thrust
A little further into the spirit air.

The wisdom one comes to with the help of ideal circumstances is nothing final or susceptible of formulation: it is not closed but open — a promise of other illuminations that may come to extend the present one. "I have left the religion of my youth behind me," I once heard Duncan Scott say, "and so have all the other Methodists of the country; but I have gone not into the United Church, but into the wilderness, and I do not feel at all lost in it."

With "The Height of Land" one must set the "Lines in Memory of Edmund Morris," privately issued in 1915, and now reprinted to close *Lundy's Lane and Other Poems.* With Edmund Morris, a painter whose specialty was the Canadian Indian, and some of whose pictures hung in Duncan Scott's office, the poet had shared many of his official journeys into the wilderness. It is these journeys, and above all the illuminations in them that he is recalling in the "Lines." Morris, whom he did not see often, was associated for him with illuminations:

> Nothing of the misuse
> That comes of the constant grinding
> Of one mind on another.
> So memory has nothing to smother,
> But only a few things captured
> On the wing.

In the "Lines" the illuminations depend on persons as well as on places; and the one that guides the poet to his final attitude towards the death of his friend comes from the life of the chief Akoose, drawn from Qui-wich, on Sakimay's reserve in Saskatchewan, and especially from the last act in it. The forty lines given to Akoose are the gravest and the most impressive blank verse that Duncan Scott wrote. They carry the weight, and respond to the phases, of the poet's emotion. The heroic response to the intimation of death is the recovery of energy and decision, the return to the scene, and resumption of the quality, of heroic achievement; and then the stoical acceptance of death. That a man can make this heroic response becomes an intimation of immortality, which had not been available to Duncan Scott when he lost his father or his daughter:

> So the old world, hanging long in the sun,
> And deep enriched with effort and with love,
> Shall, in the motions of maturity,
> Wither and part, and the kernel of it all
> Escape, a lovely wraith of spirit, to latitudes
> Where the appearance, throated like a bird,
> Winged with fire and bodied all with passion,
> Shall flame with presage, not of tears, but joy.

On those lines, by no means the most striking in the poem, but perfect in their music, and in the appropriateness of every formal element to the mood and thought Duncan Scott's name may stand. He could not have written them ten years before; but he was to write a good many of their kind in the ten years ahead.

At the end of his life Duncan Scott preferred among the volumes of his verse the collection of 1921, *Beauty and Life*. In it most of the poetic kinds he cared about were represented. His lyrical power is at its purest in "Last Year," the most perfect of his poems about Ottawa: the emotions rise and fall in it with an art that does not obtrude, and the short piece seems an almost impersonal cry, so transparent is the language, so timeless the form. The poetry of dream, at once beautiful and ominous, appears again in "Permanence." His experience with music forms the elaborate "Variations on a Seventeenth Century Theme" on which he commented in a letter to Lorne Pierce in 1927: "The author has followed closely the model set by musical composers, and the 'Variations' may be compared, in intention at least, to Brahms' *Variations on a Theme of Handel*, where the succeeding pieces have unity in variety, but are not slavishly influenced by the theme." In "The Fragment of a Letter," already mentioned, the great journey of 1906 is recalled, and along with it the illuminations. The great poem of the book is the one Duncan Scott placed first and had in mind in the choice of a title, the "Ode for the Keats Centenary," read at the commemoration in Toronto on February 23, 1921.

The ode is not a Keatsian poem in the full and obvious sense in which Charles G. D. Roberts's mellifluous "Ave" is Shelleyan. It does not derive from Keats in form, nor echo him. The poem is a consideration of Keats, not a pious exercise. Keats appears not as the poet of the senses, but as the man

> Who schooled his heart with passionate control
> To compass knowledge, to unravel the dense
> Web of this tangled life,

as the man who had in supreme degree the power of "seeing great things in loneliness." These great things are summed up as "beauty," and Keats's mode of access to them is just what Duncan Scott had experienced in his own illuminations in the north country

Where moments turn to months of solitude.

The ode is packed with pictures of the north, as it should be, for Duncan Scott, in considering Keats, is considering what in our time and place could be achieved if one had Keats's secret of seeing great things in loneliness. The discovery of "beauty" as Keats understood it, and the access to illumination as Scott himself had known it, are linked with the processes of scientific thinkers who also require quiet and seclusion. All three are alike; all three are concerned with what Duncan Scott calls "beauty," what if another poet, Wordsworth, say, or Coleridge, had been his subject, he might have called "ideality." He laments that

Beauty has taken refuge from our life
That grew too loud and wounding;
Beauty withdrawn beyond the bitter strife,
Beauty is gone . . .

Can it be induced out of the secret place where the poet and the scientist have tracked it and stream again into the general life? Duncan Scott does not think so, and the ode comes to an arrest rather than a conclusion in a grave melancholy.

If the ode has a flaw, it is the indeterminacy of the ending. The course of thought that Duncan Scott had not been able to carry to a conclusion in 1921, he began to retrace in 1922, in his presidential address to the Royal Society of Canada, "Poetry and Progress," buried in the transactions of the society and resurrected in *The Circle of Affection*. The image of Keats reappears, recording his discoveries of "beauty" and seeking to involve them in a "constant reference" to "life." Again the processes of poetic and scientific creation are linked; both are forms of the imagination, both have "ideality." But science has also the enviable power to interweave with "life"; poetry in comparison seems divorced from "life." Modern societies are remote from "ideality"; and the Canadian society seems especially remote. What is the poet to do? Duncan Scott offers examples of what poets have done. Lampman took to the woods, and his account of what he found there had "a verity and a vigour that are unmatched"; but in the end he could not stay there and returned to write not perhaps from such illuminations as he had drawn from the landscape, but in "a deep and troubled way" of "the mind and heart of man." Marjorie Pickthall – dead just a month before the address was given – had entered a closed garden with a view of mountain and sea; but the walls were not thick enough to shut out "the rumours of life" which came bringing "longing and disquiet." Rupert Brooke, who had come to Duncan Scott in the summer of 1913 with a letter from John Masefield and had appealed to his host as "a clear fine personality," was feeling for another solution of what the poet could do, and in his final poems suggested how "beauty" and "life" might be united. Wilfred Owen, facing a worse moment than Brooke, had locked himself into irony and bitterness. Newer poets had whirled into total rebellion. The way of irony and bitterness is rejected by Duncan Scott: it leads straight into a blank wall. The way of total rebellion is rejected: it leads nowhere. In their various ways Lampman and Pickthall and Brooke had been wiser; they had found forms of "beauty" and they had not lost a sense of "life". The poet has value in so far as he expresses illuminations, the "hints that his intuition has whispered"; and he may reassure himself in his loneliness, with the knowledge that when he expresses his illuminations, he promotes in sympathetic spirits "vibrations of ideality and beauty." In sharing or offering to share his illuminations he has his part, and it is a high one, in the progress that is coupled with poetry in the title of the address. It is a lofty theory of poetry, and not the worse for its loftiness; one of the few predictions that are safe to offer is that it will not be long before criticism will turn again in its direction from the present stress on poetry as an "elegant diversion" such as chess or topiary.

The ode and the address, written as he was nearing sixty, are the key to Duncan Scott's conduct of his mature life. He seldom complained of the small effect his poems seemed to have, although he was resentful when they, or anyone else's artistic works, were ignored by the few who might have gained by knowing them. He resented indifference to art or neglect of it only on the part of those who had an inkling of what it was. The Canadian Manufacturers Association had asked him early in the century for a poem which would suggest to manufacturers from other regions of the Empire the quality of Canadian life and landscape. He struck off a short piece with which he was rather pleased and in sending it set fifteen dollars as the fee. When the manufacturers returned the poem, declining to pay a fee, he was not angry, for he was not surprised. Such was the nature of the beast. He did not expect that a manufacturer would value poetry. But when the highly cultivated editor of a magazine allowed an absurd review of his last book to be printed, he was sharply indignant. This man must have known that the review was an absurdity; and must have been either negligent or cynical in passing it. Duncan Scott knew the Canadian society much more intimately and much more broadly than his contemporary poets, and he saw it more as it really was. By the circumstances of his career he knew who shaped policy and opinion, and how they did it. It was a joy to hear him epitomize a politician, or a journalist, or a man of affairs, or a snob in some bitingly destructive phrase: one person of great note and consequence he liked to call "the inspired boo-oo-tcher boy." But he did not expect such people to be regenerated by art – or by anything. He was the more resigned because in his travels abroad he had found that the sympathetic spirits in whom poetry set up vibrations were few anywhere. His work in the civil service interested him; but the centre of his life was not in his office, where he seldom came early, and never stayed late. After he retired his conversation did not run on the Indian department. The centre of his life was the search for illuminations, and for the expression of them. The search and its occasional reward was enough.

In 1923 Duncan Scott collected his tales under the title, taken from one of them, *The Witching of Elspie* – twelve stories, eight dealing with the north country from Nipigon to the Ottawa, and four with regions nearer cities or staid old towns. Most of these stories, unlike those in the volume about Viger, turn on stern and bloody happenings, and centre in characters of unusual nervous intensity. They come nearer to the narratives in verse than the stories about Viger had. In the northern tales the finest effects are not in the realization of Indians but in the suggestion of the strain that develops when a white man has been cut off from his fellows for many months, or is pent up with one or two others who are incompatible with him. The most poetic of the stories is of another kind, "A Legend of Welly Legrave," an old story of the Ottawa Valley lumbermen. Under the melodrama and the blood there is an illumination akin to what Duncan Scott had rendered in some of his narratives about primitive men and women. Most of the stories in this collection had been written long before it appeared, some, like that of Welly Legrave, before the turn of the century.

The *Poems of Duncan Campbell Scott*, the single collected edition, came out in 1926, in a handsome volume of three hundred and forty pages. The hundred and eighty poems it contains are not all he had published, not even all he had gathered into earlier books, but not many of the pieces left out have importance either as aesthetic achievement or as personal record. As he grew older Duncan Scott gave more and ever more thought to the ordering of his poems in significant sequence, and it was to be expected that when he came to collect his poetical works he would arrange them in an order more inward, more essential than that of chronology. Often his juxtapositions are for obvious reasons, as when "Avis" from the volume of 1898 follows "The Magic House"; for these are "companion pieces, although written many years apart – the spell of sight and the spell of sound." "The Height of Land" follows "Spring on Mattagami" – both had their origin in the northern journeys – and is followed by "I Do Not Ask," written as late as June, 1925, but developing an idea in "The Height of Land." The book opens with a national poem, the "Fragment of an Ode to Canada," and closes with another, "The Battle of Lundy's Lane." Most of the narratives are gathered together in the early or late pages. Towards the middle come most of the poems with subtle or complex substance, either imaginative or reflective. It is not, I think, an accident that at the exact middle of the book and in immediate sequence come the elegies on the poet's father and daughter. The most important of the poems added in the collected edition is "Powassan's Drum," written in the winter of 1925. This is the greatest of the dream poems, the most ominous, the most nightmarish, the most thrilling; into it Duncan Scott put almost every power he had – his feeling for the Indians, his feeling for the wilderness, his responsiveness to horror, his sense of the links between dream and reality, something of his reflective power, his command of intricate structure akin to that in musical works, and, to a magnificent degree, his mastery of a free verse that bends to every impulse of his spirit. The juxtaposition of this piece with the delicate "Variations on a Seventeenth Century Theme" is one of the most skilful in the collection.

The *Poems* were greeted respectfully by the few Canadians who could or cared to be articulate about their feeling for poetry. The reviews by Arthur S. Bourinot and Raymond Knister were perceptive; and in the *Dalhousie Review* Pelham Edgar, in the most careful of all his studies of his friend's work, claimed for him a place among the major poets of his time. Although the English edition was introduced by John Masefield it did not make an impact Duncan Scott's poetry has never been widely read in England, and has been ignored in the United States. It was well for his happiness that he was able to say, "I have long been quite satisfied not to be taken seriously as a poet. I don' seem to be able to gain the attention of important papers or reviews, but I am not grieving. Probably I would not be able to live up to popularity."

During the nineteen twenties his life in Ottawa became superficially at least, more varied and more stimulating. He was a founder and an active member of the Little Theatre he wrote the "Prologue," to be spoken on January 18, 1923 when the Theatre was opened, and a one-act play in prose *Pierre,* performed that same evening. *Pierre* was also performed at the Hart House Theatre in Toronto, and published in 1926 in the first volume of *Plays for Hart House Theatre.* The spurt in dramatic activity, so strong in Canada during this decade, gave him much pleasure. H had almost as much in the talk at a small dining club to which he belonged during the last quarter century of his life, listening to judges and journalists and senior civil servants, and now and then cutting through the eloquence with one of the unanswerable tart remarks he phrased so well. It was for the delectation of this group that he had privately printed a four-page pamphlet, "For the Byron Centenary, April 19, 1924: Byron on Wordsworth, Being Discovered Stanzas of Don Juan." In this he made contemptuous fun of the hypocritical element, as he thought it, in Wordsworth's moral rigorism, in the light of the revelation concerning the poet's French daughter. In 1922 the University of Toronto had selected him as the first recipient of the honorary degree of Doctor of Literature, and other honorary degrees followed.

It made him gloomy, however, that Ottawa was less and less a place where literature was practised or talked of. The civil service, which had counted in the generation before his the names of Mair and Sangster, and in his early prime, Lampman's and Campbell's, was more and more the province of men whose interest was in the social sciences. The young men coming into it from the universities were less and less often trained in the humanities. There were no new voices to arouse his hope. He had always cared for the true sciences, but for the pseudo-sciences of psychology and sociology he had no respect. The classification and analysis of individual and social traits would never point the way, he was sure, towards a solution of the problems of man's fate; they would not even provide an enriching awareness of it. Yet all around him he noticed people with good minds who were deserting the great poets and prose writers through whose works he had found his own education to distend themselves with pseudo-scientific theory and express themselves in a barbarous prose.

His wife, who had often been ill for long periods, died on April 13, 1929. Although he wrote no elegy, the few poems of this year are heavy with grief, and in one, "The Fields of Earth," he expresses his sense of his own old age, and of the distance of age from youth. In this same year Bliss Carman died, and to some of Duncan Scott's friends it seemed that if he was not nearing the end of his life his career as a poet was nearly over. The assumption was a mistake. A new, happy, and important phase began March 27, 1931, with his marriage to Elise Aylen of Ottawa. She was much younger, she shared to the full his interest in music and art, and she was besides a poet of deep insight and strong feeling. *Roses of Shadow,* a book of her poems, appeared in the year of their marriage, with an introduction by Duncan Scott. From the very beginning of the second marriage, although Elise Aylen had led a secluded life, Duncan Scott began to see more people and to meet them on easier terms. His humour became more playful, his power to live in the immediate present more sure. He has expressed much of what the marriage brought to him in the sequence of sonnets called "Twelfth Anniversary," and published in *The Circle of Affection.* In April, 1932, he retired from the service; and in 1935 in a new volume of verse he revealed the fruits of his new leisure and new stimulus.

The Green Cloister, the title for the new collection, has an obvious and also a recondite meaning. Ostensibly it points to the importance of the poem, "Chiostro Verde," a series of perceptions and reflections at Santa Maria Novella in Florence. The frescoes have either fallen from the walls or grown dull. All about him the poet sees the constant renewal in nature, in the grass and flowers, the cypresses, the pigeons. But the great performance of the artist is in decay:

> Will nothing at last be left
> But a waste wall?
> Will painting forever perish,
> Will no one be left to cherish
> The beauty of life and the world,
> Will the soul go blind of the vision?

The answer, given abruptly, is that the nature which renews itself and the art which appears to decay and perish have a common origin. It is an unconvincing answer, because undeveloped, and because given in a wrong tone, a tone of prose. The real answer is given elsewhere in the book: to the *chiostro verde* the green cloister replies.

Many of the poems were written in Europe. After he retired, Duncan Scott, accompanied by his wife, took a long holiday. "A Blackbird Rhapsody" was written at Oberhofen in Switzerland in June and July, 1932, and "Como" in the same summer; "Kensington Gardens" was written in London the following November, and "At Palma" in January, 1933. The summer of 1934 was passed in England, and led to "At Lodore," written in June, and "On Ragleth Hill," written in Shropshire in July. "Chiostro Verde" and "Evening at Ravello" were written in Italy in the winter of 1935. These poems are not literary: Lodore did not speak to Duncan Scott in the tones of the Lake poets, or Kensington Gardens in those of Matthew Arnold. He had his independent uses for what he saw, and what he drew on when he faced a European landscape was not his broad reading, but his long pondering on the problems of personality, the universe, and art. There is no hiatus between the European poems and the Canadian poems, which are in the majority. "A Scene at Lake Manitou," written late in 1933, and "At Gull Lake, 1810," written in the autumn of 1934, are vigorous Indian narratives very like "The Forsaken." Another narrative, "The Nightwatchman," has no parallel in his earlier writing. Into it enters that inventive whimsicality which was so large a part of his conversation, and so seldom an element in what he wrote. A reminiscence of his childhood, it is in the spirit, and to some degree in the form, of the poet he thought the most penetrating of writers about childhood, Walter de la Mare. "The Spider and the Rose" is another dream poem of the ominous kind. The rest of the collection is mainly lyrical.

In "A Blackbird Rhapsody" the reply to the question in "Chiostro Verde" is given powerfully. In the blackbird's song Duncan Scott hears

> the wild impromptu voice
> Of the simple love of life.

This love enables the blackbird to surpass the nightingale. For a moment the blackbird arrests his song, and mockingly utters the rapt notes of the nightingale, only to return to his usual music. He can do what the nightingale does, and has not much regard for it. He can do more. After singing all day long,

> a dauntless sprite
> Who lives without the need of rest,
> Without a mate, without a nest

he falls silent, and the poet observes him "rapt and still" absorbed in some dream beautiful beyond all performance,

> a dream of silence
> Of a day too rich for singing
> By a brooding shadow nest,
> Far beyond the mountains of the west.

It is apparent that the blackbird is rendered as experiencing an illumination. This is not that life is to be loved (but without the love of life he would not have had it): it is the recognition of an ideal realm, seldom to be reached, but indestructible, a perception of that "beauty" which like everyone else the blackbird must discover in loneliness; he however has been qualified for the discovery by his love of life. Love in a personal relationship is the qualification for the poet's illumination in "Compline," written in Northern Ontario, which has always seemed to me the special glory of the book, the deepest utterance from the green cloister. The intensity of shared love in ideal circumstances leads here to an identification with those circumstances, with the swallows, for instance, who are resting on the telegraph wires between the lovers and the sunset. The lovers pray for the present happiness of the swallows, and for their quiet death, and plead with the swallows to reciprocate the prayers. Their sense of identity with the swallows is so complete they know the prayers they have asked for will be granted them. In these poems a new element is enriching Duncan Scott's thought: the role of loneliness is not ended, but it is now complemented by the role of affection.

After the publication of *The Green Cloister* he continued for many years to be a great traveller. The summer of 1936 and the autumn of 1937 were passed in Europe. The winter of 1939-1940 was passed in the southwest of the United States and on the Pacific coast. In the winter of 1942 he had his last sight of the Canadian west, and decided that he had been right in his long belief that the Selkirks had more beauty and more suggestion than the Rocky Mountains. He was happy to return to his home and resolved not to leave the Ottawa region again.

I proposed to him that he guide me in a search through Lampman's notebooks in the hope of recovering prose and verse that should be added to the published works. The first result of the search was the collection, *At the Long Sault and Other New Poems by Archibald Lampman* which we edited jointly in 1943; subsequently two prose pieces, the essays on Canadian poetry and on the character and career of Keats, were published in the *University of Toronto Quarterly*. The return to the manuscripts he had examined so carefully more than forty years before led him to think over Lampman's personality and achievement once more and write another study, which appeared in W. P. Percival's *Leading Canadian Poets*. The selections from Lampman he had edited in 1925 under the title *Lyrics of Earth* having gone out of print, he prepared another for the series to which this volume belongs. Wisely he dropped the introduction of 1925 and restored almost intact the essay with which he had introduced the edition of 1900, when his sense of Lampman's personality was at its height. He added a number of poems from *At the Long Sault*. The long period in which he had been the custodian of Lampman's works and fame was now, he felt, nearing its end; he was happy to perform these final services for the friend whose name he had always set above his own, and happy, too, in the knowledge that the custody would devolve on T. R. Loftus MacInnes, Lampman's son in law, and for twenty years his own associate in the department of Indian Affairs. Another service of friendship was the little book on the artist Walter J. Phillips which, along with the *Selected Poems of Archibald Lampman,* came out in the early months of 1947. The study of Phillips is an evidence of the depth of his feeling for art, and the subtlety of his discrimination; it has also a special charm rarely found in his works, the charm of a gracious informality.

The last of his books, *The Circle of Affection,* was published in the summer of 1947. One's first impression in turning the pages or glancing over the table of contents is of a miscellany; but of all his books this is the most carefully unified. In the "Foreword" he remarks: "The title for the collection, borrowed from the opening story, seemed to the writer appropriate, for throughout the book a circle of affection is gradually rounded: an affection for persons and places, for his own country and other countries, an affection for moods, for passions and aspirations." There is a circle, and it is a circle of affection. The importance of affection had been emphasized in *The Green Cloister;* now for the first time in Duncan Scott's writing affection overshadows loneliness. In his ninth decade his fundamental ideas were still in development.

At the end of my essay on him in *On Canadian Poetry* is an impression of how I found him in 1942, the year in which I was most often in his company. He liked it; and for that reason, and because a number of his friends thought it just, I include it here:

It was one of the many evenings in the summer of 1942 when I talked with him in the huge high-ceilinged room at the back of his rambling house. Along the walls were low bookcases filled, for the most part, with first editions and the collected works of modern poets; on top of them were varied momentoes of his relations with the Indians; and above were the brilliant landscapes of Milne, Emily Carr and the "Seven," one of the most distinguished small collections of Canadian painting. Scott took down battered old volumes of early Canadian poets, of Heavysege, Sangster and Cameron; he spoke of his arduous canoe trips long ago up the Nipigon and along Achigan, and of his memories of London and Florence; he evoked for me the long sessions in the 'eighties and 'nineties when he and Lampman, "poor Archie," were forging their poetics; he told me of the welcome he gave to the early work of Marjorie Pickthall, and of Rupert Brooke's visit to him just before the first world war; he sought to make clear the change in the fibre of human nature that has occurred in the past half century; he gave to me the manuscript of one of Lampman's lyrics and allowed himself to be led on to read a few of his own briefer pieces. It was only a week before his eightieth birthday; the grave, gentle voice was that of an old man, but what he had to say reflected not old age but exquisite maturity. Here, I thought, as Pater presents Marius thinking of Fronto, was "the one instance" I had seen "of a perfectly tolerable, perfectly beautiful old age – an old age in which there seemed nothing to be regretted, nothing really lost in what the years had taken away. The wise old man . . . would seem to have replaced carefully and consciously each natural trait of youth, as it departed from him, by an equivalent grace of culture."

In his life Duncan Scott had been many things. At the end he was above all else a connoisseur, alert to every distinguished work in literature, art and music, drawing pleasure from the newest kinds of art and music, and a little sad because most recent experiments in poetry were too much at variance with his own practice to be accessible to him. He was touched by the appreciation of his poems a few younger critics expressed, friends for many years like Arthur S. Bourinot or Ira Dilworth, or men he scarcely knew, and greatly cheered by the brilliant campaign for his work carried on over the air-waves by one who was in the last years probably the closest of his friends, Leonard W. Brockington. In Ottawa there was a vague feeling that a poet of some note was passing his old age in the city, but one cannot pretend that there or anywhere in the world the quality of this rare spirit was comprehended. Duncan Scott knew how little his poems were read, but once more he did not repine. In reading, playing and listening to music, looking at pictures, and talking to friends, he happily spent the last years. Sometimes he was seriously ill, but he would recover quickly until in the autumn of 1947 his final illness settled on him. The last book that he asked for was George Rylands' admirable anthology, *The Ages of Man, Shakespeare's Image of Man and Nature*. Years before he had written to Pelham Edgar "When there is so little time to read and ponder why should one stray from Shakespeare?" He died December 19, 1947, and is buried in Beechwood Cemetery at Ottawa. At the close of his first essay on Lampman, who also rests there, Duncan Scott wrote: "He said it was a good spot in which to lie when all was over with life. Even if there be no sense in these houses of shade, it is a pleasant foreknowledge to be aware that above one's unrealizing head the snow will sift, the small ferns rise and the birds come back in nesting time. And though he be forever rapt from such things, careless of them and unaware, the sternest wind from under the pole star will blow unconfined over his grave, about it the first hepaticas will gather in fragile companies, the vesper sparrow will return to nest in the grass, and from a branch of maple to sing in the cool dusk."

Canadian Poetry
1935-1949

1935

At the outset it should be admitted that 1935 has not been a decisive year for Canadian poetry. Scores of volumes have come to the office of the QUARTERLY, some fat, some thin, some well printed by the great publishing houses, some botched by small presses which have wisely suppressed their names. In none of them can one discover such evidence of a new talent as Miss Audrey Alexandra Brown revealed in 1931 or Mr. Leo Kennedy in 1932. A number of our best poets have published new works during 1935; in none of their volumes is there a marked lapse from their best previous achievements: but in none of them is there a marked success in striking out along new paths, or an evident power to do better what they have done well already.

Among the most solid gains of the year are three collected editions indispensable to students of Canadian poetry: *The Complete Poems of Francis Sherman*, edited with a long memoir by Dr. Lorne Pierce, *Selected Poems (1915-1935)* by A. S. Bourinot, with a prefatory note by Sir Andrew Macphail, and Tom MacInnes's *Rhymes of a Rounder*. Sherman's work is all over thirty years old and it is perfectly congruous with the prevailing tone of that large body of quietly beautiful lyric poetry which in the last decades of the nineteenth century inspired so many with hope for the future of Canadian literature. Sherman had not Carman's command of rhythm or Lampman's sensibility to colours and forms, but he had strong emotions of a kind easily expressible in verse and a sufficient mastery of his medium to communicate them. Some of the poems which Mr. Bourinot has reprinted were written as recently as 1931, but his slender volume also recalls the work of Carman and Lampman. His touch is softer than Sherman's, and his range is narrower: the conventional aspects of Canadian nature, the more notable themes which war suggests to a sensitive mind, and love as the Victorian sonneteers conceived it. He develops his themes with a laudable economy of language, at times reaching austerity, and a sure sense of what is beautiful in a quiet way. Tom MacInnes is worlds apart from poets such as Sherman and Mr. Bourinot: he is one of the few Canadian poets who have something unusual to say and who say it with an unusual accent. Most of his successful poems are in medieval verse forms – the ballade, the cantel, the villanelle. (A form with five stanzas, each rhyming *a b a a b*, he has christened a "mirelle:" "I made up the name and form of 'mirelle' for myself in Montreal because it sounded that way.") A long postscript, dated 1912, and entitled "Somewhat Concerning Ballades" describes the source and growth of his interest in intricate and exquisite verse forms, some adaptations which the character of the English language has suggested to him, and the types of emotional effects to which these forms lend themselves. "Virility, colour and euphony are," he affirms, "the qualities most worth while in any poem." Virility he always has, although often it is simply the virility of the barbaric yawp. At his best he unites virility with euphony; colour, however, in any usual sense of that vague abstraction, is not more often present in his verse than in the work of most poets. One beautiful poem in which all the qualities he admires appear I shall quote:

THE TIGER OF DESIRE
VILLANELLE

Starving, savage, I aspire
To the red meat of all the World:
I am the Tiger of Desire!

With teeth bared and claws uncurled
  By leave of God I creep to slay
  The innocent of all the World.

Out of the yellow glaring day,
  When I glut my appetite,
  To my lair I slink away.

But in the black returning night
  I leap resistless on my prey,
  Mad with agony and fright.

The quick flesh I tear away,
  Writhing till the blood is hurled
  On leaf and flower and sodden clay.

My teeth are bare, my claws uncurled –
  Of the red meat I never tire;
  In the black jungle of the World
  I am the Tiger of Desire!

A poem such as this – and there are more than a few in the volume – stands out sharply from the quiet verses of our older poets. There is much in Mr. MacInnes's collection that a writer with any power of self-criticism would have recoiled from printing, but there is much that one will not willingly let die.

Three well-known and rightly admired poets have published books which if they do not reveal unsuspected powers have in full measure the magic under which we have fallen before. Dr. Duncan Campbell Scott has given us *The Green Cloister*, Mr. Wilson MacDonald *The Song of the Undertow*, and Dr. E. J. Pratt *The Titanic*.

Dr. Pratt's subject imposed upon him a special mode of treatment: like the stories of the Greek tragic writers the disaster of the *Titanic* is a tale familiar in its outlines to the poet's audience. In narrating a story of which the final stages are known in advance, the poet's emphasis appropriately falls upon the rôle of necessity, the emergence of tragic premonitions, the outcropping of dramatic irony. As the poem proceeds, a cold horror spreads through the reader's mind, a horror intensified by Dr. Pratt's repeated stress upon the *hubris* of the captain, the assumption of the passengers that they are in a palace-hotel. We read every line in the light of the foreknown catastrophe and Dr. Pratt has written almost every line in its light. The emotional range of the poet and his power of enduing all that relates to the sea with individual life have long been appreciated. What has not been appreciated is his command of his instrument, his rhythms and his imagery, and, in this poem especially, his use, at once exact and suggestive, of technical terminology, as in this passage:

> She
> Was feeling out her port and starboard points,
> And testing rivets on her boiler joints;
> The needle on the gauge beyond the red,
> The blow offs feathered at the funnel head.

The poem is not completely satisfying: the poker-game which is in progress on the night of the collision is protracted unduly, and the same may be said of the dinner. One would gladly sacrifice some of the lines devoted to these for a few more of the rapid memorable pictures of individual passengers in the time of crisis:

> Millet was studying eyes as he would draw them
> Upon a canvas; Butt as though he saw them
> In the ranks; Astor, social, debonair,
> Waved "Good-bye" to his bride – "See you tomorrow,"
> And tapped a cigarette on a silver case;
> Men came to Guggenheim as he stood there
> In evening suit, coming this time to borrow
> Nothing but courage from his calm, cool face.

Among the lyrists of what has profanely been called "the mapletree school," Dr. Scott's distinction has been in his success in metrical experiments and in his keen sense of the oneness of nature. Both came out brilliantly in *The Height of Land,* to name but one example; and they come out brilliantly now in such poems as *The Sea Shore* and *Compline.* No other Canadian poet can awaken such deep and serious emotion; no other Canadian poet can so convey the consolation that lies in a certainty of man's participation in the same life that finds expression in the sea, here called "the mother of sorrow," the sun, and the animal creation.

Dr. Scott does not often strike out single lines of memorable quality and it is not easy to represent the expressiveness of his poetry by quotation; but I shall venture upon a passage from *Compline:*

We will pray for you bright swallows
Now and in the hour of your death;
Now when you fly aloft in the bright air
Rushing together in a storm of wings,
Grasping the wires;
And when you fall secretly in the wilderness,
Where, – none knoweth –
Ora pro nobis.
May you remember then this northern beauty,
The pure lake surface,
And after a long light-day,
Wing weary, the rest
Of a night by the nestlings and the nest.

Mr. Wilson MacDonald is among our poets the only one who adopts the prophetic strain. He has strong and scornful opinions about the Canadian public; and in the very moment of confessing his love for Canada and his admiration for her seers, scholars, and poets he rends the community:

My land is last to living thought
    And last to walk in light:
My country, last across the world
    To leave tradition's night,
Strong hater of her seers is she,
    And worshipper of might.

So the Irish poets and prose writers were wont to speak forty years ago; and whatever indignation Mr. MacDonald excites, such poetry is a far better kind of national verse than the odes and hymns to be found in many of the collections of poems published in 1935, poems which mouth empty nothings about the heroic north. *The Song of the Undertow,* which occupies most of the volume to which it gives a title, is a long narrative of the poet's physical and mental anguish during a voyage to England thirty years ago. The poem recalls *The Ancient Mariner* in stanza form and marginal gloss,[1] and in an atmosphere of unnatural horror and distress, and, besides, in the fascination it exerts upon a reader to prevent him from laying it down until the whole tale is told. The poem is not always well proportioned and sins at times against the reasonable demand that a poet should not indulge himself in mere self-pity; but it is much too absorbing for one to be conscious of either failing as one reads.

Only a few of the books listed in the accompanying bibliography under the caption "Poetry" have been mentioned. Of the remainder a shockingly large number are worthless or, at best, have so little worth that mercy bids one avert his eyes and pass by. A few are uneven: there are passages of agreeable verse in Mr. A. M. Stephen's *Verendrye,* there are moments of vision in Mr. C. F. Lloyd's *Landfall,* there are brief lyrics of a fine intensity in Miss Sara Carsley's *Alchemy and Other Poems.* Mention should also be made of Mr. Hugh Heaton's *The Story of Madam Hen and Little Horace,* which in its text, its illustrations, and its format, is an entire success – the best example of intelligently humorous books for children that any Canadian publisher has given us. Among the French-Canadian poets Mme. Blanche Lamontagne-Beauregard's *Dans la brousse* is by far the principal achievement of the year. In *Beau jour d'été* she relates that:

> Pour la centième fois j'ai pris
> Le livre d'un grand romantique

and about this admission one's misgivings crystallize: there are too many echoes of the romantics here, too many standard romantic themes, too many facile romantic emotions.

Many books must go unmentioned. The perpetration of bad or mediocre verse is not a grave misdemeanour; and there is no reason why a critic should drag a book from the darkness in which it lies to torture it in momentary light before dropping it again into the darkness. The critic need concern himself with mediocre literature only when he has before him a book to which the reading public, or a sub-

---

[1] A poet may spell as he pleases; but why should Mr. MacDonald's publishers have allowed gross errors in spelling to disfigure the gloss, which has been set up in a facsimile of Mr. MacDonald's exquisite script?

stantial fraction of it, is disposed to assign a false importance. Mrs. Edna Jaques's *My Kitchen Window* is such a book. Mrs. Jaques exalts the cosy things in life – rocking-chairs, flower-pots, wee dresses on the line, strawberries in a blue bowl, and, of course, lavender and mignonette. Love, patriotism, even religion itself, take on a kind of cosiness in her verses, as they, doubtless, do in the minds of a multitude of Canadians. Her verses are an expression of the ordinary self of the Canadian middle class, that is to say, of the immense majority of Canadians. They stir one to fear that an Eddy Guest may be the next phenomenon in Canadian literature.[2]

Over against the vogue of such verse as Mrs. Jaques's should be set the cheering excellence of the poetry which has appeared in the *Dalhousie Review* and the *Queen's Quarterly* and in other magazines which have not maintained as generally high a standard as these. Mr. Leo Kennedy has given us one admirable sonnet (in the *Canadian Forum,* August) and Professor Watson Kirkconnell has printed privately a moving and finished tribute to Horace, of which only the first stanza can here be given:

All, all are gone: those comrades who with laughter
Joined in thy jesting and convivial mirth; –
Silent their voices, and their lips hereafter
Ashes in silent earth.

To scan the future with a hopeful eye is a national characteristic: it is pleasant to note the excellence of much of the verse which has appeared in undergraduate periodicals during the year, notably in the organs of University College and Trinity College in the University of Toronto.

---

[2]While this survey was passing through the press the publisher of *My Kitchen Window* announced a second edition.

1936

During 1936 three extremely important services have been rendered to Canadian poetry.

In January appeared the first number of the *Canadian Poetry Magazine,* "a quarterly issued under the auspices of the Canadian Authors' Association," with Professor E. J. Pratt as chairman of the Editorial Board. The editorial foreword in the April number is a statement of policy; it gives an assurance that the pages of the magazine will be accessible to poets in the new forms and in the old, to those entirely unknown on the same terms as to those of established reputation. The numbers so far published justify the claims made in the foreword; they abound in excellent and extremely varied verse.

A few months after the foundation of this magazine the Macmillan Company published the long-awaited anthology *New Provinces,* a slender volume containing poems by Robert Finch, Leo Kennedy, A. M. Klein, E. J. Pratt, F. R. Scott, and A. J. M. Smith. Many of the poems in the collection are at least ten years old; the book would have had a more formative effect if it had been published some years ago; for even the authors, in a disconcerting preface, acknowledge that their present attitude to their art differs from that which shaped the moods and methods represented in the anthology. In a word they are now a great deal more concerned with contemporary economic conditions and with political theories than they were when these poems were written. They are content to present *New Provinces* as containing "work which has had significance for the authors in the evolution of their own understanding;" but the book has more significance for Canadian readers. It marks the emergence before the general readers of the country (others have followed the tendency for some years in magazines with relatively small circulation) of a group of poets who may well have as vivifying an effect on Canadian poetry as the Group of Seven had on Canadian painting. The poems in the anthology are closer in spirit and technique to the best English and American poetry of the twenties than anything that has yet appeared in Canada, except Mr. Kennedy's *The Shrouding* and Miss Dorothy Livesay's *Signpost*.

Most of the verses in this collection are difficult – "difficult lonely music," to borrow an expression of Mr. A. J. M. Smith. Fortunately, almost in the same month appeared Professor W. E. Collin's *The White Savannahs,* the most penetrating study of Canadian literature since Professor Cappon wrote. At first glance it seems to be only a group of nine essays on individual writers (we may be pardoned for recalling that two of these essays appeared in the QUARTERLY); but from the first pages of the first essay, a study of Lampman, it becomes clear that Mr. Collin has a more ambitious purpose. His purpose is no less than to write the history of Canadian poetry from 1875 to the present and to relate this body of poetry to our culture and our economic and social order. One may properly complain that he has not kept this purpose before him continuously, that he leaves large gaps which need desperately to be filled, that he has a scale of values which is repeatedly determining his judgment, and also his selection of material and his emphasis, and which, nevertheless, is never made really clear. Still his work is extremely illuminating. Lampman is studied as a man living in Ottawa forty years ago, and it is made vivid to us exactly what it meant to be a poet in that particular place at that particular time. Marjorie Pickthall is shown as a woman living in Toronto in the years immediately before the War; and her poetry takes on new meaning when it is brought into relation with the conditions under which she lived. The intermediate figure between these earlier writers and the young men from Montreal who dominate *New Provinces* is Mr. Pratt; Mr. Collin recognizes the peculiar value of Mr. Pratt as the link, the only valid link, between the new and the old, but he fails in his otherwise admirable study of Mr. Pratt, amusingly entitled "Pleiocene Heroics," to use his poetry as a means of taking us from the world of Lampman and Roberts to the world of Kennedy and Smith. Accordingly the book breaks down in the middle; and the emergence of the Montreal group is not adequately explained. Among the members of that group Mr. Collin makes fine and valuable discriminations; he discerns in Mr. Smith a religious poet after the pattern of the metaphysicals; in Mr. Kennedy a poet all the facets of whose art bear a relation to the idea and symbol of drought and resurrection, as found in *The Golden Bough, From Ritual to Romance,* and *The Waste Land;* in Mr. F. R. Scott a poet divided between a concern for social injustice and a hunger for an absolute; in Mr. Klein a poet whose fusion of Jewish scholarship and tradition with the aspect of modern industrial society is something new not only in Canadian poetry but in all poetry.

It would be appropriate to represent the art of all these "new" poets by quotation; but space does not permit of a sufficient number of illustrations and I must be content with two brief passages. First, Mr. Smith's "Epitaph:"

Weep not on this quiet stone:
I, embedded here
Where sturdy roots divide the bone
And tendrils split a hair,
Bespeak you comfort of the grass
That is embodied Me,
Which as I am, not as I was,
Would choose to be.

And in sharp contrast, two stanzas from Mr. Kennedy's "Words for a Resurrection:"

Each pale Christ stirring underground
Splits the brown casket of its root,
Wherefrom the rousing soil upthrusts
A narrow, pointed shoot....

This Man of April walks again –
Such marvel does the time allow –
With laughter in his blessed bones,
And lilies on his brow.

154

Four volumes have appeared during the year which will be of high value to the student of the development of our poetry.

One is a new edition of the *Complete Poems* of Marjorie Pickthall. The justification of the new edition is the discovery of new manuscripts.* Few of the poems which are printed now for the first time are of remarkable quality, and none of them reveals a new aspect of Miss Pickthall's work; but any poetry of hers is worth adding to the slender store of good lyrical poetry written in Canada. Sir Charles Roberts in his *Selected Poems* reprints the entire contents of *The Iceberg and Other Poems,* along with a generous selection from eight earlier volumes all of which are out of print. The claim made in the prefatory note that the poems illustrate a great variety of tendencies and techniques, and show the author's responsiveness to successive waves of thought and attitude, is a sound one. The collection contains no new material. Interesting but less important than these collections is the slight volume containing all the poems of the late T. G. Marquis which have seemed worth preserving. Much the best poem in the book is that which gives it a title – the dramatic monologue "The Cathedral," in which Mr. Marquis presents a bishop musing on his creation and justifying his dictatorial urgency that the cathedral be built. Most of the other poems (many of them were written when the author was in his teens) are rough in form, conventional in diction and point of view.

Notice should be taken also of the anthology of light verse planned by the late John Garvin, completed by Dr. Lorne Pierce, and aptly named *Cap and Bells.* In his preface Dr. Pierce pays tribute to the spade-work done for Canadian literature by Mr. Garvin, and no less aptly points out how much we needed such a collection. "Mr. Garvin," he says, "felt that our literature and art were too solemn,

---

*The editor has failed to indicate which are the new poems. They occupy the last thirty pages of the collection (exclusive of the poem "Finis" which has appropriately been retained as a conclusion). Almost all the aspects of Miss Pickthall's art are represented in them: fine observation of nature, pious meditation, Celtic mistiness, fevered patriotism, psychological analysis. Perhaps the most admirable among the new poems are "The Naiad" and "Christ in the Workshop."

that they did not move blithely enough. . . . The absence of
this note in a more marked degree appeared to John Garvin as a serious fault, a lack of poise and detachment in our
literature, some fundamental neglect." From such a feeling
arose the present anthology. It does not accomplish its
laudable purpose. There is something forced and thin in
the gaiety of the serious souls, who have tried for brief
snatches to see life in a humorous way. Here and there one
finds a successful venture; among them are Grant Allen's
delightful fable "The First Idealist," a number of ballades
of Tom MacInnes, and that nonpareil "The Ahkoond of
Swat." It is a mournful fact that very few of the more recent
poems are comparable with these.

Among the new voices the most interesting is that of Mr.
Alan Creighton; although *Earth Call* is the first collection
of his poems, he has long been known to readers of the
poetry which appears in our magazines. He divides his lyrics into four groups: Nature, Love, Portraiture, Insurgence;
and as one turns to the later ones there is a sense of contact
with a striking personality. Most – not all – of Mr. Creighton's nature poems are somewhat conventional in idea if
not in expression; but in the other groups there are poems
in which the natural background and the human situations
are presented with remarkable directness and power. Scattered throughout the volume are innumerable lines which,
without being imitative, recall the note of Robert Frost. I
think of lines such as these:

An urge has come for soil against the hand. . . .

And under this prim tyranny – a reign
Of chair and potted plant and kitchen floor. . . .

The day had been harsh with sidewalk, sharp and dank
With house-fronts and emptiness of road. . . .

It is not fair to Mr. Creighton to represent him only by single lines; a short passage on cows will suggest more adequately his manner:

Their bodies glisten sharply red,
With shaggy brow and curving horn,
Large waggling ear, grass-bending head.

With dainty hoof and solemn lurch
They munch along their quiet search.

With a fine sensitiveness to impressions, great power of feeling, and a consciousness of the contemporary world, Mr. Creighton has made an original addition to our lyrical poetry.

Next in interest among the new voices is Irene Moody, whose collection of lyrics bears the unfortunately precious title *Attar of Song*. I could think of a number of volumes of verse published in Canada during 1936 for which that title would have been altogether appropriate; but it does not suit Irene Moody's power of communicating intense emotion or her variety and felicity of metre and structure. It does suit an occasional outburst of pseudo-philosophical and pseudo-theological verbiage, and a tendency to lusciousness of phrase. So much of the imagery in Canadian poetry is indeterminate and conventional that it gives a shock of surprised pleasure to come on a collection which abounds in vivid physical description and in no less vivid symbols of mental states. The poem "After Three Thousand Years," which deals with the intense likeness between the face of a modern girl and the effigy of an Egyptian king, is perhaps the most vivid in physical description; neither from it nor from the symbolic poems is it possible to make brief quotations which would represent adequately the art of Irene Moody.

Another new poetic voice, but one which has long been heard in prose, is that of Mr. Stephen Leacock. His *Hellements of Hickonomics*, like most of his work, is not evenly good; but there is in it an occasional fusion of humour and warm intense feeling which is one of the rarest of artistic effects, and one not to be met with at all outside of the greatest humorists. There are passages in "Oh Mr. Malthus" which are superior to anything in the whole of *Cap and Bells*. The bringing together of Malthus's anxiety about overpopulation and Wordsworth's *We Are Seven* is one of Mr. Leacock's most striking inventions. No less happy is the picture of the disorganization of society by the machine. Throughout the poem there is a power of grotesque and bizarre imagination which makes one forget

157

the negligence in expression and, at times, even the feebleness of form.

The death of King George V prompted many poets in Canada to compose elegies and funeral odes. Of these much the best is Professor G. H. Clarke's "Ode on the Burial of King George the Fifth," a poem marked by a perfect appropriateness of diction, rhythm, and tone. It suggests a comparison with what is perhaps even a finer funeral ode, the "Ode on the Burial of Marshal Joseph Pilsudski" which Professor Watson Kirkconnell prints at the beginning of his *Golden Treasury of Polish Lyrics*. The Pilsudski ode has not the finish of Professor Clarke's; there are words and even lines here and there which are not "inevitable;" in compensation there is a rapidity and a sonority which are beyond the reach of almost all other living Canadians.

There is no injustice in dismissing rather briefly the remainder of the volumes which have appeared during 1936. In them we shall find neither originality nor any large measure of power in the more conventional modes. Mr. W. B. Lane has written a poetic drama on the great theme of the capture of Quebec; unfortunately he is not so happy in treating such a theme as he was in the collection of sonnets which he published several years ago. The characters lack vitality and the style and tone waver from the vigour and raciness of the most modern diction to the set eloquence and elevated quality of the poetic drama as written a generation ago. More successful is the narrative of New France by Miss Sarah Larkin entitled, from the name of the family which she has placed in the centre of the picture, *The Trvals*. Despite the unfailing interest of the narrative and the skill with which it is related to the main stream of Canadian development, the poem does not satisfy. The tone is that of prose; and one asks why prose fiction was not the form adopted by Miss Larkin. Another narrative poem, *The Fields of Yesterday*, by Mr. John F. Ivey, recalls in stanza form, diction, tone, and substance *The Widow in the Bye Street*. It is too long, it suffers from digressions, from carelessness in expression and from a dissipation of interest; but it has in a high degree realism in the representation of nature and human character, and intensity in the conduct of the plot.

In approaching the remaining volumes of lyrical verse, I wish to quote from the excellent preface to the *Alberta Poetry Year Book, 1936-37*. Speaking of the poems appearing in the collection, Mrs. Annie Osborn remarks that their

> flaws are deplorable because, in many instances, they are palpably evidences of careless work – the disinclination to take the trouble to recast a weak line, to improve hopeless scansion in one section of a poem where the rest is passable, to find a poetic word to replace one of grating prose, to seek a better simile, or to avoid the mixed metaphor. . . . Nothing annoys the sensitive ear of the lover of poetry so much as to be betrayed by some fine lines into stumbling upon false metre; it is like missing the last step on the stairs. . . . It was a disappointment to find so small a range of subjects chosen, so grave a lack of poetic conception underlying the work, so few indications of the transcription of actual feelings or experiences.

In front of me are volumes written in British Columbia, Alberta, Manitoba, Ontario, Quebec, and Nova Scotia, to which these strictures apply in their full force. Most of them have been privately printed; they will probably have a small circulation; but what effect they have upon Canadian taste will be a weakening effect.

Despite the provision of a new organ for Canadian poetry in the *Canadian Poetry Magazine*, there has been no falling off in the quality of the verse appearing in the *Queen's Quarterly*, the *Dalhousie Review*, the *Canadian Forum, Saturday Night*, and other periodicals. Where so many good poems exist, it is difficult to single out those which seem to be exceptionally good. The poets in *New Provinces* have contributed a fair number of poems to the magazines; among these the most striking are Mr. Pratt's "Silences" (*Canadian Forum*, March), Mr. Kennedy's "Michael David" (*Saturday Night*, August 29), and Mr. Smith's "Poem" (*New Frontier*, September). Miss Dorothy Livesay has contributed several poems of great intensity and imaginative power to *New Frontier*. Among the poems written by less known poets may be mentioned Mr. Geoffrey Johnson's vigorous and delicately finished "Cloudburst" (*Queen's Quarterly*, autumn), Miss Frances Angus's "Anywhere" (*English Journal*, December), and a poem entitled "Look Homeward Angel" by an author who would not give his name even to the editor of *Saturday Night* in which his work appeared on October 3.

1937

There is no difficulty in singling out the most important book of poetry published by a Canadian in 1937: it is Mr. E. J. Pratt's *The Fable of the Goats*. This collection consists of a long allegorical narrative which furnishes the title, and nineteen other poems of varied lengths and moods. It is markedly different work from Mr. Pratt's earlier volumes, although in *The Titanic* (1935) some of its aspects are present in a less emphatic form. What distinguishes it from the body of its author's work is a daring experimentation in techniques and a keen awareness of the structure and diseases of contemporary society. That a poet who has already explored the possibilities of two or three profound moods and original themes should renew himself so fully is a heartening sign; most Canadian poets take a mould when they are young and never display any evidence of dissatisfaction with it. The monotony and the narrowness of our poetry are in no small measure owing to such an unwillingness to adventure and develop. The past five or six years of social experience have left a deeper mark on Mr. Pratt than on any other of our major poets. He is writing contemporary poetry as the best of the American poets do.

Most of his best work in the past has been in a single metrical form – the rhyming tetrameter, a measure which suits his delight in resounding rhythms, clear tonality, rapid development, and emphatic statement. The specific danger of that measure he has avoided by breaking away from a strict succession of couplets and by introducing variety of accent within the line. In "The Fable of the Goats" the rhyming tetrameter is retained. Retained too is the rush of polysyllabic music which has been one of the distinguishing marks of his poetry and which other Canadian poets are now seeking to imitate – with slight success. The first four lines of the titular poem would make one say "This is Pratt!" even if one came upon them in the dark deserts of the Waste Land. No one but he, inside Canada or outside, has quite the accent of:

One half a continental span,
The Aralasian mountains lay
Like a Valkyrian caravan
At rest along the Aryan way.

But in the shorter poems which follow "The Fable of the Goats," other and often quite novel forms occur.

The substance of his earlier poetry suggested unmistakably that Mr. Pratt was ill at ease under the cramping pressures of contemporary life and seeking to liberate himself by making a clean break for a more spacious world, either the world of primitive mastodons or the world of the sea with its heroes and its monstrous denizens. He drew his figures and their setting on a scale so grand that it was difficult to focus them clearly; he has been dominated, as Mr. W. E. Collin has said, by the "heroic imagination." Now he is pursued into his primitive world by the very pressures he formerly broke away from so sharply. He writes an allegory: wild creatures exemplify human traits, first greed, ambition, pugnacity, then peace and conciliation. Mr. Pratt has no care to disguise his allegory or even to leave it, in the manner of most allegorists, ambiguous. The fierce, bounding, heroic temperament which formerly captivated his imagination is subdued to the purest form of Christian temper; it has remained heroic for clearly it has subdued itself. "The Fable of the Goats" is an achievement; it does not take away from its high value to say that it will probably be spoken of in the future as the first of a series of poems in which a new aspect of Mr. Pratt's power will appear. It convinces one that superior things are possible in the same kind.

Among the other poems in the collection the one which is most striking and moving is "Silences." It is in a metre and mood new in Mr. Pratt's work, a mood comparable with the terror which is the distinguishing characteristic of

Mr. Robinson Jeffers. There is a tense, disturbing quiet in this poem which probes into evil implications of quietness:

There is no fury upon the earth like the fury under the
                                            sea,
For growl and cough and snarl are the tokens of spendthrifts who know not the ultimate economy of rage.
Moreover the pace of the blood is too fast.
But under the waves the blood is sluggard and has the
                              same temperature as that of the sea.
There is something pre-reptilian about a silent kill.

Anyone who heard Mr. Pratt read this poem at the meeting of the Association of Canadian Bookmen last November had one of the purest aesthetic experiences possible in our time and place.

A great disappointment is Mr. Wilson Macdonald's collection of satires, *Comber Cove*. In it he attempts, somewhat after the method of the *Spoon River Anthology,* to give a picture of the life of a small town by a succession of short, sharp character-sketches, most of which are bitterly destructive. The aim is admirable; stinging satire is needed. The stanza forms, however, do not lend themselves to the expression of the emotions which Mr. Macdonald is trying to utter; the emphasis in thought is repetitive; and the few idealized figures (included to supply a standard by which the deviations of the others can be measured) are not sufficiently impressive. On the cover Bliss Carman is quoted as having said that this collection is "the greatest satire since the days of Juvenal," an example of the bad old kind of critical opinion from which we are slowly escaping.

Another Canadian poet whom many of our critics were exalting a few years ago to the heights which Mr. Pratt securely occupies, has published a collection of verses which are sadly disillusioning. Miss Audrey Brown's *The Tree of Resurrection* contains along with much new material a few older poems, notably that poem which was the corner-stone of her reputation, "Laodamia." What this collection impresses on a sympathetic reader is the bookishness and traditionalism of the poet's sources of emotion and expression. The experiments with modern forms and simple feelings are unsatisfactory; neither the forms nor the feelings appear to have been inevitable or, once adopted, to have been handled with the power and tact which flow only from absolute sincerity. The best of the new poems are those which are literary and conventional, "The Pilgrims," "Lammastide," "Past Noon, October, To E. B. B." The grace and skill and tranquillity of some of the older poems are in these.

There is more of pure poetry in the slim brochure which Sir Charles Roberts has brought out – *Twilight over Shaugamauk and Three Other Poems*. Here and there, if not continuously in any one of the poems, the old magic casts its spell:

> From many a far and nameless lake
> > Where rain-birds greet the showery noon
> And dark moose pull the lily pads
> > Under an alien moon. . . .

> On the pale borders of evening
> > The hawthorn breaths are cool.
> The frogs pipe in the sedges
> > About the shadowy pool . . .

Sir Charles has had more disciples than any other Canadian writer now alive; they have praised him, they have winded themselves imitating him, and none of them has as yet come within measurable distance of his achievement. It is, I suppose, a desirable phenomenon in a relatively new literature, that the best of the older poets should have a group to hold a nimbus o'er his head and found a tradition of which he is the patron. In some of his recent collections, although his coterie has tried to disguise the fact, a falling off in vividness and force has been noticeable; led by the disciples the general reader has tended to neglect his earlier work, much of which was once more rendered accessible in the *Selected Poems* of 1936. A glance at the best poems in that collection and at the best stanzas in *Twilight over Shaugamauk* will sharpen one's awareness that between Roberts and his followers there is a chasm which will tolerate no leap.

At his best Mr. Lloyd Roberts is not a disciple of his father, although many of his less successful poems are imitative either of the elder Roberts or of Lampman. In *I Sing of Life,* a representative selection of his poems with a disarmingly modest preface, the general level is not very high; a few poems do, however, rise far above this level, notably a resonant hymn, "Song of Trust," a Blake-like meditation, "As We Sow," and a firm, hard nature piece, "Dead Days." In these and in a few other pieces a fund of experience and a faculty for clear design issue in poetry so striking as to astonish a reader by their superiority to the prevailing qualities of the collection. One has to go back to Lampman for Canadian writing such as this:

> The reeds creek in the dawn
> By the dead pond;
> Dry tongues respond
> From grasses yellow and drawn;
> And ever scourged by the wind,
> The alders clatter and grind.

> Vines furred with the frost
> String from the wall:
> Their bones recall
> Summer leaves long lost,
> Cricket and fly and bee
> And their low melody.

This is no mere imitation of Lampman; the diction and the movement are what Lampman might have used had he lived in our time.

Not for many years has a young Canadian writer appeared to have an ambition to be an official poet. It now seems that Mr. Nathaniel Benson has that ambition; in his collection, *The Glowing Years,* there is more verse on public themes than in any other at all notable volume of Canadian poetry since the War. He writes odes on Dominion Day, on the death of George V, on the death of Bliss Carman, and on the centenary of Toronto. In some of these odes the movement has sweep and vigour; there are passages of high rhetoric; but it is impossible to feel that the formal archaic structure is appropriate for a Canadian's tribute to aspects of Canadian history and civilization. Mr. Benson is among the poets who might meditate on the thesis advanced by His Excellency Lord Tweedsmuir in his address of last November, the thesis that Canadian themes require measures subtly (and perhaps even strikingly) different from those which have ruled in England. Here and there in Mr. Benson's collection there are poems modern, even modernist, in theme, in diction, and in structure; but in these poems he does not seem to work easily or naturally, he seems rather to be engaged in calculated experimentation. The best of the poems in the volume are those in which Mr. Benson expresses intimate experience, especially the experience of bereavement.

Fresher than Mr. Benson's talent or Mr. Lloyd Roberts's are the vigour and colour with which Mr. Joseph Schull tells the tale of *The Legend of Ghost Lagoon*. In this long narrative poem, recalling again and again the manner of Masefield, Mr. Schull evokes piracy, superstition, torture, profanity, and all the other traditional trappings of the Spanish Main. Certain defects of the poem are unescapable: it is not well proportioned, it is not unified in style, passing from archaic elegance to rough modernity without adequate justification in subject, and the central scenes (which should in a narrative like this have been brought into high relief and recounted with heroic fulness) are somewhat scamped. So much for complaint. The poem is nonetheless a heartening one; it is pleasant to find one young poet interested in the objective world rather than in the nuances of his own feelings, able to deal with character as fully as with landscape, powerfully gifted with historic imagination. It is not possible to represent Mr. Schull's narrative gift; but his imaginative language may be illustrated in a few lines:

A halberd's plunge or a cutlass slash
Letting the water into his heart. . . .

The lion leaps for the boar's red eyes. . . .

His thighbones crumple about his neck. . . .

It is an injustice to such lines to tear them from their context in a swift-moving narrative; taken by themselves they may seem crude and over-coloured; but when read in the rush of the poem they startle with their compact effectiveness. We need more poetry like *The Legend of Ghost Lagoon*.

There is vigour also in Mr. Patrick Slater's *The Water-Drinker* – in the preface rather than in the verses which follow. The preface is a sensible discursive essay on the problem of poetry as it appears in a Canadian framework. His comment on the feebleness of colonial art is admirably put:

> The writings of other days and other climes are available and should be read and enjoyed . . . . But whatever their merits it is a vain thing to attempt to improve on them by laboured imitation, which is the negation of all art. It is for this reason that little of artistic merit has ever come out of colonies, as ancient writers observed and as we have seen with our own eyes. The explanation is obvious. Communities differ from one another in quality; and whether better or worse than our ancestors or others, to produce anything worthwhile, we must be frank and be ourselves.

Mr. Slater is equally sound in the distinctions he lays down to separate verse and poetry and in his attack on the versifiers, or, to adopt a happy phrase which he uses elsewhere, the *verse-smiths*, "whose inspirational songs combine a comfortable religion with good home-cooking, and who assure our troubled hearts that in some mysterious way virtue yields a tidy profit in earthly goods." About his own verses Mr. Slater is extremely modest; he assures us that they fall far short of poetry, conceding that he lacks the power which above all others distinguishes the authentic poet – the power to find adequate words and rhythms for the emotions which crowd painfully in his mind and clamour for utterance. It is unnecessary to say more of the defects in his verse; and it is pleasant to note that they show some study of Indian and early Western life.

The clearest and most moving of the new voices is that of Mrs. Floris McLaren who has brought out a collection of thirty poems entitled *Frozen Fire*. Almost every one of her poems has a definitely Arctic landscape and makes much of the peculiar stimuli and ordeals of the far North-West. The note struck in the first poem is maintained throughout:

> The crowding spruces go,
> A still black army, down to the curving shore.

The frost lights glitter on every twig and brier
Till we set intruding feet on the jewelled floor
And shatter the cranberry bushes' frozen fire.

Despite the persistent pre-occupation with the North, and with the forms of character it develops, there is a lack of real unity in the collection and the poems seem to be unrelated facets of a personality nowhere clearly defined.

The rest of the year's poetic production must be dismissed more briefly; nor will brevity result in any serious injustice.

Four of the Ryerson Poetry Chap-Books have come out during the year. In Mr. Charles Boyle's *Stars before the Wind* there are two striking love sonnets; but the collection as a whole is marred by deficiencies in technique, and above all by unsatisfactory rhymes. Archaic forms and rhythms rob Mr. William Thow's *More Odd Measures* of reality. In Mr. Leo Cox's *River without End* there is a bewildering variety of feeling and form, and the total effect of this collection is disappointing for a poet from whom for ten years much has been expected. The fourth chap-book, Miss Helena Coleman's *Songs*, contains no fresh material.

Ship's Wake and Road's Lure, by Mrs. Christine Henderson, abounds in somewhat conventional impressions of travel, in none of which can one discern any note of the intense or the new; the appearance in this collection of two poems on the flea is a heartening omen for Canadian verse which must not pass unnoticed; and there is a poem on a Sibelius symphony which indicates sensitiveness and a willingness to experiment. Sister Maura's *Breath of the Spirit* is a slim volume in which the poems disclose technical competence beyond the reach of most Canadian poets; but the content is thin and the emotion faint. Miss Martha Martin's *Out of the Shadows* does not rise above smooth and easy melody. More old-fashioned, perhaps, than any of these, is Miss Alice Wilson's *My Sanctuary Garden* which is lacking throughout in concreteness and is in the main marked by a rough bumping rhythm. Similar in tone, but more melodious, is Mr. Gordon LeClaire's collection *Star-Haunted;* here the diction is exuberant and the emotion, apparently at least, not entirely real. In *Rhymes of the*

French Regime, Mr. Arthur Bourinot has tried to present early Canadian history in a guise attractive to children with a sense of rhyme and humour; but, like many other such undertakings, his verses are satisfying neither to the children for whom they were intended nor to the adults who were intended to peer at them over children's shoulders. The book is a disappointment coming from a poet who in another mood has done satisfying work.

Among the collections published by groups – and from year to year these increase in number – much the best is *Canadian Poems,* a small brochure containing the best of the eleven hundred poems submitted in a competition sponsored by the Calgary Branch of the Canadian Authors' Association. No more interesting volume of Canadian poetry has appeared this past year with the exception of Mr. Pratt's; and it is regrettable that the sponsors have not had their collection bound in durable cloth. They conducted their competition in a fashion which other groups might wisely imitate. They chose excellent judges; they defined types and themes, in which separate competitions were held; and they extended the terms of eligibility to welcome all Canadians. The best poems came from New Brunswick, Montreal, rural Ontario, Winnipeg, Regina – and, one of them, only, from Calgary. It is impossible at all points to agree with the judges, but the award of the Senator Patrick Burns Memorial Prize for a poem on a definitely Canadian theme imposes immediate assent. The poem which won this prize, the work of Mr. Frederick Laight of Regina, should be known across the country, and I take leave to quote it entire:

I have seen tall chimneys without smoke,
   And I have seen blank windows without blinds,
    And great dead wheels, and motors without minds,
And vacant doorways grinning at the joke.

I have seen loaded wagons creak and sway
   Along the roads into the North and East,
    Each dragged by some great-eyed and starving beast
To God knows where, but just away – away.

And I have heard the wind awake at nights
   Like some poor mother left with empty hands,
   Go whimpering in the silent stubble lands
And creeping through bare houses without lights.

These comforts only have I for my pain –
   The frantic laws of statesmen bowed with cares
   To feed me, and the slow, pathetic prayers
Of godly men that somehow it shall rain.

That is a note struck too seldom in our poetry; and in other poems by Mr. Laight, appearing in other collections or in the periodical press, it is not struck with anything like equal power.

The poetry appearing in the major periodicals of the country has continued to maintain a high level. The disappearance towards the end of the year of *New Frontier* is a misfortune for Canadian poetry; in its brief life this periodical became one of the main vehicles in this country for original and powerful poetry. In 1937 alone it published a notable poem by Mr. A. M. Klein ("Of Daumiers a Portfolio"), one of Mr. Leo Kennedy's most vigorous pieces ("Calling Eagles"), and a large group of Miss Dorothy Livesay's moving lyrics. The *Canadian Forum,* among much that is excellent, published another of Mr. Klein's poems ("Blue Print for a Monument of War") and some notable satires by Mr. L. A. MacKay. The level of poetry in these two magazines and in *Saturday Night* is higher than that in the volumes which have been noticed; and if the poetry of our periodical press is good, we may reasonably hope that the poetry appearing in book-form will steadily improve. Neither Mr. MacKay nor Mr. Klein has as yet published a volume of verse, and it is a long time since there was a collection of Miss Livesay's. When the survey of Letters in Canada for 1938 is written, we hope that books by each of these three highly individual and powerful poets will have appeared.

1938

The poetry of 1938 was markedly less interesting and valuable than that of any other year since the survey of "Letters in Canada" began. 1935 was the year of Mr. Pratt's *The Titanic* and Mr. Duncan Campbell Scott's *The Green Cloister;* 1936 the year of the anthology *New Provinces* in which the six against tradition made a massed attack on the Canadian public; 1937 the year of Mr. Pratt's *The Fable of the Goats.* No work comparable with any of these appeared in 1938.

The most valuable book of the year is an anthology, Mrs. Ethel Hume Bennett's *New Harvesting: Contemporary Canadian Poetry, 1918-1938.* The publisher and the compiler are to be congratulated on its comprehensiveness and on its very modest price. The compiler has, however, been too self-effacing: the brief biographical notes are useful, but they should have been supplemented by an introductory essay explaining how our poetry came to attempt new things and to achieve a new manner, and estimating, perhaps, how far the new things and the new manner have been successfully handled. This anthology is clearly destined to be reprinted; and it is not in the spirit of idle criticism, therefore, to say that with an introductory essay by Mr. W. E. Collin or Mr. A. J. M. Smith (if the compiler does not wish to write one) its usefulness would be hugely increased. A second edition should also be slightly more inclusive: the absence of Mr. A. M. Klein is an intolerable blemish in so good a book as this; and the representation of Mr. A. J. M. Smith, Mr. Watson Kirkconnell, and Mr. Duncan Campbell Scott is seriously inadequate. But it is a more important test that what is included in an anthology should be good, than that no good things should have been omitted. This more important test Mrs. Bennett does in the main pass triumphantly. From her collection one can see quite clearly the directions of Canadian poetry in the past twenty years: what has been of secondary importance in the period is secondary in her book. One aspect of our contemporary poetry requires, however, much more space than Mrs. Bennett allows it: satire. Perhaps it is distaste for satiric poetry that explains the exclusion of Mr. Klein; the poems of Mr. F. R. Scott included in the anthology would never lead anyone to suspect his vigour in satire; and the overlooking of the claims of Mr. L. A. MacKay confirms one in the hypothesis that Mrs. Bennett does not care for satire in verse. If the hypothesis is right, it points to a great limitation in her power to do for our poetry all that at this moment an anthologist could and should do.

It seems useful to point out the specific weaknesses of this work since, unlike most good books published in Canada, it will beyond question have a fair sale, a second edition, and a strong influence in the reshaping of our standards of excellence.

Far less useful is *A New Canadian Anthology,* edited by the spirited Nova Scotia poet Mr. Alan Creighton with the assistance of Miss Hilda M. Ridley. The editor has excluded, he tells us, all poems going beyond thirty-two lines; and although one is pleased that he has not applied the limitation with severe literalism (Mr. Gordon LeClaire's "Initiate, 1918" extends to thiry-six), the principle is vicious. It is impossible to represent many of our best poets in lyrical snatches. A more serious limitation is hinted in the remark: "In making our selections . . . we were limited to the work submitted to us." It is not clear what this means: Did the editor not invite contributions from all the poets he esteemed worthy of inclusion? Did the poets invited send in mediocre or unrepresentative poems? Whatever the statement may mean, the anthology is not sufficiently representative of our best poetry; and its real usefulness lies in the introduction of notable writers who are either not known at all or are known only locally. The QUARTERLY has, from the initiation of the survey of Canadian literature, had a specially keen interest in talent which is either unsuspected or insufficiently appreciated. A number of the best poems in this collection are by poets who have not as yet published collections of their own; and it is to them that comment here will be confined. The poems I have in mind are Mrs. Angus's "West Coast," Miss Monkman's "Sea Burial," Mr. Rowland's "Epitaph for Warriors," and Miss Smart's "Bourgeois Afternoon." Space does not suffice for representing all four by quotation; let the closing lines of Mrs. Angus's and Miss Smart's poems indicate the excellence of all four. Mrs. Angus, in a vein to be contrasted with Mr. Smith's in "The Lonely Land," ends

> Bones of an unknown past
> Rootheld by listening trees,
> Ghosts of another race,
> Echoes of older songs
> Haunt me, and keep me
> Alien to soil I love.

In the earlier stanzas, and even in the lines quoted here, there is a shade too much of the Victorians, of Arnold and Clough above all; but there is evidence of intention to renovate the old rhythms and diction. Miss Smart ends more experimentally:

> We cannot cut with hard decision
> through the pleasant web of afternoon.
> Whatever thirst is ours, whatever pain,
> we must delay the reflex and the end.
> Whatever hunger stalks the restless night,
> whatever death yawns in the void of dawn,
> we must delay, procrastinate our force.
> Our feeling shall be after, after this;
> it shall come after, after afternoon.

Appreciative comment on these lines would be superfluous; it is not superfluous to draw attention to the ambiguity of effect in the sixth line.[1]

---

[1] Why did Mr. Creighton include photographs of his contributors?

The account of Canadian poetry in 1937 closed with the expression of a hope that during 1938 Mr. A. M. Klein, Miss Dorothy Livesay, and Mr. L. A. MacKay would issue collections of their recent verse. Under the pseudonym of John Smalacombe Mr. MacKay has given us a brochure of seven pages entitled *Viper's Bugloss*. Short and uneven though it is, unsatisfactory as I find the selection, which omits Mr. MacKay's most polished and ingenious satires, this little book is, if not the most nearly perfect, the most significant of those with which this survey has still to deal. Mr. MacKay's range is notable: it runs from the elaborate richness of

> Float slowly, swimmer, slowly drawing breath.
> See, in this wild green foam of growing things
> The heavy hyacinth remembering death.

to the brutal clarity of

> . . . you'd look like a headless hen
> Hung up by the heels, with the long bare red neck
> stretching,
> curving, and dripping away
> From the soiled floppy ball of ruffled feathers standing
> on end.

The poem from which these last lines are taken is probably the bitterest ever published by a Canadian, unless that eminence be reserved for the one preceding it. More nearly perfect than any other in the brochure is a slightly irregular sonnet which appeared many years ago in the *Canadian Forum*, and which Mrs. Bennett and our other anthologists have unaccountably missed. Yet "Hylas" is one of the few Canadian poems in which tone and form perfectly harmonize; it is one of our few anthology pieces:

> Between the blue that burned the swimming bay
> And the green welter of the tangled land,
> Nosing blood-browed against the grating sand,
> The tarred bulk of the mighty Argo lay.
> But the tall young Theban thrust his idle way

Through the tough thickets with brown arrogant hand
To where the little river seemed to stand
Dozing, beneath the dead mid-swing of day.
And saw there kneeling by the shining stream
Through the still depth white slender bodies rise:
On his strong wrist cool fingers wrapt unseen;
Unfathomably in blue quiet eyes
His soul drew down, and he as in a dream
Sank through the still bright water quietly.

It would be an interesting exercise in criticism to set that sonnet alongside some of the riparian sonnets of Lampman; one could then see clearly the movement which has gone on in our poetry in the past thirty years, a movement which without breaking sharply with tradition (Greek poetry and the Hellenic verse of Morris and Hérédia lie behind this poem) has ventured into a new region of suggestiveness and terror shot through with beauty.

Some of the directions of this movement may also be defined by comparing with her earlier collections Mrs. Louise Morey Bowman's *Characters in Cadence*. The range of the latest collection is notable: it is full of references to the great Romantics and of reminiscences of them; but in rhythm and image and subject it more often recalls the American poetry of the past thirty years, especially the imagists. The variety both in tone and subject, and still more in essential point of view, is disquieting: there is too much of the mocking bird in the book. But for the first time one is convinced that in Mrs. Bowman there is the possibility of a poet of high importance, I should not hesitate to say of an importance higher than Marjorie Pickthall's.

Another notable collection is Mr. Kenneth Leslie's *By Stubborn Stars and Other Poems*. The title-piece is a sequence of twenty-seven sonnets in which with a simple music and a deliberately circumscribed choice of imagery the author sets down intense, and chiefly painful, moments in the development of a love. Rather against one's expectations, the fusion of a simple tone with a complex temperament is a happy one and the effect is one of continuous intensity. Less satisfying are the more experimental verses which follow; in some of the rhythms he attempts Mr. Leslie does not appear to be fully at ease; and in diction the balance between old and new for which he aims (so it seems) is not accurately struck. Still, in the two rather long poems with which the collection closes, he does seem once more to be at ease: one which deals with the Spanish War is intense and complex without perhaps being as profound as the sequence of sonnets; and the other, a fable of Robert Frost and "Cobweb College," is a delightful mingling of an original tone and the peculiar tone of Frost himself. The effectiveness of this piece makes one wonder again why Canadian poets have not appreciated how fully they could appropriate Frost without crippling anything essential in themselves. Of all American poets Frost is the one whom most Canadians may most safely study: I hope Mr. Leslie's success may lead other Maritime poets to saturate themselves in *North of Boston* and *New Hampshire*.

A sequence of sonnets occupies the central part of Miss Kathryn Munro's *New Moon*; in tone and in diction it is less striking than Mr. Leslie's sequence, but it is fresh and authentic. In general Miss Munro is at her best in short-lined stanzas, where she is obliged to lop off her epithets which have a tendency towards conventional lushness. The lyric "Burial" shows what she can do when she is austere in form.

III

The year's most notable attempt at handling a great Canadian subject is Mr. O. J. Stevenson's *The Unconquerable North and Other Poems*. The work which supplies the title is one of the most ambitious of all handlings of the Canadian theme; it duly celebrates the Canadian landscape, and turns to speak sympathetically of the actual terms of Canadian life on the farm and in the factory. Somehow it fails to move; and as one seeks the explanation of the failure, noting the intense sincerity, the wide knowledge, the power to organize and to fuse, the defect appears – it is a defect in language; and the reading of the collection as a whole confirms this criticism. Mr. Stevenson, it is sad to say, would have been a truer poet, if he had not spent his life in reading and teaching the English poets. Their splendours of phrase have left a mist between his eyes and his subjects. His failure – it is not an absolute failure, one need scarcely say, but a failure in adequacy to a supreme subject – is the scholar's, the belletrist's failure.

Down the Years is introduced by a very careful and subtle critique written by Mr. E. J. Pratt. He observes that "it has always been a matter of psychological curiosity to watch a critic step out of his professional tract and enter a territory known to him only as an observer and analyst." From a critic, Mr. Pratt concludes, one expects flawless technique; he may or may not conceive his themes as a creator does, but once he passes from the conception to the expression he will not fail his readers. Mr. Morgan-Powell sets himself some arduous technical exercises; but it is in his simpler poems that he is at his most attractive – in these he has a fluidity of movement and a strength of feeling which, as Mr. Pratt suggests, the long practice of criticism is little likely to develop.

Standing out sharply from most of the year's poetry by the adroitness of touch and humorous vigour which characterize it throughout, Mr. Arthur Stringer's *The Old Woman Remembers and Other Irish Poems* is a considerable reinforcement of the small body of our light verse. It abounds in such charmingly unemphatic lines as

> I love to stop and quietly listen
> To those voices, night or day,
> Where some rapt-eyed son of Erin
> Stands lying his soul away.

Like all finely poetic humour Mr. Stringer's is strengthened by a foundation of grimness and tenderness exquisitely fused.[2]

In *Leaves in the Wind,* a selection from Mrs. Virna Sheard's poems, many notes are struck: most effective among them are the notes of rich sweetness and of wild

---

[2]Mr. Stringer's little volume of 57 pages very properly has its title on the spine. It was published in the United States; had it been published in Canada the spine would bear no mark of identity whatever; and one would have to take the book down from its shelf to know what it was. When will Canadian publishers – who now bring out books extending to a hundred pages and costing two dollars, without any lettering on the spine – learn that their practice is both inconvenient and ugly?

humour. In our sage and serious verse it is seldom that one comes on lines such as this Carrollian stanza about penguins:

No matter what the hour may be
Penguins are dressed to dine,
And have a gentle dignity, –
Stuffy – but yet benign,
As though their minds dwelt much on soup,
On walnuts, and on wine.

Mrs. Sheard cannot maintain such a level throughout a poem; but it is much for a Canadian to have reached it at all! Space does not permit illustration of her imagery which is, in a number of instances, original within the tradition of our poetry to which in all her serious poems she is faithful.

IV

Of the booklets containing the results of the year's competitions, the best is that published by the Poetry Group of the Montreal Branch of the Canadian Authors' Association. All the principles governing the competitions of this group are not equally intelligible. Prizes for the best lyric, the best sonnet, the best hymn, are self-explanatory; but why should there be a prize for the best Maritime poem, the best "Who is Great" poem, the best bird poem? Notable among many good things are Mr. Leo Cox's "Labrador Sunday" and Miss Robina Monkman's "Ebb Tide."

The level of verse in the periodicals continues to be surprisingly high; the *Canadian Poetry Magazine* has in each of its quarterly issues printed a large number of admirable poems, some of them traditional, others boldly experimental; and in the *Dalhousie Review*, the *Queen's Quarterly*, the *Canadian Forum*, and *Saturday Night*, there has been no lapse from the high performance of 1937. In places where readers of Canadian poetry are not so likely to find them, good poems have been appearing. Notable among the poems which are in danger of being overlooked are Mr. Watson Kirkconnell's prairie narratives in the Saturday supplements of the *Winnipeg Free Press* and in the *National*

Home Monthly, and Mr. A. M. Klein's "Childe Harold's Pilgrimage" in *Opinion.* Mr. Klein's poem, in his richly erudite and allusive manner, traces the relation between Gentile and Jew from Pharaoh to the present; of all Jews his plight is worst who has from communication with the Gentile abandoned his religion and divested himself of his prejudices, for that Jew can neither pray nor fight, he can only endure. It is a tragic tale, enforced by that grim quickly-melting humour which runs through all Mr. Klein's poems. Mr. Kirkconnell has attempted something in the manner of the *Tales of a Wayside Inn.* Snow-bound in a rural hotel in Manitoba, a group sit about a fire and tell tales which represent the picturesque aspects of Manitoba life: the stock-fairs, the clashes of mining prospectors, the psychology of the *métis,* the development of the Slavic Canadians. The series is not yet complete; and it is as yet impossible to speak of its design or central motive as clearly as one would wish; but it is not too soon to speak of the vividness and dramatic imagination Mr. Kirkconnell exhibits.

1939

In 1939, more than in any other year, Canadian poets have been preoccupied with stresses and blockages in the national society. Those of us who have long believed that in our verse there has been far too much meteorology will take a special pleasure in noting that, from undistinguished scribbling up to the authentic poetry of Mr. Pratt, there has been a new vigour and clearness in the presentation of social life. The poets have also shown that verse alive with anxiety and packed with reflection forfeits nothing of the sensitivity to nature which has long been the one constant virtue in poetic writing in this country.

No poem represents the emphasis of the year so well as *The Wind Our Enemy,* by Miss Anne Marriott, published as a Ryerson Chap-Book. In it we have the first striking presentation in verse of the tragedy of drought. After a spirited prelude, in which the themes are suggested, she paints the wheatfields in their productive glory; the rest of the poem reveals the effects on farmers and their families of year upon year of drought – first a wry fortitude, then a grudging acceptance of relief, pathetic efforts at communal amusement, degeneration of fibre, an indestructible residue of irrational courage, all set against the background of caked earth, shrivelled grain, and gaunt farm-animals. It is a great subject. Miss Marriott's technique is firm and at the same time infinitely plastic: she can state and she can suggest, setting side by side scraps of significant conversation in impoverished language and bursts of high poetry. She has achieved the most impressive single poem of the year.

Much of Mr. Arthur S. Bourinot's *Under the Sun,* a collection of thirty-four poems, remarkably varied in form and tone, is social verse. One of the most careful craftsmen in the whole range of our poetry, he has hitherto been conservative in the choice both of themes and forms; in his new collection he shows himself keenly aware of the Canadian society (and of the international framework to which it belongs) and of the most successful contemporary modes of experiment in verse. In "Transients" a restrained but deep compassion finds a perfect vesture in short lines, full of moving reiterations, and conveying, by these and by the turn of phrase and the avoidance of sharp or strong stresses, the helplessness of the wanderers. Much the same is his success in the bitter "Wrestling Match" and the more subtle "Not Long Ago" in which the theme is the helplessness in the grip of great social forces not of transients but of us all. Many other themes are treated in this collection. The spirit of Wordsworth hovers over the tragic pastoral "John Ridd." Even Wordsworth's stolid humour is there:

> A man of great physique and ponderous bulk
> Who held his car upon the rutty roads
> By force of his brute strength, and if there was
> At any time a doubt of Darwin's theory
> Here in his flesh was truth personified.

The chief weakness lies in the abundance of imitation, conscious or not; and it is astonishing to find in "Flying Geese" the rhythm, verse structure, and even the tone of Mr. A. J. M. Smith's great lyric "The Lonely Land." But even the poems in which the notes of others are audible impress by an undoubted integrity of feeling and a scarcely broken perfection of form.

Another poet with a grave anxiety about the national life is Mr. Alan Creighton, who has published his second collection, *Cross-country*. Unlike Miss Marriott and Mr. Bourinot, he is threatening:

> Pushed to the end of the pier,
> After years of fighting day and night,
> We are ready for revolution.

Unemployment, the régime of big business, the verge of war, the insecurity of all relationships – even marriage – with a revolution around the corner, these are his worries, and he speaks (unlike the two poets mentioned, his social verse *speaks,* it does not *sing*) of them with spirit and defiance. He closes a collection in which nature, love, and simple relations between individuals have their places as well as the poetry of society, with a forceful social statement, in which he repudiates a regional and an imperial society, and asks for a "country" to be born of a new world which he sees

> ... forming
> In the ether and skies
> Of an untouched land,
> Enveloping, comfortable,
> With many friends.

Mr. Creighton's social poetry is not so deep, is not so variously and immediately moving, as the social poetry of Miss Marriott and Mr. Bourinot; but for its vigour, warmth, and clarity we are grateful. Vigour, warmth, and clarity mark his best nature-poetry, and his very striking poems of love. In these there is an easy frankness unusual in our verse, and unfortunately marred here and there by a too adorned phrasing such as spoiled some of the strongest and most sincere love poetry of Edgar Lee Masters.

Over-decoration continues to enfeeble the poetry of Mr. Gordon LeClaire, whose *Though Quick Souls Bleed* is the largest collection published during the year. The fatal injury of over-decoration can be seen even in so short a poem as "Scarlet Manna"; in which, as in many of the poems, there are social implications:

> Fresh-gleaned from a Vimy field,
> Fomented by scarlet rain
> And youth's marrow-dust, they sealed
> A flagon of topaz grain
> To be planted on some Gaspé plot –
> A "beau geste" to honour the dead.
>
> May no millstone grind wheat from the spot
> Lest we strangle on the bread.

Mr. LeClaire's emotional quality is intense: this poem is no more violent in feeling than most in the book. It is a pity that his language is softish, and his structure complex and often unclear. The poems that result from the odd fusion of violent feeling and lush expression are almost uniformly disappointing. Some severity in comment on Mr. LeClaire's poetry may be pardoned: there is a possibility that he will, in certain circles, be mistaken for one of the major poets of this country. In a pamphlet of four pages accompanying the volume it is reported that the Montreal *Herald* has hailed his poems as "fine as anything in contemporary American or Canadian verse," the *American Weave* saluted him as "the preeminent Canadian Poet," the *Leamington Post and News* affirmed that he "seems not to know any limit of creative genius or beauty of expression," and the *Macon Telegraph* distinguished him from Milton to Milton's disadvantage. Usually, the pages of this survey are reserved for those among our poets who appear to disclose something remarkable either in performance or promise; but it is no less its province to comment upon work which seems to have had exaggerated praise and to which virtues of a very high kind have been much too hastily ascribed.

Much more modest in scope and more limited in intensity is Mr. Richard Callan's collection, *Chains of Harmony*, in which our traditional preoccupation with nature dominates the first two-thirds, leaving scant space for reflective poems on human and social conflicts. Still, it is in these poems that Mr. Callan's thought and feeling seems freshest and strongest. What pleasure Mr. Callan could give us is almost completely destroyed by an insensitive rhythm, and a lack of congruity between form and substance.

Hackneyed diction and inability to escape from light rhythm are the defects in Mr. William Thow's little chapbook, *Poet and Salesman*. The light rhythm is quite appropriate to the title poem, and in it even the worn diction serves its end – grim comedy – but in the more ambitious pieces such as "Killed in Action" rhythm and diction work such havoc to the effect as these opening lines exemplify:

> Having been born where love and *lore* are strong
>   He learned to read the hearts of *mere* and mountain,
> Where *fays* and *fauns* and *kelpies* all day long,
>   *Conjure their spells* beside the guggling fountain . . . .

The rough realism of "guggling" is merely comic in its

ornate setting; and what gravity survives rhythm and diction is annihilated by the feminine rhymes. Mr. Thow's technical insensitivity is the more regrettable, that he has much to say and feels deeply what he says. Other volumes in the hospitable Ryerson series of Chap-Books to which his work belongs are Mr. C. F. Boyle's *Excuse for Futility,* Miss Lillian Leveridge's *Lyrics and Sonnets,* Miss Carol Coates's *Fancy Free,* and Miss Isobel McFadden's *Reward and Other Poems.* Mr. Boyle shows more technical expertness than in his preceding collection (1937) and again writes some striking love poems. The intensity which distinguishes these from the other poems in his brochure runs through all the darker pieces in Miss McFadden's collection, in which there is also a great, but very uncertain, power of phrase. Power of phrase is exactly what Miss Leveridge lacks: her easily flowing, pleasant, sincere verses leave no imprint on the mind.

Miss Coates is quite unlike the other chap-book writers. She explains in a brief and carefully weighed foreword the influence upon her of Japanese civilization, especially its painting and poetry. Of Japanese poetry (and implicitly of her own) she says:

> Eastern art excels in suggesting what it does not say. Therefore a ruthless selection of significant detail is of paramount importance. A poem may consist of less than a dozen expressions . . . The function of the reader is an active one – to become a creator . . . . This is done by reflecting with more than usual care upon the tonal and rhythmic qualities of word, savoring to the full each literal and emotional connotation.

Many of the poems in her collection will not, it seems to me, support the close scrutiny she invites: the words often seem merely approximately good, and the substance thin. But when Miss Coates is at her best, as in "Ashes" –

> These ashes that now stir idly in the wind
> have played a double fire –
> for the words
> ere they crumbled in the flame,
> burned on my cheek,
> thawing the chill of loneliness
> from my heart –

she vindicates her theory. Even when she fails, one welcomes the careful experimentation.

Less welcome is the experimentation of Mr. John Murray Gibbon. The many readers of his *Melody and the Lyric* will recall his theory that lyrics are best written to a tune. So Burns often wrote; and so Mr. Gibbon writes in his *New World Ballads*. The theory is attractive, and in the past great things have been done in accordance with it. But a theorist about poetry is not often happy in illustrations of his theory. Mr. Gibbon is very far indeed from being a Burns: he has nothing of Burns's strength and little of his sweetness. Ballads more effective than his are to be found in Mr. Alfred Biggs's *Songs of Limehouse and Other Verse*. The "other verse" is weak; but in more than one of the songs there is a rough strength.

Two collections of a much more old-fashioned sort are Edna Jaques's *Beside Still Waters* and Isabel Graham's *Be of Good Cheer:* their character is perhaps sufficiently indicated by these titles. Edna Jaques is notably more interested in humanity than in nature; and in a Canadian that is a merit. Her approach to people or to society as a whole is, however, no deeper than what we see in these two stanzas in which she evokes Collingwood, where she was born:

> New bread with flaky crusts and lots of jam,
>   Cookies with scalloped edges crisp and thin,
> Gardens to dig for treasures in the sand,
>   Small creeks to wade and fish for minnows in.
> Old ladies primly sitting on the lawn,
>   Green tangled hedges growing wild and dense,
> Old-fashioned flowers nodding in the sun,
>   We peeked at them through knot-holes in the fence.

Sometimes the tone is graver, or the subject more complex; but there is never more poetic depth. One sees why Edna Jaques is popular: she is probably our most genuinely popular writer of verse. But her popularity is not a very consoling fact to anyone who would wish a literature in this country, profound and penetrating and great. She enables us to see what Canadian taste really is. Miss Graham is more old-fashioned; she has less directness and simplicity, more dignity and variety. Like Edna Jaques's, her rhythms are almost always light; and there is a painful incongruity between these rhythms and the substance of her more ambitious poems.

The year-books of the poetry societies are often among the most interesting volumes of verse commented upon in this survey. In 1939 they were all disappointing, the least depressing being that which came from Victoria, with poems by Mrs. McLaren, Miss Marriott, and Mrs. Angus.

Among the poems appearing in periodicals, the most notable were Mr. A. J. M. Smith's nightmarish "The Bridegroom" *(Canadian Forum,* January); Miss Anne Marriott's beautifully sharp and clear "Woodyards in the Rain" *(Canadian Forum,* April) – one of the best impressionist pieces done in this country; Mr. Charles Bruce's moving and expert "Words Are Never Enough" *(Canadian Poetry Magazine, July);* a number of brief, high-pitched, and very feminine poems by Miss Joyce Marshall; and Dr. Duncan Campbell Scott's noble and resonant "A Farewell to Their Majesties" *(Saturday Night,* June 17). With this last Professor G. H. Clarke's "Ode on the Royal Visit to Canada," an impressive example of rhetorical verse, careful in structure, vigorous in phrasing, invites comparison. None of these is perhaps so moving as "Haunted," by Mrs. Mary Quayle Innis:

> When I come suddenly.
>   To an open door,
> Something I can almost see has gone through it
>   Just before.
>
> From the dark pane
>   As I draw near,
> I see the silent, the invisible face
>   Disappear.

In the presence of those eight lines, comment is stilled; as it is almost stilled too by Mr. Pratt's verses (like Mrs. Innis's they appeared in *Saturday Night):*

> To the poets who have fled
> To pools where little breezes dusk and shiver,
> Who need still life to deliver
> Their souls of their songs –

There are roses blanched of red
In the Orient gardens, Japanese urns to limn
With delicate words, and enough wrongs
To exhaust an Olympian quiver,
And time, be it said,
For a casual hymn
To be sung for the hundred thousand dead
In the mud of the Yellow River.

These lines, abounding in echoes, bursting with substance, varying from foot to foot, seem at first utterly unlike the verses of Mrs. Innis. They have the same absolute integrity; and at the end of this review of our poetry in 1939, it is pleasant to note that 1940 will bring Mr. Pratt's heroic narrative of the Jesuit Martyrs.

1940

In 1940, along with many works of minor distinction, three volumes of great importance and astonishing originality appeared: Mr. Pratt's *Brbeuf and His Brethren,* Mr. Klein's *Hath Not a Jew . . .,* and Mr. Kirkconnell's *The Flying Bull and Other Tales.* It was a great year.

The history of Canada abounds in great subjects for fiction, drama, and poetry; and it has been a standing complaint that writers have either declined to present them at all or have presented them in a manner so painfully inadequate that silence seemed better. The choice of one such subject by our noblest living poet is a white milestone in the development of Canadian literature. For dealing with the heroism of the Jesuit Martyrs Mr. Pratt has remarkable qualifications. He is a scholarly poet and a great deal of patient digging into records and of travel in Huronia preceded the composition: the facts are sound. He has in all his work shown a passionate imaginative sympathy with the heroic ideal; and in the moments when religion has been an element in his poetry his emotion has been strong and noble: the note is true.

The soundness of the facts together with the truth of the note has enabled him to reconstruct the conditions spiritual, intellectual, and material, in which the Jesuits made their difficult way into the wilderness of Ontario, impressed affection, respect and fear upon the savages, and steadily contemplated (for long years before its endurance) the fate of martyrdom. Others who have attempted to present in imaginative writing the same great subject have found it impossible to individuate the members of the Order, all concentrated on the same exclusive end, and tempered by the same self-repressive discipline. Mr. Pratt, like Miss Cather, was happy to discover the peculiarity in

Nol Chabanel, incapable, do what he would, of accustoming himself to the filth and grossness in the Indian way of living; he has also lingered rather affectionately over De Nou's incapacity to acquire the speech of his flock; but with many of the principal figures, with Gabriel Lalemant and Jogues, for instance, and even Brbeuf himself, the quest for individuation has not been wholly successful. Brbeuf is the towering lord, and by the elaborate presentation of his states of mind, as well as his exploits, he is securely kept at the centre of the mental stage, even when someone else is the momentary theme; but from Jogues and Gabriel Lalemant his difference is merely one of degree.

How serious is the failure to individuate? It was no part of Mr. Pratt's conception to make his martyrs, even Brbeuf, rounded complex human figures. They are heroes on the epic plane, for whom we are to feel not sympathy or pity so much as unwavering and unvaried admiration. We know that there will be no flinching from the torture, no hesitation as to duty. Each successive evidence of epic heroism, far from astonishing, merely confirms expectation. We are perhaps a little curious not about the measure of their calm strength, but about its source; Mr. Pratt, recognizing the soundness of the curiosity, satisfies it at the close of Brbeuf's torture in a passage among the most moving and finished he has ever written:

Nor in the symbol of Richelieu's robes, or the seals
Of Mazarin's charters, nor in the stir of the *lilies*
Upon the Imperial folds; nor yet in the words
Loyola wrote on a table of lava-stone
In the cave of Manresa – not in these the source –
But in the sound of invisible trumpets blowing
Around two slabs of board, right-angled, hammered
By Roman nails and hung on a Jewish hill.

Such poetry as *Brbeuf and His Brethren* aims not at the realization of human figures but at the communication of epic emotion, and this is possible without individuation of character.

It is possible, in part at least, because of the movement of the verse. Wisely Mr. Pratt has abandoned his rushing trenchant octosyllabics; and as a result this is the quietest of his poems, the most meditative and the most elevated, marked by such lines as

Before the casual incident of death.
Within the grass and reeds along the shore.

Blank verse has seldom had a slower movement than it has in this poem, most notably in the conclusion,[1] too long a passage to be quoted, but well represented by its perfect closing line:

And prayers ascend and the Holy Bread is broken.

The poem is notable too for its imagery. In his earlier poetry, in spite of an occasional unforgettable image such as the comparison of the cachalot to Gibraltar,

Silent and sinister and gray
As in a lifting fog at dawn
Gibraltar rises from its bay,

the emotional effect depended to an extraordinary degree on sound, and scarcely at all on picture. In *Brébeuf* there is a multitude of great images: the comparison, for instance, of wild geese to wedges driven through the zodiac, of Brébeuf's great height to a totem-pole, of iron chips drawn by a magnet to the swarming of bees. The poem is moreover packed with vivid and accurate vignettes of savage life and customs.

Mr. Pratt has given us something great. Some of the qualities that enriched his earlier work have been held in abeyance: rollicking would have been improper, humour and exuberance of any sort could be but sparingly introduced; the only kind of vigour appropriate was a chastened and quiet vigour; expansiveness was unfitting. In place of such qualities we are given, along with craftsmanship of the

---

[1] A limited edition appeared before the end of 1940 in which the last fifty lines were expanded to about seventy-five, and what is here described as the conclusion (the passage beginning "Three hundred years have gone but the voice that led") was clearly divided from the rest of the poem and entitled "The Martyrs' Shrine." The conclusion in its new and expanded form has greater intensity of emotion, partly because it more strictly contemplates the heroic past as the antecedent of the present. The Macmillan Company have presented the poem, in the limited edition, in a format of striking excellence.

most considered fineness, loftiness and calm.

For at least ten years the poems of Abraham Klein have been appearing in Canadian and American periodicals. In the epochal anthology, *New Provinces* (1936) he was represented by two long pieces, a rich-textured and learned study of Spinoza, "Out of the Pulver and the Polished Lens," and a robust and acrid study of Jewish life in contemporary Montreal, "Soirée of Velvel Kleinburger." The present collection contains neither the "Soirée" nor anything like it: Mr. Klein has preferred to limit it to those of his poems which deal with Jewish life in religious or universal terms, supposing, perhaps, that the local and immediate, if it were wholly secular, would strike false notes in the record and celebration of the race and its culture. In such a decision I believe he has made a mistake: to root his Jewish characters in their specific environment, to speak of streets and restaurants in his own Montreal was exactly what was needed to complete the effect of vitality which his work so magnificently achieves. We may hope for a second collection in which the local, the immediate, and the secular will have a generous and even a predominant place.

The great rabbis fascinate Mr. Klein's imagination, and he has the power to make them live for us as complex human individuals, each with some astounding oddity, the Baal Shem Tov, for instance, Master of the Name,

His memory ever splendid like a jewel,
His, who bore children on his back to school
And with a trick to silence their small grief
Crossed many a stream upon a handkerchief.

The ceremonies of the cult fascinate him no less, and again in these he presents vigorous humanizing touches, as when a junk-dealer raises his voice in the synagogue:

While litanies are clamored,
    His loud voice brags
A Hebrew most ungrammared.
    He sells God rags.

As this last passage suggests, the presentation of the Jewish religion is charming, homely, and wholly human. One of the most delightful of the poems is a little lyric on Reb Simcha, who, when the point of a pin was placed on a page of the *Talmud,* could immediately recite the word two hundred pages beneath the point, and of whom Mr. Klein divines

> . . . that in Paradise
> Reb Simcha, with his twinkling eyes,
> Interprets in some song-spared nook,
> To God the meaning of His book.

And there is Elijah who, to the annoyance of his fellow-rabbis, crows and dances in the market-place, tosses his skull-cap in the air, and as it falls

> . . . catches it neatly
> Right on his bald spot.

What to most Gentiles had seemed forbidding and alien is rendered perfectly familiar, unexpectedly attractive.

A loftier and even stern note sounds in other poems. At the end of "Childe Harold's Pilgrimage," a poem recording the varieties of Jewish tribulation since the diaspora, Mr. Klein speaks in his own person, stating his own mode of life and his counsel to his race:

> 'Tis not in me to unsheathe an avenging sword;
> I cannot don phylactery to pray;
> Weaponless, blessed with no works and much abhorred,
> This only is mine wherewith to face the horde:
> The frozen patience waiting for its day,
> The stance long-suffering, the stoic word. . . .

It would be an error to say that this is his only attitude: if it were, the joyous jesting, the intimate familiarity with sacred things, would have been impossible. To be aware of the outsider's frown is to be incapable of a light and happy handling of one's religion.

In the Jewish tradition one of the chief glories is erudition; and Mr. Klein's poetry is erudite. In some quarters Mr. Klein has been rebuked for his difficulty; but the rebuke is mistaken. Mr. Eliot, one of his principal masters in form, has once and for all demonstrated that learned poetry can be deeply felt, deeply imagined, and a perfect communication to its proper reader. The time has come when it should be frankly said that the comments on contemporary verse made by critics to whom Mr. Eliot is still something of a drunken helot are without any validity.

The third major volume of the year is Mr. Watson Kirkconnell's *The Flying Bull and Other Tales,*[2] a collection of seventeen narratives, the first preceded by a general prologue and each of the others by a briefer prologue of its own. The tales are told in the hotel of a Manitoba town, where travellers are marooned by a blizzard, and local worthies, unable to go about their tasks, find the warmth and jollity of the room a magnet. The resemblance to the general scheme of the *Tales of a Wayside Inn* is patent; but from the learned man of letters that Mr. Kirkconnell has proved himself to be one might have expected a really Chaucerian prologue in which the personalities, behaviour and apparel of the group would have been fixed for us once and for all. One might also have expected – something that Longfellow as well as Chaucer has given – a variety of metre and stanza: throughout all the prologues and all the tales he keeps to rhyming octosyllabics, reminiscent of Mr. Pratt. There is little effort to establish characteristic idioms for the several tales. We are warned that in "The Drummer's Tale" we shall have to do with

A salesman supercharged with slang,

and there is indeed more slang, usually happily employed, than in any other tale, but even here the difference of manner is not marked. The language of "The Poet's Tale" is more learned and elaborate than that of the other narrators. In general, however, the resources of differentiated idiom have been refused.

For these wasted opportunities there is rich and varied compensation. The language is almost always realistic in diction and in pace, with lapses only now and then into the worn ways of poetic phrasing; there is in many a line a vivid imaginative power; and the vigour and quickness of the narrative seldom abate. The substance of the tales is more interesting than the form. In seven of them Mr.

[2]Another narrative, quite worthy of those in his volume, is *A Western Idyll,* which Mr. Kirkconnell issued separately in the Christmas season.

Kirkconnell deals with the subject of his special competence, the lives of New Canadians – Hungarians, Czechs, Bulgarians, Poles, Russians, Ukrainians, Germans, Swedes, and Icelanders; and, in some, racial differences play a dramatic role. In one gripping tale of a boy's killing of a Winnipeg policeman and then committing suicide there are reflections which remind us that the poet is the author of a treatise on unemployment; and in general there is maturity of thought which could only have come from close observation of the Canadian scene and careful reflection upon it. What is most impressive – and it is something his previous writings had not prepared us for – is the power to communicate grisly horror. Such horror is a recurrent theme, lending a tonal unity to the collection, and in the final tale, the poet's own, it culminates in a nightmare of the race of man hunted down by dinosaurs and pterodactyls of steel; on this tale the last comment is – and it is made by the wisest and gentlest of all the personages, a *métis* priest:

My guess is that he dreamed it waking
And that its trend is all too true.

Again and again in *Bar-Room Ballads* the old familiar note of Mr. Robert Service resounds. Who but he would begin a ballad with a queer mixture of Swinburne and a rowdy song:

Now Fireman Flynn met Hank the Finn where lights of Lust-land glow,

or declaim – is this Swinburne plus Sandburg? –

Now there was I, a husky guy, whose god was Nicotine.

In this collection there are half a dozen ballads in which he returns to the frozen north which his imagination was the first to animate and populate. These are good, in their kind. It is a pity that they are hemmed in by personal lyrics in which the disguise of the tough guy – a thorough and a pleasing one – is dropped and a sentimentalist talks of saccharine things. Not all the personal lyrics have a sentimental flatness or syrupiness. There is a sonnet written in Warsaw on the outbreak of the war in which authentic strength of feeling is controlled and patterned by a sharp sense of form; there is a poem on war-time parades, where the emotion is so violent it could not be contained in its form and the effect is raw and hoarse; and there are some charming reflective pieces (why will Mr. Service insist he cannot think and does not like to observe the process?). It is curious to note the eleven books of verse he would have on the bookshelf of his affectionate admiration: *The Rubaiyat, The Ancient Mariner, The Ballad of Reading Gaol, A Shropshire Lad,* the verse of Burns, Bret Harte, Eugene Field, Henley, Kipling, Chesterton, and Masefield. All are vigorous emphatic poetry, very masculine, very intense, very rebellious. But one had not expected to find Housman named; and little of Housman's art has found its way into his own work. If it had – but Mr. Service is too old for conjecture about his potentialities to be useful.

Lava has the same general qualities as Miss Irene Moody's previous collection, *Attar of Song* (1936). Tribute was paid in these columns to the intense emotion and the variety and felicity in metre and structure which distinguished the best pieces in that volume; and reference was made also to the lusciousness of phrase and the pseudo-philosophical verbiage which marred it. The weaknesses are there in the new volume, in increased proportion – all too often they are so obtrusive as to nullify the excellences. In the later pages there are some of the strongest emotional reactions to the war that Canadian literature has yet registered; but the reaction is too often crude, too seldom heightened and refined by artistic contemplation and patterning. Finer war-verse than Miss Moody's, indeed the finest in 1940, apart from Sir Charles Roberts's contributions to *Saturday Night,* comes in Mr. A. M. Stephen's *Lords of the Air.* In many of his poems there is a fine blending of vigour of feeling, strenuousness of thought, and resonance of line.

More finished and more satisfying in form, Miss Frances Angus's collection of lyrics, *As We Are,* is long overdue. For years in many Canadian periodicals, and in some outside Canada, her poems have been steadily appearing, always firm in language, clear, fine and controlled in emotion. Brought together they reveal an unexpected breadth in her response to nature: the sea shore, the hills, and the great lakes all move her profoundly. Here is genuine poetry, limited in theme and aim, but rarely defective in performance. Another volume formally satisfying is Miss Phyllis Comyn Clarke's *From the Canadian Prairies,* which contains, along with a few other brief pieces, a score of sonnets. The sonnets especially have a precise and tranquil beauty; but Miss Clarke's poems have less intensity than those of Miss Moody or Miss Angus, and in her collection there is some monotony of tone. Miss Joan Buckley's *Green Flame* is introduced by Mr. Wilson Macdonald, who describes her work as "dance-rhythms for the soul." The rhythms are perhaps the least impressive quality in the collection: what strikes one most and most repeatedly, is a strange power of phrase, giving an astonishing and even memorable quality to lines and stanzas, but leaving one usually disappointed in the total effect of the poems. In Mrs. Janet Pollock Graham's *From Hill and Dell,* despite much outworn diction and some conventionality in the approach to experience, there is a steady sweetness of melody. Among the new Ryerson Chap-Books the most distinguished is that of Mr. Arthur Bourinot, *Discovery.* Many of the qualities of form and feeling that marked his larger collection, *Under the Sun* (1939), commented upon rather fully in this place a year ago, reappear in the five poems in his new booklet. His readiness to experiment continues to be notable; but one wishes that in his experimental verse Mr. Bourinot could demonstrate the fine economy of phrase that gave beauty to his sonnets. In *The Pioneers and Other Poems,* Mrs. Glynn-Ward gives vigorous and melodious rhythms, often in the form and tone of ballads, but the words and even the rhymes leave one with a wish for more fineness and precision. Such fineness is an almost constant trait in the little collection of Miss Verna Loveday Harden, *Postlude to an Era,* introduced by Mr. Nathaniel Benson. In the softer pieces there is an admirable marriage of feeling and expression; but in the poems where the feeling has energy, and there are many of these, the expression disappoints by its persistent lightness and simplicity of music. In Mr. Fletcher Ruark's *Red Wind and Other Poems,* his first collection since 1934, dignity and depth of thought, and a measure of intensity of emotion, are too often betrayed by language. Language is also the betrayer, and rhythm as well, in Miss Margaret Harvey Wilton's *Pageantry of Days,* in which the choice of theme and an occasional line promise superior performance to come.

Two poems quite unlike anything so far mentioned, and each appearing as a brochure, claim special consideration: they are Professor George Herbert Clarke's *McMaster University, 1890-1940, Commemoration Ode* and Mr. John A. B. McLeish's *Not Without Beauty.* Mr. McLeish's poem, about one hundred and fifty lines in length, is a remarkable fusion of rugged realism and vivid imaginative picture, echoes of Eliot and Sandburg effectively combining in it with suggestions of a more individual idiom, the whole communicating the feel of a railway town in the evening. Undoubtedly Mr. McLeish is one of the most original poets to appear in Canada in the past decade; and his originality, applied as it is here, to the evocation and interpretation of experience, is a power for whose later realizations we shall look with more than mere curiosity. Professor Clarke conceives the solemn ode in the grand manner of nineteenth-century poetry, filling it with pictures and reflections, and manipulating with expertness a complicated stanzaic scheme. In his work there is much to admire: but the flame of originality is not there – in none of the pictures or words or thoughts is there anything which can halt us in delighted surprise.

So rich was the year in poetry that it is impossible to comment at the usual length on the booklets of the poetry societies or the verse appearing in periodicals. Neither the booklets nor the periodical verse differ notably from those of previous years: the main organs continue to furnish generous space for the poets and to exercise, on the whole, real discrimination. One exception to the silence which the limits of space impose must be made in favour of Mr. Ralph Gustafson's group of eight poems published in the April number of the *Sewanee Review.* In these pieces there is a continued expertness and finish throughout a great variety of forms and moods: from Mr. Gustafson a lyrical collection of original vigour and fineness will come, we hope, before the end of 1941.

1941

Last year it was with Mr. Pratt's *Brébeuf and His Brethren*[1] that the survey of Poetry began. No one will dispute the claim of his *Dunkirk* to the place of honour this year. *Dunkirk* is not one of his principal works; it takes its place rather as a brilliant experiment which suggests widening and deepening power and points to something in the future grander and bigger than itself. It is doubtful, however, if in the whole history of our poetry any volume has had so wide a distribution and such an immediate effect. From the popular recognition that the poem has had it would be foolish to deduce that our poetic taste has improved: verses about the wistaria by the verandah, and the moon through the pines, and violet eyes, are as likely as ever to win places in scrap-books – and poetic competitions – closed to Mr. A. J. M. Smith and Mr. Abraham Klein. Still, it may be hoped that a poem read often for purely extraliterary reasons may bring some of its readers to a purer taste. It may be hoped that they will be affected for longer than a moment by such lines as:

> Children of oaths and madrigals . . .

> If pierced they do not feel the cut,
> And if they die, they do not suffer death.

In the former, a summing up of the English people, Mr. Pratt has quietly achieved one of those jarring juxtapositions which give one of its principal beauties to modern verse; and in the latter, with equal quietness, he ends a passage in which, after a rough mass of mechanical terms, he

---

[1] The Governor-General's medal for poetry was awarded to his work, and seldom has a committee's decision been so obviously right.

voices the feeling of desperate men pitted against the panzers, a feeling in which awe and infinite fatigue blend with an inarticulate questioning of the essential nature of things.

The subject was perfect for the poet. His preoccupation with the huge and powerful, with great ships and great primeval beasts, makes him sensitive to the force of German machines. His ever-growing sympathy with man, which has given to his recent works a sense for the tragic formerly lacking to his approach, enables him to communicate pity and terror together, in the section where the English wait helpless on the beaches. The savoury incongruities of human contacts abound as the makeshift flotillas of rescue set out from the English shore. The reader remembers the passages in *The Titanic* which described the life on that ship just before the iceberg crashed into her; but in *Dunkirk* there is a sharper naturalism in the dialogue and in the brief descriptive comments, and there is a frankly comic quality in the rhymes. The comment made last year that in *Brébeuf* Mr. Pratt held his comic and humorous powers in restraint does not apply to *Dunkirk*, in which humour and tragedy, the heroic and the pathetic jostle one another with rugged effectiveness.

The final note is, as always with Mr. Pratt, the heroic. The sea becomes a *deus ex machina;* fog and fleet combine to rescue those who had appeared irreclaimably lost. After the varied excitements of the piece a calm sets in with the fog; the worn-out men, the motley ships, move in silence towards the white shores, up the hidden harbours and the quiet rivers. The calm is not one of exhaustion: it is the calm following upon triumph. As one reads the last lines, different as they are in rhythm and diction from the close of *Brébeuf,* it is of that noble epilogue that one thinks, with its perfect final line:

And prayers ascend, and the Holy Bread is broken.

II

In 1941, far more than in 1940, the theme of the war was running through our poetry: the increased emphasis shows how closely and quickly Canadian poetry catches the surface, and some of the depth, of Canadian life.

After *Dunkirk* the most impressive of the poems related to the conflict was Mr. Ralph Gustafson's *Epithalamium in Time of War*. Like so much of the best in contemporary verse it fuses an Elizabethan largeness of sound with a peculiarly modern ellipticalness and compactness of meaning. So few will, for the present, read it[2] that a rather extended quotation may be forgiven. The closing movement, with its rich reminiscence of Gerard Hopkins, is this:

Now is the holy time, sweet noon.
Within this chapel's candled dusk
Does love lack loss, place glory on.
Gain gladness! Against these eastward two,
Take angles, sights, high orthogon;
Mortally, measure against, risk,
Arrive at, solve, survey His sun!
God's binder goes. Golden through
His gates they come! Now belfry, ring!
Love, them, each living thing, renew!
To her, to him, His blessings bring.

Here is inspired imitation, which goes near to the core of Hopkin's method, going as it does to what is most personal in his rhythms and diction. In the passage Mr. Gustafson's own personal stamp is obvious – the lightness of musical and intellectual pace, easily distinguishable from Hopkins's quickness, in a kind of daintiness.

The slim brochure *Canada Speaks of Britain*, issued by Sir Charles Roberts, in the interests of the War Services Library Council, has three parts, the first with eight new poems responding to various phases of the present war, the second with three poems representing his poetry at the time of the first World War, the third reprinting the lyrics of peace in the little chap-book *Twilight over Shaugamauk* (1937). It is interesting that Sir Charles's temper, tone and diction should have altered so little in the past quarter-century: in the new pieces there is a slight tendency towards greater simplicity (a simplicity suggesting Housman in the

---

[2]Privately printed in an edition of one hundred, the work is a notably beautiful example of the printer's and the binder's craft.

powerful "Epitaph for a Young Airman"), a tendency a little more marked towards broken rhythms; of vigour there is scarcely any loss, in intensity a gain – "Forget Not, Thou," is probably the fiercest poem of any aesthetic merit to come out of Canada since the present war began. Sir Charles has never written a sonnet more carefully designed or more firmly phrased than the poem which gives this collection its title. Line after line is a triumph of art:

> Smite her, and we are smitten; wound her, we bleed . . . .

> Stands she, and shall; – but not by guns alone . . . .

> > . . . her own
> Will, hammered to temper, – keeps her whole . . . .

It should be said that this sonnet was composed at the time of the heavy bombings – late in the summer of 1940.

Another brochure, similar in intent, is *Lift Up Your Hearts* by Canon Frederick George Scott; the themes and the forms are much the same as in *Canada Speaks of Britain;* but Canon Scott's verse, charming and musical as it almost always is, lacks the concentration and the vitality of Sir Charles Roberts'. A like criticism is invited by Mr. Arthur Nash's little collection of lyrics entitled *The Drama of Dunquerque.* Echoing constantly the metre of *The Ancient Mariner.* Mr. Nash's verse is injured by a general negligence in language – a satisfaction with the approximate word or phase – which not even the swiftness of the movement can obscure.

The anthology *Voices of Victory: Representative Poetry of Canada in Wartime,* has been the subject of a scathing review-article in the *Canadian Forum* (February, 1942). When that article is read in conjunction with the afterword to the volume, the impression created is that the little book is the most confusingly complicated undertaking in the literary history of this country. The nucleus was a competition with prizes, conducted by the Poetry group of the Toronto branch of the Canadian Authors' Association: the three prize-winning poems and twenty, thought (for reasons sometimes exceedingly hard to discover) deserving of honourable mention, begin the book. It is curious that six among the twenty have no relevance to the war, and some of these six moreover are the dreamy stuff that suits a heavy summer afternoon. The poem awarded the principal prize does relate to war but it also belongs to lotus-land. Twenty-seven among those whom the Poetry group of the Toronto branch of the Canadian Authors' Association considers the eminent poets of Canada were invited to contribute, but enjoined against taking up too much space. Their work is (for reasons not quite so hard to discover) mixed up in strictly alphabetical arrangement with a dozen poems written by members of the sponsoring group. One American poet insisted on his inclusion; and the sponsors, thinking perhaps (and this time the reason is not at all hard to discover) that the plan of work was already in irremediable confusion, could not say him nay. At some stage in the compilation, Dr. Earle Birney, who subsequently wrote the *Forum* article, served as judge, throwing out a number of pieces which were promptly restored. Professor Birney's name is not one in the long list of those thanked in the luxuriant apparatus.

In the preface the hope is expressed that the collection "might make utterance for the Dominion." The volume contains poems unaware of the war, poems opposed to war, poems gloating over war, and poems – a very few – responding with power and insight to the development of the war. If the sponsors' wish was to emphasize to the point of distortion our national uncertainties, the divided counsels that impede our effort, they have succeeded. I do not attribute this aim to them: I prefer to think that in gauging the aim of the book as in everything else they were muddled.

Here and there the collection contains excellent pieces: none perhaps so much as Mr. Leo Kennedy's address to the intellectuals entitled "The Eagles" – it was written in 1937, its theme was the Spanish War.

III

The Ryerson Chap-Books were this past year more numerous and more varied than usual. Among them the outstanding work is Miss Anne Marriott's *Calling Adventurers,* which consists of the choruses in a radio-drama, entitled

"Payload" and having to do with flying in the far north. In his second book on Canada, M. André Siegfried remarked that every country has its vital dream about which its most powerful imaginative energies cluster; the Canadian dream, he suggested, is of the limitless cold-lit spaces of the north. Few of our aesthetic expressions have dealt with it, and M. Siegfried would say that our imaginative maturity – on which our social maturity partially depends – waits upon our understanding of the crucial role of this northern dream. Some understanding of it Miss Marriott displays, although her choruses have not the power she had through-out *The Wind Our Enemy* (1939). Her new work is not so sure in style or tone, it is not so vivid in perception, not so deep in feeling. Miss Marriott is less at home in the north than on the drought-ridden prairie: she approaches the north more externally, more as surface than as reality. Still, her choruses are full of striking lines, and here and there she finds a memorable way of suggesting some aspect of the northern dream, speaking of a land of "mud-green grass-haired muskegs," of "gray lakes flung like polished stones on to the land," of "traps of glare ice, blue smooth treachery," enchanting

Men whose bones ache in cities,
Who long for a land too large for them.

What is striking in Miss Amelia Wensley's *At Summer's End* is an uneven quality of diction, rising in a few passages to imaginative distinction, but too often imitative and at times even quite inappropriate in tone. Her most successful poems are nature-pieces. Nature is also the theme of Mrs. Mary Matheson's fifteen sonnets in *Out of the Dusk,* and again one's attention fastens on the diction. Some of the lines are eighteenth-century – weak eighteenth-century – in diction, and in rhythm, as for instance:

Dawn rides triumphant o'er the silver plain
And shakes his golden head in laughter gay.

Within one sonnet are packed the loosely romantic "span," "scanning," "girds," "daunt," "fray," " 'tis," "cleave," and "bosom." There is a conspicuous lack of clearness, sharp-ness and intensity. Mr. Nathan Ralph's *Twelve Poems* are preceded by a passionate lament of Thomas Wolfe's. Between its rude intensity and the rather gentle melancholy of the poems it is hard to establish an emotional connection. Mr. Ralph's treatment of nature – and much of his work has nature for theme or at least for symbol – is undistinguished; and in his treatment of human feeling the subject is rarely matched by the work, the image or the rhythm. Mrs. Mollie Morant's *The Singing Gipsy* has two quite different styles, one rich and romantic, suggesting Tennyson, another vigorous and rather bare. The rich style is weighted with the words and phrases of nineteenth-century verse and seldom carries the weight with the erectness that springs from original and intense feeling. The bare style is seldom sustained through more than three or four lines, and the effect produced when the styles mingle is not a happy one. In the thirteen little pieces that make up Miss Sara Carsley's *The Artisan* the predominant note is the slightly old-fashioned grace that has marked so many of her poems. "The Little Boats of Britain," a Dunkirk piece, is strikingly different from the others: it is vigorous and eager, but surely the movement is too rollicking for the theme. In Miss Doris Ferne's *Ebb Tide* there is more depth than in any of the other chap-books, Miss Marriott's excepted, not intellectual depth, but personal depth, richness and maturity of being. The collection is not even in excellence; the tribute to Nijinsky has an oddly bathetic end, and the symmetry of "Unease" is simply mechanical; but at her best, in certain lines of the title poem, and in the sustained imaginative vitality of the sonnet "Memory," she accomplishes very good things indeed.

Several numbers have appeared in a new series, the Carillon Poetry Chap-Books, published by the Crucible Press under the editorship of Miss Hilda Ridley. These are notably larger than those in the Ryerson series, and some of them have fuller biographical information; but they lack the attractiveness in cover-design, type and paper that has always distinguished the Ryerson Chap-Books, and their poetic standard is sadly inferior. The most interesting to come out this past year is Mr. William Dobree Calvert's *Ypnos;* but it is no service to Mr. Calvert, who has a rich imagination and a striking variety in themes, for the general editor to assert that "there are lines in this poem that equal those penned by Keats and Wordsworth." Some of the most horrible lines in the language were "penned" by these two poets; it is a poor compliment to anyone to say that his best is better than the worst of theirs; and the meaning which I think the general editor intended – that Mr. Calvert's best lines are as good as the best of the two romantic masters – is a foolish compliment against which poets should be ensured. A word should be said of Miss Kathleen Earle's *Spindrift,* which, amid much that is uncertain in tone and diction, has lines and even stanzas of notable power.

Among the publications of groups much the most striking is the *Victoria Poetry Chapbook.* An astonishing number of the most original and accomplished of the younger Canadian poets are in British Columbia, and among these the most promising are in relation with the Victoria poetry group. Of special distinction in this collection are the poems of Miss Anne Marriott, Miss Doris Ferne, Mrs. Floris Clark McLaren and Miss Pauline Havard.

Another quarterly has come to join the *Canadian Poetry Magazine* in the service of Canadian writers of verse. Mr. Alan Crawley and some other poets in British Columbia have initiated *Contemporary Verse,* a genuine "little review," mimeographed and very thin. The first number, issued in September, set an admirable standard, maintained and even raised in the second, drawing on poets in other parts of the nation and in exile. Mr. A. J. M. Smith's "The Face" startles with that vital imagery of which he has the secret and abounds in those strange, somewhat blunt verbal effects which suggest the individuality of his ways of feeling. It is significant of his evolution as a mind and a person that the poem ends on the note which was Mr. Eliot's in "Ash Wednesday":

And he may live by grace
Who wills to act.

Mr. Leo Kennedy is represented by one of his gay pieces in which delicacy and volume combine to produce an effect of depth exceedingly rare in our humorous verse. The other poems are all admirable in their diverse ways. The hospitable greeting given by the *Canadian Poetry Magazine* was another instance of Mr. Pratt's kindness; and I join with him in saying that this new venture merits not only eulogy but support.

Mention may perhaps be permitted here of the collection of Canadian verse which occupied the April number of *Poetry*. I was asked by Mr. George Dillon, the editor of that magazine, to undertake such a collection, in order that American interest in Canadian writing might be quickened at a time when all that touches Canada has taken on a new life for Americans. The issue was well received in the American (and Canadian) press; and it is a source of gratification that the group of lyrics contributed by Mr. A. J. M. Smith won an important award.

IV

It remains to notice some volumes of varying worth and tendency. Among them perhaps the most interesting is Mr. Leo Cox's *North Star*. Many of our poets publish their first collection of verse ten or twenty years too late; some console themselves for the delay by issuing a chap-book or two, not appreciating, perhaps, how inadequate a basis a chap-book provides for the observation and estimate of a poet's range. *North Star* comes much later than one would have wished in a career which has elements of great interest. One need only look at the table of contents to note the special place Mr. Cox has begun to fill, as the poet of the Quebec landscape in its bolder and sterner aspects, of Labrador, and of the waters of the Gulf. For stimuli so powerful the emotions that the poems record are surprisingly gentle; of him as of so many Canadian poets one must say that there is an edulcoration of some of the loftiest material in the world. Again and again one comes on such phrases as "old grief in sweet Romaine," "the misty lanes of old Bonne Bay," "mirrors the cloudy patterns of the moon." Such phrases have an undeniable beauty; but they seem dissonant in the setting of bleak grandeur that Mr. Cox prefers. When he abandons his favourite themes, he is less at ease, less individual, and therefore less interesting. The leading piece, "Ode after Harvest," is full of agreeable echoes, chiefly of Keats, from whose odes are taken the stanza and the rhythm. The more meditative poems also fall short of excellence: feeling and thought are not so well fused as feeling and picture were in the poems about Quebec.

In his preface to Mr. Arthur Bourinot's *Selected Poems* (1935), Sir Andrew Macphail commented on the "close scrutiny of nature, selection of the beautiful, largeness of idea, depth of emotion, and delicacy of phrase," all of which were to be found in the volume. To the poems in *What Far Kingdom*[3] some of these phrases do not seem wholly appropriate. Mr. Bourinot has for some years sought to liberalize his practice; and he has not often or for long at a time succeeded in achieving an effect of beauty in freedom comparable to the beauty in restraint that marked some of his earlier sonnets, especially those in the sequence called "In Memory of My Mother." In his most recent collection he is various in form and tone, ranging from the dramatic monologue through the nature lyric in the manner of Carman to the epigrammatic comment. The monologues are always interesting, but they do not set the impress of the character upon the turns of thought or phrase and in the end the effect produced is not dramatic but narrative. The nature lyrics are more moving, but for all their felicities of diction, and sometimes of movement (it is in his rhythms that Mr. Bourinot is least evenly excellent), they do not picture as Lampman could or suggest with the strange power of Duncan Campbell Scott. The epigrammatic comments are more satisfying; but in them one misses that weight of significance, that constantly widening aura of suggestion, that mark the epigrammatic comment of Robert Frost. High standards are implied in the names mentioned; but it is by such standards that Mr. Bourinot's poetry requires to be judged.

Like Mr. Bourinot, Mrs. Carol Cassidy has been expanding and varying her expression since in 1939 her chap-book *Fancy Free* appeared. Of her work in *Poems*, as of his, one may say that although the experimentation is admirable the finest effects she has yet attained are those in the old

---

[3] The last five poems in the collection are reprinted from the chap-book *Discovery* (1940).

manner. Her years in the Orient and her sensitive response to Japanese poetry led her to an extraordinary competence and often a sharp, clear beauty in the pieces in which she pictures or reflects. Sometimes she is imaginative as in:

When you lifted your voice
it was as if you snared
a frail and beating butterfly
between your thumb and forefinger,
and crushed its innocent loveliness
to a cruel powder.

Sometimes she is merely descriptive, but with what insight!

Japanese prows are optimistic
and haughty.

They tilt their noses proudly,
whether in a baffling sea,
or beached,
waiting for battle.

In everything that is crisp and compact she is a distinguished artist. However, it is probably the longer poems in this collection that point to her future course, poems in which emotion dominates picture. In these there is a fine aesthetic quality which may be called the "effect of distance"; ideas, feelings, even objects, take on simple contours, as if seen from another world. But the effect of distance seems aesthetically incompatible with occasional sudden rushes of warmth which communicate a shock that does not seem to have been designed. With the astonishing technical powers shown in the brief poems, it is proper to hope that sometime Mrs. Cassidy will present large subjects in a large way without a flaw.

On Mr. Arthur Stringer's *The King Who Loved Old Clothes* and Mrs. Edna Jaques' *Aunt Hattie's Place* no comment is needed. These poets have for many years written without significant change in manner or in theme. The limitations which have been noted in previous surveys exist today as conspicuously as ever. Miss Clara Bernhardt's *Far Horizon*, on the other hand, shows a maturing of the poet's sensibility and an increased command of techniques. In the sequence of seven sonnets with which the little brochure closes, the advance in power is specially notable. A new tendency is also evident in Sister Maura's *The Rosary*, a sequence of fifteen meditations on the mysteries of the Blessed Virgin, preceded and followed by simple hymns. Richness of language and definiteness of design cannot conceal, or compensate, rhythms that fail to satisfy partly because of occasional awkwardness, partly because of incongruity with the substance.

Only the briefest comment is possible upon the quality of the verse appearing in periodicals. There is more light-hearted verse than usual; the war bulks larger, as it does in the verse appearing between boards; the balance between traditional and experimental forms is still heavily in favour of the former. Perhaps it will not be invidious to call attention to two admirable pieces, both by writers as yet little known, Miss E. Garrett's "Fable," which came out in *Saturday Night*, and Dr. Earle Birney's "David," which he gave, as one would expect, to the *Canadian Forum*. "Fable" is a brief, rhetorical meditation on the loneliness symbolized by the unicorn; "David" is a long narrative of a tragic ascent in the Rockies; both are individual and both have structure and unusual emotional power.

1942

In 1942 the most notable book was a first collection, Mr. Earle Birney's *David and Other Poems*. The title piece alone would have sufficed to make it so. David is a narrative of a kind new to our poetry, matter-of-fact in manner and, until the crisis is reached, matter-of-fact in substance also. It is a tale of two young men climbing mountains along the British Columbian coast, David an experienced mountaineer, Bobbie a novice. The early sections of the poem – it comes just short of two hundred lines – are rich in pictures and impressions, in passages such as

> Then the darkening firs
> And the sudden whirring of water that knifed down a
> fern-hidden
> Cliff and splashed unseen into mist in the shadows

and

> Coming down we picked in our hats the bright
> And sunhot raspberries, eating them under a mighty
> Spruce, while a marten moving like quicksilver scouted
> us

passages which for all their detail are full of vitality and suggestion, urging the reader to participate fully in the experience of the characters. These early sections carry also a load of learning, the mountaineer's learning of rocks and fossils, a load perhaps heavier than the prevailing note of simplicity requires. The two characters are securely realized, the relation between them is warm without ceasing to be simple and clear. The tragedy comes quietly; Bobbie's foothold gives way and David instinctively turns in a trice to steady him; the added strain is enough to make David slide, and at once he is gone. It is all over in an instant, and the quickness is an essential part of the effect Mr. Birney is trying to produce. The central scene is yet to come: it is the dialogue between the two when Bobbie has made his way to where David lies partly paralysed. Mr. Birney has found simple words, brief phrases, which bear the weight of David's plea to be pushed from the ledge on which he is caught and die in a six hundred foot drop, and of Bobbie's plea that he wait till help can be brought. Bobbie yields, staggers back to camp, and

I said that he fell straight to the ice where they found him,
And none but the sun and the incurious clouds have lin-
                                              gered
Around the marks of that day on the ledge of the Finger,
That day, the last of my youth, on the last of our moun-
                                              tains.

It is impossible to overpraise that close: magic has entered in with the last line, giving an unpredictable extension of meaning, and at one stroke raising the experience of the poem to another level where pain and constraint and self-reproach are no longer matter-of-fact but full of tranquil-lizing imaginative suggestion.

David does not stand alone. I cannot fully share the admiration that has been lavished on the topical poem which closes the collection; I wish that the last third of *On Going to the Wars* had been suppressed and that it stopped with this passage of rough idealism:

I'll stand by those who strive to chart
A world where peace is everyone's,
A peace that does not rot the heart
With hunger, fear and hopeless hate,
Nor rust the cunning wheels nor still
The subtle fingers, peace that will
Unlock to every man the gate
To all the leaping joys his hand
Creates. For no less prize I stand.

This is admirable in itself and as an end, and since it comes at the bottom of an odd-numbered page I at first supposed it was the end. What follows seems to me much less strongly felt, much less clearly and vividly said. In the closing section there is a lack of that finish and richness of feeling which mark, for instance, the admirable *Dusk on English Bay,* one of the most moving war poems to come out of Canada. Here there is not space for comment on other pieces in the little collection – twenty-one poems in all – but space must be found to say that in Mr. Birney's work there is authentic originality; he owes nothing at all to earlier Canadian writing and scarcely anything – when he is fully himself – to recent verse anywhere else. He has a harsh and intense sensibility which make his pictures and rhythms fresh and living, and his technical accomplishment is brilliant, at times bewildering.

II

In 1941 Mr. Ralph Gustafson printed privately a beautiful little book with a delicate epithalamium for his sister. Almost uniform with it he has now brought out, again in an edition of one hundred copies, *Lyrics Unromantic,* a series of twelve love poems. In tone and form the range is remarkable: sometimes there is perfect simplicity as in

> A silent harbouring
>   Of nothing read,
> A silent remembering,
>   And it is said

and sometimes in elaborate and contorted poetry he is no less happy

> As though a clutch of stars
> Was a logicked thing;
> An esoteric moon
> A mastering!

It ought to be said that these stanzas lose much of their power when lopped off from their context, for Mr. Gustafson is the sort of poet whose texture is a unit whether it is all of a piece or a mosaic of fragments. If space sufficed I should like to quote an entire poem so that I might substantiate the judgment that in this collection is the most carefully wrought poetry of the year. Much as there is to praise and praise warmly, one may regret a constant resort to parenthetic thought and feeling and an occasional instance of obscurity so heavy that one wonders whether the editions are limited to one hundred copies because the author has lost interest in a larger and more miscellaneous audience than that of his close friends and a few fortunate reviewers.

Hardly less interesting than *Lyrics Unromantic* is *Salt Marsh,* the third of Miss Anne Marriott's chap-books. The first, *The Wind Our Enemy,* a narrative of drought on the prairies, at once gave her a secure place among the best of the younger poets; then came *Calling Adventurers,* a set of extracts from a radio drama, which could not produce a powerful total impression and showed no significant advance in texture; now *Salt Marsh,* a collection of thirty lyrics, enables us for the first time to surmise the range of her mind and art. The variety of theme is notable – love, religion, society, nature, each with several aspects; and the variety in form is no less notable, though not so easy to express. Miss Marriott has three main styles; one is smooth, corresponding to the kind of work she has described in one of the poems in this booklet.

> Words were easy other years, they came
> smoothly to talk of stone-brown streams, or trees
> that sang in sunlight, broken green and gold –
> no pain in these.

another is sharp and quick, the style of *Traffic Light,* for instance, in which objects are mentioned without being fully realized; and the third is tense and crammed, the style which abounds in compound epithets such as "rain-pitted" and "colour-roused," and more important, perhaps, in successions of pictures of what has somewhat repelled her sensibility, for example in *Salt Marsh* itself,

> Mud-green crabs scuttle sideways – in – out –
> slit-caved burrows. A flung-string clutter
> of washed weed shines – orange wire – on rush tops
> marsh buttercups' flat yellow.

It is this third style that seems most personal and interesting. It may be, however, that the second style would permit without any loss to its values a fuller realization of what it presents, and that it offers a better vehicle for great poetry. There is no doubt that what I have called the third style gives enormous emphasis to a very few aspects of the poet's sensibility, and accordingly threatens to establish what would be a mannerism rather than a manner. *Salt Marsh* is the most valuable of the year's chap-books, but what it reveals of Miss Marriott's range does not fully show anything beyond what *The Wind Our Enemy* showed or suggested and that poem will continue to be thought the highest of her achievements.[1]

An unusual and moving collection, though one not comparable in formal value with Mr. Gustafson's or Miss Marriott's, is Mr. J. S. Wallace's *Night is Ended*. It is a poignant book. Mr. Wallace has just emerged from two years in confinement, presumably as a supposed communist, and in his bunk at Petawawa and his cell at Hull wrote most of the best work in this volume. He has two accents – the martial and the melancholy: the martial poems, like so many of their kind, are over-rhetorical and verbally not more than half alive, but the melancholy personal pieces are often wholly admirable in their intensity, economy and clarity. Now and then, especially in the poems on Spain, the martial poetry borrows some of these virtues.

III

Among the smaller collections of the year the Ryerson Chap-Books were outstanding. One of these, Miss Marriott's *Salt Marsh* has already been mentioned. Five others were added in 1942. Mr. Ernest Fewster's *Litany before the Dawn of Fire* consists of five poems of moderate length, each of them eloquent and dignified, and the first a solemn ode in the old-fashioned manner. Mrs. Barbara Villy Cormack's *Seedtime and Harvest* is a group of unpretending simple verses recording the feelings of a farmer's wife during the more active half of the year, feelings which are not

---

[1] *Calling Adventurers* received the Governor-General's award for poetry in 1941. It is understood that Mr. Pratt's *Dunkirk* was *hors concours*. Once more the judgment of the committee was intelligent and acceptable.

fully communicated since the responses she makes are so often stock responses. Mr. Hyman Edelstein's *Spirit of Israel* has two poems only, each of which seeks to suggest the life of the Jew in the big city, neither succeeding as Mr. Abraham Klein has so often succeeded, in realizing the splendour of the Jewish religion or the pain of Jewish contact with an alien world. What Mr. Edelstein has to say is important and at times profound but the manner of his saying it has little of Mr. Klein's depth and nothing of his magic. The characters in Miss M. Eugenie Perry's *Hearing a Far Call* do not come alive and the situation is not so treated as to disguise its essential commonplaceness, but there are passages in the narrative which have a pleasing music and in pure narrative Miss Perry is notable. Miss Mary Elizabeth Colman's *For This Freedom Too* is the most interesting of the group. More than half of her sixteen pages go to one poem, *Hunger*, a bewildering piece, in which the development does not seem very certain and the emotions, if eager and tense, are expressed with such a flagging that all too often they become faint or commonplace. In the other poems, written in a quiet conversational manner, the power is conspicuous. They all have to do with the war and make one of the most thoughtful responses to the war.

The lack of intensity in language prevents Mr. James Edward Ward's *This England* from being the impressive and moving work intended. The time when a poet might write of a "verdant dell" or "tranquil vale" or of "lyric ditties" is not 1942. The diction of Mr. Gordon Dagger's *The Prospector and Other Poems* is sharper, and the rhythms have often a genuine music, but the approach to the material is radically unpoetic. *Afterdusk*, by Miss Mary Frances Edwards, abounds in genuinely poetic matter, but between this matter and the reader intervenes a medium of expression that is flat and often prosaic. Similarly in Miss E. Lillian Morley's *Watchwords of Liberty* the language stifles the undeniable emotion. Most of the poems in Miss Dorothy Dumbrille's *Last Leave* have to do with the anguish of a wife and mother in war-time; these read like extracts from a diary and the reader is made uncomfortable by an intimacy which is not always appropriate. In some fashion poetry must generalize emotion; and here it is wholly particular. *The Sky Was My Friend* is a memorial volume; after the death last spring of Miss Mary McCullough of Ottawa, her mother, with the aid of Miss Anne Marriott and Mr. Charles Clay, gathered the best of her work. Miss McCullough had the love of natural detail which has marked so many of the poets of the Ottawa valley, but the sifting of her verses has not been sufficiently severe: her reputation would stand higher if most of the poems with themes other than that of nature had been left out. The touch is uncertain, but there are moments of genuinely charming achievement.

More interesting for one reason or another than those volumes which have been surveyed in this section are four collections with which it must draw to a close. In Mrs. Lyon Sharman's *Town and Forest* an original mind with a delicate sense of language and a sharp imagination expresses itself in a great variety of moods. Mr. Arthur S. Bourinot's *Canada at Dieppe* is a stirring narrative, evoking our French origins and ties, and achieving in its carefully handled presentation of the great commando venture a notable variety in metrical form. Mr. John Elmoran Porter's *Furrow in the Dunes* has rich imagination and, in its simpler forms, a satisfying music. *Rhymes of a Western Logger,* as its title suggests, is another book in the Service tradition; but the vocabulary is so technical that the author, Mr. Robert E. Swanson, supplies a copious lexicon at the end. The technical language justifies itself by a frequent vigour of imagination. But as is usual in books of this sort the situations, characters and reflections – these last are abundant – are drawn from stock, and the poems do not arouse the emotions that Service at his rare best could be sure of stirring.

In the periodicals, notably in the *Canadian Poetry Magazine, Contemporary Verse,* and *Saturday Night,* the quality of work has been at least maintained. A tendency towards greater clarity and vigour can be easily discerned. A Montreal group has begun to issue a provocative and accomplished little mimeographed journal called *Previews.* The space I should like to give to these vehicles must go, however, to works of greater scope important to Canadian poetry as a whole.

Forty years ago William Archer brought out his *Poets of the Younger Generation* and among the thirty-three included there were three Canadians, Carman, C. G. D. Roberts, and Duncan Campbell Scott. When in the intervening years has an English critic of Archer's distinction mingled Canadian poets with English in a book of criticism, or even in an anthology? Within the period that has seen the rise of E. J. Pratt and the Montreal men our poetry has circulated within a national wall, and American as well as English readers have not cared to know what was going on inside. The appearance in the Pelican Books of Mr. Gustafson's *Anthology of Canadian Poetry (English)* is an attempt, which promises success, to get our poetry over the national wall, and accordingly it is an event of extreme importance. Wishing to show the range as well as the quality of our poetry he has presented selections from fifty-eight authors, and to none of them has he allowed more than six pages in the hundred of which the text consists. The principle of variety is one of the many good principles on which an anthology can be built, although I should not have used it for the purpose Mr. Gustafson had in view – to interest and impress the English-speaking world with our poetry. I should have included one of E. J. Pratt's narratives in full, and what do we find of Pratt's in this book? Three lyrics, the close of *The Titanic,* and about seventy-five lines from *The Cachalot,* a good passage relating the struggle between the whale and the squid. It seems altogether unlikely that a reader to whom Pratt's work is unknown could conceive from the five pages assigned to him the essence of the power he has demonstrated in tragic and heroic verse. It would surely have been better to leave out some of the minor figures, and thus ensure sufficient space for Pratt. Lampman is another on whom Mr. Gustafson might have relied for greater aid; the five Lampman pieces are admirable, but in none of them is the poet's reflective power impressive (and it often was) nor does any of them show his Keatsian manner at its ripest. No anthologist should be expected to include anything that he thinks wretched, but once he has decided to include a poet he may be expected to represent him by some at least of the work on which his reputation is based. It is surprising, therefore, that the three pages allowed to Marjorie Pickthall – three seems scant allowance when two are given to Francis Sherman – should be occupied by *Palome*. Earlier in this survey I expressed admiration for Mr. Gustafson's own poetic gift but I question his wisdom in including five poems of his own composition, good as these are. Whatever criticisms the anthology may merit, it is a great service to our poetry. Scarcely any of the hundred and thirty poems it contains are really unpoetic; most of the poets are represented on the level of their best work; no poet of eminence is left out. If I can imagine an anthology which would be more effective than this, after all every anthology leaves the reader who is familiar with the material "anthologized" with a sense of opportunities missed and emphases misplaced. It is a pleasant sense, and one of the reasons why anthologies are interesting to read.

Of two other anthologies it may be said that the execution falls far short of the idea. *Montreal in Verse* was inspired by the tercentenary of the city: none of its thirty-two pieces[2] is likely to be long recalled as an important or moving comment on our greatest city, and few of them are to be compared with the best work of their authors. *Flying Colours*, a collection of patriotic verse primarily intended for use in schools, is uneven: the Canadian section is in the main good, the English, spotty, the American and Australasian, exceedingly weak and not fairly or generously representative.

Two books relating to the past of our poetry claim the one mention in passing, the other extended comment. The Ryerson Press has done a notable service by gathering into one collection at a moderate price five volumes of Bliss Carman's verse which originally appeared between 1902 and 1905, *From the Book of Myths, From the Green Book of the Bards, Songs of the Sea Children, Songs from a Northern*

---

[2] If Mr. Alan McLachlan had waited a few months, he would not have opened his *Rhymes of a Montrealer* with the words

Since poets lack, to sound her praise
The layman dares. . . .

Garden, and *From the Book of Valentines.* The same house has issued Mr. Carl F. Klinck's biographical and critical study of a poet who was unfriendly to Carman, Wilfred Campbell. This, like Chittick's Haliburton and Connor's Lampman, is a Columbia doctoral dissertation and fully as valuable as either of its predecessors, less exhaustive than Chittick's book, not so deft as Connor's, but more aware of the importance of literary connections and more skilful in the handling of intellectual history than either. Specially useful are Mr. Klinck's chapters on the evolution of Campbell's political ideas and on his varying attitudes towards nature. From a vigorous Canadianism Campbell passed to an imperialist faith more rigorously consistent and more flamboyant than any other Canadian man of letters has professed since Confederation. Mr. Klinck follows the development with careful objectivity, showing the part played by revulsion from the United States (where Campbell had lived not too successfully) by his sentimental attachment to Scotland, and notably to the chief of the Campbells, the Duke of Argyle, by his pleasure in consorting with "the Great of the Earth in Palaces" (by which even Kipling was revolted), by a family link with the Greys, and by what is perhaps the strongest of all imperialist motives, discontent with the narrow dimensions of the Canadian scene. The treatment of Campbell's nature-theory and nature-verse is not so clear, and some of the distinctions Mr. Klinck draws between Campbell and his more gifted contemporaries are ingenious rather than convincing. The man who emerges from the book is neither attractive nor impressive. He thought that George Meredith was an insidious corrupter of morals, that the Roman Catholic Church had instigated the First World War, and that there was an active conspiracy in Canada and the United States to prevent the recognition of his poetry at its true worth. These ideas are not merely misguided; they are foolish and could not have been held by a mind of quality. Flightiness, a disposition to make enormous claims for himself and his work, an inner lack of solidity are betrayed again and again, although Mr. Klinck has sought to interpret Campbell's temperament with imaginative sympathy. In Mr. Gustafson's anthology Campbell is represented by one exquisite nature lyric – *Along the Line of Smoky Hills* – and after reading the life one wishes that Campbell had kept to subjects such as this, lived out his time as a Church of England rector in little Canadian towns and never met the Great.

1943

Since these surveys began in 1936 I have counted as fat years those which brought new works by E. J. Pratt and as lean those in which he was silent. It was to be feared that 1943 would be among the lean years; but in its last month came *Still Life and Other Verse,* a little collection of fifteen lyrics and brief narratives. Mr. Pratt has never been happier as a lyricist than he is in two, at least, of the poems in this latest collection, "Come Away, Death" and "The Invaded Field," the pieces by which he chose to be represented in the Canadian issue of *Poetry.* With them must be set the title poem, in which he makes powerful and beautiful use of a device somewhat new to his practice, the framing of famous lines and images in ironic contexts. Indeed "Still Life" is his most sustained study in irony, an assault dangerously polite upon the dwellers in ivory towers, those who need stillness about them if their hearts are to flow into verse. Underneath the surface courtesy, but not far enough underneath for the surface to be unruffled, is a grim stress upon the intensity and the significance of the times, the multitude of great themes calling imperiously for a poetic treatment adequate to their burden of splendour and pain. Once the surface cracks wide open to let horror loose:

> To-day the autumn tints are on
> The trampled grass at Marathon.
> Here are the tales to be retold,
> Here are the songs to be resung.
> Go, find a cadence for *that field-gray mould
> Outcropping on the Parthenon.*

This is a new note for Mr. Pratt; with his strength he allies a new softness of touch, a radiance quite different from that play of lightning and the aurora borealis which in their more spectacular ways have coruscated through so much of his greatest work.

In some of the narratives the old note of "The Cachalot" sounds again; it can never sound too often for a reader of that incomparable piece. Nowhere else in this collection is it so strong and clear as "The Submarine," in lines such as:

No forebear of the whale or shark,
No saurian of the Pleiocene,
Piercing the sub-aquatic dark
Could rival this new submarine.

It is fascinating to compare Mr. Pratt's treatment of this mechanical monster of the sea with his earlier treatment of cachalot and squid, iceberg and storm. The opening lines are so masterly in their ease that their technical distinction will be missed; after them come a full hundred in which Mr. Pratt's unique texture is constant. The longest and perhaps the most impressive poem in the set is "The Truant," where the essential likenesses between Mr. Pratt's more theoretic passages and the intellectual pieces of E. A. Robinson become clearer than in anything else Mr. Pratt has done. His thought has not the complex richness that Robinson's had, nor does he leave that peculiar excitement of mystery that marked Robinson at his rare best; but there is more force in Mr. Pratt, and I think, an even greater emotional integrity. In this poem there is a powerful Hitler-symbol; and indeed everywhere in the volume war is either a theme or a substantial part of the framework of feeling. Ever since "The Fable of the Goats" appeared in 1937 it has been interesting to watch the primitivist and the idealist conflicting within Mr. Pratt, the primitivist elated by the ideal simplifications of character brought about by a common experience of battle and strain, the idealist appalled by the horror of loss and degradation. *Still Life* complements *Dunkirk:* now it is the horror that dominates.

Beside Mr. Pratt's book I must set Mr. A. J. M. Smith's first collection, *News of the Phoenix and Other Poems.* Twelve of his poems appeared in *New Provinces* (1936), and ever since then I have eagerly awaited a first collection of his poetry. The first feeling at sight of the book must be one of disappointment. It is a little book; it holds but thirty-nine poems, spread over about as many pages, and among the thirty-nine are the twelve from *New Provinces,* and several others well known to readers of more recent anthologies of Canadian verse. One had hoped for evidence of greater fertility; but Mr. Smith is an exigent critic, and more severe towards himself than towards others. Such exigence has been rare in our literature; and this shining example may be educative.

The collection reveals an exigent temperament. In one of the most admirable poems in the set Mr. Smith espouses the "cold goddess Pride" and announces that it is to the "barren rock" he addresses his "difficult lonely music." In another, his most explicit exercise in criticism, he counsels a younger writer to aim at achieving the effect

> of a hard thing done
> Perfectly, as though without care.

The tone of that, as well as the idea, recalls the elder Yeats, to whom, in a memorial essay in the QUARTERLY, Mr. Smith paid significant tribute, speaking of him as an "eye made aquiline by thought." Well, Mr. Smith too is aquiline, and it is temperament as much as thought, as it was with Yeats, that has made him so.

The eagle's vision is in that picture of the Canadian landscape called "The Lonely Land." This is a scene girt with sharp jagged firs, and pines that a ceaseless wind has bent, spume is blown high in the air, and at the centre are wild ducks calling to each other in "ragged and passionate tones." The essence of the scene is stirringly caught in these lines:

> a beauty
> of dissonance
> this resonance
> of stony strand,
> this smoky cry
> curled over a black pine
> like a broken

and wind-battered branch
when the wind
bends the tops of the pines
and curdles the sky
from the north.

In this harsh world Mr. Smith takes an austere and intense delight. The natural setting for his beautiful "Ode: on the Death of W. B. Yeats" is almost the same. His Ireland has nothing in common with George Moore's or Elizabeth Bowen's: it is no place of soft contours, rich greenery and gentle rain; his Ireland is the bare hills and rough coast of Synge and of Yeats in his elder years. If a tree is conceded blossoms, it is a twisted tree; if a white swan flies through the poem, the air is cold and the clouds above upheave.

Almost equal severity stamps the religious poems with which the collection closes. In 1936 religion was a minor theme in Mr. Smith's work; it was scarcely more than an armoury of imagery. Now it is almost in the dominant place. The choice of religious topics is revealing: Good Friday, Calvary, Christian death. A line or two here and there is infused with gentleness:

And His face was a faded flower
    Drooping and lost;

but lines such as these are among the least successful in the book. The main effect is that of the Bellini portrait of Christ: haggard, stricken, at odds with life.

Mr. Smith's theory of poetry leaves an honoured place for light verse. In the introduction to his anthology *The Book of Canadian Poetry* he quotes with approval Mr. Auden's warning that it will "do poetry a great disservice if we confine it only to the major experiences of life." "Far West" is a lightly satirical suggestion of a London girl's feelings as "among the cigarettes and the peppermint creams" she enjoys a movie about cowboys. More acrid are "On Reading an Anthology of Popular Poetry" and "Son-and-Heir." In these Mr. Smith's disgust with *bourgeois* values has a searing strength. "Son-and-Heir" is an arraignment of *bourgeois* civilization in terms of the reveries an average *bourgeois* couple might have as they plot the ideal future for the baby. In the comment on the anthology he speaks of the "sweet sweet songs," the "soft melodious screams," the "old eternal frog in the throat that comes with the words, *Mother, sweetheart, dog.*" Read first, these satirical poems will help prepare one for the emotions that lie within and behind the more difficult and more important pieces.

A proud, hard, noble and intense book, *News of the Phoenix* leaves the regret that Mr. Smith has not been more fertile, or, if he has kept back much (as I for one presume), that he should not have given us some peeps into the laboratory in which he works his wonders.

II

None of the other books the year has brought belongs on the same shelf as *Still Life* and *News of the Phoenix*. There has been, however, at least the usual amount of attractive verse. Miss Audrey Brown's *Challenge to Time and Death* is clearly better than her *The Tree of Resurrection* (1937), although I do not find anything in it to equal the earlier "Laodamia" or one or two other pieces in her *A Dryad in Nanaimo* (1931). The fantastic is a large part in her charm, such evocations as this, inspired by the humble clop of the milkman's horse:

Dappled and clouded
   So daintily they trod
On small hoofs of ivory
   Silver-shod.

Ordinarily the effect is less definite. She speaks of a "road enamelled with the rose," of "meadows piled with drifts of daisy bloom," of "dim heather-purpled hills of dream." With most of us now a little of such quietly rich description goes a long way. War is the theme of most of the poems in the collection; and the note is extraordinarily old-fashioned; a few great words are over-used, words like "gallant" and "glory", blacklisted by Mr. Hemingway and most of the sharpest sensibilities of the time. In strong contrast with most of the poems is a long piece "Remittance Man," which has a straightforward energy and dramatic imagination not often found in Miss Brown's work. Even in it the quietly rich descriptions come now and then:

> And the keener-than-emerald-coloured alley and lane
> Jewelled with jade of leaves –
> And the blue eggs of the robin under the eaves . . .
> . . . the wind tossing almond boughs apart,
> And petals of pink pearl
> Lightly dropped on the lifted face of a girl.

One wishes away these effusions of a soft sensuousness, and wonders whether Miss Brown could sustain throughout a poem of this length the note of

> I go down to the half-post-office, half-store,
> Trying to keep the expectancy out of my eyes:
> A dozen droning flies
> Enter with me through the snapped-back door.

Mr. Wilson MacDonald has always looked askance at critics, and in the foreword to his *Greater Poems of the Bible: Metrical Versions, Biblical Forms and Original Poems* he asserts: "The frost of criticism is now upon the song of the world, seeking to destroy it." I have never met, read of, or heard of a critic who sought to destroy the art which was the subject of his own writing, although I freely concede that every critic may now and then seek to "destroy," that is to discredit, a work of art which he believes mistaken. The sentence I quote is one of many pronouncements in Mr. MacDonald's foreword flung out in a rage or an exaltation without any evidence offered in support. Mr. MacDonald's undertaking seems to me one hard to justify. Some of the greatest passages in the Bible (for example *I Corinthians*, XIII) he retains almost unaltered; to others he gives a metrical scheme definite and modern; sometimes he removes archaisms and obscurities. The test of his book must clearly lie not in the passages he retains as he found them but in those he refashions, and particularly in those where the changes are fundamental. As an example of his work I shall cite "The Lord's Prayer":

> Our Father, who are in Heaven,
>   hallowed be Thy name;

let Thy desires and our desires
    be evermore the same.

Thy will be done, O Lord, on earth
    as it is done above.
Forgive us by the measure of
    our own forgiving love.

Preserve us from the tempter's hands
    and every evil thing.
Give us this day our daily bread,
    and let us ever sing:

"Thine is the kingdom and the power,
    O Lord of sinful men,
And Thine the glory evermore,
    yea evermore, amen."

With this evidence offered in support, I shall say that Mr. MacDonald has based his work on a misconception of what constitutes poetry, with no fear that this attempt to "destroy" him may be interpreted as an attempt to "destroy" what he calls "the song of the world."

Three long poems, very different from one another as they are, may come next. *Shadowed Victory,* from the practised hand of Mr. Arthur Stringer, is a slow-moving deeply-felt novel in verse. A Saskatchewan farmer loses his girl to a soldier; she joins the CWAC; the soldier is killed at Dieppe; she is blinded in the blitz; meanwhile the farmer has made a marriage founded upon a curious mixture of passion and respect from which love is absent; and at the close, after the blinded girl's return, appreciates the measure of his loss. The blank verse is always competent, and at some points very moving; but some magic of diction, some fullness of insight, some power of sudden illumination is lacking. Another long war story in verse is Lieutenant-Commander Frederick Watt's *Who Dare To Live,* on which I shall offer no aesthetic comment. This tale of personal experience in the convoys (with a romantic fiction as the warp) is dedicated to two comrades now missing; much of it was written aboard; and it offers a stirring, sometimes a thrilling account of heroic incidents and the toll such incidents take of personality. As Cowper said of his castaway:

> And tears by bards or heroes shed
> Alike immortalize the dead.

These tears are a hero's; I am not sure they are a bard's. *The Closed Book* by Dr. Wilmot B. Lane, professor emeritus of ethics at Victoria College in this University, is a philosophic presentation, with much copiousness of example, of conflicts within individuals and societies. It will remind Professor Lane's students of that vast store of reading and that intense imagination which marked his lectures. Space does not permit an account of the elaborate intellectual scheme of the poem; but one may say briefly that the work lacks the fullness of poetic conception, and in the detail of image, rhythm and verse paragraph is insufficiently vital.

There were but three Ryerson Chap-Books in 1943, and one of these, Miss Eugenie Perry's *Hearing a Far Call*, was inadvertently included in the preceding survey. Miss Evelyn Eaton, the well-known novelist, catches in the two dozen brief pieces which make up *Birds before Dawn* fugitive moments and crucial incidents of undoubted beauty. Her touch is so light that the feeling does not often come through in the intended intensity. In *Journey into Yesterday* Miss Irene Benson, in a manner that is always solemn (and often over-solemn), writes with something of the charm that Carman had in his graver moments. The level of the Carillon Chap-Books continues far below that of the Ryerson series. Of the three that appeared in 1943, Miss Phyllis Pettit's *Promise,* Miss Laura Ridley's *Christmas Eve*, and Miss Mariel Jenkins' *Beauty for Ashes*, the last is much the best. Miss Jenkins shows a clear grace of form, and in a few poems a strength of feeling, sometimes betrayed by her defect in verbal power.

A number of small books, many of them simple booklets, remain. Miss Dorothy Dumbrille's *Watch the Sun Rise* has the same painful intimacy as her preceding collection. She is simple and clear, and often expert, but nothing of the magic of great verse has entered into her work. In *They Shall Return and Other Poems* Mr. J. Lewis Milligan shows that there has been no decline in his management of the musical old-fashioned manner that has so long been his. In approaching Mrs. Amabel King's *The New Crusaders and Other Poems* one is pleased by the admirable decorations by the versatile Wilson MacDonald but worried and indeed put off by the statement on the jacket that she was the prime mover in the anthology *Voices of Victory*, commented upon in the survey for 1941. In the best of Mrs. King's poems there is grace; but the collection should have been cut by at least one half, and the diction of the remnant (here is the chief formal weakness of our poetry) considered and reconsidered with Horatian care.

III

Two anthologies await comment. From the *New Directions* company in Connecticut comes a beautifully produced volume called *A Little Anthology of Canadian Poets*, edited by Mr. Ralph Gustafson. To use a phrase of Mr. A. J. M. Smith's, quoted when his collection was discussed, this is a book of "difficult lonely music." Except for Mr. Pratt, Mr. L. A. Mackay and Mr. Leo Kennedy, the poets of simpler spirit and freer manner are not here. What is lost in comprehensiveness is gained in unity. I was surprised by the absence of Miss Anne Marriott and Miss Dorothy Livesay, who are poets in Mr. Gustafson's kind, and much superior to those who occupy his last pages. But the test of a small anthology is not what it leaves out, but what it admits; and there are but one or two dubious pieces in this. For the distinguished little magazine *Voices* Mr. Gustafson undertook another anthology of our recent poetry; and again he achieved an excellent representation, this time more comprehensive.

Mr. Gustafson would be the first to say that neither of his anthologies has the importance of Mr. A. J. M. Smith's great *Book of Canadian Poetry*, which he reviewed at length in the January number of the QUARTERLY. His review and those of three other works lightens my task. One of these is Miss Elsie Pomeroy's biography of Sir Charles Roberts, reviewed by Professor Pelham Edgar in the autumn number. Miss Pomeroy's book came out just a few months before Sir Charles died: it has served both as a homage at the close of an incredibly long poetic career, and as a memorial tribute to one who had seemed too robust to die. Some of his admirers have complained now and then that the comments on Sir Charles' work in these surveys were grudging. If there is any ground for such complaint, it lies in the fear I had lest his great age, the strong loyalties he evoked, and the immense influence he had come to wield should prejudice the reception throughout the country of some kinds of poetry that he did not fully appreciate. In his own poetry at its best – and much of it was very good indeed – there was mellow beauty and dexterous art. *Full Tide*, the excellent little magazine of the Vancouver Poetry Society, devotes a number to his memory; and since this organ does not circulate as widely as it might, I should like to quote from the tribute paid in it by Dr. Duncan Campbell Scott:

> I could hazard the opinion that few writers have used oftener the term fellow-craftsman; this word was an index of one of his qualities; he thought of all poets and versifiers as members of a guild and if he praised indiscriminately, it was for that reason. I think the praise came from a sense of comradeship and from a feeling of kindness for writers of all calibers. . . . He was a leading Canadian for Canada and Canadians. . . . This was generally recognized and I note its record in a late issue of the Literary Supplement of the London Times. "His aim – early and late – was to give Canada a sense of nationhood, and Canadian literature its own distinction." This was a worthy aim and one can only hope that he was satisfied after a long and strenuous life, with its accomplishment, in degree at least, for its full attainment would be impossible for any man.

With all that Dr. Scott here says of Sir Charles I concur.

The two other works, reviewed by Professor W. E. Collin in the January number, I may not comment upon: one of them was the fruit of collaboration between Dr. Scott and me, and the other was wholly mine. It is not improper to say, however, that to some serious misinterpretations I shall make reply in an appropriate place.

1944

After the *Collected Poems* of E. J. Pratt, reviewed at length
in the January number of the QUARTERLY, the most important contribution to the *corpus* of our poetry in 1944 came
from Mr. Abraham M. Klein. Mr. Klein was one of the six
represented in the anthology *Poems by Several Authors*
(1936); and four years later a collection of his verse *Hath
Not a Jew* . . . came out in New York. Perhaps because the
anthology did not circulate very widely and the collection
was published by an American house, Mr. Klein has not
been as well known in Canada as the merits of his poetry
require. It is perhaps unfortunate for the growth of his reputation at home that the two volumes he has given us in
1944 were brought out in the United States. *The Hitleriad*
seems to me the less valuable of the two. It is a Byronic
poem, a rich mixture of satire and burlesque, in which Hit-
ler and his associates are impaled on the twin spears of
laughter and derision. The double effect is not as strong as
the poet hoped; the satire does not reinforce the burlesque,
nor the burlesque the satire; rather the lines are clouded by
the varying intent. Almost all Mr. Klein's verse leaves an
impression of haste. It is not a wholly unfortunate impression: it suggests spontaneity, intensity, conviction; but the
advantages are bought at the high price of more than occasional carelessness, and the careless details are not always
successfully carried by the vigour and colour of the general
effect. In his *Poems,* especially in the first section, his
Psalms, his work is more careful than it has ever been. In
"Psalm IV", subtitled "A psalm of Abraham, touching his
green pastures," he has attained an exquisite purity of note:

> From pastures green, whereon I lie,
> Beside still waters, far from crowds,

I lift hosannahs to the sky
And hallelujahs to the clouds,

Only to see where clouds should sit,
And in that space the sky should fill,
The fierce carnivorous Messerschmidt,
The Heinkel on the kill.

They'll not be green for very long,
Those pastures of my peace, nor will
The heavens be a place for song,
Nor the still waters still.

In his Psalms – there are thirty-six – he is remarkably varied both in topic and feeling, and he has usually found appropriate forms. The forms I should question are, for instance, in Psalm VI (where the rhythm fails to rise to the height of the feeling) and Psalm X (in which the idea is not adequately embodied). Compared with the characteristic poems in *Hath Not a Jew* . . . , most of the Psalms have a sobriety and tranquillity of expression which comes as a surprise in Mr. Klein's verse. The second group in the collection, "A Voice Was Heard in Ramah," resembles more closely what Mr. Klein has given us before. The choruses in "Ballad of the Thwarted Axe" are marked by those brilliant unexpected but wonderfully suitable images which abound in Mr. Klein's treasury, for instance:

The blade that's eaten by the flint
The better eats the bone!

Headsman, headsman, catch that breath,
That is as sharp as lime!
O, it will eat away the limbs
Of any judge's crime.

In this second instance Mr. Klein's known power to remake a nursery rhyme for grave and even frightful meaning appears once again. The third part of the collection consists of a single long narrative in Spenserian stanza, "Yehuda Ha-Levi, His Pilgrimage." The poem is splendidly romantic, and has that high colour and sharp impetuosity that we look for in Mr. Klein, but the details lack the finish and aptness that distinguish his Psalms, and the antiquation of language is not maintained with the patient skill that alone could justify its introduction today.

Not far below Mr. Klein's work may be set Miss Dorothy Livesay's *Day and Night*. Although I believe that her preoccupation with radical conceptions of social reform has narrowed her vision as a poet – and has made her one of our least dependable critics – no one could read her new collection and not find in it passages of an excellence which outruns any intellectual synthesis. Sometimes it is the rhythm that seizes on one:

Are you waiting?
Wait with us
After evening
There's a hush

Use it not
For Love's slow count:
Add up hate
And let it mount.

What a threatening flood is just held back by those thin and nervous lines! Sometimes it is the images which pounce out; few revolutionary poets have found to express their sense of the present phase of society an image comparable with:

We are asleep on the long limb of time.

Many other images are there to remind us that a part of Miss Livesay's sensibility does not live in the fetid slums, or in megalopolis, or in the mechanized society of her ideal future, but just in wind and sun and rain as she has known them in rural Ontario or British Columbia. Turning from the details of her work to the passion that gives it much of its rush and colour, we must pay homage to a revolutionary creed fiery enough to form striking aesthetic expression. Still it is true, I think, of most of her verse, as of most of Mr. Auden's, that it lacks that opulent wholeness of being that marks great poetry, Mr. Eliot's and Keats's, and in our North American terms, Mr. Pratt's. The great poet's vision is not narrow, but extremely broad; his variety is informed by a unity that no poetry can have unless the whole of life is seen as greater than its parts, greater than the sum of its parts.

Flight into Darkness, Mr. Ralph Gustafson's collection, notably beautiful in format as all his volumes are, is less easy to appraise than Miss Livesay's work. None of our poets is more concerned with minutiae, and yet it is in craftsmanship that his main limitation comes. Most of the more carefully wrought poems in this volume are extraordinarily lacking in music. To illustrate this charge it would not be fair to quote single lines, and indeed it is only by the reading of whole poems that its full force can be felt, such poems as "Crisis," "The Valiant," and "Lyric Sarcastic." My space does not allow for such extended quotation; but it may be that these stanzas will suggest the shortcoming:

> You shall harvest (moths circling the moon)
> And you shall still work a work with your hand.
> But you shall say This harvest's bitter
> The fingers blunt.

And even more:

> What brink and bastion bound can make
> Against the common sea delays
> Of dart and dazzle, crumple rake
> Of sun off earth's cornice, rays?

With Mr. Gustafson these things do not happen by chance; and it is therefore right to insist that, for some sensibilities at least, there is an unredeemed harshness and roughness in passages that he has carefully considered. Mr. Gustafson's language is usually dense; his lines and phrases carry an unusually heavy freight of meaning and suggestion; and the emotions he arouses have a way of fading out obscurely (but also quickly, an odd combination). I should say that *Flight into Darkness* is the most difficult volume of verse to come from a Canadian in the decade since these surveys began. Still the difficulty is not in all the poems, and in some even the quickest reader will find a disciplined and smiling charm.

The contributors to *Unit of Five* are Miss P. K. Page, and Messrs. Louis Dudek, Ronald Hambleton, Raymond Souster, and James Wreford. The book has not the unity its title claims for it. Miss Page and Mr. Souster are relatively simple poets with a strong sense that the present social order is unendurable. Mr. Souster has much more frankness and volume than Miss Page; he states his resentments and compassions as readily as Sandburg or Masters; and indeed his rather old-fashioned warmth reminds one of the earlier practitioners of free verse in the United States. It is impossible to read him without emotion. Miss Page is much more tense and clipped; she relies on implication, but what she implies is always easy to grasp. Although to each of these writers no more than a dozen pages have been assigned, an effect of monotony comes before their verses have been read through. I do not think that the monotony can be ascribed to the forms they use, or to their imagery, but it may well come from the starkness of the responses they make to the world in which they define themselves; they merely keep on stating or suggesting that it is a bad world, that it dulls life, that they pity the victims and hate the machine. Given a greater range either Miss Page or Mr. Souster might develop into a significant poet. Mr. Dudek is the bridge between them and the other contributors. He has variety in theme and tone; sometimes he is as simple and perhaps half as warm as Mr. Souster; sometimes he is as enigmatic and as crammed with unfocussed imagery as Mr. Hambleton. His variety seems to be experimental: I do not find any core of unity within it, the mark of a strongly feeling, clearly thinking personality. In Mr. Hambleton's work, and even more in Mr. Wreford's there is the complication and the (I have no doubt deliberate) unmusicalness which come into so much of Mr. Gustafson's verse. Now and then, as with Mr. Gustafson, the complication and the unmusicalness are thrust aside and the energy of their intelligences, the vitality of their imaginations are revealed.

II

Among the books remaining the most interesting is Mr. Dick Diespecker's *Between Two Furious Oceans and Other Poems*. The title poem derives from Whitman, and abounds in evocations and eulogies of aspects of the Canadian scene. Here, and in the long poems following there is energy and flow, but without that philosophic curiosity and that power to picture in a word which were so strong in Whitman and lent a poetic tone even to most of his catalogues. In his short poems Mr. Diespecker is definitely mediocre; but if he could attain concentration and sharpen his pictorial power, in longer works he might achieve effects of great interest. He is the best of the new voices of the year. Mr. Joseph Schull acquired a more than ephemeral reputation by his *Legend of Ghost Lagoon (1937)*. His new book, *I, Jones, Soldier* is a narrative with flashbacks in a spare concentrated idiom, all too close to the usual level of estimable prose. The gravity of his subject – the history of a soldier's career during this war – has confined Mr. Schull whose highest qualities, as the *Legend* showed, were in fancy and humour. His poem is, however, the best of the war poetry of the year. *Barbed Wire Ballads,* by Lieutenant Tom Melville, comes to us from *Oflag* VII/B, and was written piece by piece "to whittle away a few hours of a monotonous existence." A pleasure in writing as well as reading verse in the Kipling-Service manner, is more common among young Anglo-Saxon males than most people realize. W. H. Drummond rather than Kipling or Service is the master of Squadron Leader Carroll McLeod, the author of *Dat H'ampire H'air Train Plan,* a set of seven ballads marking the crises in an airman's career. In the texture this verse is really very unlike Drummond's, especially inferior perhaps in the rhythms; but in the overall effect there are vestiges of Drummond's charm.

Except It Die, by Mr. Elkin Lamb, impressively printed and decorated with Blakelike full-page illustrations by the author, is a visionary record, the sense for language unfortunately falling far below the level of the noble ideas and feelings the poet is groping to formulate. *Ypnos,* volumes III and IV, show Dr. William Dobree Calvert in a less mystical or visionary state than their predecessors. His verse continues to be extremely uneven, and inevitably the large number of weak and unshaped poems damages the effect of the few which are superior. That Dr. Calvert can achieve delightful verse the following dialectal stanza will establish:

Ha-done! Ha-done wi bellerun,
Hodmedods an nippadors,
Swiffs an meece an clapperclaws,
Liddle gells a-hollerun.

For the gloss the reader is referred to Dr. Calvert.

Among more conservative poets perhaps Mr. Arthur S. Bourinot, in *Nine Poems,* is the most agreeable; in "Now Is the Earth Made Glad" there are charming couplets. In *Candled by Stars,* Miss Jean Waddell deals with many of the themes of romantic poetry, but in an unoriginal fashion. Only when a poet's rhythms and images are stamped with something peculiarly his own can writing on these themes produce the shock of poetry. Although the themes in Miss M. Eugenie Perry's *Canteen* touch on war, the interest is rather in the handling of a woman's impressions and contacts, subtly altered by the background of war. The language, like Miss Waddell's, is deficient in creative vitality. *Lanterns in the Dusk,* by Laura Nixon Haynes, is quiet musical verse, marked by religious feeling. *Jeunesse and Other Poems,* by Kenneth Knatchbull-Hugessen, introduced by his father, is a memorial volume. The author died in 1942 at the age of seventeen. The best pieces in the group have a brightness and an integrity of feeling that sets them among the more promising sort of undergraduate verse. As Senator Knatchbull-Hugessen wisely says: "It is impossible to say whether his poems were the early indications of a talent which would have continued to grow and develop with the years, or whether on the other hand they were only an adolescent's need of self-expression which, as time passed, would have taken other forms."

On *Roses in December,* by Edna Jaques, it is unnecessary to comment in this place beyond remarking that it is exactly like the earlier collections from the same pen.

It remains to speak of the "Ryerson Poetry Chap-Books," this year a somewhat disappointing batch. Most of the pieces in Mrs. Elsie Fry Laurence's *Rearguard and Other Poems* do not rise above the average of verse in the women's magazines, though the title piece has a warmth and music that sets it off from the rest. *Legend and Other Poems,* by Miss Gwendolen Merrin, is quiet conventional verse. Mr. Austin Campbell, in *They Shall Build Anew,* achieves a predominantly rhetorical effect. Sister Maura, a practised poet, is more original, but in *Rhythm Poems* she drops far below the level of her best work. The most satisfactory of the group is an elder poet, Professor Frank Oliver Call, from whom little has come during the past decade. His thirteen *Sonnets for Youth* have a balanced and mellow beauty without the intensity that marks the best work Mr. Call has done. The quality can be measured by the closing lines of "Frozen Garden":

Only one word, one voice, one quickening breath
Can wake this garden from its dream of death.

1945

Those of us who have watched for the appearance of Mr. F. R. Scott's poems in the magazines and anthologies of the past two decades have also looked forward to the year which would bring a collection of them. That it would be an impressive book no one could have doubted. It is more impressive than I had expected – it reveals that Mr. Scott is among the few modern poets who can be read at length with unwearied technical pleasure, with intellectual satisfaction, and with unresting poetical excitement. *Overture* is one of the best volumes of poetry this country has seen, and what I have elsewhere described as the wall that Americans have raised against Canadian poetry should not prove high enough to keep out Mr. Scott. His poetry is the expression of a man who is living intensely and sensitively on all levels, spiritual, intellectual, political and sensual. It is the expression of a man who, very much a citizen of his own country, is also a citizen of the world. I do not know of any book in prose or verse in the past five years which more powerfully shows that we in Canada, or some of us, enough of us to matter, have come of age.

The first great strength of this poetry is a core of belief. No one who knows the history of poetry can doubt that it is of immense advantage to a poet that he should believe firmly, and that his belief should be comprehensive, enlarging to the spirit, and so substantial as to command at the very least the reader's ungrudged respect. It is, above all, of use to the poet that he should believe in mind, not the *siccum lumen* (as I need scarcely say) but mind as Wordsworth or Coleridge conceived it. "Every time", wrote A. C. Bradley forty years ago in *English Poetry and German Philosophy in the Age of Wordsworth,* "has the defects of its qualities; but those periods in which, and those men in whom, the mind is strongly felt to be great, see more and see deeper than others. . . . And when the greatness of the mind is strongly felt, it *is* great and works wonders." The belief in the greatness of the mind has been rare in recent poetry, Canadian or other. It is strong in Mr. Scott's.

It rings out again and again. "To Certain Friends" is addressed to men with comfortably full minds but no intention or ability to do anything with them. It begins with agreeable lightness on the surface:

> They show great zeal collecting the news and statistics.
> They know far more about every question than I do,
> But their knowledge of how to use knowledge grows
> smaller and smaller.

> They make a virtue of having an open mind,
> Open to endless arrivals of other men's suggestions,
> To the rain of facts that deepens the drought of the will.

> Above all they fear the positive formation of opinion,
> The essential choice that acts as a mental compass,
> The clear perception of the road to the receding horizon.

Mr. Scott has not been unobservant when he has attended the meetings of our learned societies, or listened to the patter of comment in our senior common-rooms. At the close of the poem the note is a deeper one and angry:

> They will grow old searching to avoid conclusions,
> Refusing to learn by living, to test by trying,
> Letting opportunities slip from their tentative fingers.

> Till one day, after the world has tired of waiting,
> While they are busy arguing about the obvious,
> A half-witted demagogue will walk away with their
> children.

This poem is such an attack on a disease of the mind as only a man who passionately believes in its right use could conceive.

The mind, Mr. Scott holds, will help us to plan and establish a great society. To do so we must drop much that has charm, for the charm, he thinks, is a tie with things which are far from charming, antiquated, crippling to the mind, intolerable to the alert moral sense. I continue to think that Mr. Scott is for dropping too much. In the title-poem he is for dropping Mozart, by which he means the states of being that Mozart can arouse in those who love his work . He is for dropping tea-parties and bric-à-brac – partly this is mere sentiment, for Mr. Scott like the other poets of his group has ears that are closed to the beauty of Victorian poetry, and eyes resentfully critical of the Victorian minor arts. Perhaps the examples of both had an almost peculiar badness in Montreal and Quebec when Mr. Scott was growing up. But the mind he will never drop:

> And if the ultimate I, the inner mind,
> The only shelter proof against attack
> Sustain these days, carry this banner out
> To the clumsy dawn: A green seed
> Lies on the ground under a leafless tree.

Many of the poems express Mr. Scott's socialist plan for the great society. They escape the flatness which curses so much proletarian verse , partly because Mr. Scott generally avoids abstract polysyllables, rhetorical exclamations, and all the rest of the dreary apparatus of inflated prose which some versifiers demand that we accept as being a finer distillation of poetry than Yeats' lyricism. The essence of Mr. Scott's social ideal is mind in society, the planned society; and in his way of conceiving this he is no naive rationalist, he is indeed very much of a mystic. For partisan reasons he would not perhaps appreciate the comparison; but his "socialism" is much akin to the Prime Minister's, one of whose recurrent quotations is: "We are members one of another." By both political leaders mind is conceived in a generous sense, inhibiting neither to poetry nor to religion.

There is one reflective lyric in the collection which I should set beside Mr. Leo Kennedy's "Words for a Resurrection" and Mr. Pratt's "Silences," that is, in the very highest range of reflective lyrical verse in the past quarter-century. This is "Advice":

> Beware the casual need
> By which the heart is bound;

Pluck out the quickening seed
That falls on stony ground.

Forgo the shallow gain,
The favour of an hour.
Escape, by early pain,
The death before the flower.

There is no reason why this, in its almost perfect purity, should ever age; and its wisdom will stand the strictest test, and emerge a living thing. There are a number of poems in this vein, some of them weakened by the closing lines in which Mr. Scott almost always tries for a climax and sometimes comes to ruin, others almost as perfect as "Advice." Among the triumphs I should place "Dedication," "November Pool" and "Below Quebec." Among the poems with disappointing endings are "Calvary," "Devoir Molluscule" and "Union." In "Union" the three final lines seem an obvious appendage, and I suggest to Mr. Scott that he consider the poem as it stands and then the poem shorn of its appendage; perhaps he will agree that everything he wished to convey is conveyed without it, and that by dropping it he will enable the poem to rest in perfect proportion. "Teleological" is, I think, a poem of an inferior texture throughout; but in it also the final lines are loss.

Between Mr. Scott's poems and those of Mr. Earle Birney's second collection, *Now is Time*, there are many resemblances. Mr. Birney professes the same belief in mind, speaking with respect of a "map of a reasoned future"; his counsel to a World Organization is that "the iceberg is elective" for the dangerous fogs are projections only of our wills and thus are under our control. A social idealism, the same in final aim, animates him. He has almost the same pleasure in the precise vision, the firm touch, with him a harder touch.

Perhaps the essential differences are that Mr. Birney is more dramatic, and more bitter in temper. There is no narrative in this collection to remind us of *David*; instead we are given elegies. One of these is already widely known: "Joe Harris 1913-1942." This is in a highly successful poetic prose, and is intended, as its biblical captions emphasize, to be not only a lament for an individual and an account of his life and death, but a generalized accusing picture of the plight of a generation of poor Canadian boys upon whom a cruel necessity forced first a depression and then a war. "For Steve," in long stanzas with a curious and stirring effect of assonance, recounts a story which is much the same, but told with even less concentration on the individual, and a more wide-ranging concern with the Canadian economic and social problem,

> the human fissures
> that cleave the lanky land from which we grew.

"Man on a Tractor" belongs with the elegies, in the framework of thought at least, although in this poem the individual survives the worst that depression seconded by war can do against him. The poor of the tractorman's generation (which is also Joe Harris's and Steve's, and roughly speaking is the generation following Mr. Birney's) had in the thirties an exceedingly raw deal. Mr. Scott is aware of this; it haunts Mr. Birney. His poems are packed with references to the plight of the unemployed. He speaks of the "ceaseless palsy of boxcars," the "slammed doors," the "graceless gingerly handout," the "stale handout," the "kicks in the rump or three day hungers," the "yardbulls ahead," the "pinched slumboy." The poor people, rural or urban, have been ridden mercilessly and smugly by the rich, "fat and unheeding":

> sprouting thicker than wheat are the towers
> of its traders, shining more than the headstone
> his father saved from a lifetime's farming.

What Chesterton called "the impudent fatness of the few" is never far from Mr. Birney's mind. The rich are on high either in their towers, or as hawks circling over the helpless flocks, and when they descend it is always to hurt. Their life is seen from below angrily, and without any real sense of motive. The dramatic quality in Mr. Birney's poetry suffers by the contrast between his ever-ready sympathy with the poor, a sympathy grounded in understanding, and his summary unconvincing presentation of their masters. His bitterness of mood forces its way into almost everything he writes, sometimes to give it greater energy and vigour, but often to weaken a note of delight or triumph, or to destroy a touch of reality.

The personality set before the reader in Mr. Charles Bruce's *Grey Ship Moving* is extraordinarily attractive without being strongly individualized. The poems express, often in narrative form, the moods and thoughts of a man nearing forty,

> With a tentative foot on the door-step of middle age,

who has been living in easy but not luxurious fashion, busy in his brown-walled office in a large inland city and a trifle bored in his suburban home set well back from the street, very often mindful of his childhood along the Nova Scotian coast, stopping to

> consider where the mackerel run
> And three grey fish-huts on a windy beach.

He is maturely introspective, often questioning the wisdom of his choice of an urban inland life so much at odds with the impulses of his blood. The war has taken this man from his rut; it has brought to him an unexpected variety of scene, width of association and range of action. Trite as the phrase has become, it is impossible to avoid saying that the war has brought perspective. And an admirable truth of perspective is the main virtue in this man's spirit. Broadly typical in its concerns, its regrets, it maturities, of so many Canadians, indeed of so many North Americans, this personality expresses itself in a quiet casual-sounding agreeable medium, thoroughly in keeping with its essential qualities. *Grey Ship Moving* is extremely pleasant to read. It is minor poetry, but the poetry is authentic:

> There is virtue too in a grey and dragonish sea.

In *Sandstone* Miss Anne Marriott reprints *The Wind Our Enemy* with which her fame was established in 1939, and half of the poems in *Salt Marsh,* her chap-book of 1942. To these familiar pieces she adds fourteen that are new. In noticing *Salt Marsh* in the survey of three years ago I said that nothing Miss Marriott had done since *The Wind Our Enemy* had equalled that stark and vivid evocation of drought on the prairie. The poems which now appear for the first time are more impressive than most of those in *Salt Marsh*. They are above all impressive as lyrics. The peculiar reputation that *The Wind Our Enemy* gave her, they will not reinforce; but they point to a greater power in pure lyric. In many of the new poems, as in many from *Salt Marsh*, there is a fundamental disharmony between the kinds of emotion Miss Marriott wishes to record, and the kinds of diction and rhythm she prefers to use as her instruments. Put simply, the emotions are gentle, the instruments rough. In the landscapes, and Miss Marriott is very much a poet of landscapes, the gentle and the rough are brought together with an interesting effect, but at the cost of discomfort to the reader's sense of ideal unity.

True Harvest is uneven, as all Mr. Arthur Bourinot's collections have been. The title suggests that the volume will carry some of the poet's essential meanings; and it does deal with serious issues in a serious way. War, death, growing old, the national future weigh upon him; and the grave mood they fashion is held even when he ventures a little less seriously into the past in dramatic monologues which present the last days of the widow of Samuel de Champlain and the pain of Ariadne deserted by Theseus. Except in a few passages which are prolix the monologues are successful. More striking are two short poems on the grave, "Utter Silence" and "Only to Rest." Stanzas from the latter will suggest the seriousness of mood and the severe beauty of the form at its best:

Nothing is heard
Under the ground –
Not even a word,
Never a sound.

Cities may break,
Great nations pass,
The flesh will not wake
Under the grass.

With *Here and Now,* by Mr. Irving Layton, the editors of *First Statement** open a new series in which two other volumes, Mr. Patrick Anderson's *A Tent for April* and Mrs.

---

*The magazine has since been reborn as the *Northern Review*.

Miriam Waddington's *Green World,* appeared before the end of 1945. Mr. A. M. Klein, Mr. F. R. Scott and Mr. A. J. M. Smith have joined with a number of younger writers to make of Montreal once more what it was in the late twenties and early thirties, the most adventurous experimental centre of Canadian poetry. The group or groups have expressed themselves in a number of magazines; and now, in this series, a more important form of expression has been devised. It is excellent that a group of poets with kindred views and techniques should come together to make publication easier and more effective for themselves, and I hope, for others in sympathy with them. I have deplored more than once the late date at which so many Canadian poets publish their first collection of verse, Mr. Smith, for instance, at forty-one, and Mr. F. R. Scott at forty-six. Perhaps through the new series poets may begin to have that impact which verses in a magazine, or even in a chap-book, cannot provide, before they pass thirty. Another reason for satisfaction in the existence of the new series is rather a reason for dissatisfaction concerning the general relation between poets and publishers in Canada at present. The five collections so far noticed have all come from one house, the Ryerson Press; aside from them, and from the *First Statement* publications, there is but one significant book to notice, and it is not a true book but a small brochure. Wise as the decisions of the Ryerson Press have proved, it is exceedingly unhealthy that all poetry should come through the channel of one publisher.

Here and Now is an appropriate title. Mr. Layton's thirty-two poems are saturated with Montreal and with the political and social problems of the immediate present. He complains:

> Since Auden set the fashion
> Our poets grow tame;
> They are quite without passion,
> They live without blame.

I do not see what harm there must be in living without blame – the belief that drugs or drabs are the catalysts for poetry is outmoded – and in Mr. Layton's poems there is very little passion, except in the trivialized form of resentment. No one will ever call him tame, however, and his rich chunks of experience are unfailingly interesting. In Mr. Patrick Anderson's *A Tent for April* there is a spirited delight in language for its own sweet sake which is rare in our poetry. Sometimes his gambollings are heavy as in "Writer," which opens with this stanza:

> He turns his deadskin memories to the day
> and he dies daily writing his doom's diary
> while body's queer career is his carrier
> in time across a plain of life and paper.

More often they are so light as to be elusive. Images pour out in a wild flood as in his remarkable hermetic love poem "Summer's Joe," an instance of his method at its best. The multiplication of the levels on which he is seeking to communicate has probably led to some stifling of the real self from which he writes. Too many of the poems leave the impression which is often created by the work of young poets of energy and intensity and technical preoccupation: that the poet had no clear conception of what he most wished to say, or how it would be best to say it. The two dozen short poems in Mrs. Miriam Waddington's *Green World* – Mr. Anderson's volume ends with these two words – express her revulsion from the social structure of the time, her pain in personal relationships, and even a dark view of natural beauty. These are essentially urban poems, of Montreal and Toronto,

> far from snows of winnipeg
> and seven sister lakes.

They are set in a framework of reflection concerning world-wide misery and catastrophe:

> All hope and hear the Spaniard's curse
> Even in dreams.

> I see over your shoulders the years like a fascist army.

Personal relations are ruined by solipsism:

> So tell me your misfortunes, lay your plans,
> I'm listening with one ear to my past.

And the general effect of the poem which closes with these lines, and is ironically entitled "Sympathy," suggests that both ears are responsive only to the poet's past. Love is dismissed as "idiot female ecstasy." In Mrs. Waddington's poetry there are no crises of despair or pessimism; it is slow-moving and bored. One may wish, after reading a number of her pieces in succession, for a sharper focus, a more perceptible progression.

To the most interesting poetry of the year there remains one addition to make, not of a book but of a brochure. Mr. Pratt's *They are Returning* runs to just over three hundred lines. In it he essays to suggest the experience of the Canadian soldier during the years of war, and to draw the future as with personal good fortune and national wisdom it may take shape. His conception of his subject allows him a number of couplets of masterly narrative; some resonant outbursts of names

Like Buchenwald of Maidanek or Lidice

and above all, perhaps, some examples of his unmatched power to translate scientific fact into the magic of poetical language:

They could direct the pale-gold
Drip of the plasma or the *mould*
Into a median vein and see
It re-enact
The Resurrection from the Dead.

The rhythm is grave and stirring, and the form elaborate and distinguished. In the thought there is the dignity, the stoicism that befits one of the masters of our poetry expressing himself on one of the greatest occasions in the history of Canada. *They are Returning* is an occasional poem: it does not fall below its great function.

Mr. Ira Dilworth's *Twentieth Century Verse* has a special significance for the student of Canadian poetry: it is the first noteworthy selection of modern verse in which a large number of Canadian poets are set side by side with the American, the English and the Irish. If the book has the circulation it deserves, it may acquire for Canadian poetry a large new audience. Of the eighty-four poets represented fifteen are Canadian, a liberal proportion indeed. Mr. Pratt, as a narrative poet, presents a difficulty to the anthologist; and it is certain that in seven pages, all that Mr. Dilworth allows him, he cannot be given his fair chance. But why confine him to seven pages, when a much more generous allotment is given to Stephen Bent, Mr. Birney and Miss Audrey Brown? I miss a sonnet in the selections from Sir Charles Roberts, and regret the exclusion of Robert Finch, Leo Kennedy and A. M. Klein. In general Mr. Dilworth's choice of Canadian poets and poems is happy; and his brief biographical notes are accurate, interesting and illuminating.

II

The longest poem of the year is Mr. Andrew Merkel's *Tallahassee*, a narrative of Confederate raiders, coming to its climax in the account of the run of the *Tallahassee* from Wilmington to Halifax and away again, in the teeth of Federal men-of-war. In a narrative poem the reader does not, and should not, expect the high finish of the ode or the elegy; but Mr. Merkel is so rough and ready in manner as to distract the attention almost constantly from what he has to recount, and to rob his tale of most of its excitement. The printing is careless in the extreme, and many of the stanzas have been mangled by the misgrouping of lines. *Banner in the Sky,* by Miss Lilian Found, has a preface by Mr. Wilfrid Eggleston which is a model in a genre where it is so easy to be officious, or absurd, or portentous, or cowardly. "Her primary concern," he says, "is the underlying thought, not the superficial finish. Of some of her own lines the dictum applied to Thoreau may also be relevant, that the 'thyme and marjoram are not yet honey'." They are indeed very far from honey; for Miss Found's thought is an essayist's rather than a poet's, and much more than superficial finish is lacking. The thought is solid, however: Miss Found could stock a dozen minor poets in ideas, and not observe the loss. Mr. Lloyd Douglas's preface to Mrs. Dorothy Sproule's *Poems of Life* is as unfortunate as Mr. Eggleston's is apt. "The Dorothy Sproule poems," he says, "vibrate with spiritual energy. . . . Their power is rather

that of the quiet storage-battery than the noisy dynamo."
There are other jewels in the page. The poems are harmless, and some of them have charm; but it is difficult to do them justice after such an opening blast. Mr. H. H. Langton's preface to Miss Helen Fairbairn's *From Dawn to Dusk* is a mere certificate of acquaintance; and I am at a loss to know what function it could possibly serve. Miss Fairbairn's verses belong to the late Victorian manner, are elaborate and melodious, and very often delightfully dexterous. Like many late Victorian poets she does not leave the impression of strong belief in anything she says. Professor O. J. Stevenson's *A Group of Poems* belongs to a kindred but simpler tradition; his mastery of his medium is not so striking, and his sense of his substance is a little stronger, although the substance is slight. The *Poems* of Miss Laura Bedell are always competent, and, unlike many of the collections noticed in this paragraph, have sentiment without sentimentality; but they are powerless to seize upon one's emotions or mind. *The Moving Finger,* by Miss Mary Matheson, has many resemblances to Miss Bedell's *Poems,* but is less dexterous, and less finely controlled. *Vistas Grave and Gay and Here's to Happiness,* two little collections by Mr. T. B. Gleave, have won not only popularity but critical approval. It is easy to understand their popularity, but difficult to conceive why the critics (in a preface we are told that Mr. Gleave does not write for them) were pleased. *The Sojourner,* by Mr. Arthur C. Nash, is a series of musings in poetic prose. *God's Plenty* is Canon J. E. Ward's reshaping of the story of Ruth in a dramatic form; the verse is eloquent, and some of the songs are pure, but dramatic intensity, in which the biblical narrative is so rich, is flagging.

The "Ryerson Poetry Chap-Books," one of the most useful media for Canadian poetry, are slightly more numerous than usual. One half of Mrs. Hermia Harris Fraser's *Songs of the Western Islands* are on Indian themes, and call up agreeable memories of *Hiawatha;* the others touch on the immediate present and, although in these the expression is not often at the height of what is felt, something of the intensity of the feeling reaches the reader. In Mrs. Dorothy Howard's *When I Turn Home* what one misses is again the power of phrase by which such feelings and pictures as she offers are made memorable. The same comment applies to Mrs. Eileen Cameron Henry's *Sea-Woman*. In *And in the Time of Harvest,* by Mrs. Monica Roberts Chalmers, there is a greater originality of phrase and rhythm and a greater power in presenting ideas associated with feeling. Dr. Vere Jameson's *Moths after Midnight,* a somewhat larger collection, pleases by the variety of themes and forms, and also because here we are addressed by a fully adult intelligence, working on broad experience. The level of performance is uneven. "A Name" seizes upon the old theme of the incongruity and queer importance of names (Christian and patronymic) and makes of the perception the opportunity for a fine imaginative excursion. "Miracle" is a doctor's experience, sharply drawn.

With the "Chap-Books" it is natural to associate another valuable medium, the publications of the poetry societies. Of the three that have come to the QUARTERLY this year, from Montreal, Alberta and Saskatchewan, the first is much the most satisfactory. It is the smallest, and reflects more editorial discrimination. Doubtless exclusions present difficulties even to courageous editorial committees; but if the purpose of poetry groups is something superior to self-glorification or mutual applause, if it is to serve the interest of poetry, in their organs should appear only the truly poetic. If there is not enough of the truly poetic available for publications on the present plan, it is a simple decision to reduce the size of the brochures and to extend the intervals between appearances.

Three little booklets by Miss Evelyn Cook, undated and privately printed, have a sincerity and delicacy which lead one to wish for them a wider circulation. Miss Cook's talent is uneven for all its charm, and she too has much to gain from a more general circulation and a more critical audience than she has allowed herself. Hers is an interesting new voice, and with mention of another such voice, a stronger one, this survey must end. Four of the poems of Bertram Warr appear in the October issue of *Contemporary Verse,* a quarterly which takes on a higher distinction with every year. Bertram Warr was born in Toronto in 1917, lived there until 1938, spent that year in wandering through

Canada, at the end of it left for London, where "against his convictions he was drafted into the RAF" in 1941, and was killed in action over Germany in April, 1943. A memorial volume is planned to contain his journal as well as his poems. English men of letters noted the quality of the poems he contributed to a variety of magazines and anthologies. In the four poems now available to us there is a deep and sombre imaginative power, and an art which is adequate either for pure fancy of a grim kind or for strict realism informed by mature emotion. "Stepney, 1941" is one of the most striking poems precipitated by the war.

1946

The *Poems* are Mr. Robert Finch's first volume. Even for an English-Canadian poet they appear somewhat late, for Mr. Finch is forty-six. He has however achieved a considerable reputation, and the book has been eagerly awaited. Mr. Finch was one of the six poets represented in *New Provinces* (1936), with which the contemporary phase of our poetry began to attract critical notice. His pieces in the Canadian number of *Poetry* (April, 1941) were among the most individual. He had striking poems in Mr. Gustafson's two anthologies, the *Anthology of Canadian Poetry* (1942) and the *Little Anthology of Canadian Poets* (1943). In Mr. A. J. M. Smith's *Book of Canadian Poetry* (1943) he stood with F. R. Scott at the head of the section significantly named "The Cosmopolitan Tradition." Most of the old favourites are reprinted in the *Poems,* but there is also much that is new.

There has never been anything in Canadian poetry at all like Mr. Finch's work. As I write, one of his early paintings hangs in front of me, an exquisite study in line, sharp, emphatic, decisive, but saved from all hardness by an astonishing delicacy in colouring. Emphasis and delicacy, so extraordinarily combined in his painting, come together to produce in his poetry a unique effect. He delights in the monosyllable, the quick clean phrase, the short line, the simple stanza, but he delights also in the suggestive epithet, the approximate rhyme, the fantastic, even bizarre image. The complex effect that comes of so strange an association appears in such a nature piece as "Etobicoke Autumn":

> Under the white bridge
> In the hush between gale and gale
> The water tugs edge over edge
> Over ochre shale.

The barbs of the willow leaves
Point from bent stems
At a black stove-pipe on pink eaves
As the wind aims

Misses and rips the cloud-butts
Loosing a gale again
Till the rain falls like ripe notes
And the nuts like green rain

And the pickers cramming the sleeves
Of sweaters are fanned
Through the rain of nuts and breves
To the hot-dog stand.

Extraordinary care has gone into the composition of his poems. In "Poet on Poet" he contrasts two kinds of poetry, and there is no doubt to which his own belongs:

His lines run wherever his pen goes,
Mine grope the miles from heart to head;
His will tire before he does;
Mine will move when I am dead.

In poetry as in painting Mr. Finch cares immensely for the expressiveness peculiar to the medium; and it is because he cares that he can make so luminous a critical statement as his sonnet "Words":

There are words that can only be said on paper.
It is fortunate they are few. All others shrink
On paper to the thinness of dried ink
And fade at the mind into forgotten vapour.

There are words that can only be said once
And have all been said before that fact is plain.
In a sense no word can ever be said again
And none can be said again in the same sense.

There are words that have to be said or written,
Answers and questions, times to be observed,
But most words die in a cause they have not served
Or bite forever what never should be bitten.

And then there are the words that are left unsaid
And the undetectable words used in their stead.

I should like to quote other poems of the same delicate just-ness of expression, such as "The Reticent Phrase," "Being Remembered," "The Formula"; but there are other aspects of Mr. Finch's work which must not go unmentioned.

The least satisfactory of these is the satire on vulgarities. The chief surprise the *Poems* reserve for one who has read all Mr. Finch's fugitive publications is the copiousness of his satiric vein. It is difficult to be delicate in satirizing the coarse, or precise in satirizing the shapeless. I do not think that Mr. Finch, amazing as his ingenuity is, has satisfacto-rily solved the difficulty. Occasionally he appears to recog-nize what a difficulty lies in wait for him, as in "At Niagara" – a comment on a stupid response to the glory of the falls – and abandons delicacy and form. The poem has vigour and point, but it lacks a poetic residue.

Emotion is curbed in most of Mr. Finch's poetry. In a phrase or rhythm it suddenly assumes power, only to be checked. Now and then it animates a whole poem as in the admirable "The Captive":

> Though you were ice
> My heat would melt you,
> Though you were iron
> My fire would smelt you,
>
> Though you were silence
> I, a sound,
> Would fill your most
> Reluctant bound,
>
> Though you were music,
> None should hear
> Without the office
> Of my ear,
>
> And were you wings
> You could not get
> Beyond the soaring
> Of my net.
>
> So might I do,
> And these might be,
> If you should ever
> Set me free.

This is a fine poem, and one which discloses some of Mr. Finch's affiliations. Unlike any of those I have previously quoted or cited, it might have been written by Mr. A. J. M. Smith or Mr. Frank Scott. It shows Mr. Finch's allegiance to the Metaphysicals, and his liking for Emily Dickinson.

The collection is full of good things, and now that Mr. Finch has consented to publish a book of his poetry, I hope its reception will persuade him to give us more, much more.

II

The essence of what Miss P. K. Page has to say, and something of the fine and simple art with which she says it, appear in the poem from which her collection takes its title:

> For we can live now, love:
> a million in us breathe,
> moving as we would move
> and qualifying death
>
> in lands our own and theirs
> with simple hands as these
> a walk as like as hers
> and words as like as his.
>
> They, in us, free our love,
> make archways of our mouths,
> tear off the patent gloves
> and atrophy our myths.
>
> As ten, as twenty, now,
> we break from single thought
> and rid of being two,
> receive them and walk out.

As ten, as twenty! Where so many poets and lovers have prized their experience because it appeared to them unique, and gloried in a *solitude à deux,* Miss Page requires to be convinced that it is common, accessible to all. Otherwise it would be an experience to be rejected. Multitude and solitude preoccupy her, the need of community, the fear of

256

peculiarity. Her set of values is emphasized in many appropriate ways, best of all perhaps by the arrangement of her poems. The group at the end of the volume is an excellent instance of her skill in arrangement. In "Landlady" she presents a horrifying portrait of a purely parasitic emotional life, in which the solitary landlady spies and pries with revolting astuteness. The three poems that follow present attempts at escape from solitude through love. Then comes an arraignment entitled "Only Child." The effect is clinched by the powerful short poem that concludes the collection:

> The mole goes down the slow dark personal passage –
> a haberdasher's sample of wet velvet moving
> on fine feet through an earth that only
> the gardener and the excavator know.
>
> The mole is a specialist and truly
> opens his own doors; digs as he needs them
> his tubular alleyways; and all his hills
> are mountains left behind him.

In "Generation" and "Election Day" Miss Page accounts for the primary value she sets upon universality. It is characteristic of her that the autobiographical piece "Generation" should present no experience peculiar to her, but simply what she believes the *élite* of her age have undergone. Spain, she declares, was their awakening. After they came to understand something of what was happening in Spain, all the tribal ways of their parents ceased to count. Nothing exclusive was any longer good enough. "Election Day" is a more vivid poem, and her attitude towards the conservative elders comes through it very well:

> Colonel Evensby with his narrow feet
> will cast his blue blood ballot for the Tory
>
> and in the polling station I shall meet
> and smiling, rather gentle overlords
> propped by their dames and almost twins in tweeds,
> and mark my X against them and observe
> my ballot slip, a bounder, in the box.

Late in the evening, when the returns are in and the Conservatives have won – at Miss Page's years it can only have been a provincial election – she walks through the wealthy avenues:

> The neighbourhood
> is neatly hedged with privet still, the lights
> are blinking out in the enormous homes.
> Gentlemen, for the moment, you may sleep.

The young *élite* – Miss Page does not speak of an *élite*, and in her terms of thought she cannot, but it is of an *élite* she is thinking – have had at least one tremendous reward. They may have had their lives torn up (if not ended) by the war that followed upon Spain; but it has brought thousands of them to remote parts of the earth, and given them, as they look upon a map, a sense of the world's oneness that no other generation in Canada ever had. They have grown safely into multitudinousness, solitude has few dangers for them. This is Miss Page's reading of their experience.

For my part I think it is far too hopeful a reading. But this is a critique of poetry, not of political attitudes. The poetry Miss Page has developed about her constant theme is strong in its intensity and simplicity. It has dignity and it has beauty. To say of an epic poet that his attitude towards his material is partial is to admit a fatally limiting defect; but what lyrical poetry is not partial? One would need to go a long way back to find a great lyrical poet who expressed a broad and central attitude towards any large part of life. Is there any one between us and Robert Burns?

III

A remarkable vitality of language is the quality in Mr. Patrick Anderson's *The White Centre* that first makes its way with the reader. Not all the poems have vitality. From "The Machine," to take a striking instance, it is quite absent. But when the vitality is there, and it usually is, the effect is unmistakable. It animates these lines on the Canadian wilderness before the first white men came:

when resinous currents streaked its boughgreen waves
and soundless arrows
were slipping like fish through fathoms of spruce and
balsam:

or in a very different, much more economical manner it
animates this stanza on a stream:

And there were beds of stones
baked white by the brown water
and feathery islands where
the birds chilled with their beaks
the beaches of white stones.

Mr. Anderson is a natural lord of language, a born word-
man. But he is also a man whose senses are remarkably
impressionable. When he writes without a basis in sense-
impressions the effect is thin and dry.

The collection as a whole defines an interesting personality. The personality is much more multiform than is usual
in Canadian poetry, and it is significant that Mr. Anderson
came to Canada only after he had graduated at Oxford and
studied in the United States. Poets of Canadian birth and
mainly Canadian experience are less curious, less eager,
less various than the author of *The White Centre*. Most of
them are, however, more fully in possession of themselves,
less likely to experiment in somewhat contradictory directions. Mr. Anderson has already become an influence upon
a number of the younger poets, and he will certainly bring
enrichment, if perhaps also a degree of confusion.

Mr. Louis Dudek, like Miss Page, was one of the contributors to *Unit of Five (1944)*. In *East of the City* the themes
are almost the same as those that preoccupied him two
years ago, and the treatment of them is not significantly
different. Mr. Dudek is sensitive to the surfaces of things
and of persons, and many of his best passages are the records of his simple responses to what he sees and hears. He
is also concerned with the social system, and bent upon its
reconstruction: he often bursts into indictments of injustice
and calls for summary action. The two main levels of his
poetry – the sensual and the intellectual – remain separate,
and there is little reciprocal enrichment. Perhaps what one

misses most is what Mr. Finch has in such perfection, the distinctive power over words, the individual word, and the arrangement of words in broad units. When this power is lacking a poem may yet move, it is true, but it is scarcely poetically moving, for what it has to deliver is not enhanced by the poetic medium.

The "New Writers" series, which began in 1945, had but one addition, Mr. Raymond Souster's *When We are Young*. Another contributor to *Unit of Five*, he shares Mr. Dudek's social doctrines, and his delight in surfaces. What distinguishes his verse is its warmth. Where so many poets impose upon the expression of their feelings the discipline of a constantly vigilant intelligence, Mr. Souster allows his almost unrestricted play, with a long emphatic line, an apparently casual collocation of words, and a movement of ideas as simple and clear as in popular verse. He is extraordinarily readable, and often a moving poet. His themes are few – physical love is the chief of them – and a not unpleasing monotony runs through the collection and before long lulls the critical sense. I hope that he will develop a greater interest in pattern; whether he does or not, I shall look for his next collection with a lively interest.

IV

Mr. Ernest Fewster's collection, *The Wind and the Sea*, gives exactly what its title promises, and something more. It is a carefully organized sequence of odes first on the wind and then on the sea, followed by a miscellany of shorter and simple lyrics on related themes. Wind and sea have mystical meanings for Mr. Fewster. Unfortunately the words are in the main worn counters, and it is crucial to poems on topics such as his that the words be fresh and living. The best poems in Mr. John Coulter's *The Blossoming Thorn* – an engagingly modest title – are the simple melancholy pieces. The formal elegies and the humorous and satiric pieces fall quickly into the prosaic or conventional. Mrs. Doris Ferne's *Paschal Lamb* and Miss Reba Hudson's *Brief for Beauty* have much in common; Mrs. Ferne has the broader range and the more experimental approach to structure, Miss Hudson the greater competence in verse.

Mrs. Mona Gould's *I Run with the Fox* has at its best the tripping movement and fugitive touch of light verse; in the poems where the feeling is graver the movement and the touch are not appropriate. Mr. Frederick Watt, the author of the naval narrative *Who Dare to Live*, turns in *Landfall* to occasional and reflective verse. In the speed of narrative the roughness and thinness in his verse texture could be obscured, but in the new collection they force themselves on the reader's notice. Mr. Robert Allison Hood's *Ballads of the Pacific Northwest* are misnamed. The poems are long-ish narratives, in unrhymed verse, and anything less like songs or ballads it would be difficult to conceive. Based on early journals and on well-chosen secondary sources, they recount the exploits of explorers and settlers from Vancouver to Moberly and John Cameron. The sober rather prosaic quality of the verse is suggested by the final lines which explain Mr. Hood's admirable motive:

> When we look back
> upon these stirring stories of the past
> and see what common simple men have done
> under the plan of Providence Divine
> to shape the destiny of the Northwest,
> whether selfishly or otherwise, in faith and hope,
> it steels us with fortitude to face the future.

There were nine new "Ryerson Poetry Chap-Books" in 1946, more than in any year since the series began in 1925. Miss Audrey Alexandra Brown's *V-E Day*, the hundred-and-twentieth in the set, is an ode contrasting the horrors that have passed with the calm that has followed. It is a work of feeling, not of thought; and perhaps a simpler form would have expressed with fuller appropriateness what Miss Brown wished to say. The language and music are marked by the purity and grace of her poetry at its best. The other "Chap-Books" are of quite uneven merit. There are moving poems on death in Mr. Goodridge MacDonald's *The Dying General*. Mr. George Whalley's *Poems 1939-1944* have an attractive economy. Mrs. Marjorie Freeman Campbell's *Merry-Go-Round* is a narrative of contemporary life, written with vigour and directness uncommon in our poetry – in which this valuable *genre* is unaccountably neglected. Vigour and directness also mark Mrs. Norah Godfrey's *Cavalcade*, but the language falls far short of her high intention. In Mrs. Margot Osborn's *Frosty-Moon* and Mr. R. E. Rashley's *Voyageur* there are pictures of the prairie sharp enough to stir one's memories. Sharp pictures of many sorts are drawn in Mrs. Doris Hedges' *The Flower in the Dusk*, but feeling is not so aptly rendered. One of the poems in Mrs. Verna Loveday Harden's *When This Tide Ebbs* is a meditation on old Trinity College, closing with lines that in a more mature culture would not be forgotten:

This is where Lampman walked on that May morning,
With Robert's *Orion* in his hand.

How many of the passers-by on Queen Street have heard of Lampman's name?

The poetry societies have been busy. *The Vancouver Poetry Society, 1916-1946: A Book of Days,* is a useful compilation. It provides a history of the Society, uneven in tone and value, but with many facts and impressions on which historians may draw; biographies of the charter-members, present practising members, and honorary presidents – the order may be unusual, but is eminently just; and a small number of poems representative of the work of members past and present. Too little local literary history is written in Canada; and even when the performance is not wholly satisfactory it is welcome. The most interesting of the annual publications of the societies is *Profile,* which comes from Ottawa. The judges, Miss Anne Marriott and Mr. Wilfrid Eggleston, were admirably chosen; the brochure is beautifully produced; and much of the verse, in the main by young and relatively unknown writers, has charm as well as competence. Like all such publications, in Canada, and elsewhere, it is too generously inclusive.

This has not been one of the most notable years since the QUARTERLY'S survey began; but the number and variety of promising books has made it one of the most interesting.

1947

The death of Duncan Campbell Scott at eighty-five came in the last month of a year in which three of his books made their first appearance: a critique of the art of W. J. Phillips, a selection from the poems of Archibald Lampman, and *The Circle of Affection,* a miscellany of his own verse and prose. The new Lampman retains almost everything from the selection of a quarter-century ago entitled *Lyrics of Earth,* adds a considerable number of poems from *At the Long Sault* (1943), and restores a few pieces which have not been accessible since the Memorial Edition of 1900 ceased to be reprinted. The introduction is substantially a reprint of that to the Memorial Edition (there are a few corrections of fact), which is on the whole the best of the many tributes to Lampman's power that Scott wrote in the course of the forty-eight years by which he survived his friend. The Ryerson Press has given the book a handsome format, and I hope that this edition may long remain in print as a means for making acquaintance with the most adequate of Canadian poets in the sense that he achieved perfection in the kinds of poetry he preferred. He wrote much outside those kinds, and I believe that he was moving to great achievement in a more dramatic kind. Whatever differences in opinion there may be concerning Lampman's poems in other kinds, only sectaries will question that his evocations of nature and his sonnets on ethical themes have the beauty of adequacy. Only a few pages in *The Circle of Affection* belong to this section of "Letters in Canada." A few poems from Scott's earlier years which had escaped his notice when he collected his verse in 1926 now appear in a volume for the first time; some of them have charm and power; but the chief interest in the poetic part of this miscellany lies in poems written since the publication of *The Green Cloister* in 1935. Among these the tribute to his second wife, Elise Aylen, on the twelfth anniversary of their marriage is pre-eminent. The intense emotion is expressed in the strict form of a short sequence of sonnets, and the high success is the more remarkable since the sonnet is a medium that Scott did not often essay, and one to which he did not feel much attraction. Another striking piece is "Amanda," a dream poem verging on nightmare, which carries one back to the title-piece of Scott's first collection, *The Magic House* (1893). To set them side by side is to see that whatever the years may have taken from his poetry they added more.

A learned quarterly is an inappropriate place to lament the failure of the Canadian public to value Scott's poetry – or his prose for that matter – as its quality deserved. It is not inappropriate to say here that the failure of the Canadian universities, and especially of their English departments, to see in Scott a poet whose work would reward the closest interpretation is an example of the immaturity of our culture. His death severs the last link with the greatest movement in our literature. It also ends one of the great careers and admirable lives in our history.

II

In the spring of 1945 it was intimated to Mr. E. J. Pratt that the facilities of the Royal Canadian Navy would be at his disposal if he should care "to spend some time at sea in order to gather material and atmosphere for a poem." Mr. Pratt went to the east coast the following summer, and spent some weeks at sea and in naval installations ashore. He read many files of records, and talked with a large number of naval personnel. When he had evaluated the role that the Canadian navy had played in the war, it seemed to him that the ideal subject for a representative narrative would be an incident which "would combine dramatic intensity with the eternal tedium of a convoy." Among alternatives the one that finally satisfied him was the voyage of S.C. 42 in the autumn of 1941, from Halifax to Londonderry by the northern route. The convoy consisted of sixty-six merchant ships, travelling at eight knots, and meagrely protected by a single destroyer, the *Skeena,* and three corvettes. This convoy when it had reached northern waters was the first victim of an assault by a wolf-pack of U-boats, and lost sixteen ships in the course of two successive moonlit nights, the attack continuing at intervals during the intervening day. On the day following the second assault, five British destroyers met the convoy and put an end to its ordeal. In 1941 *asdic* was the most powerful scientific aid to the defence of merchant ships; but *asdic* ceased to be dependable when the assault was delivered not by one but by many submarines, penetrating the lines of the convoy, and offering simultaneous and confusing attack. Once convinced that here was his subject, Mr. Pratt obtained from the commanding officer of the *Skeena,* Captain James Hibbard, "the use of his log and the Report of Proceedings," and also "his personal narrative" of the convoy. This material – precious beyond all else for his purpose – was supplemented by conversations with others who had been in the company of the *Skeena* at the time of the convoy.

The narrative is called significantly *Behind the Log.* The emphasis is placed at once on Mr. Pratt's imaginative reworking of his material, on his perception of the human traits which lay behind official entries:

Just here the log with its raw elements
Enshrined a saga in a phrase of action.
"The *Empire Hudson* listing badly, crew
And officers were disembarked. Someone
Reported – 'Secret papers have not been
Destroyed, mersigs, swept-channels, convoy route,
And codes, the CODES!' And as there was a chance
The steamer might not sink, *Kenogami*
Was ordered to embark an officer,
Return him to the listed deck to find
And sink the weighted papers – *which was done.*"
This stark undecorated phrase was just
An interlinear item in the drama,
Three words spelling a deed unadvertised,
When ships announced their wounds by rockets, wrote
Their own obituaries in flame that soared
Two hundred feet and stabbed the Arctic night. . . .

This passage will also show that the familiar Pratt rhythms recur with undiminished power in *Behind the Log*.

The narrative is in three main blocks: the conference in port at which the merchant captains are briefed; the anxious week in which, unattacked, the convoy makes its slow way to the north; the attack. There follows a short but exceedingly fine concluding passage in which under the guard of the five British destroyers the convoy proceeds to port.

The conference is in the vein of the passage in *Dunkirk* describing the improvisation of the rescue fleet. Here (and in a few later passages concerning fledgling sailors) Mr. Pratt gives his exuberance its head. It is certainly not his intention that the report of the conference should be a simple transcript of the real thing: rather it is the real thing in its essence, buoyant, with the Elizabethan heroic humour in which Mr. Pratt is always at home.

In the second block, the narrative of the anxious week preceding the attack, occur some of the most elaborate and startling of the images Mr. Pratt's scientific learning provides for his poetry, and some of his surest perceptions of the tensions of prolonged crisis.

The third block, the narrative of the attack, is the core of the poem, and it is here, properly, that Mr. Pratt draws on his greatest resources of style. It is no longer the style of *The Cachalot,* or *The Titanic,* nor is it closer to the style of *Brébeuf and His Brethren.* What is happening to his style is analogous with what happened to Yeats's: it is assuming a new austerity. There is loss in the transformation, loss that is inevitable, but should not be regretted, since in the new style an effect of peculiar intensity can be attained. There is also a loss that is not inevitable: when the new style becomes wholly flexible to Mr. Pratt's intentions, it will produce greater effect than it produces here, or will produce it more continuously. The danger incurred in the new style is the danger of prosaism; and there are some lines, not many but enough to be noticed, in which the manner lapses into the prosaic. But in the happier passages what a fine and new effect the style provides:

It took three minutes for the merchantman
To dock her pigiron on the ocean floor.

> Survivors from the *Stargard*
> Who would for life carry their facial grafts
> Told of the scramble from the boiler rooms
> Up canted ladders and the reeling catwalks,
> Only to find their exit was the sea.

The beautiful quiet close, with its music of names, now of a Scandinavian harshness, now with all the softness of Irish, and its rhythms like those of a sea with long gentle waves, is comparable with the close of *Brébeuf*. If it has a fault that is its bevity. Perhaps we require more time to pass securely into the final mood.

Ten Selected Poems by Mr. Pratt is for use in schools. Among the ten are *The Cachalot, The Titanic, Brébeuf and His Brethren,* and *Dunkirk*. There are seventeen pages of notes by an unknown hand; many are so illuminating as to convince the reader that the poet either wrote them or revised them. The preface, signed merely "The Publishers," is much less successful. This text-book is surely destined for a long life; and I urge the Macmillan Company to replace the inadequate preface by a statement from Mr. Pratt on the scope and intention of his poetry, or if he should prove unwilling to write one, from a critic of unquestioned competence. I have called *Ten Selected Poems* a text-book: it will also provide at the modest price of a dollar and a quarter an excellent sampling of Mr. Pratt's work for the general Canadian reader.

III

Miss Dorothy Livesay's *Poems for People* is a collection somewhat less striking than her *Day and Night*. It has the same general qualities as the preceding book: the sharp perceptions of the surfaces of objects and persons, the easy mastery of varied forms, the powerful rhythms, and the urgency of thought on political and social issues. The language is somewhat less rich, the emotion somewhat less vehement. In a number of the poems there are tracts in which the form seems less inevitable, less appropriate to the idea. In a word some of the poems in the new collection fall short of that wholeness of impression in which Miss Livesay has so often been strong. But *Poems for People* is an important book.

On the jacket of *The Flowing Summer* Mr. Charles Bruce makes a perceptive comment on his poem: "*The Flowing Summer* sprouted as a story and was written first in prose. But I had been thinking of how narrative verse is so frequently concerned with the heroic, . . .(the suspension points are in the text) wondering whether certain aspects of the undramatic continuity in common living could live again in poetry. And almost before I knew it *The Flowing Summer* was being worked out in a simple verse form; a form in which if I were lucky the happy accident of poetry might occur." *The Flowing Summer* is a very quiet poem, the story of a summer spent by a young boy, Toronto-born and bred, on the Nova Scotian farm of his grandfather. The incidents are slight – the pulling in of nets full of herring, the cutting and stooking of grain, the ransacking of the attic for the toys and books of his father. All the personages have a pleasant equability and normality – everything that they do or say or feel is simple and intelligible at the quick reading the poem invites. Where then is the poetic element, the thing that is to justify the choice of verse as medium? It is in the poet's mood, in the angle of vision from which the simple persons and slight events are contemplated. The poet is unobtrusive; but he is everywhere. It is he who shapes our responses to all that occurs. The method is Wordsworth's: a situation is chosen from common life and treated within the vocabulary of ordinary men, and yet raised to poetry by the effort of the imagination, in Mr. Bruce's case a moral imagination, a sympathetic insight. As so often happens in Wordsworth's longer rural poems the effect is not uniformly happy; there are fine and moving passages, but there are also passages in which the thud of prose ruins the mood. But like everything that Mr. Bruce has published in verse *The Flowing Summer* has charm and is almost unscarred by fad or oddity. It reads well now – not superlatively, but well; and it has a better chance than most poems written in this decade of being read in the long future.

At the opposite extreme from Mr. Bruce, often so near to

the prosaic, is Mr. Tom MacInnes. *In the Old of My Age* is an interesting postscript to the *Complete Poems,* published twenty-five years ago, and now happily proved incomplete. The new volume, appearing after the poet's eightieth birthday, is not unnaturally less imaginative, and above all less fanciful than his earlier performance; reflection has grown more vigorous, and it is fascinating to see what were the ideas that underlay the sprightly but seldom superficial verse that charmed us long ago. Unfortunately the verbal texture has become thin and detracts from the poetic effect. But almost every piece is marked by Mr. MacInnes's peculiar manner, by an aesthetic identity rare in Canadian poetry.

To pass from a poet of the older generation to one of the middle, Mr. Arthur Bourinot's *Collected Poems* disclose a movement from the strict forms which were current when Mr. Bourinot began to publish to the freer media that characterize the most original verse of the past decade. Mr. Bourinot is an accomplished and sensitive craftsman, and his forms are seldom arbitrary. If they have altered it is because he has altered: he has received the impress of the time, and if he has lost something that he had when he wrote the admirable memorial sonnets to his mother, he has gained in sweep and force.

Mr. Raymond Souster, one of the youngest generation of poets as yet worth consideration, has published in *Go to Sleep, World* a collection very like his *When We are Young,* which came out last year, and from which only two poems are retained. The title of Miss Livesay's *Poems for People* suits his book better than it does the products of her subtler and more learned art. Nature, the city street, love, melancholy, a keen fear of the pressures of society upon the ordinary man, a vaguer somewhat desperate belief in the value of the individual in himself – these are the chief themes of the collection. It is obvious that they are themes that belong within the emotional life of the normal Canadian, of the normal person in this time. What Mr. Souster requires is confidence in a ruthless editorial adviser; until he finds and trusts such an adviser his verse will not have the impact it ought to have. I wish it would have that impact, for Mr.

Souster is one of the extremely few poets in Canada who have an idiom that permits real communication with the average reader.

IV

Among the chap-books of the year Mr. A. M. Klein's *Seven Poems* is outstanding. All seven touch on aspects of the national life in extraordinarily illuminating fashion, and in a language which if less rich in texture than Mr. Klein once employed is firm and imaginative. The shortest of them, "Air Map," will give a notion of their force and illumination:

> How private and comfortable it once was,
> our white mansard beneath the continent's gables!
> But now, evicted, and still there—
> a wind blew off the roof?—
> we see our fears and our featherbeds plumped white
> on the world's crossroads.

Songs from Then and Now, by Mrs. Ruby Nichols, the 127th Ryerson Chap-Book, and one of the best in the series, is unhappily titled. It is a sequence of love poems in two contrasted moods, but the constant intensity of emotion is much more significant than the contrast. Despite occasional infelicities of diction and rhythm this little book is one of the most successful of the year. The emotion has found a medium through whose imagery and movement its force passes to the reader with almost complete adequacy. Emotion is as strong in Mrs. Doris Hedges' *Crisis*, and here there is unusual breadth of mood; but the language is rhetorical rather than finely poetical. The poems seem to have been set down in a rush, and the poet to have believed that the force of feeling would blind the reader to the frequent thinness of realization. The lyrics and sonnets in *As a River Runs*, by Mrs. Dorothy Howard, express a cultivated personality and without exception give pleasure. But the words and rhythms in which Mrs. Howard expresses her feelings are too often worn, and do not remain in the mind after the booklet has been laid aside. The largest of the Ryerson Chap-Books for 1947 is Miss M. Eugenie Perry's *Song in the Silence, and Other Poems*. "Song in the Silence" is a moving narrative: it turns upon the effect of deafness in a young girl's life and love, and the change brought about by a hearing-device. The language is somewhat too decorative for so austere a theme, but the grasp on character is firm. Most of the other poems are in one of Miss Perry's accustomed manners – ornate, reflective, accomplished. The chap-books from other presses are of a disappointing quality.

V

A Whip for Time, by Mrs. Elizabeth Harrison, is accomplished verse, and a pleasure by the deft arrangement of sound and image and the sure evolution of the emotion. If the texture is surely woven, the total effect is slight. This is Mrs. Harrison's first collection. I look forward to a second. *Sunday-Monday*, by Mr. Harry Amoss, is an expression in an idiom often gnarled and sometimes grotesque, of an original and impressive personality. The collection is startlingly uneven; and like Mr. Souster, Mr. Amoss would gain by trusting a ruthless editor. *Coffee and Bitters*, by Mr. Nathan Ralph, is a series of pictures expressed in language marred by a persistent and apparently deliberate thinness of texture. In *Always the Bubbles Break* Mrs. Irene Moody reveals the same qualities as in her much earlier *Lava*; intense but seldom successful effort is the dominant impression. The best of the poems in Mrs. Margaret Fulton Frame's *Phantom Caravan* have grace and melody; but both the range of feeling and the idiom are so conventional that no lasting effect is produced. Arthur Tooth failed to return from a bombing mission in May, 1942. Fiction had been his chief literary concern, but like many a prose writer he occasionally preferred to express himself in verse. *Flight's End* is a memorial collection of his poems. A smaller volume would have been a wiser choice; but in the best of the pieces Mr. Tooth is sincere and vigorous and at home with words. Guy Victor Waterman served with an artillery unit and was killed in Holland in December, 1944. *Work Unfinished* reveals a more formed personality than *Flight's End*, and a sharper visual power. But like the other memorial volume it expresses the author in a medium over which his mastery was far from complete.

Dr. Vere Jameson's *The Sultan of Jobat*, privately printed, and accompanied by a vigorious preface on the delights of humorous verse, has poems of delightful hilarity. But in invoking Burns as his master, Dr. Jameson invites the question why he did not attempt the portrayal of the hypocrisies and pretences in our society with the devastating directness of Burns. A satiric poet of Burns' kind at work in Ontario today would be a greater boon than a great newspaper.

1948

During the past two or three years the practising critics of Canadian poetry have been assailed by a few apologists for some of the younger poets. Two accusations have recurred. In one we are presented as so backward-looking that we have no awareness of the future. The future, it is said, will be scientific and collectivist. But the future will not be determined by science. Science does not make values. Values are in the custody of theologians, humanists, and artists. It is quite possible that the future will be collectivist in a degree that most of us on this continent find it difficult to conceive. Yet there is no reason for supposing that the arts as we have known them for millennia will perish or undergo such changes as would make them unrecognizable. They may be subject to persecution and distortion; but the arts have met those ordeals before, and have not been ruined. Despite the powerful impact on art of the society in which it is created, the essential concern of art is with the humanity, not with the political and social framework of man. To suggest that collectivism will lead to a greater kind of art or an art essentially different from what we now have is mere dreaming. From the dreaming, as from dreaming about the restoration of Laval's Canada or Durham's, admirable poems may come, but it is no basis for a criticism. The apologists may not be aware of it, but what they are assailing in the practising critics is not a hostility to collectivism, or an unawareness of its nature, but a lack of enthusiastic belief in its necessity and beauty.

In the other accusation we are presented as applying an over-lenient, and therefore implicitly insulting standard, in our criticism of Canadian poets, one that we do not or would not apply in writing of English or American poets. Here a distinction is needed for clarity. The criticism of poetry as of any art must first interpret. If in the exercise of his interpretative function a critic writes chiefly of what is genuine in a poem, what is notable, what is *there*, rather than of what is spurious, what is negligible, what is not there, his doing so need not mean that he is abandoning another of his functions, the making of judgments. Careful interpretation, conducted with insight and a measure of sympathy, must precede judgment, and in writing of recent or contemporary poets it is much wiser to make sure that one's interpretation is adequate than to press on to judgment. The history of criticism is strewn with examples of how the slighting of the critic's interpretative function has led to false and absurd judgments. The practising critics in Canada have been more concerned, in the exercise of judgment, to establish that poems are genuine than to declare that they are great. When an English critic writes of Walter de la Mare, he does not keep repeating that de la Mare's lyrics may be all very well in their way but will not bear a confrontation with Shelley's, nor does an American critic writing of Robert Frost's monologues remain in a state of nervous awareness that they do not have the rich close texture of Browning's. It is obvious to anyone that there has not been in the range of Canadian poetry anything as impressive as the best writing of the few best English and American poets of the past hundred years; but there is no reason in this to require of our practising critics that they bewail the absence of something to equal *The Waste Land*. When I say that 1948 has been a year of exciting achievement in Canadian poetry, I mean that at least half a dozen poets have brought out books in which there are genuine poems which offer delight; I do not mean that Shakespeare will be required to move over, or that the Nobel prize was awarded to Mr. Eliot only because Sweden has not heard of our strength.

II

The first thing to say about Mr. A. M. Klein's *The Rocking Chair* is that this small collection of thirty-seven poems is an important political fact.[1] The two subjects that Mr.

[1] Seven of these poems had already appeared in a brochure a few years ago.

Klein had cared to render in his earlier collections were the Jewish tradition and the somewhat segregated Jewish community in contemporary Montreal. In introducing *Hath Not a Jew* . . . Ludwig Lewisohn remarked that Mr. Klein was the most Jewish poet who had ever used the English tongue.

What Mr. Klein now renders with insight and sympathy, quite from within, is that element in our national society in which there has been the most acute prejudice against the Canadian Jew. The rocking chair is the symbol for French Canada. There are several bridges by which Mr. Klein has crossed over to become as an imaginative artist a part of the French culture in Canada. He has long delighted in Montreal – he has cared for it with a rhapsodic intensity no other Canadian poet has shown for his city. The great historic mountain is his special landscape, as necessary to his spirit as the Lake country to Wordsworth:

> And you above the city, scintillant,
> Mount Royal, are my spirit's mother,
> Almative, poitrinate!

Those strange polysyllables are extraordinarily apt; for the moment we glimpse a French poem within the English. Mr. Klein cares for all ancient cultures, especially for those which, like the Jewish and the French-Canadian, have a vigorous present and an immense promise. He cares for all religions, especially for those with elaborate and sensuous ceremonies, and an antique hierarchy. He cares with greater feeling for something that is very deep in the Catholic religion in the province of Quebec, a quality of amenity and sensitive kindness to those in trouble. "The Cripples" is an exuberant hymn of praise for Brother André and the Oratoire de St. Joseph:

> How rich, how plumped with blessing is that dome!
> The gourd of Brother André! His sweet days
> rounded! Fulfilled! Honeyed to honeycomb!

In "For the Sisters of the Hotel Dieu," with a more lyrical emotion he exclaims:

O biblic birds,
who fluttered to me in my childhood illnesses
 – me little, afraid, ill, not of your race, –
the cool wing for my fever, the hovering solace,
the sense of angels –
be thanked, O plumage of paradise, be praised.

I have already passed far beyond the political importance of the book to the revelation of its poetic force and beauty. It is not evenly good, but in the best poems there is a bold, full utterance and a fine profusion of imagery, depending on a buoyancy and force of temperament very rare in Canadian poetry, and rare, it is right to add, in the poetry of this age, wherever written.

Mr. Klein has the richness of nature that would equip a dozen accomplished and interesting poets. That is his greatest strength. It is what links him with E. J. Pratt, to whom, in many of the most learned passages in *The Rocking Chair,* the reader's mind quickly turns in reminiscence. But suddenly Klein will strike another note, more like that of Kenneth Fearing, and here much less clear and true, the note of irony and self-distrust. The largeness of Klein's habitual utterance leads one to think that the irony and self-distrust are external things, something the poet has found imposed upon him by the fashion of the age.

To Canadian critics who have believed that the Canadian element in a book was worth mention and analysis Mr. C. Day Lewis's introduction to *The Wounded Prince* by Mr. Douglas Le Pan is a valuable document. The closing paragraph has this passage:

He is a Canadian. He is also in his poetic thoughts and themes a European. He is not the first poet in whom the New and the Old World have met; but I am not sure he may not be the first in whom this partnership will remain an equal one. A great deal of the imagery of *The Wounded Prince* comes from his native land. . . .When he is concerned with the landscapes of the mind, too, and with what is called "the contemporary predicament," his brooding has "the features of Horatio" (as distinct from Hamlet's); there is a certain bluntness and dependability about the surface of his poems, a sense of largeness and open-airness and physical well-being, a tendency not to whittle down the heroic nor to wince at the sound of trumpets, qualities which derive no doubt from a New-World heritage and give to his verse its individual tang and strength.

This is admirably seized. The landscape in Mr. Le Pan's poetry is from Muskoka or the Georgian Bay, and in almost all his better poems the landscape matters. It is vigorously realized, and congruent with the mood. In "Canoe-Trip" he passes from landscape to reflection, to what should be called in Herbert Read's term "felt thought":

> What word of this curious country?
>
> It is good,
> It is a good stock to own though it seldom pays dividends.
> There are holes here and there for a gold-mine or a
> hydro-plant.
> But the tartan of river and rock spreads undisturbed,
> The plaid of a land with little desire to buy or sell.
> The dawning light skirls out its independence;
> At noon the brazen trumpets slash the air;
> Night falls, the gulls scream sharp defiance;
> Let whoever comes to tame this land, beware!
> Can you put a bit to the lunging wind?
> Can you hold wild horses by the hair?

It is difficult to end the quotation, for Mr. Le Pan's poems have a close texture, they are genuine wholes and they are packed with pleasing phrases as the clearings he speaks of are "enamelled with blueberries." His volume may not be one that the runner may read, but its obscurities are not very black, and for a poet in possession of modern techniques, he is straight-forward and uncomplicated. The weakest of the poems are those whose motive is romantic love, and in such a limitation Mr. Le Pan proves himself once more a part of Canadian writing. Where imagery is compact the words are sometimes only approximately right; but when an image is elaborated Mr. Le Pan's feeling for language appears to become surer. The lyrical and reflective poems that make up *The Wounded Prince* somehow leave an impression, partly by style, partly by tone, that Mr. Le Pan could manage a long narrative or a dramatic poem – and it is some years since any Canadian poet has made me wish that he would turn to a longer form.

The poems in *Deeper into the Forest* (a title taken from Grimm's *Tales*) are difficult, the most difficult of the year; and Mr. Roy Daniells is aware of their difficulty, and regrets it. In an appendix he offers a few notes on lines and phrases, on the pattern of the notes to *The Waste Land*, and also considers the more elusive kinds of difficulty that his poems present:

> No piece in this book is designedly or wilfully obscure, though a line here and there may seem difficult at first reading. (And at second and at third reading, no less, and not only a line, but quite often a passage, and sometimes a poem.) From the images supplied by the unconscious mind, or as was once said, by the Muse, the maker of a poem must accept those best embodying his impulse; he must shape them on the page in the fixed words provided by the language, as best he can; the result will seldom answer fully to his vision or intention. The reader is asked gently to hear, kindly to judge, to piece out imperfections with his own thoughts.

Many of the poems, especially in the section from which the collection takes its title, well from very deep in the unconscious. The store of words and images from which Mr. Daniells clothes his emotions is unusually rich: he has at his most intimate disposal not only the idiom of modern poetry and the poetry of the Renaissance but that of myth and folk-lore generally. The characteristic poems in this and other parts of the book are profound and extraordinarily anxious. The poems in lighter fashion, although they too have a note of anxiety and thus of some obscurity, will probably give more immediate pleasure than the others. It will be unfortunate if the collection comes to be judged by these more penetrable poems; for in them Mr. Daniells is simply another very clever poet. How clever, "Buffalo" will suggest. From the beginnings of civilized life in Manitoba down to the present, the buffalo, Mr. Daniells says, has been an implacable foe to progress. The close of the poem with its private message for academics runs:

278

Even mighty smiths like true men must confess
His power than theirs proved very little less
And still he stands far out Fort Garry way
Strong to obstruct, tenacious to delay.

Of the more difficult poems, it is with "Farewell to Winnipeg" that a reader should begin: the image of Louis Riel is at its core, and that image with its train of associations is much more easily grasped than most of those with which Mr. Daniells works. That the other parts of the book reward repeated readings, and slowly release a weight of religious and spiritual meaning I can give an assurance, but within the limits of this survey no proof.

The two main themes in Mr. L. A. MacKay's *The Ill-Tempered Lover* are passion and politics.[2] This collection undoubtedly contains the angriest poems a Canadian has published. In twenty sonnets and lyrics the poet traces the rise and then the rejection of a love. The earliest poems are so gentle that they may fairly be called idyllic; the beauty of the girl melts into mild natural backgrounds. The emotion mounts as the lover appreciates that his intense passion is not returned; now he is cast loose from his moorings, and even the pace of the poetry takes on a wild energy and freedom. In "Or as Andromede" he expresses his disquietude through a beautiful use of two Greek myths, and in the following poem, a bare quatrain, he expresses it with vigorous directness. Then in "Stript Bare, Strung up on Tiptoe" the sadistic imagery which is to dominate the remainder of the love-sequence appears with an appalling force and concentration. The denunciations begin. The intensity of the desire to belittle, to disdain, to hurt, is proof of the force of the poet's feeling. But of what feeling? What is disconcerting is that only after his rejection does the feeling become really intense. What is expressed seems rather wounded pride than wounded love. The poet seems much better able to express hatred and the related emotions than any of the elements that are usually thought to be central to love. It is difficult for the reader to participate in the poet's

---

[2]The fourteen poems that made up *Viper's Bugloss*, published under the pseudonym of John Smalacombe ("Ryerson Poetry Chap-Books," no. 79, 1938) are all reprinted in this collection. Most of the other pieces are also ten years old, or more.

feeling; the imaginative effort he is invited to make is too much of a strain, above all, too protracted a strain, for the later poems in this sequence to be read as they were intended to be read.

In the political poems there is a continuous jet of satire and invective. The League of Nations was a congress of hypocrites; the Spanish policy of the democracies was crypto-fascist; the Second World War was the fault of us all; the contribution of the Canadians who remained at home during the war was insignificant; and finally, a not unexpected climax, mankind is a pretty miserable lot. There is a specifically Canadian set of satires and invectives: our literature has been dull and stupid, and our criticism worse because too benign; our national policy in the nineteen-thirties, a true mirror of our lives, was cheap, materialistic, and confused; a few Canadian types are portrayed as deluded, vulgar, and frivolous. Mr. MacKay is not of the satirists who mingle attack with advocacy. The only values I can discover are silence and having a low opinion of ourselves; and even these qualities are less admired than merely opposed to their detestable opposites. Again that defect in love that appeared in the first part of the collection is notable. The political poems abound in dexterous and vigorous passages, and some of the couplet are brilliant:

> Why, we aim to be
> The Empire's, nay, the whole world's granary.
> A lofty mark, i' faith; to find our place
> Just in the belly of the human race.

The final and briefest part is miscellaneous. The idyllic quality in "Hylas" has a beauty that would be noticed anywhere, and is extraordinarily pleasing after all the rage and sneers that have gone before.

The Strait of Anian, Mr. Earle Birney's new collection does not need detailed comment since so much of it is reproduced from his earlier volumes. It is in two part "One Society" and "One World." Almost all the poems in the second part were in *David* (1942) or in *Now is Time* (1945), and it is good to see them restored to print. In the few poems in this part that are now collected for the first time Mr. Birney continues his commentary on the political and social signs of the times. "Man is a Snow," one of his most finely textured pieces, seems out of place. It is a poem about man, not simply political and social man, with this admirable close:

Man is a snow
that cracks the trees' red arches.

Man is a snow that winters
his own heart's cabin
where the frosted nail shrinks in the board
and pistols the brittle air
while the ferns of the lost world unfurling
crusten the useless windows.

In the first part of the volume, along with "David" and some other early pieces, Mr. Birney gathers a number of comments on Canada. The most impressive and in many ways the most satisfying of the new poems is "Prairie Counterpoint," in which there is a strong but delicate realization of the prairie landscape and atmosphere interwoven with conversational passages of great energy on the estrangement of the young generation from the land and the region. The platitude of their ambitions is rendered with a greater moderation than Mr. Birney often cares to attempt. This part of the collection is framed by two fine poems, "Atlantic Door" and "Pacific Door"; anyone who knows Mr. Birney's passion for British Columbia could foretell that the Pacific would liberate his feelings and focus his imagination and intelligence as the Atlantic could not. I am sorry to miss some poems from this collection that were in the earlier ones, especially "Joe Harris."

In "Letters in Canada: 1946" I considered at length Mr. Robert Finch's *Poems. The Strength of the Hills* is a collection twice as large, and much more than twice as finely produced, in the beautiful format of the new McClelland and Stewart series of Canadian books, the "Indian File." The new volume is as winning as the old, but so much like it in substance and manner that I am not prompted to offer a detailed critique. Mr. Finch is one of the few living Canadian poets who often combine with mastery of form (and for his mastery scarcely any praise would be too high) a uniqueness of vision which makes his poetry for page on page a series of unexpected, moving experiences. On one point of form, but a point of importance because the device recurs in so many of his lines, I am dissatisfied. Instead of hovering about a vowel, whether for emphasis or for some unusual musical purpose, he prefers to repeat it bluntly. The blunt effect does not seem in keeping with the delicacy of the other techniques that mark his verse.

The motive of the best poems in Miss Audrey Alexandra Brown's *All Fools' Day* is expressed in "The Reaper":

> Look well, who love all lovely things,
> The hour is, but the hour has wings.

Miss Brown loves all lovely things, and looks well at them. Her poetry is essentially a capturing of moments which she values for their intensity, aware that they are on the wing, occasionally moments in her own reflection, but far more often moments in which she has responded to something outside herself. Flowers at the very start of spring, a glimpse of the sea or of a special expression in a friend's face, candles shining in a mirror, the howl and emerald eyes of a wolf (not lovely to her, this last, but remembered because of the sharpness of the impression, and the intensity of the mood that gathered about it) – it is about such sudden experiences as these have brought that her poetry achieves its most satisfying forms. In this collection there is more verse of an intellectual cast than Miss Brown had previously published; but there is not the power to make poetry of an idea, and if her intellectual passages command respect they do not rise to the intensity so often realized in the renderings of what the hour with wings had brought. Miss Ethel Kirk Grayson's *Beggar's Velvet* has some affinities with Miss Brown's verse; but where Miss Brown depends equally on image and music, Miss Grayson is as nearly a pure imagist as any Canadian now writing. Her images are delicate, highly stylized (often oriental), and profuse. They carry the best of her poems. In the parts of the collection where a subject unsuited to velvet and brocade required a barer style, the effect is much less pleasing, almost prosaic. In Mr. George Whalley's *No Man an Island*, the best of his *Poems 1939-1944* are reprinted, often with interesting changes. Most of the poems in the present collection are new. Primarily this is a record of Mr. Whalley's emotional and intellectual experiences during his years in the Navy. Many of the poems are well wrought; all are interesting; but they read as if they were only incidentally rendered in verse, and their chief values would survive in prose.

There were six additions to the "Ryerson Poetry Chap-Books." This series has been as carefully planned as anything of the kind can be; and it is no accident, one may be sure, that three of the new booklets are by established writers, one with a famous name, and the other three by poets who are as yet unknown to any broad audience and are clearly at the beginning of their careers. The title of Mr. Arthur Stringer's *New York Nocturnes* was used long ago by Charles G. D. Roberts; and it is of Roberts and Carman as they wrote in their New York years that this work reminds one. It has their soft music, Roberts' direct observation of detail, and Carman's romantic feeling. Mr. Stringer's special quality of sweetness is found once more. The larger part of Mr. John A. B. McLeish's *Not without Beauty* is given to one poem in which he evokes, without overt nostalgia, a country town on a summer night. The town is sympathetically rendered with a moving appreciation of the deserted moonlit square and of the unformed being of the youth who is the central figure. The best of the nineteen poems in Mrs. Lenore Pratt's *Midwinter Thaw* are pictures of the Newfoundland landscape. Of the three younger poets, Miss Margaret Coulby is the most obviously promising, and has made the greatest progress towards a poetic style adequate for her needs. There is a striking and imaginative personality in *The Bitter Fruit,* and in some of the poems a fine feeling for structure. In *Myssium,* by Mr. Albert Levine, there is more sharpness of perception and more vigour of intelligence. But in style and structure his poems are less mature. In Miss Genevieve Bartole's *Figure in the Rain* there are two interesting poems, and "Canadian Farmer," although uneven like everything else in the booklet, has lines of power.

In *Omar from Nishapur,* with a due mixture of the humorous and the grimly serious, Dr. Vere Jameson presents a supposed recantation of the *Rubaiyat*. Much of it is delightful, but there was only one FitzGerald. One can no more vie with him than with Milton.

1949

The poetry of 1949 is less striking than in any year since "Letters in Canada" began. The poverty is unlikely to persist, and is not wholly unwelcome to one reader: it gives me a chance that I have hoped for, space for an attempt to see the poetry of the past fifteen years in brief perspective.

These years are among the most interesting in the development of Canadian poetry. In retrospect the landmarks seem unmistakable. With *The Titanic* in 1935, and again with *Brébeuf and His Brethren* in 1940, E. J. Pratt appeared at the height of his power in versification, organization, and interpretation. Nothing in the praise given these poems in "Letters in Canada" now appears excessive. In 1950 Pratt's reputation is even more secure than it was when these surveys began. I grow tired of hearing the charge that his writing is not in the main stream of modern verse; of course it is not, but should anyone care? What is wrong with most poetry that falls outside the main stream is that it imitates without enrichment some old formula. Pratt imitates nothing: his best poetry offers a strong pleasure not to be found in any other writing, past or present. The publication in 1936 of *New Provinces* associated with Pratt, Robert Finch, Leo Kennedy, A. M. Klein, F. R. Scott, and A. J. M. Smith. The importance of this small anthology was emphasized in "Letters in Canada: 1936": "It marks the emergence before the general readers of the country (others have followed the tendency for some years in magazines with relatively small circulation) of a group of poets who may well have as vivifying an effect on Canadian poetry as the Group of Seven had on Canadian painting." All that now seems at fault in that judgment was the implication that "general readers" would look into the anthology. Few of them did. It sold slowly; the publisher did not push it very hard; and it was not as widely discussed as it might have been.

But *New Provinces* is a landmark. The poets it introduced have been the authors of a number of the most interesting collections in the interval between 1936 and the present; and their mark is upon the best books by other experimental writers that have come out in this period. The *New Provinces* poets have not been widely read; they have not counted for much in the general culture of the country. This is because of their language, which they did not devise but share with most of the best contemporary poets in the United States and some in England. This, much more than the sometimes bewildering irregularity of their prosodic patterns, or their preference of myth to lyricism, or their occasionally uncompromising subtlety or learning, is what scares away the larger audience. The boldness with language is not only easy to account for, it is practically inevitable. Conservative critics in the universities, and more vociferously in the newspapers (where the reviewing of poetry is usually in weak hands) have been saying that the experiments are not only unattractive but gratuitous, and should be called off. They cannot be called off. There is no direct way back to the quarries from which earlier poets drew their marble. Sooner or later another quarry will be found where the marble is of superb quality. Then poets will no longer concern themselves so much in experimenting with language; they will take idiom more or less (although never entirely) for granted, and without the noisy heaving and straining that have been so characteristic of the past fifteen years in Canada, they will express their impressions, feelings, and ideas in a way that can be more generally shared.

Already there are signs that the period of extreme concentration on linguistic experiment is passing. *The Rocking Chair* – another landmark – is much more accessible than Klein's earlier verse. Earle Birney and Dorothy Livesay, owing a good deal to the kind of poetry the *New Provinces* men wrote, although not perhaps to any individual poet, have repeatedly combined with a sensitive use of language a set of feelings and ideas that can be apprehended with no great effort. In less profuse language, and with less rendering of feeling, Anne Marriott and P. K. Page have done the same. The rich imaginative force of Patrick Anderson may perhaps take the same path.

What lies ahead in poetry is probably a period of less myopic concern with the medium, more interest in structure, and a wider range of impressions, feelings, and ideas. Perhaps the audience for good poetry may grow in Canada (the C.B.C. is at last in a faltering way beginning to do something that may be helpful); but I am not persuaded. The culture of English Canada is becoming more and more a culture founded on the social sciences; even the physical scientists, who are likely to absorb most of the first-rate minds in this and the next generation, are turning to the social sciences rather than to the humanities as they enlarge their interests, and their awareness of responsibility.

The distance between the kinds of good poetry written today and the kinds that seemed experimental twenty-five years ago is made plain by a reading of the *Collected Poems* of Raymond Knister, edited by Dorothy Livesay. Knister died in 1932. In the last six years of his life he wrote prose fiction. As early as 1926 he "collected and revised" his poems, intending to publish them under the characteristic and delightful title "Windfalls for Cider." What is now printed is the book he put together: his poetical works collected, but not complete, an author's own sifting. Dorothy Livesay who knew him well has written a substantial and infinitely illuminating study of his personality and work, the best of her critical essays on poetry.[1] She takes Knister as a case of the experimental author denied a hearing in Canada – most of his poems came out in *The Midland* – and as a case of the lonely artist committed, partly by temperament and partly by circumstance, to introspection of a tragic cast. Although she does not explicitly say that his drowning was suicide, suicide is the natural ending for the person and the life Miss Livesay has described.

The poems do not seem to me as pervasively good as they do to the editor. Some are good; and these are more than enough to justify the publication of the book – it is not

---

[1] Miss Livesay is mistaken in listing the now eminent Jamesian scholar Leon Edel among the poets.

a mere work of piety, but an enrichment of our useable tradition. Knister is at his best when he is recording the aspect of a thing, an animal, or a person, and his own response to this. He had most sensitive perceptions, and an exquisite awareness of the form that would convey them. "A Row of Horse Stalls," ten poems that originally appeared in *This Quarter,* are delightful renderings of perception. But, introspective and brooding, he often could not stop with rendering his perceptions and his delight in them: he was impelled to add what he thought, and this he did not often manage with any height of economy or insight. The first poem in the collection, "The Plowman," has much to say about furrows, and no poet has known them more intimately. The next to last stanza runs:

> The horses are very patient
> When I tell myself
> This time
> The ultimate unflawed turning
> Is before my share,
> They must give up their rest.

Already the movement from aspect to symbol makes one uncomfortable. Then, with what seems to me a thumping heaviness the poem ends:

> Someday, someday, be sure,
> I shall turn the furrow of all my hopes
> But I shall not, doing it, look backward.

This is what we could have done for ourselves, with the dominant image of the furrow clearly set in the earlier parts of the poem; and doing it for ourselves we would have done it to much better effect.

Poetry written today on Knister's sort of subjects would have more implicitness; and it would not be denied a hearing. There are at least three magazines in Canada where poems of quality, no matter how unlike the styles in vogue, would be not only printed, but prized.

Charm in rendering the aspect of things and people also marks *Invitation to Mood*, by Carol Coates, a collection in the same vein as her chap-book of 1939, *Fancy Free*.[2] The distinctive thing in her poetry is admirably described by Professor Thorlief Larsen in a few paragraphs which might well have been promoted from the jacket to a place in the body of the book. Her characteristic form is the *hokku*, adapted to the opportunities and limitations of English, and in some degree to the personal modes of the poet's feelings. Mr. Larsen rightly notes: "When one has read four or five of these poems the rhythms become established in the mind, so to speak, and one comes to expect them just as one does the rhythms of conventional verse." What needs to be added is that one remains conscious that the rhythms established are novel, and there follows a pleasant blending of confidence in pattern, and awareness of its strangeness. In Miss Coates's poems everything is clear and sharp when she is at her best – the pictures as clear and sharp as Raymond Knister's, although not so strong. The form loses its appropriateness and becomes a vexation when the content is vague (as in the closing section called "Transcendental Mood"), or the tone ambitious (as in the tribute to Winston Churchill, "Chosen of Men").

Almost every one of the forty-two poems in Mr. James Reaney's *The Red Heart* is interesting. A few are trivial; a few unconsidered; almost all the rest uneven.

The first group called "The Plum Tree" is the most satisfactory. These poems, like those in the second group "The School Globe," are evocations of moments in the poet's experience as child and boy in Stratford, Ontario. Mr. Reaney's use of nature centres in the sky – his titles prepare one for this, "The Clouds," "The Sun Dogs," "Suns and Planets," "The Heart and the Sun," "Clouds." The sky is what cannot be reached, and what matters most. The imagery is strong, without being rich or intricate: the sky, in Mr. Reaney's universe, does not need to be rendered with complexity or nuance. In other poems of this first group there is almost constant reference to things that fall – in the first poem, admirably chosen for its place:

---

[2]No poems from *Fancy Free* are reprinted in the new collection; but happily it does contain a dozen of the best poems from a hand-produced limited edition brought out in 1941.

In the opium-still noon they hang or fall
The plump ripe plums.
I suppose my little sister died
Dreaming of looking up at them. . . .
And there is no listener, no hearer
For the small thunders of their falling.

This is Mr. Reaney at his best. Unless something is dropping the world is ruled by ennui: nothing initiated on its surface has significance, or intensity. The droppings from the sky have intensity, but what their significance may be, the poems do not suggest.

The sense of ennui is everywhere in the collection. Mr. Reaney appears to be vulnerable to boredom beyond any other Canadian who has taken to writing. I can understand how one might be bored by living in Stratford, but not how one can found a poetic career on it. The intensity with which he can be bored has enabled him to achieve a few striking passages, but a lyric poet who is prone to be bored is very much like a producer with a boring character in his cast: the audience is likely to miss the fine strokes of characterization in a general effect of ennui. In the later parts of *The Red Heart* the boredom is relieved by wit, but the wit of a really bored person is likely to be forced. "The Great Lakes Suite" is a would-be witty sequence, but the effect, if it is achieved at all, seems much too trivial for a book. In general Mr. Reaney's wit is trivial, and appears to come from the shallows rather than the depths. T. S. Eliot has linked with the mood of boredom, the mood of horror and the mood of glory. Mr. Reaney links with his boredom horror. He finds horror especially in the fact of physical death and in the sexual interests of ordinary people (he has a strong sense of the difference between ordinary and extraordinary in everything), perhaps of all people except himself and those who love him. I do not think that his poetry of horror comes off as well as his poetry of boredom: but it will more and more, perhaps, be Mr. Reaney's principal "line." As to the mood of glory – there is none of that.

The Red Heart is the first collection of a young poet. It reads so. It leaves one eager to see the next.

So does a smaller book, the most interesting of the "Ryerson Poetry Chap-Books," Thomas Saunders' *Scrub*

Oak. This is poetry very much after the earlier manner of Robert Frost, that is to say, after one of the best manners in the poetry of this century. Robert Frost has always been absorbed in the people and the places of his own New England, but the absorption has not blunted his interest in the general nature and plight of man. Thomas Saunders, who writes from Winnipeg, is absorbed in the people and the places of rural Manitoba. He renders them with power, with a fine balance between sympathetic insight and stern detachment. This is a harsh world, somewhat like the world of F. P. Grove's western novels; and the modes of writing that Robert Frost has used for the harsh world of Vermont and New Hampshire suit it. Two short passages from "Rural Slum" will show what Thomas Saunders can do:

> The low hills seemed to brood
> Above them, while the muskeg reached to coil
> Its soggy arms about the land. The walls
> That sever life from death had here grown thin.

and:

> No land less loves
> Mankind – and no land holds men more. They live
> In rural squalor. . . .

Among his poems I find a few that are the best of the year.

The other three "Ryerson Chap-Books" are diversely interesting. John Murray Gibbon's *Canadian Cadences* are mainly applications of his well-known way of allowing the words and structure of a poem to be suggested by a musical work. The outcome is not evenly successful, but is always worth study. In *Last Mathematician* Hyman Edelstein continues his trenchant, erudite verse, the form sometimes buckling beneath the stress. Marjorie Freeman Campbell's *High on a Hill* has less unity in form or feeling than the others. The best of her poems are those of grief.

More Lines from Deepwood, although privately printed, must not go unmentioned. Arthur S. Bourinot turns quickly from manner to manner, theme to theme, in the dozen poems that make up the brochure. In those that reflect the Ottawa country-side (where Deepwood lies) and in those that grow out of Indian legend Mr. Bourinot achieves his usual blending of delicacy with ease.

Causeries

A Fine Novel
on The West
(September 27, 1947)

Last week I was asked, as one who had lived in Winnipeg, what was the finest novel of the Canadian West. I quickly thought of two deeply sincere and tragic novels, Frederick Philip Grove's "Settlers of the Marsh" and Sinclair Ross's "As For Me and My House." Both are notable novels, and besides each of them gives some feeling of what it means to live in the Canadian West, how the milieu imparts something of great importance to the day-to-day drama of human relationships. But the book I actually named gives, I believe, a deeper sounding of life in the West than either of these; and yet it remains unknown to most Western Canadians because it is written and beautifully written – in French.

The book is M. Georges Bugnet's "La Fôret" (published by Les Editions du Totem, Montreal, in 1935), a novel of the Peace River country where the author has lived most of his adult life. Georges Bugnet, novelist, dramatist, poet, and critic, is one of the really important Canadian writers. In him an intellect and spirit of a very high order unites with a long experience of life in the wilderness; and the result has been a literary work in which the materials of the frontier have been wrought into designs of lasting beauty, and their meaning presented with an unwavering courage. His "Nipsya" in the beautiful translation of the late Constance Davies Woodrow, is known to English-speaking Canadians, or at least was known some years ago – a copy of it is now hard to come by.

"The Forest" is in some ways an even finer performance. It relates the tragic struggle of a young urban Frenchman and his wife with the formidable nature of primitive Canada. They come from France with a romantic wish to pioneer beyond the end of the steel. They take up land beyond all the farms in the district, on the edge of a great lake, in the midst of a green forest.

They arrive at the beginning of the short northern summer. With the aid of a kindly elderly practical French-Canadian couple on the next farm – drawn with an affectionate realism that never forces a note – they build their cabin and barn; they make a garden and clear a few acres; the next summer they harvest their first crop, damaged severely by a hailstorm, and try, vainly, to live off the land. The wife, a delicate, sensitive, super-civilized girl is oppressed from the very beginning by the scale of Canadian nature – the hugeness of the forest and the lake, the force of the winds from the north, the length and coldness of the winter. Even the Canadian mosquito seems to her to have a force of penetration beyond its European cousin.

Her husband is toughened and coarsened by the tremendous efforts he makes to subdue the wilderness. But his energies are increased beyond his wife's belief. In doing his utmost to make his dream come true he becomes another personality. To her he seems to have changed into an element in the nature that surrounds her. M. Bugnet's insight into the characters of both husband-and-wife is at this stage of an acuteness exceedingly rare in our fiction. The simple French-Canadian couple, although they cannot express their ideas in adequate words, are not far behind the author in understanding the process of character change. A conversation between the two women in which this process is the subject touches on deep perceptions without any loss to plausibility. It is an artistic triumph.

The calm competent French-Canadian family, the children of Canadian nature, work not against nature but with her. Nature is an uneasy partner, but they know her ways, and thus can yield and can take the lead at the right moments. The contrast between the two households helps to give the novel its firm design.

Towering over both is the nature that M. Bugnet knows so intimately, with his senses, his imagination, and his intelligence. M. Bugnet conveys the glint of the trees in the strong summer sunlight, the glorious ruin of the autumn, the smell of the rank northern flowers, the color and movement of the lake, the sound of cracking ice and of the gale beating upon the timbers of the cabin. The details are admirable; but they are never included for their own sake.

What interests Mr. Bugnet is the spirit of nature, the austere immensely strong entity that routs the civilized invaders – the husband too is defeated, and will relapse into his former urban self and return them where they belong.

It is a great and tragic book written out of experience controlled by reflection. We do not have many such books. It is a pity that most of us cannot read this one.

Ten Best
Canadian Books
(February 28, 1948)

In the days of our grandfathers every reading person enjoyed lists of the "best books". It was stimulating to draw up your own list. As you struggled with it you learned a surprising variety of facts about yourself. You realized how many books there were that you always had intended to read, had even bought, but had never got into. When you reached down some novel or record of travel that had once seemed to be the peak of perfection and began to scan it, suddenly it crumbled into a dull mass of type. It was equally stimulating to make some one else's list a target of ridicule. Every one had a good time. The end product was excellent; people heard of, or were reminded of, good books, and went off into corners to read them. Like many of the ways of our grandfathers the diversion was useful, and it could stand revival.

I am going to offer a list of the ten "best" Canadian books, limited to those written in English. I have never seen such a list, and I have been surprised as it took form. My courage will not go beyond giving ten equal first places – giving the authors' names in merely alphabetical order.

Charles Cochrane: Christianity and Classical Culture
Mazo de la Roche: Jalna
F. P. Grove: Over Prairie Trails
Archibald Lampman: Poems
Stephen Leacock: Sunshine Sketches of a Little Town
John Macnaughton: Lord Strathcona
Sir William Osler: Aequanimitas etc.
E. J. Pratt: Poems
Sir Charles G. D. Roberts: Animal Stories
Duncan Scott: Poems

All but two of these are widely known. About Cochrane's and Macnaughton's, which are not, there is much to be said, and in the hope of enlisting readers for them I want to explain why I think they deserve their places.

"Christianity and Classical Culture" has been praised by Harold Innis as the first major Canadian contribution to the intellectual history of western man. W. H. Auden has described the discovery of the book as an epoch in his life. Charles Cochrane, Ontario born and bred, died in 1945 at the age of 56, after spending his whole mature life as a teacher of ancient history at the University of Toronto. Towards 1930 he began to write his great book and finished it only after ten years of the most strenuous thinking.

The great moment in Cochrane's life was his realization of the depth and power of St. Augustine. Any one whom he buttonholed and made listen to his interpretation of "the saint", as Cochrane called him, will never forget the experience. In his book Cochrane looks back over the ancient world, particularly the Roman world, almost through the eyes of Augustine. He brings immense learning, the sharpest kind of synthetic power, and spiritual insight to his great task. If the style were a little finer, and if Cochrane had been more explicit in the statement of his religious convictions, his book would belong on the same shelf with Arnold Toynbee's. It has a sure place on the shelf below.

Macnaughton's book has had a curious history: it was resurrected only to be buried again. The history has never been given in print, so far as I know, and I have pieced it together. It was commissioned for the original Makers of Canada series, but the manuscript, like almost everything that Macnaughton wrote or said, was found too hot to handle. When after the lapse of a generation the series was revised, W. L. Grant was editor in chief. One of the most courageous of Canadians, and unusually sensitive to literary art, Grant decided that such a masterpiece could not remain unpublished. But even Grant could not conceive of its coming out with all its invective unpruned.

Macnaughton had ended his active career – he circulated

like current coin through the universities of Canada, said his great friend Leacock – and retired to England. He had also mellowed. Grant asked permission to make some cuts, and it was granted. Appearing only in the shelter of a learned series, and differing radically from the conventional biographies that shouldered it to right and to left, it has never had its chance. "Lord Strathcona" is a very great book. In the fullness of his power to make a reader feel persons and places, in the magnificence of his rhetoric, in the lurid splendor of his invective, and above all, in his unfailing grasp of issues deeper than the political and the economic, Macnaughton achieved a biography like no other on a Canadian subject. It was as if Carlyle, belatedly, had come out and lived among us, taking notes and storing up his rage and humor till the great occasion came.

Mavo de la
Roche's Jalna
(April 3, 1948)

In the list of ten outstanding Canadian books that I gave a few weeks ago only one novel was included, Mazo de la Roche's "Jalna". The reason that Canadian novels are so rarely good, the main reason at least, is that they lack credible and interesting characters, sufficiently complex to exercise the reader's imagination, and sufficiently human to lay hold on his feelings. There never was a really excellent novel that did not make a strong appeal to the imagination and the feelings in that manner. In the old grandmother, Adeline Whiteoak, Miss de la Roche developed such a character, the most impressively vital human being that I have come on in a Canadian novel, and complex as well.

There would be much less doubt concerning the excellence of "Jalna" if Miss de la Roche had not continued during the twenty-one years since its appearance to write about the Whiteoak family and their manorial estate, although she long ago exhausted her perceptions about this brood of her imagination. The second book in the chronicle, "Whiteoaks of Jalna", although inferior to the first in clarity of outline and imaginative force, kept much of its power. But with "Finch's Fortune" the decline was deep, and I ceased to read Miss de la Roche. When I picked up in 1946 the most recent in the series I could hardly believe that it was from the same hand as "Jalna". It was thin and tired, there was not an atom of dramatic force, and the life in the characters was as sluggish as in the dullest moments in Howells. It must be almost impossible for a reader who makes acquaintance with the Jalna series by one of its late numbers to believe what a fine work "Jalna" itself is.

The inferiority of sequels is an old story. Miss de la Roche might have been put on her guard by what happened to the novelist who seems in many ways to have been her model – Galsworthy. "The Man of Property" is a very fine novel. The portrait it offers of Soames Forsyte has a devastating reality, and the society in which Soames moves is in a more superficial way convincingly real. But when Galsworthy decided to write a "saga" of the Forsytes his powers left him, and from that fatal day nothing that he wrote could rise to the qualities of his early fiction. The failure of sequels (to which Byron's "Childe Harold, III and IV," and Trollope's "Barchester Towers" are the striking exceptions in English) is a very mysterious affair. One would suppose that a world in which a writer's creative imagination had found a congenial expression would be a good place for him to revisit. But the fact is that with sequels in fiction as with revisions in poetry it is seldom that the original elation can be recaptured.

Like "The Man of Property," "Jalna" needs to be read as if it never had been "continued". Read in and for itself, "Jalna" cannot fail to move. The Whiteoak family, the three generations gathered under the high ceilings of the old country house near Lake Ontario, has an irrepressible vitality. All the Whiteoaks have color and fire. They have resisted the dulling pressure of southern Ontario, that land of sober-suited cautious-living Puritans. It is true that each generation loses something of the magnificent energy, the tireless delight in life and eagerness for experience of old grandmother Adeline. But all her offspring preserve her mighty stamp, even if it becomes somewhat effaced in their softer material.

Whenever Adeline Whiteoak appears the pace of the story is accelerated, the scenes take on a more vigorous life, all the other characters, even those who are not Whiteoaks, rise to the challenge of her primitive force. And Miss de la Roche's style rises too, and becomes almost winged, but when Adeline dies midway through "Whiteoaks of Jalna" the life departs. In "Young Renny", the fifth of the novels, Miss de la Roche returned to the time when Adeline was alive. But she could not revive her key character: at eighty the old lady appeared as merely a shadow of the cursing battling centenarian of "Jalna."

"Jalna" is the book to read not only because of the portrait of Adeline. The old matriarch brought the whiff of life into all the people she spoke to, asked to kiss her, or just glared at. We have all known persons who could bring that whiff into others. Stephen Leacock could. Sir William Osler appears to have been another; he could bring back to life patients whom every one else had despaired of – by being Osler. The power to work this particular magic is reserved to personalities of the rarest vitality. One of the best examples in any book is in the chapter "Inside the Gates of Jalna" where the old lady brings a new reality into the character of the rather effaced prim American her grandson had married. Once Adeline has wrought her effect on this girl, Miss de la Roche can keep her alive. But without Adeline the novelist was lost.

A Pioneer Historian
of Canada
(August 7, 1948)

George MacKinnon Wrong, who died in Toronto this summer at 88, was a shaper of Canadian culture and civilization. English by birth, Wrong chose to have a wholly Canadian career: not only did he live and work in Canada, Canada was also the centre of his thoughts, studies, and writings.

When he became professor of history at the University of Toronto in the early 1890's, he had no training for the study of Canadian history, and indeed there was then no place where such training was provided. That the history departments of our universities and schools are now full to overflowing with men and women admirably trained in Canadian history and finding in it their chief interest, is in no small degree Wrong's work.

He founded the "Review of Historical Publications relating to Canada," a priceless tool to other workers in the field and saw it grow into the "Canadian Historical Review," a periodical that bears comparison with the best historical magazines in other countries. He reshaped the history courses at Toronto to allow for a close study of the problems that confront the writer and the critical reader of Canadian history. He wrote textbooks for the schools (widely used across the country) that made our history, and particularly his favorite period, the French regime, exciting to the average student. Meanwhile, in a long series of books he was contributing to the scholarly interpretation of our country's development from Jacques Cartier to Laurier.

It was important to Canada that for thirty-five years the head of the Toronto history department was an appreciative friend of French Canada. Thousands of students derived from his lectures – and he was a model lecturer, entertaining, eloquent, and beautifully clear – an understanding of the intellectual and moral virtues in the French Canadian tradition. He provided an antidote to Ontario bigotry, and wherever Wrong's books have penetrated bigotry has been sapped.

He was also deeply interested in the United States. One of his best books is "Washington and His Comrades in Arms," written for a top-flight American historical series. At a time when American history was neglected in Canada – as American literature is today – Wrong lectured upon it, and interpretated it with great wisdom and above all with a fine sense of its relevance for Canada.

With his interest in the new civilizations of this continent went wide knowledge of the continent from which they have sprung. He was at home not only in the political development, but in the arts and letters of Europe, and especially of his native England.

At the moment his writings are a little undervalued by professional historians. This is because we have not yet quite emerged from a quarter century in which Canadian historians (like their brethren in other lands) have made the economic factor in history their primary concern. Wrong did not lay a heavy stress on economics; history for him was chiefly constitutional and social, military and diplomatic. It is true that he should have dealt more fully with economics, but his writing will serve to redress a balance that the economic historians have disturbed.

His literary gift was magnificent, and many of his students learned more about writing from him than from his colleagues in English. His style is almost flawless. He was a master of narrative – he could describe a battle or the progress of an expedition with a skill that reminds one of Macaulay or of Parkman. He was also adept at the character sketch. Whatever he wrote, he composed his details with an exquisite sense of proportion, and produced admirable general impressions. He would relieve a dull tract by a suave witticism or an incisive aside. He was always readable in a high degree, and at his best (he required space to achieve his best effects) he was captivating.

His personality was like his work – benignant, urbane, shrewd, and in the grand manner. Wrong may not have been one of the original powerful minds of his time, he may not have had the force that enables a man to develop a great new seminal idea. But he was something only slightly less valuable than an original and powerful mind. He was a richly stored, admirably organized, wholly civilized mind. No Canadian has worked more effectively towards the civilizing of us all. Those who have never read a line Wrong wrote are nevertheless the better for his activity among us. His influence has become a permanent element in our national life.

Frederick Philip Grove:
In Memoriam
(August 28, 1948)

The death of Frederick Philip Grove is an occasion for melancholy thought concerning the plight of the creative writer in Canada. Grove did not begin to depend on literature for his living until he was well into middle age. He had a small family. He was extremely industrious. He wrote chiefly in the most popular of all literary types: the novel. But he lived in poverty, and probably could not have lived at all if his wife had not assisted in maintaining the household, and if he had not supplemented the meagre proceeds from his books by work of other kinds. When he was almost seventy he worked for a season as a manual laborer. The highest official literary honor in Canada is the Royal Society's gold medal: Grove sold his medal to buy the cheapest radio he could find.

When I was one of the editors of the "University of Toronto Quarterly" I asked Grove to write on the position of the Canadian novelist. The article, "The Plight of Canadian Fiction" appeared in July, 1938; and I continue to believe that it is a statement of great interest and importance. Like almost everything that appears in the academic quarterlies, it received little popular attention; and now that Grove is dead I should like to bring it to the notice of a larger audience.

Grove's image for the state of Canadian literature is among the most brilliant I have ever seen. "We have a bookshelf reaching from Halifax to Victoria; and on it stands one single book, written by a Frenchman transient in Canada". Ten years later what can be set beside the incomparable "Maria Chapdelaine"? What other serious book continues to be widely read year in and year out? Perhaps the poems of E. J. Pratt, whom Grove admired with intensity. But two books leave the shelf a horrible vacancy.

For the vacant bookshelf the responsibility rests, says Grove, with some combination of these four factors: writers, publishers, critics, and the public.

The publishers seem to him to have done well. Indeed any one who has known as he did the enthusiasm and idealism of the late Hugh Eayrs of the Macmillan company or of Lorne Pierce, who still presides at the Ryerson Press, cannot doubt for an instant that our publishers care more for the muse than for money bags. Again and again they bring out books that they know will lose money because they believe those books important.

The critics do not fare so well. I have alluded to the fissure between the academic publications stresses this fissure. The academic critics seem to him to be informed, discriminating, courageous – but what they write does not have a serious impact on the public.

The popular critics do not, in his opinion, know their job. They tend to judge books by the breadth of their appeal, not by the depth of their vision or the beauty of their form. The books they recommend to the public are not often the best books; and thus they clog the channel from the serious writer to the readers he covets. There is more truth in this charge than we may like to admit. People are writing about books in media with large circulations who do not know what a good book is, and would not care if you told them.

Worst Offender

Grove's heaviest blows are for the public. The public is not interested in books as it is in some other countries – Sweden and Denmark are examples that come to mind at once. The public in Canada is extraordinarily indifferent to books written by Canadians, or about Canada. "Canadians are at bottom" says Grove "not interested in their own country". Certainly there can be no considerable Canadian literature, certainly there can be no career as a serious creative writer in Canada, if this is so.

It is somewhat less so than it was ten years ago. The last war led a large number of Canadians to think new thoughts about their country, and their own relation to it. The troubled relations between the two great world-powers, between which we now lie, forces us to go on thinking those thoughts. So far these new thoughts have not aided literature in any decisive way – we are an unaesthetic people, and will probably always be less concerned with the arts than the Swedes or the Danes.

But it is nevertheless true that a serious young writer would find it a little easier now to make his way than it was for Frederick Philip Grove when he published his first book, which was also his best, "Over Prairie Trails". That beautiful record of the Manitoba countryside in all the seasons of the year is the most remarkable literary work to come out of the west. The best way to mark Grove's death is not to pursue our melancholy train of thought any further, but to read "Over Prairie Trails", and if one has read it before to read it again. It bears many rereadings. Perhaps if there had been more writers like Grove (for the writers too have a responsibility) the critics and the public would have been saved from their sins.

The Achievement
of Morley Callaghan
(January 22, 1949)

The appearance last fall of Morley Callaghan's short novel "The Varsity Story" directed attention to one of the best Canadian authors, who has been out of the candlelight for the past decade.

A play of his, originally scheduled for Broadway in 1939, has had its premiere in Toronto this winter. His short stories have begun to appear again in leading magazines. This is a good time to look back over what he achieved between the publication of his first novel "Strange Fugitive" late in the 'twenties and that of "More Joy in Heaven" which closed his first productive period, in 1937.

What obviously distinguishes Callaghan from other Canadian prose writers is a peculiar quality of style. Our prose, good, bad and middling, has always been stiff — the prose of people who dress up to write, who are trying to write a little better than they really can.

Canadian writing has achieved some very fine effects, but it lacks ease. Even Leacock is not often really at ease. Callaghan always seems to be. His sentences are as unambitious as a lazy boy on a hot day.

This easy style of his is exactly the right medium for the kind of people and problems with which he is concerned in his novels and short stories, and for his attitude towards both. His collected fiction might well bear the title of Hans Fallada's novel "Little Man, What Now?" It is the little man, or little woman, lost in the big city that he cares about, the sort of person with a vague aspiration and a basic goodness, but doing a lot of things he ought not to do simply because he feels lost and grows confused or desperate.

Callaghan hides his own cultivation as carefully as a writer like Thomas Mann exhibits his. He is a graduate of the University of Toronto, and of Osgoode Hall. He went to France before the golden nineteen - twenties were over, and became a friend of Ernest Hemingway and James Joyce. The cafes of the Boulevard du Montparnasse were his graduate school.

He returned with a wide knowledge of modern literary theories and a curiosity about all kinds of art and thought. Living in Toronto he has spent a great deal of his time with the men who have made the Pontifical Institute of Mediaeval Studies one of the great centres of study for the Middle Ages.

One of his novels is dedicated to Jacques Maritain, the greatest of the visiting professors the Institute has had; and Callaghan is more at home with a professor of philosophy than with the boy behind the lunch counter or the girl at the cashier's desk. But you would never guess it from his writings.

It is the boy and girl he wants to write about, not the professor; and he does not want to write about them as a philosophic novelist might, to illustrate some abstraction or prove some theory. He wants to write about them as human beings, as if they were the people he lived with, worked with, played with, and as if he were absolutely one of the group.

Callaghan is a Roman Catholic, and the Catholic church plays a very large part in his fiction. There is nothing stiff in his approach to the priests who figure in so many of his stories. They are as human as the girl at the cashier's desk. They are good priests, all of them; but they are often confused, and the city is often too much for them. No other Canadian writer has made religion so much a part of the common stuff of life.

But if Callaghan is very close, fraternally close, to the people he writes about, he never allows his emotions to boil over in the fashion of Thomas Wolfe, and spatter the page with exclamations and rhetorical phrases.

He does not say much about his feelings towards his characters and their problems, he lets his ideas express themselves in the true idiom of the novelist, the plot and the setting. Before we reach the middle of any book of his we feel the closeness to the characters that Callaghan feels himself and wants us to feel. There is his great success.

"The Varsity Story" is not typical of his work. The institution he writes about seems more important than the people who move about in it. It was never like that with the cathedral in some of the earlier books, or the business in which one of them centred.

His return to writing, or rather to publication (for he has written a good deal during the years he has not published) stirs the hope that he will give us another novel as moving as "Such is My Beloved," or a short story as memorable as "A Sick Call."

Lampman's Literary Executor

(February 5, 1949)

It will be fifty years on February 10 since Archibald Lampman died at the age of thirty-seven. He had published two small collections of poetry, the first "Among the Millet" at his own expense, and "Lyrics of Earth" at a small Boston press. In the magazines, American and Canadian, his verses had been welcomed for almost twenty years, and he had won a modest reputation as a poet of the Canadian landscape, and as a sonneteer on moral themes.

His name might easily have become a shadow like that of George Frederick Cameron, who also died in his thirties, if he had not, among much ill fortune, attached to himself as friend and literary executor, Duncan Campbell Scott.

The way in which Scott watched over Lampman's works and fame from 1899 until his death in 1947 is a very bright chapter in the development of Canadian literature. Scott was a busy man, with a career in the Department of Indian Affairs and another in poetry; but he let nothing interfere with his duty to Lampman.

The year after Lampman's death he produced a memorial edition, the "Poems," which runs to more than five hundred pages. In this he gathered practically everything that Lampman had published in verse, and extracted almost an equal amount from the poet's notebooks and scribblers.

Only one who has pored over Lampman's manuscripts can do full justice to Scott's energy and skill. Often Lampman would write out a poem nine or ten times, and each time he would pile up alternative readings in the margin or between the lines. He seldom indicated which version had pleased him best. The memoir preceding the "Poems" is a model of literary biography and appreciation.

In 1924, to mark the quarter century after Lampman's death, Scott published a selection from the poems, entitled "Lyrics of Earth." What Scott had in view was to recommend Lampman to a younger generation of readers by showing him at his best. His taste was so sure that only half a dozen poems of notable beauty were omitted.

Nor did his zeal stop with this performance. When I asked him in 1942 to go over with me the score of scribblers and notebooks he was delighted. Our joint search brought to light two dozen poems not previously published, and yet good enough to require publication. At every stage in the preparation of "At the Long Sault and Other New Poems," his interest was keen and his judgment superb.

Scott then formed the plan of bringing out a new volume of selections, which would retain practically everything in "Lyrics of Earth," restore a few pieces from the memorial edition, and add what was best in "At the Long Sault."

In 1947, a few months before he died, at eighty five, he saw through the press the "Selected Poems of Archibald Lampman," a climax to all he had done in nearly fifty years of service to his friend.

Lampman is much more than a shadow in Canada today, but it would be pure delusion to claim that he is widely read. Critics have spoken wisely of him – there is a very readable and sympathetic biography and estimate by Professor Carl Conner, and there have been half a dozen valuable essays.

He is secure in the standard anthologies, and he has a place in many textbooks. I wonder if there is much more that writers can do for him. Or publishers. Or booksellers. Or librarians.

If there is anything writers and publishers and booksellers and librarians can do for Lampman, it is by finding more readers for poetry generally, and by helping those readers to appreciate that good poetry offers far more than catchy rhymes ever will.

It is discouraging to anyone who cares for poetry to look at the poetry shelves in a typical Canadian department store. For one copy of Lampman, or E. J. Pratt, there will be half a dozen of the latest work of some catchy rhymester . . . (or more often rhymestress) and all the half dozen look as fresh as if they had arrived from the publisher that morning.

Meanwhile the collected poems of Duncan Campbell Scott are out of print, and there are not enough people who care to make a new printing at all likely.

Is a Canadian Critic
Possible?
(January 13, 1951)

Last month at Carleton College in Ottawa there was a session on the topic – is a Canadian critic possible? The answer depends on some definitions.

What is a critic? He is a sensitive reader who can explain his responses and evaluations. In the great Ode on the Intimations of Immortality – which I think the most splendid poem written in our language in the past 250 years – the poet declares that a child six years old is a "mighty Philosopher." If on reading the poem you dismiss Wordsworth's phrase as silly, you are insensitive and any critique of the ode you may write will be worthless.

If you claim the phrase is profound but can't tell how and why, you are sensitive but not a critic. The critic not only perceives where the profundity of the phrase lies; he explains why it lies there, and shows how the phrase adds a rich strand to the pattern of the ode.

It is certainly possible to be a critic in Canada. We have a number of them – at least a dozen. I have been reading belatedly the last work of one of the best – "The Story of the Iliad" by E. T. Owen, formerly professor of Greek at the University of Toronto, published by Clarke Irwin in 1946.

Owen, who died soon after the book came out, was painfully modest – not an exceptional trait in a Canadian writer of quality – and it is probable that only the knowledge that death was near persuaded him to publish the reflections on Homer's art that had collected during 30 years of teaching his poems.

The purpose of his book is to explain why Homer arranged his diverse and copious material just as he did, why he elaborated one episode into a great show-piece and

313

forced the pace in presenting another, why he gave special, often comic, function to the gods, why his poem and its many parts affect us as they do.

Owen was sensitive to the art of the Iliad, as sensitive as a great conductor is to the music of his favorite composer. He adds to this sensitiveness a power of lucid cogent explanation. Almost always he thinks Homer was right, even perfect, in his art, and he can say exactly why this is so.

If "The Story of the Iliad" had been cited in the discussion at Carleton College, someone would have protested, I think, that this was not at all the kind of book desired from a Canadian critic. It is a book that might have been written in France or in England – although there are few persons in any country who could have achieved it.

When there is complaint about the quality of Canadian criticism, what is meant is not that there is little good critical writing in Canada but – a much narrower charge – that there is little good critical writing about Canadian literature.

It is true that in most countries where criticism has flourished – and particularly true in modern and contemporary times – it has found a main theme in the literature of the country where it is written. Not much of the best Canadian critical writing is on Canadian themes.

There is no book on a Canadian poet that compares with Owen's book on Homer, or with A. F. B. Clark's book on Racine. But there is no Canadian poet who could support such a book.

Even the narrower charge that there is no adequate critical writing about Canadian themes is not strictly true. Duncan Campbell Scott's essay on "Poetry and Progress" involves Canadian authors and problems in its consideration of its great and broad subject. It is a penetrating and distinguished piece. J. M. Cappon's two books on Sir Charles Roberts are fully equal to their subject. Scarcely anyone in Canada cares to read Scott's essay or Cappon's books, as the publishers will tell you.

What is really lacking is not Canadian criticism in any sense of the term but an audience for it. As I have said before in this place – and expect to say again – Canadians do not care what other Canadians think.